AND
THEN
THERE
WERE
CROWS

ALCY LEYVA

Thank you for
your support and
I hope you
like the book

Nov 11th
2019

ISBN (print) 978-0-9997423-2-7

Cover design by Najla Qamber

Edited by Melissa Ringsted

Interior design layout by Rebecca Poole

Publication date July 3, 2018

Black Spot Books

ACKNOWLEDGEMENTS

To my family for their support
To my boys: A.L's + M.A.
To my partner for everything she gives
To the little story that could

EPISODE ONE:

ROOM APARTMENT FOR RENT- CONTACT ASAP

"HELLO. MY NAME is Amanda Grey."

I stuck out my hand and stared at my reflection.

The large mirror I managed to drag from my room into the living room told no lies. I looked like a complete idiot in the stupid pants suit thingy my sister had left behind when she moved out. The ensemble consisted of a white top and black bottom.

I look like a fucking penguin.

"Hey. I'm Amanda."

Too informal.

"Greetings. I am Ms. Grey."

Too foot fetish madame.

"Yoo …"

I fist bumped my reflection which, unsurprisingly, looked ashamed to meet me halfway.

I just wanted to keep my apartment. It's not anything those hippies living in NoHo (North of Houston), or the yuppies flocking to DUMBO (Down Under the Manhattan Bridge something), or even the dummies squatting in RATCHET (Right Around Thelma's Chicken Hut on East Twentieth) or whatever the hell has been fantastically acronymed for the sake of a rent hike—my point is that anyone else would have pulled the same thing to stay where they are. Well, that's what I want to believe. Because that's what New York life is like. You find a place with lots of sunlight, with at least a 1:4 rat to roach ratio, and within walking distance to a supermarket and/or train and/or bus to get you to that train or bus or what-have-you, and you plant yourself. You sit and wait and hope you can stay afloat when the next rent swell smashes into you.

Checking the time, I saw that I only had a small window before my guest showed up. I skipped the salutations and went right into practicing my smile.

My reflection said it all. I was dressed like a Crayola marker. I had nothing to do with my hair, so I rubber-banned it and prayed for the best. With funds being the way they were—as in, nonexistent—I had run out of actual soap that morning, so I Febreezed the hell out of my clothes and threw them on.

To top it all off, the best smile I could come up with after ten minutes of practice was pretty damn hideous—it bunched up the light freckles on my nose to look like a smeared map of Europe. Too many teeth exposed on top, too few on the bottom. I felt like a clown, I looked like an idiot, and I smelled like a couch in an "Autumn Breeze."

Leaning my head against the mirror, I gave my forehead three straight bumps. Knock-knock-knock.

And then, there were three knocks on my door. He was here.

I sighed. *You're an idiot, Amanda Grey.*

Dragging myself to the door, I thought about the stupidity that had stuck me in this horrible position to begin with. I was a screw up. Had been all of my life, but this time was major. Fucking epic. I had gone from a twenty-coughcough-something girl living in her parents' apartment in my little section of Queens, to the person days away from getting her entire family evicted. Sleeping out in the streets.

Walking toward my apartment door, readying myself to welcome the warm blooded stranger -waiting patiently behind its wooden frame, I knew that I was possibly about to headline a serious shit show.

What I didn't know, as I slid open every lock, hearing each one click open one by one by one—this *was* New York—was that all of my social weirdness and worries, each and every misplaced fear and phobia, was just the tip of the iceberg; that the guy waiting on the other side of my door was about to bring the whole thing to another level. A screw up of literal biblical proportions.

So as I reached for that door handle, I knew that my back was against the wall. My last week had already been hell on earth. The Craigslist roommate ad I had slapped online had subjected me to the most obnoxious and wretched scum this rich, beautiful city has to offer. And strange doesn't bother me. Trust me, I'm all for the weird. But awkward? I've officially hit my awkward quota for the year, thank you very much. Want a glimpse? A few of the "greatest hits"?

- I got into a heated, almost violent, debate because one guy objected to one of my lifestyle choices. I mean, what you do in your home is your own business, I agree. But to me, it's painfully obvious: Trix is an edible cereal while Cap'n Crunch should only be shot at zombies and insurgents.

- One girl said that I had to call her parents back home to pledge that I wouldn't give her "the lesbianism."

There was one guy, just one, who got all the way through the entire vetting process, I mean the entire thing, and was shaping up to be the perfect fit. He was smart, calm, and vaguely handsome, so I wouldn't have to worry about taking number twos with him nearby. Better still, he was paying cash. Upfront! I gave him the apartment contract and he whipped out a pen to sign.

But then he looked up and asked, "Do your feet stink?"

I froze as he stared at me, waiting for an answer.

"No!" I crossed and recrossed my arms because I didn't know what to do with them. Dropping them on my lap, I tried to smile, but my lips came up so broadly that it hurt my face.

Angrily, he put his pen away and stood. "That's a real shame," he said, and then walked out of my apartment, and out of my life.

Wishing for some change of luck, and feeling that I needed something in the "win" column, I turned the knob to my front door and slowly opened my life to my fourth and final candidate.

His bio stated that he was fifty-four, and Gaffrey Palls did seem that old, but an old guy built like a small house. To me he looked like what a retired linebacker would be if he ate nothing but cement and other retired linebackers. Otherwise, there was nothing too alarming about him. He even wore a suit: long, gray dress coat, fine pair of ironed pants, and his shoes shone. Palls' face sat stern, cleanly shaven, all business.

3

Considering all of the crazies that I had paraded through my home, this was like a breath of fresh air. Still, I made sure that everything was in place before I invited him in: I kept the cell phone in my hand with 9-1-1 all ready to press dial; three cans of mace sitting in strategic locations around the apartment; and my trusty safety alert whistle around my neck. Hell yes, I was ready.

And hell yes, I was dead wrong.

As I closed the door behind him, Palls stood in the space between the kitchen and my living room; the sheer size of him made him look like a sumo wrestler navigating a doll house.

As he stood there, I tried my best not to fidget too much. My parents' apartment was on the line. They were away on vacation and had left me to mind everything back home, with rent all up to date while they traipsed around the globe for a month and a half. But then came the bouncing checks, the mail with the red letters stamped "IMPORTANT" on the front. Housing had backlogged our rent as missing for three months. Three entire months in the hole! I did what I could using the account they had left for me, but that was starting to dry up. My parents were long gone, unreachable. My only other family member, my younger sister, was as approachable as the bubonic plague. I didn't have friends, let alone rich friends who had two thousand dollars to spot me.

So that's how I got to that point in time, nervously wringing my hands as a complete and total stranger stood in my living room. Me, Amanda Grey: someone who could only take being in public spaces for five, maybe six minutes tops before wanting to set fire to something.

I stepped around him, trying to hide how desperate I was. I was drowning in the fact that I really needed this to work; that Palls need-ed to be some kind of savior because I was at the end of my rope, up shit's creek, and et cetera with all the other doom-filled propaganda. So to break the ice, I threw on that goofy smile I had been practicing and extended my hand.

"Hello, um, Mr. Palls. I'm, uh, Amanda Grey. Er. Nice to meet you, finally."

Palls stared at my tiny peace offering. Then he smiled, exposing these rotten, misshapen teeth. One canine zigged, the other molar zagged. It made me recoil a bit.

The next thing I knew, he lunged at me, slamming his hand around my neck. The moment I tried to scream, he crushed the breath right out of my throat and lifted me off of my feet. With one arm, he tossed me aside, sending me crashing against my fridge. I only managed to avoid breaking my neck on the hard surface by turning my head at the last second. Not being my first ass kicking—and in no way was it to be my last in this bloody story, unfortunately—I fought off the metallic taste of blood in my mouth, the slippery spots swimming in my sight line, and my broken wrist, to get to my feet and call for help.

With my cell phone smashed somewhere, I grabbed my whistle, fumbled with it, put it to my lips. But no amount of adrenaline could put the air back into my lungs, and Palls, wasting no time, quickly wrapped his tree trunk arms around me in a bear hug.

I managed to get my arms free, but slamming them against his face and shoulders felt like I had entered a fistfight with a freight train. The moment a few of my ribs gave out, punctuated with a warm, wet crunch, my whole body seized. I coughed and blood splattered Pall's face.

So I did the only thing I could do in that situation—I took my whistle and crammed the sharpest side into Palls' eye until it tore open the entire lid. He tried to jerk his face away, but with my palm flat, I jammed the whistle passed those tiny folds of flesh until the whole thing vanished into his head.

I remember that there was this dull pop as it sank deeper into the socket. Even with an object lodged into his skull, Palls didn't budge. So I grabbed the cord, tore the entire whistle out of his face, and crammed the whole thing right into his big, fat mouth.

He let go of me right away, but that didn't mean much on my end, what with my eyes sliding in and out of focus, black to fuzz and back again. I could hear him nearby, thrashing around like an animal, crashing into everything in my apartment, while the whistle lodged in his windpipe made this gargled zwee-zwee sound that was all wet, all mucus.

Then Palls—all two hundred plus pounds of him—face-planted right in front me, his skull driving down like a spike that made a small dent in my hardwood floor.

Gaffrey Palls died staring at me. I still remember the red string hanging out of his throat, the way the crooked veins in his only good eye sprouted out like dying fireworks.

A part of me wanted to say something to cut the silence. I wanted to say something smart like "Boom" or "Yeah" or "Please help me someone because I believe there's a small chance that I'll most definitely bleed to death here."

I never got the chance.

I heard this thick crunch and a hefty wet splatter as Pall's knee snapped like someone had hit it with a sledgehammer. Then his left leg. Then both of his arms. Suddenly, a storm of crows burst out of the Gaffrey Palls' body and descended on my trashed apartment.

The crows—black feathers slicked and glistening, bodies roughly the size of small dogs—loitered around my apartment. Each one sported a black number printed in thick typewriter font at the center of each crimson-colored eye. There were five.

One of the crows—Number 2—hopped over to my tipped over box of Trix and began scarfing down one black beak-full after another. It may have been the concussion speaking, but I nodded to myself because I thought that even freakish crows know what's up: Trix is where it's at. Fuck a Cap'n Crunch.

Only one of the crows seemed to see me, seemed to care that I was even there at all. It stood larger than the rest with a small crest of white feathers above its beady red eyes, a number 5 etched into them. It launched itself at me, striking at whatever I couldn't cover up in time with its blade shaped beak. It tore into my ears, nose, fingers, shoulders. Before I could fight it off, my door imploded with a crash, scaring all of the crows into the air.

A man entered from the hall. I recognized him as the old-ish looking gentleman from upstairs. He lived alone, didn't talk to a soul. I once rode the elevator with him. He smelled of wet pigeons. He came into my apartment swinging a bat, but the crows took flight and burst through my street side window.

Running to check through the broken glass, the man then looked over at me. "You okay, Grey?" he asked, which I found weird because he had never talked to me before. "I'm Barnem. I am a Seraph ... the highest order of angel," he added, which I also found weird because I always thought he was Albanian.

I heard a chirp.

One last bird—smaller, more disheveled—climbed out of Gaffrey Pall's mouth, and with its gray feathers barely grown out and tiny legs wobbling, the creature fell flat on its face and then shook itself off. It blinked at me and chirped again. Number 6.

Barnem yelled and drove the bat down over his head. But the bat missed completely as the chick used its tiny wings to fly a crooked path to my feet. Then its body started changing, warping, swelling. The matted feathers grew tough and leathery; the beak turned into six sharp fingers, three on each hand; the body bubbled like black taffy. What stood in front of me was impish, standing four feet tall with two round hands ending in claws. Its feet were hooved and its legs were arched backward like a doe's. Even for its size, the round, dark belly wobbled when it walked. Its head was shaped like a partially inflated football. And where there should have been horns sprouting up on either side, two soggy flaps, which ... I'm not sure if these were supposed to be stand-ins for ears or what, but otherwise, that's all it had in the "features" department. No eyes, no nose.

As it leaned toward me, it began to growl. The vibrations sank into the floor, the walls. My broken table and shattered dishes began to rattle. Every light bulb in my apartment popped, sending glass and ghostly sparks everywhere. A tear formed around the base of the shadow's head, one that stretched the entire base. A mouth was opening for the first time. It drew closer.

"KFRM!"

The creature slapped a paw over its mouth.

Barnem shot me a look and shrugged. I would have shrugged back, but, you know, the blood loss was impairing my muscle responses.

"KFRM!" the demonic oompa-loompa squealed again.

"Uh. B-bless you?" I said.

7

The creature started heaving, wrenching, snapping its neck from side to side. Along with this twisted sound came a phlegmy whooping, followed by a dry, drawn out wheeze like a car failing to start. The mouth became sucked into his head and its round belly rocked like a water bed. It fell on all fours, gagging and then suckling up air until, like some cat from hell, the creature hocked up a brown ball of mucus which splattered onto my chest.

Spitting out as much of the liquid as I could, I cleared my eyes enough to spot what must have been a ten-inch stack of hundreds and a print of my Craigslist ad soaked in thick grime, just lying there.

For me.

I stared at it.

For a long time.

Barnem, still brandishing his bat but no longer up to using it, called out to me, "You can't be really thinking about accepting this, Grey? It's a demon!"

Beside me, my trashcan laid turned over. Among the garbage sat the "final notice" from my building. I was days away from getting my parents evicted from what was our home, our way of life. And yet sitting on my chest was my answer, my shred of good luck. My way to make all of those worries melt away.

Barnem began massaging the bridge of his nose with the tips of his fingers, then mumbled something about the fragility of the mortal spirit, and about going out for a smoke. He didn't say anything about my door—which he had kicked in, F-Y-I—and stepped over the fractured wood, dragging the bat behind him like a defeated child.

The creature retreated a few paces and spit up a black luggage bag with wheels. Clutching its handle, the demon opened its mouth to smile. The size of its maw was large enough to swallow me whole. But what disturbed me more was that instead of razor sharp teeth, I found myself staring at swollen gray lumps. No teeth, just nubbed gums.

Snapping its jaws shut with a sharp clop, it then pirouetted on the spot and strode off, managing to walk over the mangled corpse of Gaffrey Palls—a solid th-thump from its rolly bags for his troubles. And then it slammed the door to its room.

Barely a second passed when the door flew open again and music came pouring out of the room. With one of my towels dragging around its waist and another tied around its head, the pudgy little demon strutted its way to the bathroom and used a light ass-bump to slam the door shut.

As the hiss of the shower came on, I found myself able to take a breath. Cradling my broken wrist in place, I managed the strength to stagger to my feet and take a good look around. Amidst my ringing headache, broken glass, and the amniotic goo—the realization of what I had signed up for began to billow in my mind like a cloud.

With its rent swells, fare hikes, rubbery bagels, pizza rats, taxis that smell like bathrooms, bathrooms that smell like crime scenes, and the Mets, I struggled through the first-third of my life trying my ever-loving best to survive this sardine can packed with 8.5 million people that insist on rubbing, bumping, and burping on each other in the name of basic human interaction. I had managed this by maintaining the little square feet this city would allow me and by keeping the outside world where it needed to be: on the *outside*. I was perfectly content with this and it's safe to say that I had a good thing going.

And then there were crows.

"I REBUKE THEE, YOU FOUL, DISGUSTING MESSENGER OF BEELZEBUB! I REBUKE THEE! MAY YOU FOREVER BE BANISHED TO THE LOWEST RUNGS OF THE DARK PLAINS, OH HELLSPAWN, AND MAY YOU FOREVER BURN IN ETERNAL DAM—"

"—only for a limited time. Enjoy the Double Bacon Back Barbecue Crisp. Why have a bacon burger when you can have bacon stacked atop bacon ... atop bacon ... atop bacon? That's right. Seven layers of bacon, lathered in secret sauce and stuffed in a half-cooked bun. The Double Bacon Back Barbecue Crisp. And when the ambulance asks you to describe that debilitating pain in your chest ... just tell 'em 'Mmm mmm mm'!"

This was how I spent the next three days. Nothing fancy. Nothing flashy. This was all my impish roommate did to pass the time: horror movies and commercials. The horror movies part I get, I mean, it's a demon. Even without actual eyes to see, it shouldn't be that much of a surprise that a creature like that would get off watching people getting dismembered and tortured. The same goes for when it used my laptop to rip a bootleg of *The Exorcist* and watch it every other second of every other day; twice if nothing else was on. I mean, the same crab-walking, puke-spewing little girl, over and over, doesn't get old. It's one of my favorite movies, but seeing this little hellspawn enjoy it so much was off-putting. It always viewed it in this silence—the kind of quiet a normal person watches a documentary. Or a home video. Package that with the fact that it had the stature of an overweight seven year old, and I don't have to tell you—all levels of creepy.

That's the first, most typical thing that took up its time. All understandable, right? Creepy but understood to an extent.

The commercials ... the commercials were weird on an entirely different level.

The creature never spoke, not a word, but it did murmur and purr from time to time, and only when watching commercials. And of course, it had *no eyes,* so who knows how it was managing to watch anything at all. Any commercials. All commercials. Phallic looking kid's toys, women's sanitary napkins made to smell like Belgian forests, Pinot Grigio flavored dog food—the demon watched them riveted as if taking the most profound of mental notes. A few times I saw it raise a claw to where its chin should have been and lightly tap there, like a human-being thinking. And when a show would start—or restart—it would throw its hands up in the air, grumble, and then grab my phone to play six more levels of *Sugar Spank* until the next show break.

Yeah. It fixed my phone. It also fixed my kitchen, my fridge, my window, and picked up Gaffrey Palls and put him away.

That's right. I said "put-him-away".

In New York, it's not uncommon to come across a used condom lying on the ground. It's totally gross and totally the reason why we New Yorkers stare at the ground half the time (that and certain levels of eye contact ... I'll tell you about that later). Palls was like these used condoms: worn, wrinkled, and spent. Without bones or organs, I watched as Gaffrey Palls—now a crunchy and empty waste—was rolled up and placed in my new roomie's room like a cheap poncho.

The demon even took the liberty of fixing the broken wrist and ribs I picked up the night before. With a quick tap of its claw, my skin folded up into itself like a tiny puckering mouth, sound effects and all. Below the surface, the muscle, tendon, and bone waltzed, cha-cha'd, and in no time, the whole thing was moving just fine. This was the only time it paid any attention to me at all.

Like I said, it spent those first few days on my TV, and I didn't feel the need to say something to the guy/gal/thing (insert proper pronoun for a demon here) that was paying the cable bill. So I lay on the sofa, laptop on

11

my lap, looking for the next source of income. Because sure, the demon had paid my entire rent for the next twelve months, but from what I could tell, it didn't eat. And I still did, so ...

For those three days, Barnem the Seraph would come by and stand outside my apartment. How would I know? *Because I could see him!* With my front door still lying flat on the ground, I could see him glaring at me. Honestly, the demon had taken care of everything, but it left the door for the super to fix. And Barnem, with his bloodshot eyes and five o'clock shadow growing in, stared at me until I invited him in.

"Yes. Barnem. Yes."

The Seraph straightened his shoulders and stepped in. He stood behind the creature as its short legs swung from the green recliner without touching the ground. On the screen, a commercial for self-warming prostate gels played as Barnem slapped his hands together and raised them slowly over his head. He began chanting.

A torrent of wind whirled about the room.

The floor shook and plaster fell from the ceiling.

His chanting got louder.

And louder.

"This again? What are you doing, Barnem?" I shouted without looking up from my laptop. The creature grumbled and tap-tap-tapped the volume button on the remote.

"I'm trying to evoke my spiritual weapon," Barnem screamed. And continued to scream. The wind erupted at his feet and my walls vibrated. His body began to hover, ever so slightly, from the ground. My toaster unplugged itself from the wall, skipped across the floor, and committed suicide out of my window.

Slowly, I got up, pushed the chanting angel's floating body aside, and headed toward the kitchen.

"Want some lunch?"

"Sure," he said, giving up instantly and falling onto the couch. The wind, the chanting, the small-scale earthquake clicked off like a switch. "It's not those awful ramen noodles again, is it? Because you keep coming up with really shitty ways to cook that stuff."

"It's cheap and my parents bought enough for me to fill a bomb shelter with. Ch-ch-check it out." Opening my freezer, I removed a tray that sported tiny toothpicks poking out of the cubicles. I pried one out and shoved the brownish creation in Barnem's face. "Ramen pops!"

"A new low, Grey," he muttered, but he dumped one into his mouth anyway.

The creature, as if abiding by some internal clock, jumped up and turned off the television. Then, scratching the back of its head and yawning, it dragged its feet to its room to close the door and lock itself away. It did this ritual every day at 1:34 p.m. Three days had gone by and I've never been able to look inside that room.

I banged on the door. "I swear, you'd better not be getting ram's blood on the floor and walls or the super's taking our security!"

Barnem hated the ramen pop so much that he had a second one. He was unemployed and I'm not really sure how he came up with rent. Who knows, maybe angels get insta-money powers, too? Barnem wasn't saying a thing about it, but it didn't take a genius to see that he and my new roommate were tied in some way. And something told me it had a lot (see also: *everything*) to do with why a grand old Seraph was living in Queens to begin with.

The first three days followed the same routine. The demon would watch its commercials in the morning and Barnem would take over the TV in the afternoon. He watched nothing but news reports for what he called "the oddities" every day. And every day, he gave up after two or three hours.

"Still nothing," he said, scraping the edge of his face with the remote. "This is a real terrible thing you've done, Grey."

"Says the guy who ate the whole tray!"

"Not that. The Shades, Grey. Your little stunt a few nights ago has unleashed these evils upon the world."

The Shades.

This is what he called the six crows that had sprung up from Gaffrey Palls. Each one, he explained, was a harbinger of death; a vicious demon capable of throwing the world into unending darkness. I guess I lucked out because my roommate was not part of that equation. Ol' blobby barely did anything. Couple that with the Seraph himself, who—minus his attempted save the night Palls came calling—was pretty un-marvelous in every single way. I must admit that this made me pretty damn hopeful. Three days had gone by without anything weird outside of those two. It made me hopeful that life was ready to return to its normal kind of weird.

But there was one of us that was none too happy about that fact.

"It doesn't make sense," Barnem muttered, turning off the screen and tossing the remote aside. "If it were going to happen, it should be happening right now. I should be able to spot these things already."

I closed my laptop and removed my glasses. "How can you tell what's on the news already isn't one of those Shade thingies?"

"Shootings in schools? Cannibalism? Home invasions," he said, rattling off a list of the most recent news, "all man-made sin. All very human problems. The brand of chaos the Shades will bring ... *should* be bringing by now, is going to be unlike anything you've ever seen."

"Well that's good, right? Back to business as usual."

I watched his face, just his face, as some dull emotion ran through it. I'm not sure if angels are supposed to have emotions, but Barnem definitely did. And the one showing on his face at the time was saying that he was less worried about the lives of the people when these things ran wild. That not only was Barnem the Seraph expecting some bad shit to go down, he was also, in a way, looking forward to it.

Then, the creature waltzed out of his room.

Barnem peeked over at him without turning his head. "You say he hasn't left the apartment yet, right?"

"Nope," I replied with a sigh, watching it go through my CD collection. It seemed to be in a Neil Diamond sort of mood. When Barnem didn't say anything else, I pressed the issue. "So what's the story with the little guy? Just a few days ago, you wanted to slay it. And now? It's a Shade, too, isn't it?"

Barnem stood up, but instead of lunging at the creature, he stretched his back. He still smelled like wet feathers and I tended to get extended whiffs of it whenever he moved too close. "Least of my problems. This

14

one's the runt of the litter. You saw how he came out, all scraggly and tiny?"

The demon slipped a CD into its dark palm and let out a hissing chuckle. *Jane's Addiction*. It scurried off to its room and closed the door.

"He *is* pretty useless," I said casually. "No maniacal laughter. No fiery embers. I mean, at the very least, I was expecting him to go outside and lick an orphan or tip over an old lady. No. Nope. Nothing. He doesn't even leave hairs in the bathtub after a shower. He has to be the worst demon I have ever met. But, and I really hate to say this, he's been the best damn roommate I've ever had."

Still lying on my back, I stretched my arms and yawned, but when I opened my eyes, the angel's face was hovering over mine, almost nose to nose. Barnem was bent over the sofa where I was lying, staring me down.

"You have no idea the scourge you have let loose upon humanity," he said with a blank expression, eyes dead.

"Scourge. Got it," I replied with an even blanker expression, my lips barely moving.

"You have to find the other Shades. You have to make this right or else the end of mankind will be on *your* head."

"Right. About that. Barnem, I'm pretty sure where you're from, information comes in scroll notifications or trumpet blows. But down here, we have Wikipedia. That's right. I looked you up and it says that you Seraphs are really 'go-getters', you do the jobs that need doing. That you kind of get off on it, actually. So I think you can go kill the nightmare leprechaun in the next room and then find the other Shades yourself. 'Kay?"

Barnem's eyes began to bulge. "Grey. I'm going to need you to listen."
"Sure."
"Really listen, okay? Are you looking at me?"
"I am."
"Really look at me."
"Barnem. I'm looking at you. You're three inches from my nose. I cannot not look at you."

The seraph gritted his teeth and said, "My 'job', as you put it, is as a herald. A herald, Grey. A herald!"

15

"A herald. Got it. Click! Save as."

"Not a messenger. Not a floating tongue of flame. And thank God I wasn't made into one of those lazy ass harpists who sit on a cloud all day ..."

"Sounds annoying."

"... just plucking away. They aren't even playing anything, you know that? It's a harp. They don't receive special training or anything. For passing their fingers back and forth on something? You don't see me demanding special treatment for an instrument with the same instructions as a cheese grater. But I digress ..."

"You do."

"It's simple. I call the name of the creator when He returns. I slay the beast on earth. I use my spiritual sword to slay the beast. But now you have scattered the Shades, which means no spiritual weapon, which means there's no balance in the world, which means— Oh my god!" he practically screeched. "Are you asleep?"

Peeking through my closed eyelids, I spotted Barnem slapping on his coldest glare. I realized that it was impossible to tell how old he was. Seeing him from time to time in the hallway—his uncombed, rust-colored hair, the thick creases dug into his face like warfront trenches, the way his skin always looked dirty—I kind of took him as any old looking young guy. Or young looking old guy? Whatever. On second thought, there were a few things that didn't seem to fit that judgment call completely. His high cheekbones were of the supermodel variety. And he always stood in this posture and walked with a stride that reeked of a completely unnecessary superiority complex. In short, the guy reminded me of a homeless man who thought he owned the street only because he slept on one every night.

"Are you going to say something, Grey, or are we going to lay there until kingdom come?"

I blinked my eyes a few times before rolling them. "Is staring one of your super powers?"

"I don't have super powers, Grey. I'm from the holy book, not a comic." Barnem stood up straight and shook his head. "And so tell me again why you don't see any of this as even a bit off-putting? You nearly died a few nights ago."

"But I *didn't* ... which, let me say, would have ruined my entire week." When he shot me a sour look, I added, "Aw c'mon. Did you leave your wings *and* your sense of humor back home? Look at the life I'm living, Barnem. My rent's paid up. Your spooky Shades? Haven't heard a peep from them. I probably have the Devil's nephew living in my house, but it doesn't even have friggin' eyes let alone anything even remotely evil in the works. I'm even finding the time to become a bodega gourmet. I'm living the dream. Zero. Nothing. Nada. No consequences. My life is totally 'regret light' right now."

Barnem wasn't having it. "Is there any logical reason why you're so amazingly aloof about things?"

I shrugged. "Maybe it's because I was homeschooled and never learned the true weight of possible circumstances?"

Barnem scratched the back of his head. "Where the hell do you come up with this stuff?" Making for the door, I could hear him mutter under his breath, "Spent thousands of aoens on earth and this time He manages to pair me with the most frustrating person ever created."

I was going to tell him to watch his pronouns but without saying anything else, his holier-than-thou-ness strutted out of my apartment.

I did have a point. It had been already three days and my life had returned to the status quo, boring business as usual. That's what I wanted, really. Sure my parents might show up at any minute, but I thought I could figure something out in the clutch. The apartment was still there and that's what was important. It's what I kept telling myself, anyway.

Flicking on the TV, I knew that some weird stuff had gone down, true, but then what? I had lived a perfectly average life before and I was in control of everything again. Barnem could go take the knot out of his sanctified panties somewhere else. When the TV came on, it was in the middle of a news segment.

"*... and neighbors say that they have never seen anything like this,*" the news reporter said before cutting to a fat, balding eyewitness standing on a street corner. "*Yeah. Freakiest 'ting, ya know. Been livin' here for, I dunno, twenny, twenny-five years? And I never seen nuttin' like dis.*"

The camera panned up.

Above their heads, standing out against the blue sky, embedded into the telephone lines the city ran from pole to pole were the severed heads of twenty or so dogs and cats, evenly spaced; their tattered furs still wet, and their severed necks still dripping down onto the street. The camera panned around the entire neighborhood—every single phone line, street lamp, and traffic light was covered in them. It looked like every pet in a three block radius had been strung up in bloody decorative fanfare.

The first thing I thought was how strange it was that a news crew would show something so graphic on daytime television. The second thing I thought?

"Well that's fucked up."

The demon snatched the remote from my hand and chucked itself into my dad's favorite chair. It scanned channels until it found what is looking for.

"**Attention.**

Power.

Poise.

The new Vilagios' Secret bra.

...LIE...

It's all you need to do is

...LIE...

He can't resist your

...LIE...

Especially created by our Male Lingerie Scientists. This one of a kind invention is padded and re-padded, but not for your body, for your self esteem.

...LIE...

For when it's obvious you can't look like our models, at least you'll get him to think so.

THE LIE BRAAAAAA ...

(Vilagio's Secret waives all liability for what you look like when product is removed. Elastic buckles on the Vilagio's Secret Lie bra pose a serious choking hazard for children below the age of five and men above the age of seventeen. This product, and all affiliated products, including

Vilagio's Redacto Thigh Creame, should not be used in conjunction with any form of contraceptive. Product is not sold outside of the U.S. territories. Bra is not made for most women)."

As the next commercial buzzed onto the screen, I sighed and rolled onto my back. Pinky hooking one of my ramen pops, I took one lick and nearly threw up on myself.

"WELL THAT'S FUCKED up," Barnem said, staring at the spectacle in the distance and crossing his arms.

"That's what I said," I mumbled, and quickly regretted it. I didn't want him laying his whole doting guilt trip nonsense on me. Okay, so I admit it. I knew damn well that I had screwed up. I just, you know, didn't need the constant reminder. I was going to fix it. Okay, at very least I was looking into it, right? I got the gravity of the situation. So when Barnem said that we had to go out and see this pet freak show for ourselves, I only gave him ten to fifteen excuses why he should go alone. And then, after he caught me trying to use my fire escape as a means of egress, and then faking my death in the bathroom—he didn't buy me drowning in my bathtub—I willingly volunteered to go. Honest.

There was already a huge crowd when we got there. Wading into them set needles prickling against my skin, but I kept this to myself and tried to breathe through it. I guess as soon as the news had dropped, everyone came out to witness the freak show for themselves. Barnem had forced me to jump on a train with him to Styeklesci Boulevard, deep in the heart of Brooklyn where the dogs and cats had been strung up like ornaments during a psychopath's birthday. I only went, mind you, because I was on a mission. I needed to convince this dick-ish Seraph to leave me out of his little spiritual adventure. And I was going to be my charming self to make sure that message came in, loud and clear.

Even though the police tape kept us far away from the actual scene, I could still make out the city worker pushed up on a cherry picker, using pliers to remove the animal heads from the cables and slowly stuffing them into oversized garbage bags. How they got up there, especially with the skulls spliced through the telephone line, was on everyone's mind and, by the amount of phones being whipped out, social media feed. Of course, only one of us in the crowd might have an answer to that, but the big shot Seraph wasn't talking.

Looking around, I noticed the community was the exact opposite of my little neighborhood in Queens. Styeklesci was a prime example of how the city tries to force change. The neighborhood was stuck in assimilation limbo, flashing the typical bouts of gentrification and rebellion: a mixture of worn down houses wedged between housing projects, factories, and all crammed block to block with lanky condos. No matter how many boozy brunch lounges and coffee stops and vinyl stores sprout up all over the place, it didn't take a genius to see that there were people still struggling. Not beautiful, not harmonious—a rampaging collage of freshly inked tattoos, old men hollering at women while balancing on stolen milk crates, licensed dog walkers, bodegas, and crackheads. Most of the young hipsters walking around with their five dollar triple mocha, double soy, single caf fraps, names scribbled on the labels, had absolutely no idea what a piping hot two dollar chop-cheese with extra onions does for a person's soul.

This all reminded me of the reason I had bunked up with a demon in the first place. My little section of the city hadn't come to this. Not yet. And more than anything, I knew my parents were proud of the life we had started there.

"So what's the call, Seraph Supreme? Is this one of your Shades or not?"

He didn't answer right away, and when I turned to Barnem, he was still looking at the corpse show, but now he was holding a can of beans. Using his fingers to scoop the brown mush out and stuff a pile into his mouth, he smacked his lips and ignored me.

"When the hell did you—"

Spotting his victim, I snatched the can from Barnem and handed it back to the flabbergasted homeless man sitting behind us.

Barnem didn't even flinch. He licked his fingers and grumbled a,

"Yeah. Only the beginning. And you can joke all you want about this, but it's your job to fix it."

I yawned, both because I was tired and inappropriate. "Agree to disagree."

The man in the cherry picker took another furry lump down and stuffed it in the white garbage bag. Even from where I was standing, you could see his fingers smeared in blood.

"You really don't see the gravity of it all?"

"No. Not really. So someone went all pet crazy, Barnem. Call a priest. Or PETA. Just leave me the hell out of it. Far away. Different zip code." I could spot how this rubbed him the wrong way, more than usual. I usually keep from talking about myself. But for some reason I turned to him and said, "I'm not built for this, okay? I'm not. All of this is so outside of me, Barnem, and trust me, that's where it belongs. All right? I'm not exactly the right person who does well with pressure. Or social interactions. Or family. Or discussions on climate change, stem cell research, or public bathrooms."

"I understand—"

"I'm not done. Or the American Dream. Or backwash when you share a water bottle. Or toy poodles. Or UFO sightings."

Barnem scratched the back of his head. "Are you done?"

I held up one finger.

"American football. All right, I'm done."

"I understand who you are, Grey," he said coldly. "Trust me. I've lived over you for years now. I know you can't keep a job to save your life. I know you used to be close to your sister and that she hasn't been back for what, over a year? Petunia, right? I know you were homeschooled but you're very bright." Before I could ask him how he came to know me in so much detail, he waved me off. "Your mom liked to talk when we met in the elevator."

Hearing about my mom from a complete stranger was a trigger. I set my fist together, pushing the grooves in my knuckles until they fit against each other. I hated that feeling of someone telling me about my life, of someone feeling this power over me. I didn't want anyone to have any knowledge about me, not without my permission. It was like someone raking their nails against my insides. With my anxiety on high alert, I started clack-clack-clacking my knuckles together. It's been a thing I've been doing since I was a kid. The odd pain that spins around my wrist when I do this, the one that shoots up my forearm and caps at my elbow makes me feel so real that it keeps me rooted in the here and now. I do it to keep me grounded before I leap off of the page. Before I spin off into space.

Barnem wiped away an equally bored tear from his eye. "Not going to rant in response?"

"I don't rant!" I replied, blowing up on him. The old lady in front of us turned around to shhh me with her penciled in eyebrows, but I was too far gone. Feeling cornered always flipped me from meek little mouse to a goddamn personification of the Macy's fireworks! "Don't think bringing my mom into this changes anything," I snapped, shoving my finger in the Seraph's face. "You can't guilt me into this. Absolutely not. And you definitely can't play the whole 'God's plan' card. Poor planning on the Creator's part, if you ask me. Should have Googled me and found out that I'm the last person—the last— that should be in charge of this. Plus, I barely believe in fate. The fact that some runway model slips and falls on her face isn't God's plan. It's called gravity."

"It's also oddly satisfying."

"Of course. That goes without saying. Wait! Where are you going?"

Barnem had turned through the crowd and started walking away.

"Wait," I huffed, catching up nearly a block down. "What about the ... the mess? You haven't fixed any of it."

He didn't even stop or slow down to respond. "Don't care."

"Oh, and I'm supposed to?"

"Doesn't matter."

I was in a half jog trying to keep up with him. "Unfair!"

Even though he was in the middle of the road on a green light, Barnem stopped and whipped around on me.

"No. You know what's unfair, Grey? What's unfair—"

A car, speeding to grab the light, narrowly missed hitting Barnem. It slammed on the brakes, skipped the sidewalk, and hit a lamp post, flush. Above the broken glass and blaring car horn, Barnem continued.

"What's really unfair is that I've had to stomach centuries worth, *centuries*, of colonization, governmental subterfuge, and something called '90's Ska music'. Do you know what I'm talking about, Grey?"

Behind him, a woman—her blood-soaked hair plastered to the side of her head—climbed out of the passenger seat and limped over to the hood. Her foot was bent off to the side, dragging along the concrete. She was sobbing.

"Uh. Not really. But, Barnem—"

"Really? It's like white people rapping and doing really bad Caribbean accents. Actually, never mind that, never mind. Don't try to change the subject."

The woman slid herself over to the driver's seat. She started calling out, "Bailey, oh my god, Bailey," as smoke crawled out of the smashed engine.

"Humanity's been screwing this world up since the cave paintings which, in my opinion, and I'm allowed to have it, weren't really that good."

The bloodied woman banged on the window. A small crowd was gathering, but everyone was too busy choosing which filter would bring out the plight of the woman better.

"But the Shades? The Shades are going to tear this place apart. If you haven't been paying attention, they're already at work, Grey, fucking up the already fucked up. They bring out the absolute worst in your people by hanging around. The animal carcass thing? Only petty stuff. Only one of them blowing off some steam. You haven't seen anything yet."

The woman snatched a selfie stick from a young couple trying to frame themselves correctly with the wreck and used it shatter the rest of the glass. Diving in to hug the man crumpled on the steering wheel, she checked his pulse and started screaming,

"And it's because of you, Grey. All of it. No matter how many times you deflect or make jokes or polish it up with some half-assed philosophy of yours. You're wrapped up in this now."

A news crew from the pet massacre swooped in alongside the car. They asked the woman how it felt to lose someone so close to her. She told them that he wasn't dead. The reporter spun back to the camera and promoted a later segment about how nine out of ten women are in denial about failed relationships. I heard a vlogger nearby critiquing what she was wearing at the time of the crash.

Barnem placed his hands on my shoulders. "I will probably have to wait for several more centuries before the Shades come back together. But this mess, this one, Amanda Grey, is on you. You're right. You're the last person who should be in the middle of this. So you get your wish. You can go back to your sheltered life, go back to those four walls you've holed yourself up in all of these years, now with a hellbringer for roommate. See how long the world is going to last now that you've made that selfish decision." Satisfied with himself, the angel gave me a light tap, grumbled a, "Have a nice life," and then walked off in the direction of nowhere in particular.

I watched as street performer started piling into the gawking sea of humanity to take advantage of the crowd, making it impossible for the ambulance to drive in.

I called in Barnem's direction, late but still with reason, "Hey, that sounded like a rant to me!"

With Barnem the Worst Angel Ever having walked out of my life, I focused on getting my partially shitty existence back on track. I returned to my neighborhood in under an hour, and after a quick trek through its aisles to setup one of my famous dinner, I stood at the supermarket checkout line, watching as the bag boy/man shoved my seven cans of kid's spaghetti and a few carrot sticks—all the makings of perfect Friday night—in bags for me to carry.

I tried my best to shake the weight of the day, of the last couple of days, and keep my eyes on the prize. I can't say that I've ever lived an easy life, but it was mine and mine alone. My parents were a big part of it, and at the very least, I had managed to keep their livelihoods intact. I was totally sure that what had happened—an event which included angels and demons and murder and prophecies and ramen pops—was going to last as long the flu, or the fanny pack fad of the 90's.

I was so caught up in telling myself that everything was now okay that I didn't notice that the bag boy/man was staring at me so hard that I could spot the red veined trails in his eyes. He had a round face and his slicked back black hair tied into a ponytail. He was one of those guys that could have been either fourteen or forty-nine; like he had been dragged through his timeline on his face. He sported more tattoos than actual clothing, with two full sleeves of everything from a floating eye and bloody roses, to a Gumbi smoking a fat joint with a big Mexican flag behind him that sported the phrase "Estamos Pasando La Vida". The ink even spread up his neck, stopping behind the gauges in his ears.

Going out in public always puts me in two different positions. First it makes me a jittery fool that can barely cross a street without me wondering if a crazed driver was secretly planning to hunt me down and run me over. Or back up into me. Or skip the curb because he fell asleep at the wheel. Or fall on me from a top floor parking lot. Look, you get the idea. I'm sometimes a nervous wreck, and all the other times I want to head-butt everyone in the face: Christmas carolers, fruit vendors, meter maids ... you name it. Whatever I have, whatever makes me the way I am, probably has a really, really long medical name which means nothing. Means nothing and everything. It made my life a living hell growing up and kept me out of school. Mom and Dad felt that I didn't need to be hopped up on meds and counselling and instead homeschooled me, kept me safe. Of course, that didn't stop kids from being cruel little turds. It wasn't long before my sister heard someone call me "Mental Mandy". Of course, she then beat the living crap out of a boy twice her size for calling me that. Like, the kid had to go to picture day the following week still sporting that purple eye.

I managed to strap a leash on it. I taught myself how to focus and flush those voices in my head before they swelled like an ocean of sound. Before I start drowning. Staying indoors was perfect for me and I never complained; never thought that I was missing out in life. I only came out when it was necessary—chores mostly—but every time, it was like landing on an alien planet. People are weird, sick creatures; mouth breathers. And there were occasions where I needed to assert myself, because New York was a city where your entire existence was a challenge; where you have to elbow, uppercut, and dropkick your way to brush your teeth in the morning.

This whole damn city seemed to breed ogglers. But that doesn't mean I would let a man shove his eyeballs in my personal space. He was larger than me and was reeking of a cologne that was so potent, it probably had a European name that meant lighter fluid. So I stood back and went to my go-to in this situation. I puffed up my chest, bugged out my eyes, and waited there until he ran away. I even sent a little tremble through my lips for good measure.

Feminism deserves its own Haka.

But unlike all of the other men I've ever encountered, this one didn't back down. He kept staring. My bags were packed and ready to go, but those cold eyes were buried into me. And I sure as hell wasn't backing down. So the two of us stood there, in complete silence.

"'Scuse me." The cash register girl, in her triple-thick Dominican accent, tapped the front of the card machine.

Without looking, and keeping myself as inflated as possible, I swiped my ATM card and punched in the pin. Snagging the receipt from her, eyeballs permanently on the freak, I growled a, "Thank you. Have a good afternoon," (because manners) and scooped up my bags. Our eyes stayed locked as I walked backward out of the automatic door and into the busy Queens street.

That afternoon, I arrived back at the apartment that had been recently hijacked by the usual suspects: a demon flopped on its chair, flicking through channels, and an overbearing angel rummaging through my fridge and complaining about a cup I left in there that contained either old milk or new cheese. But these two were nowhere to be found.

What I didn't expect was the landlord standing in the middle of my apartment, hands sitting firmly on his hips, and an expression on his face as if the world were coming to an absolute end.

Little did he know how close he was to this being the truth.

"*Grey*!" With the unfurling 'r' rolling like a snare drum falling down a flight of stairs. "Grrrey! This! What's this?" he bellowed.

"It's a door," I replied dryly, and set the bags down on my countertop with neither demon nor Seraph in sight.

"Yes, yes. It's door. Certainly, it's door. Of course, it's door." He paused and set his hands up to pray. "But, Grey, why is door not doing what door is built to do? I work on building fixes. Right? My job. Pipe on fourth burst, I fix. Blackout on twelve, I fix. Elevator rat problem, I fix. Door not being a door, I don't fix. I find new tenant."

I felt bad for my super, Lou … especially for that last part. I heard the rats were staging a fight club in there on the weekends. Outside of my family, Lou was the only other person who was sweet to me. Lou, who was from some place in Europe, was real big on the how's and why's of our tenement. He went out of his way, superseding even some health codes, to make us all feel right, feel welcomed. He was the glue that held this place together. Every brick. Every awkwardly placed mousetrap.

Lou had a knack for sweating even when standing still, which always allowed the pinkness of his nipples to show right through the white T-shirt he wore. He must have a drawer full of those shirts. He stood large, a long torso, six-eight or six-nine, and always walked around with an odd clumsiness, as if he had just sprouted up in height the night prior.

"Talk, Grey," Lou groaned. "Was walking by with new tenant—"

I jumped up. "New tenant? Who said anything about a new tenant?"

"Hey."

I had been so caught up with Lou that I didn't see him standing there. He was too much of a hipster to be snagging an apartment in my building. The sneaker-shoes. The plaid button down with the scrunched up sleeves. The clean shave of his head. He had dark skin and these eyes that seemed to change color from dark chestnut to hazel depending on how the sun hit them.

This is all to tell you that he was attractive. Not that I found him attractive, mind you, just that he was. It was obvious. Obvious in the same way a vegetarian shows you what they brought for lunch and you say, "Ooh. That looks tasty," but you only say that because you have no inclination, and no future interests, of ordering it. Ever. He was attractive because he was supposed to be.

"Donaldson is moving into 6b," Lou said coldly, "and while walking by, I see door."

"'Door not being door'. I get it, Lou." I pulled a small bag out of the closet and rummaged blindly through it while Lou wasn't looking. As soon as he turned back to me, I handed him the stack of hundreds. "Here's the rent owed. Two months, plus this one, plus the next, and a bit leftover for the door."

Lou held the stack in his hand but didn't count it. Lou loved the tenement, he treasured working there. But he didn't want anyone to know this because, I think, he seemed to be taking a cue from what he thought a super should be: a grumpy, grump who always asks for rent and walks around with a pair of needle nose pliers … just in case something needed needle nose pliering. My parents didn't think it was a gimmick, but I felt it was. I would catch him singing while making repairs, a calm expression on his face when he thought no one could see him. He only barked and grumbled because he loved it so much, because he cared. He was the kind of person that was put on this earth without a sense of irony or sliver of pessimism. I honestly think that he never believed in the American Dream, but fully believed in making it possible for other people. That's why I never took his gruff persona seriously.

Lou folded the cash and stuffed it in his back pocket. Bottom lip sealing his mouth shut, he tipped his head toward me and made for the door. He was almost gone when a loud crash came from behind my roommate's closed door.

Lou narrowed his eyes at me. "You keeping a pet, Grey? I told your parents: children but no pets."

"No, no," I replied, trying to keep my voice from shaking. "Just put up a bookcase in there. Guess I didn't secure it."

Another loud crash.

"And fort made out of cereal boxes."

A shattering of glass.

"A wine rack?"

I smiled and Lou mumbled something to himself, but he walked out of the apartment. Behind him, Donaldson hopped over the door and approached me. He stuck out a hand.

"Nice to meet you," he said, his voice a lot deeper than his first *hey*. "I guess I'll be seeing you around?"

I didn't reach out to shake it. I had had enough of shaking the hands of strange men in the middle of my apartment, thank you very much. I only told him, "Yeah, I'm sure that's a common thing for you to say, but you probably won't see me around. And even if you do, our relationship will probably degrade to meeting awkwardly at the mailboxes with nothing to talk about or me acting like I don't see you running when the elevator door is closing. Not being a bitch or anything. Just would rather save us that awkward navigation of our nonexistent friendship. No offense."

I sensed his body tense up. He froze, locked up. Men always look like they turn to stone when I draw that big, fat line in the sand.

"None taken." He pulled his hand back. And since I probably looked like *I* was the one whose heart had stopped, he added, "That was both clear and succinct, probably rehearsed but still a lot of fun to hear. I actually still think we can be friends in some vein and will attempt in the future to engage you in a way that you feel comfortable."

He then hopped over my door and left without turning around.

"Weirdo," I muttered under my breath.

My roommate came out, dragged its feet to recover the broom and dustpan, and slothed its way back to its room.

That night I ate my kid's alphabet spaghetti to the sound of a broom and the muffled—and possibly Satanic?—vocals of Celine Dion.

SEEING DONALDSON STANDING in my doorway the next day was pretty weird. In hindsight, it should have stood out even more to me, I guess, but I was focused on the demon behind my door and not the man trying to get to know me. I honestly wasn't sure which one freaked me out more.

Luckily, it was too early for the demon to clamor out of its den, and I hadn't seen Barnem since we went to the pet carcass debacle. My building wasn't exactly known to have a revolving door of tenants. Everyone who was there had been for the long haul. And even though he stood out to me—the way he dressed, the way he spoke, the way he was able to digest my sense of humor—I didn't expect to see Donaldson again. He had moved in two floors above me, which might as well have been Mars in terms of distance. Not at all uncommon for people like him, after meeting me once, to fall into a blank space of complete nothingness, leading us to never speak again.

Luckily, watching him step into my apartment gave me the jurisdiction to be my typical charming self.

Lifting my gaze from my laptop, I gave him a sour look and asked, "Hey, buddy, where the hell are we living? Twelfth century Prussia? No one knocks anymore? C'mon!"

Donaldson glanced at my door, still not being a door, and slowly knelt down to give it a light knock.

I went back to the screen and fixed my glasses. "Who is it?"

Laughing, Donaldson walked in. He held up the plastic cup he was holding and shook its dark brown liquid. It looked like syrup infused saliva.

"It's coming out of every spout in my apartment," he grumbled. "I think some of it's even coming out of my doorknob, but I'm not sure how that's scientifically possible."

I didn't look up at him. "It's Tuesday, Donaldson. Lou pours ice-tea mix into the pipes to boost morale. What can I do you for?"

"Right. Well I just came down to ask where you recommend to eat. Preferably on a budget."

"Your own home."

"Hmmm. And what if my home isn't stocked up yet? Any place for takeout?"

"Burly's is open right now," I suggested.

His brow furrowed. "The burger spot across the street is open at 10 a.m.? Who in their right mind would have a burger at …"

I snapped my head up and stared at him.

Exactly forty-nine minutes later, I fixed the knot on my drawstring pants and sat back in my stool. Burly's was a tight fit: only ten tattered, spinning stools in the entire joint. It was like someone found a grill in a closet, fired it up to see if it worked, and turned around to see folks dishing out their orders. There weren't any menus in Burly's and that's because they only sold two things: an overcooked hockey puck called a burger and an overcooked hockey puck with cheese. The place was run by an old Polish couple. Pops—with his ultra-thick glasses and three re-maining hairs slicked up and over—ran the over-greased grill with what seemed a quiet rage that had been slowly brewing over the course of sixty years. He stood at the stove, slouching in his stained apron, as if he was guarding the gates of Heaven. His wife, a woman that only went by the name of Lady—with her large hazel eyes and a mole in the shape of Lyndon B. Johnson—manned the register and plates

I hadn't been to Burley's in a long time, so maybe that's the reason I leapt at the opportunity. Besides, I was really getting sick of the ramen patties I had made for breakfast and was then repackaging for dinner. Yes, I had money from my demon roommate, but I was being frugal about spending it. Just in case.

Unfortunately, I had forgotten that when someone invites you out to eat, you sort of have to be ready to do something absolutely horrifying.

Socialize.

Donaldson silently nodded his head as he held up what was to be his last bite. "Thanks for the recommendation. Helluva choice, Amanda. One thing bothering me though. Why do they call it Burly's?"

"Dunno," I replied slowly, and glanced down at my plate. "Maybe that's how they thought the word 'burger' sounds."

He smiled with his eyes. "And I can't say I've been to a place that lets you bring your own toppings."

"Yup. Free toppings of your choice, no matter the choice. You went safe with that bag of Doritos, Donaldson. Never took you as a wuss."

He shrugged. "I'm new here, remember? How was your … hot sauce and Pepto Bismol burger?"

I untied my hair from its "safe to scarf down food" position. "Don't knock it. It was both delicious and decisively protective of my stomach lining." When he shot me a thumbs up, I averted my gaze again. "True story. My sister and I always used to come here. We wondered what would they *not* cook up here. I mean, if I came in with a human foot, would Pops slap that on the grill like nothing? Or if I came in with a burger, would they throw that burger *on top* of another burger? Can I make a burger burger?"

Donaldson chucked the last bite in his mouth as Pops' metal spatula filled the place with the sound of a Kung-Fu sword fight. With his mouth clear, Donaldson asked, "A burger burger? Sounds blasphemous."

"Sounds like lunch," I replied boldly.

Donaldson laughed. "Can I ask you a question?"

"Not really."

"You said you came here with your sister? Why don't you come here often?"

I stuffed fries into my mouth and mumbled a bunch of random things. "I'm allergic to bees. And airborne viruses. And this damn recession is kicking my ass."

Donaldson nodded again. "You do that a lot, you know?"

"Do what?"

"Deflect."

"Deflect." I rapped the counter with my fingers. "You've only known me for ... what, twelve seconds, Donaldson? You think that by buying a gal a burger, you can try to diagnose her?"

He sat back and crossed his arms, but his face showed that he was still amused. "Not saying that at all, and I'm not trying to mess up your Zen in any way. I'm new to the building and I'm attempting to get to know someone. You know, just communicating."

I smacked my lips and burped out an, "Overrated.

Donaldson slipped me a slightly credulous look. "So you don't go out? I can believe that. But what about online?"

"Nope. Don't even have it on my phone."

The way Donaldson leapt up, I might as well have elbowed him in the crotch. "I call shenanigans! You're kidding, right?"

"Donaldson, I do not and shall not kid you. I lack the desire, capacity, and charm to kid."

Wanting to prove him wrong, I slowly handed him my phone the way someone hands another human being a napkin they sneezed in.

Donaldson flicked through the screens. After he was done with his inspection, he handed my phone back and exclaimed, "Well, Grey, you have my respect. Being without the social media nonsense ... that must be an easy life to live."

"Well I'm learning that the hard way," I admitted. "You know, I used to enjoy my 'Lady Cave'." Donaldson did a double-take. "That sounded a lot better in my head. What I'm trying to say is that I have—unwillingly, mind you—been exposed to an alarming amount of television; an 'assload', I would say, if 'assload' were a proper unit of measurement."

"Noted," Donaldson agreed.

"I thought I was bad, but this entire society is built on insecurities. How many views did you get? How many likes have you nabbed? Upvotes, downvotes, ten items or less. You have to stress over your opinion about someone else's opinion on something someone wrote on a bathroom stall. You have to worry about missing that trend that will make you feel dumb. Otherwise, how else will you learn to feel the social/emotional struggle of being a left-handed dentist in New Guinea? You have to 'catch" texts.

You have to 'count' characters. I used to be too busy slowly rotting away in this physical existence, or waiting for baked potatoes to finish, but now I'm busy being swallowed up by a culture of 'spin-off offshoot reboots'. Of people I don't know doing things I can't care less about for amounts of money I will never see. Do you know that there's a hit show where a guy, his wife, and their twelve children drive cross-country renovating shoe boxes for stray cats? It's called *The Whole Kitten Kaboodle*."

Donaldson feigned covering his ears. "I'm pretty sure I'm dumber for knowing that."

"No, you know what's worse? What's worse is that I saw every episode, every season, every single one. Because everything is processed now into recording shows that you would not be able to watch otherwise. Basically, TV is watching TV for you and there's still not enough hours left in the day for me to finish my laundry *and* safely forage for food." I took a breath and passed my hands over my face. "Just makes me wonder if I was really missing anything by minding my own business all these years."

"Well, Grey. Hell is other people."

I know Donaldson meant well by the comment, but the cold hand of irony struck me across the face nonetheless. A knot formed in my gut, the same way it did every time I sensed a stranger getting all up in my space bubble. It was moments like these that made me more comfortable to be as aggressive as humanly possible, so I gave him a side eye. "Just because you listened to one of my rants doesn't mean you can be my friend."

Typically, this comment was enough to keep someone in check and give me space for some breathing room. But Donaldson just smiled. "I'll take your defensive comment to mean that you enjoyed yourself but still don't want to look weak in front of me."

I shook my head. "Donaldson, I'm pretty sure that you were created when a lonely wizard enchanted a thesaurus just because he wanted someone to speak to."

Donaldson bowed. "Possible."

I balled the napkin up and tossed it into my plate.

Sensing that the conversation had now run its course, Donaldson handed the bill and some cash to Lady. She grinned and America's 36th

President gave me a knowing nod. While she rang him up, he tried one more time.

"You know, you don't have to call me Donaldson. The super kept pronouncing my name wrong, so I let him hang onto the last name. But you can call me Jeff. Or Jeffrey."

The name clashed like cymbals in my ears and my body seized up. The sound of it was so close to a certain bastard I murdered in my apartment ... too close. Donaldson must have caught on because he quickly added, "Or not. Didn't mean to twist anything up here."

"Right. Well ..." I hopped off the seat and headed for the door. Lou was coming to fix my door and I needed to be around to curb his questions about the demon I was housing. To me, fixing the door was important. It was the only thing that had been separating me from the rest of this city and I didn't need to breathe in any more of it.

And then something hit me. Before I crossed the street, I whipped around in time to catch him coming out of Burly's.

"Donaldson."

"Yeah?"

I put my hands on my hips and stood so close that I hoped he could feel how serious I was.

"Are you flirting with me?"

"I—"

"Because if you are, you can stop. You paid for me to eat. I thank you. My stomach thanks you. You're also not too horrible to talk to."

"Um. Thank ... you?"

"You're welcome. And I actually wouldn't mind doing this again as long as you're *not* flirting, you're showing *no* romantic interests in me, and you-don't-have-any-inclination-to-occupy-space-within-my-vagina." I spouted every worth emphatically.

"*Whoa!* H-hey." He looked around. "Promise. None of that. I mean, I'm not doing any of that. Okay?"

Satisfied, I crossed the street and headed right for my apartment. When I got there, the demon ignored me and laughed as the little girl crab-walked down the stairs once more.

37

THE NIGHT EVERYTHING changed … Excuse me, the night when everything that had already changed, *changed again*, started off with a call that I never expected.

It was only a few days after Donaldson showed up in my apartment and I was knee deep in laundry. In fact, I had so much of it piled up that I couldn't carry it all. I stuffed some underwear into my pants, wedged my bras between my armpits, and even carried a roll of socks in my mouth, so that I could heave, carry, drag, and furiously kick the entire load from the bathroom to my apartment's washer.

Okay, so the washer was just my mom's metal washboard, a hunk of metal old enough to be salvage from the Titanic, and a large steel basin in the center of my living room. My life lacks very little romance, I must admit. And even though I saved off several cardiac arrests, the demon, fully entranced by the television set, didn't even lift one shadowy claw to help.

Barnem was still MIA, but it wasn't even something I cared about anymore. If he was gone, then good riddance. Lou still hadn't fixed my door, something about the hinges needing to be specially ordered. So for privacy's sake, I propped the door up over the opening, at least to give the illusion that folks should stay the hell away. Unfortunately, it only attracted hallway foot traffic. I can't explain it, but more than once, someone peeked into the space, right when the demon was on one of its advertisement benders. Both times, I had to roll up a magazine and whack it on the blobby head until it scurried back to its room while I yelled, "Shoo! Shoo!" That was before I found my bed full of burnt flakes of what was left of my magazine collection. Message received.

That's the whole picture. That's where I was when the call came in ... elbow deep in soap and suds. That's where I was when *she* called. Petunia. That's my lovely sister's name. That's the name we—meaning me and my great parenty folks—used to call her. From the moment she was born to right about the second before her prom date pinned the corsage on her. Petunia.

Now she went by Ingrid. You believe that? Petunia to Innnnnngrid. How someone goes from the light, fluttery name of a flower to the sound a bear trap makes when someone drops a refrigerator on it is beyond me. Ingrid. CLANK. PLUNK.

Spotting her name on my caller ID—properly labeled by yours truly as "OMGWTFFML" with Sauron's theme from the *Rings* trilogy as a ringtone—I grumbled a half-assed, "Hello," when I picked up.

We were close as kids, Petunia and I. She used to dress her Barbies in ornate dresses and I used to use my G.I. Joe's to practice the proper ways men should approach a lady—"I understand that your glittery star ball gown and lack of a left arm does not give me the right to disrespect your space or your intelligence ..."

That seemed like lifetimes ago. I guess I would always remember Petunia Grey: the bubbly little girl who would, without hesitation, object to the big, fat family hug our parents gathered us up for every night when we were kids. The same girl who, when that inevitable hug landed and we were all huddled in our little circle, and Mom and Dad's bodies were covering us up like large, gnarled trees with dull heartbeats, would have a giggle fit that would last long after I chucked a pillow at her head to shut up. Sometimes, it would last all night if she didn't fall asleep with that silly little smile on her face. I remember that Petunia would give the best hugs, too. Ingrid, on the other hand, didn't believe in any of that. Ingrid was the kind of woman who would look at you leaning in for an embrace and ask if she could outsource that shit.

"Mandy, darling," she said. "How are you? How've you been? What is life?"

"Nothing, Petty."

She absolutely hated that nickname, so I used it often. Hearing it, she paused. Shook it off. "I was only …" The barb seemed to latch back on. She fought it off and continued, "I was only calling to check in on you, dearie."

After a year of not hearing from her, she hit me with a dearie *and* a darling in the first minute of the conversation. This coming from the same girl, mind you, who once drank so much water out of an open pump one sweltering summer night that she threw up in the hair of the Newman's kid from downstairs.

"You never call to check in, Petty."

"Oh, give me more credit than that, Mandy. My older sister is locked away in an apartment in Queens and I can't see how she's doing? Are you working? How are you making ends meet?"

This is how Ingrid spoke most of the time, with questions in triplicate and wrapped in a nasally faux accent that convinced herself that she wasn't from Queens; convinced people from Queens that she wasn't from England, and convinced people from England that we Americans learned our English accents from our ambassador, Madonna.

"Sure, no, and I'm fine," I answered in sequence.

"Aw, honey."

"I gotta go, Petty. I'm in the middle of something important here," I said, dunking a pair of my underwear and watching it pop right back up to the surface.

"But how are you, Mandy? Are you eating well? Have you heard from Mom and Dad?"

"Fine, hell no, and just … no, Petty."

"It's a shame," she said, obviously leading to something, "They leave and don't send word or even mail. I guess it must be an issue with their location. I mean, when I spoke with them, they didn't have a clear line …"

I nearly dropped the phone "When? When did you speak with them?"

"Oh," she said, surprised. "Oh yes. About a week ago, darling. I was out shopping with Blake. Oh, you remember Blake, dear? He hasn't changed one bit. Still the husband who shops and shops. Hooked on retail therapy, I keep saying, but he barely listens. Anyway, when we returned, they called, just as we were walking in the door. They sounded good. They asked me to call you and check in."

40

"*They* asked *you*? A week ago? Why didn't you call me sooner?" I was practically shouting now.

"You sound cross. No need to be cross. Look, Mandy, I have even better news than that. I am ...-" Some of my hair fell into the metal tub. I flicked it out and cursed, missing entirely what my big, dumb, fat headed sister said. " ...I hope that's all right. Is it? Should I make other plans? When should I—"

"Yes, fine, and I don't care. Gotta go, Petty. My apartment is on fire and I have an early day tomorrow. Talk to you later. Bye."

But as I drew the phone away from my ear, I heard Petty say, "Fabulous, darling. I'm at the airport now. My flight lands at 8ish, around there. Gate 7 via Grand Line. I only ever fly Grand Line."

A sat up and fumbled with the phone again, this time saving it from dropping in the tub.

"Petty. Petty. Wait a second."

"Did you know they raised their seat prices, dear? Does that make any sense? I mean, I can fly coach, but why would I?"

"No, yes, and because you're stuck up bitch. But, Petty, what are you doing? Why are you getting on a plane?"

"I'm heading to the terminal now, Mandy. Love, please, for the sake of everything, don't come in a smelly cab. You know Saint is traveling with me and he complains when he's around cabbies smelling like they had spent all day in a sweat box and tried to douse it in five dollar cologne."

"Petty—"

Hearing the click and a dial tone made me furious. I wadded up a ball of soaked underwear and flung it across the room where it slapped up against the wall and slid down in one squishing heap.

The demon looked at the splotch mark and cocked its head at me. Disgusted, it turned off the television and walked to its room where it shut the door.

41

I DUG THROUGH my dirty laundry, fetched some tolerable clothing, and squeezed through my front door/cave hole, hoping that if I got to the airport in time, I could convince Lady Ingrid to turn around. Convince or scare, I wasn't sure yet. Let's say that I realized that if renting out a room to an inhabitant of the netherworld didn't nab me a one way ticket to hell, I figured punting a small dog would—at the very least—bump me to first class travel when I do.

Without any frequent cabs—the ones I did see, the green cabbies, were parking to call it a night—it forced me to run two streets over to Belvadere: a busy little strip lined with hookah lounges and falafel spots. The yellow cabs frequented this area, picking up the drunk folk, and replacing them with sobers. The fastest way was through a side street on Fisher. The inverse of Belvadere, this block only housed small Mom & Pop shops: a Pawn Palace and a community garden, both of which were already shut down and gated up for the night.

As I ran over the uneven sidewalks and cut across Mike's Autobody Shop, I was trying my best to shake the thoughts starting to bubble up in my brain. But the more I attempted to douse them, the more I tried to ball these thoughts up and chuck them to the deepest, darkest corner of my already heavily cluttered psyche, it only made the voices and explosions ring louder between my ears, shaking up my brain stem, plucking the nerves in my teeth. The constant pounding started to bleed into my steps as I ran, each one landing like an asteroid, each step wiping away civilizations and cities and people going about their daily lives, trying to paint, and park their cars, and Facebook stalk exes.

Living with my parents had curbed the frequency of the attacks I had, but this was suddenly different. When it came to family, I was always going to lose myself trying to not let them down, even my prissy, thick-headed sister. I had managed, up until that point, to avoid a complete and utter meltdown; to deter my very own, very intimate flame-filled Armageddon. Even with the world coming down all around me. Even with my door not being a door, my normal life not being normal, and my new life—the one now re-released with bonus gore and religious imagery—I had thought that I could wrestle my rabid life to the ground and beat the shiny rainbows out of it until my knuckles bled.

However, as I ran along that abandoned street, with nothing but my heart thumping in my throat, I knew that I had been fooling myself. Even though it had been five years since my last one, I knew what a panic attack felt like. How it coils about your lungs. How it reaches up your ribcage and gnaws at the lining of your throat. I lost myself while running. I went cold. I couldn't feel my arms pumping, my legs striking the street. I sensed myself moving, clattering—a sloppy marionette with jumbled strings and useless flopping body parts. And I knew that the largest, most pressing question was threatening to burst my skull open like a wet melon. I knew this so much in fact that I couldn't help blurting it out to the empty block in front of me, out into the street lights overhead, to the New York night air.

"Why did Mom and Dad call Ingrid and not me?"

And then it hit me.

Not an answer.

A fist.

It flew from out of the darkness to my left. I heard the scrape of a footstep seconds before, and my flinch actually saved my life. The knuckles landed flush against my temple with a force that sent me sprawling out on the concrete.

With my head swimming, a dull thud of pain vibrating behind my eye sockets, and my ears wailing like sirens, it was hard to hide the fact that I smelled the guy and his ammonia-scented cologne before I got a good look at him. This all helped me recognize the asshole as soon as he came out of the shadows.

 4 3

The bag boy/man from the supermarket.

He was wearing ripped jeans and a white tank top, which exposed all of the tattoos on his body. From his neck down, there was barely any space on his skin that wasn't scratched into with ink, with even a few in the linings of his ears. The most notable addition to this gang-banger ensemble was a hunting knife, large enough to make even Rambo blush, which he turned in his hand, over and over.

Then something happened, something that never happened before. The whole nervous wreck, mental breakdown I was having—the one that usually flooded my senses, strangled me, scattered red and yellows on my vision, set ants running through my skin—stopped. Just like that. It was like a switch was flipped in my head and the world became suddenly so much clearer, sharper, as if the edges of everything had been traced over in heavier, darker outlines. Like every color had a clear and distinct sound and taste and feeling.

With this new clarity, I scrambled back on my hands and knees. He could have stabbed me at any time, but he kept drawing closer, which put his nuts within striking distance of a straight kick from my right leg. I gladly rung that bell, and he fell to all fours, sending the knife clattering to the ground. I stood up to run, but he blindly reached out and tripped me with his arm. On the ground again, I turned over onto my back and, as he reached out for my ankle, I drove my knee into the side of his head. The sound his skull made smashing against the green dumpster made me sick to my stomach. So I did it three more times for good measure.

Seeing the opening, I got up to run but was suddenly scared when I heard a voice say, "Stupid."

It was the bag boy/man. As he stood up from the concrete, I saw that most of his skull was a deformed lump, as if it were made of paper mache, and his jaw hung limply off of his face like a broken swing. More and more dark blood poured out of this wound and down his tattooed neck. From out of his dislodged chin, a crow's head with a wisp of white on the crest peeked out at me, its red eyes sporting the number 6. It squawked, looked down the street in both directions, and then stuffed itself back into the man's dangling skin a like a train conductor. Clumsily, this odd shell of man found his knife and pointed the business end at me.

It was hard to see in the streetlight, but the tattoos on his skin were moving, swerving, pulsating with their own lives. His tanned skin had become this fucked up tapestry of things no one should see: a certain cartoon mouse stuffing handfuls of meat from the belly of his duck friend into his mouth; a dong-shaped rocket ship making circles around the man's throat. Even Gumbi had grabbed a big breasted woman and sat her on his green lap as he took a big toke of his blunt.

"Know what ... you cost me?" The distorted voice was not coming from the man's mangled face, but the odd slurping from his throat sure was. Every time he breathed in, all that followed was this sloppy gurgling sound. "You ... cost us *everything*! Palls ... was supposed to carve you up. Easy kill ... easy kill. You were served up ... to us like a fat goose on ... a silver platter. Your meat ... hanging from the rafters. That ... was my idea. Mine."

He took a step forward. Black feathers fell out of his swinging chin.

The moving tattoos began to get faster in their fucking and killing and cannibalism. Their eyes began glowing red.

"You ... screwed that up. So I came back ... to finish the job. Gotta get ... to you before the others do."

Off to the side, by a garbage pile, I spotted a broom. I quickly scooped it up and got it ready to put to good use. Demon or not, there was no way in hell I was anyone's late night snack.

But then, standing a few feet from us, a little farther down the street, we suddenly noticed that we weren't alone. In the shadows, within the blackness of the alley nearby and out of the halo of the streetlight, someone was standing there. I'm not sure how long it had been there, or even *why,* but its outline seemed darker than the world around it: a deeper shadow, humanoid in shape but all wrong. Jagged and flowing, as if its skin were black flames.

At least that's what I thought at first.

When it stepped into the streetlight, I sighed. The squat little body of my roommate waddled out, its little hooves click-clocking its blobby body into view. It smiled—dull gray nubs for gums in its wide mouth—and it waved its sharp claws as a silent "Howdy" to the both of us. The darkness and evil from before was gone, and instead of a second helping of menacing evil, there stood this ridiculous looking thing with doe legs and a round belly. With his featureless head, it looked like a pathetic stray—nothing like the horror brandishing the knife nearby. The little black flaps of his ears were even propped up the way a dog looks when it sees someone it likes.

"You," the possessed man grumbled at it. "Always around … for scraps. Fuck off." When the demon didn't fuck anywhere off, with some of his eyeball now drooping out onto his chin, he repeated, "Scram!"

My roommate threw his hands up, as if to say that he wasn't there for any trouble. But even with his claws in the air, he started walking toward me.

I gripped the broom handle tighter. Now there were two of them and they were getting closer. Closing in. *This is what I get*, I thought. My week had been rough enough without the hellspawn and the doom. Now it was a matter of who was going to kill me first.

Taking my chances with the little guy, I charged at it. He didn't react to this at all and stood perfectly still as I drove the handle down across his head. However, I ended up swinging at nothing but air, losing my balance, and hitting the ground.

And then there was this pop.

A wet, split of flesh.

I turned around to see that my roommate had leapt onto the man's chest, clasped him by the shoulders, and clamped its mouth over the man's entire head. I remember muffled screaming, a barely audible crow squawking, the man flailing at the air with his knife, and then a nasty crunch of bones. With one quick drag to the ground, it began the process of swallowing him whole. Slowly.

My roommate's body swelled as the possessed bag boy/man's legs kicked at the air. The rest of him was already sliding down the stretching black gullet, finding its way into the protruding belly. My roommate bucked his head back, the way an animal kicks more of the meat to the rear of its throat. Between the crumpling bones, the muffled screams of panic, and the frantic punches coming from inside the creature's stomach,

4 6

I could only sit there and watch, on the verge of throwing up but too scared to. I watched as the shoes slid in and vanished. Watched as the screams died to moans, down to whimpers, and then died.

Following this, there was a moment that nothing happened—a long pause after the most violent thirty seconds I had ever seen in my life. And then my roommate's body continued to expand, twist, buckle, flatten into impossible shapes. This wild ink blot, contorting itself like a cartoon drawn by a raging alcoholic, shot up into the sky.

The stars seemed to go out as the night around me began swallowing up every source of light possible. The air grew thicker, like trying to inhale syrup, making it almost impossible to breathe. Small charges of crackling black energy leapt from its skin, striking the concrete, the walls, the street signs. The parked cars that were struck began wailing, horns honking, high beams sending columns of pure light through the darkness, windshield wipers pumping away. I dodged a few of the strikes myself as they arced around like black lightning bolts.

Then everything drew back into the creature's body, slowly at first, but then with a force that felt as if it were trying to suck me in, too—a black hole in the middle of Queens.

Suddenly, the air softened. The stars blinked back into the world. Even the parked cars each slammed shut, one by one by one. And when it was all done, the round, impish body it had before was gone. Now what stood in front of me was six feet tall, with gangly arms. Its legs, no longer hooved and fragile, bent at rounded knees and flexed under its weight.

Sensing me nearby, the demon staggered over to where it heard my drawn out breaths. Around us, rubber-necking neighbors began filing out onto the street, poking their heads out of their windows to find out what was going on. A few whipped out their phones to call 911, others to film me lying in the middle of the street as this silhouette drew close.

The demon stopped and lowered its head over me.

There I was again, lying at the feet of this creature, having survived my second life or death situation in a week. But unlike the time in my apartment, I was fully conscious of what was standing in front of me—the nightmare that had moved into my spare room, took over my bathroom, hijacked my TV.

Tilting over me, it was easy to see that its head was now two times larger. Even the little flaps on the sides of the head were longer, more rigid, with a curl that ended in a sharp point. Two seams began forming around the front of the head. The creature stood, scratched at them like a kid picking his scabs, and bent downward again. After a few repeats of scratching then staring, the seams tore open, and two yellow, perfectly circular eyes blinked back at me.

I'll admit, as my senses suddenly came back to earth, as the world around me quieted and dulled itself back into some semblance of normalcy, I should have been happy that I wasn't dead. I mean, twice in one week, I had come seriously close to losing more than my sanity and my apartment. And both times, I had managed to come out of it (somewhat) intact. I should have been grateful. I get it. No doubt. That should have been front and center, my first thought.

But the truth was, staring up at those large, yellow eyes—eyes as large as dinner plates—and having seen the demon attached to those eyes *eat* another human being, made me realize that I had been lying to myself the entire time. That there was no coming back from this, no way of getting my life back. Petty was on her way to raise hell. My parents could be coming back at any moment, any second, and all of them would finally find out how much I've let the whole thing go to shit.

And there was something else. Call it a premonition or whatever. Part of me started realizing that there was a time coming when I was going to wish I had died in that alley, under the sputtering streetlights and honking cars. That I was going to regret that it was Palls, not me, who choked to death in my apartment that night.

In that moment—and this is all the point, the whole "lesson" to this whole first bloody chapter—that somehow, someway, I was going to look back on my first week and realize that all of it was a joke, that all of it was nothing, a veritable cake-walk, freaking Fiji, compared to what was really coming for me.

"KFRM!" the demon hiccuped in a deep voice, a whiff of thick after-shave on its breath.

"Bless you," I said softly.

EPISODE TWO:
OCCULT OF PERSONALITY

ONLY A DAY after Petty had shown up announced, the same night I was forced to watch a demon—my roommate—munch on a human being, I actually woke up to find a video of the whole thing on the internet. Sure, you couldn't tell it was me exactly. But I knew. Filmed from a cellphone, the clip was of a blurry but scared to death woman sitting in the middle of the street and a long shadow looming over her. The schmuck holding the camera phone was adding his own screaming commentary the entire time. Several hundred "Share" button smashes later and the video hit a million views in a few hours, two million by morning.

I had gone viral.

At first, the Internet did as the Internet does. Conspiracy theories, slow motion takes, message boards dedicated to finding out if it was a hoax or not. I even found a few groups talking about combing through my neighborhood, because the video featured the sign outside the auto body shop down the block. But when that well ran dry, the public affection mutated and not even an hour after posting, a "remix" video was released. On this version, the audio was bumped up with the guy's voice on the video autotuned so badly that it sounded like a seal having a five-minute orgasm. Within a week, downloads of "Run Bitch, Ommagahd!" had tripled the amount of views on my video.

Then the guy on the clip hit up the late night talk show circuit. Then it was made into the slogan for bean-stuffed hot dogs. And like that, my one hundred seventy hours of fame via the viral video labeled "A Demon in Queens?" sank quietly into the dark ether of the web.

I enjoyed living in a swipe left society where there was zero surface area left for absorption. Not with text crawls and phone buzzes and poop emojis firing at us from all sides, at all times of day. On trains, on bathroom stalls, commercials for commercials hidden in remastered, rebooted pre-sequel movies (in 3D!). That's why I tried to not stay around in public after my attack. Left all of that the hell alone. The supermarket delivered my groceries and I duct taped a poncho to stand as my front door. I didn't want to become the wild weird world walkers I had tried to be part of a few weeks ago. The ones with the dumbfounded faces and glazed eyeballs—a side effect of becoming so oversaturated with information that most of it's expired before you can even process any of it. Flushed before it caused you serious harm.

If only siblings were the same way.

Picking up Petty at the airport, I'll admit made me feel a bit split. The good and the bad.

First, she was my little sister that I hadn't seen in a year.

And that's as far as the good stuff goes.

Petty had a way of speaking that was always wrecking ball material, like blows to your gut. I always felt wasted after talking with her on the phone and I wasn't looking forward to spending any time with her. Luckily, neither did she. As soon as she hopped in the cab, she asked to be taken to a hotel. I don't know what her problem was about staying in my parent's house or why she even flew back here in the first place, but she kept to herself the entire ride. After getting my ass kicked, I was damn thankful for the silence.

This is how it continued for the next few days. She didn't call or come knocking. She stayed to herself. Again, it made my life easier so I didn't ask why. I had my own problems back at home.

The next morning, my roommate's door swung open and he slunk out. On the demon front, where blobby hung out mostly in his room, this version of him was always in the kitchen or on my couch. The only time he showed any signs of life were when he watched commercials. He still loved doing that, sometimes chuckling to himself. But now with his big, yellow eyes glowing and his overall clumsiness, he came off as a loafing teenage stoner. Couple that with my fear that he was going to make an hors d'oeuvre out of someone and you can already see that I was on edge every time. I didn't worry about my safety. The guy still didn't seem to care about me at all.

That's not entirely true, I thought, as he took the controller and plopped down in the chair with his long legs over the side. A piece of me started wondering if he had shown up to somehow, I don't know, save me? That he had scarfed down that guy as a way of coming to my rescue? It had been rattling around my mind for a long time, but I quickly bound it up and flushed the thought away. I didn't want to think about what that meant.

So there I was, stuck in a holding pattern between my god awful sister and a lazy demon. I needed some kind of stupid miracle to make things right. Instead, I poured myself some cereal.

And then the news came on.

"A new local story out of Manhattan," the newscaster at the scene explained. "'We just want to be heard'. That's the sentiment being held by the cult calling themselves 'The Beguilers' who, this week, have up set up shop here in Washington Square Park."

The news crew was busy interviewing one of the cultists while the rest of the flock, only four or five others, pranced around and beat a drum wrapped in cellophane. All of them wore linens which looked like curtains from a 99 cents store. All of them sported shaved heads, men and women alike. And in the middle of those shiny heads, all of them had carved a symbol of a clock on their foreheads.

"We are the Beguilers," the lead idiot said, looking right into the camera. "We are followers of the true dark. We hear the songs of the Tower of Night."

Suddenly, another man jumped onto the screen. He wore black guy-liner and held up a sign with a sorry ass looking snake on it with the speech bubble saying, "U Don't Sssspeak For Me!!!".

"We, the followers of the Eldest Snake, the truest believers of our Dark Lord, are disgusted, and in fact, a bit insulted, by the lies being spread by the so-called Beguilers and we believe that any association and /or comparison to these weekend fanatics gives the true servants of the Darkest Heart a bad name."

"The Beguilers are *the* disciples of the Heart of Endless Torment," the lead baldy said, moving his way back into frame. "We enthrall the masses to sip of sin. Give your blood to the Eater of Screams. Follow him to ... Really, Donny? You're going to shove me now?"

"Screw you, Phil."

"Screw me? Reeeeeal mature!"

"Real mature is your shitty offshoot cultist hacks trying to act important."

"You wanted to leave, Donny, so we let you leave. No one said any-thing. No one got in your way."

"And what ended up happening?" Donny exclaimed and poked his finger in the air emphatically. "Look who took charge after that! And what are your qualifications for that position? Hmm? Um, well, Phil here carves a stupid clock into his forehead with a paperclip, so let's all vote him in, right? The voices spoke to me like they did to you, Phil!"

Crossing his arms, Phil shook his head slowly. "Always patronizing. At least I don't look like I found my followers waiting in line at a Shake Shack."

Donny slapped Phil in a headlock, Phil tried to punch Donny in the gut, and the reporter's arm got snagged on Phil's garb, making for one action packed segment of news.

I totally bypassed the drama of the two grown men going at it on live television, too focused on what I saw over the reporter's left shoulder. Right there, right in that spot, was a homeless man that wasn't actually a homeless man in the background, scaring away a bunch of pigeons from their dinner. The man, wearing sunglasses and a trench coat, scooped up the breadcrumbs and shoved them into his pockets. I wasn't 100% sure if I saw this right, so I dashed to the screen and nearly pushed my nose through it. It wasn't until said non-homeless man dumped himself on a park bench and threw his head back to snack on his perfectly harvested bounty that I realized who it was.

After almost two weeks, I had found Barnem.

"Captain Cross,
Whisk us away on advent-uuure.
Captain Cross,
The sea winds are a-blowing,
Fore the mast,
And change ye sails.
Oh, Captain. My Captain.
Land ho! Land ho!"

As I got dressed to head out, I couldn't believe that I was hearing that song. I can't even say how many times I've heard it growing up and was doubly shocked to see the demon watching it. So shocked, in fact, I kind of stood there watching it myself, wondering what the hell I saw in the show as a kid.

The room looked like a mockup of a pirate ship, but a terrible one with cutout waves and mobiles with little boats on them. As an adult, it was painfully obvious that the whole thing was being done on the most anemic budget ever and, therefore, was the hottest mess you will ever witness in a kid's show.

A colorful parrot puppet appeared out of a box (who the hell keeps a parrot in a box?) as the children sitting on the carpet ended their Captain Cross song.

"Aw, what a crackerlicious day we had, kids!" the puppet parrot squawked.

The children went apeshit as a man walked out from a side curtain, allowing the camera to sweep over him. It was Captain Cross. Given on a public access channel, the *Captain Cross Show* was a staple of growing up for most children, but you sure couldn't tell that from the man's slouching posture and bored expression. He was dressed as I remember him: a sea captain with a blue double breasted jacket and black buttons, a fanciful hat with a single feather curling out of it, black tights and dandy boots with silver buckles. What I didn't remember was that horrible spray-on tan that made it look like someone drew a man's face on a tangerine and slapped a powdery white wig on it. Even the man's eyepatch sagged, never really standing in place.

Cross fell into his large wooden captain's chair and crossed his legs as if the world disgusted him.

"Hello, children. Today was exciting, huh?" The words falling out of his mouth were were barely audible. He then looked right into the camera and asked, "What was your favorite part of today, lil' lubbers?"

It was easy to see, with this extreme closeup of the man, that he was in his late fifties, with thick age lines around his forehead and bad make-up trying to hide the puffiness under his eyes.

"My favorite part was when our friend, Cracker Barrel the parrot, learned where the treasure was hidden," a little blonde girl sitting a few feet from him said. The sticker on her chest said her name was Caitlyn.

The Captain sighed. "Please don't be a rude little bitch, Caitlyn with a 'y'. There's already enough of those in the world."

IT ONLY TOOK me an hour to get into the city, but I ran at full speed from
Bleecker until my lungs burned. Luckily, when I got to the park, I spotted
him within a minute or two. The angel hadn't budged an inch from his
spot on the bench.

He wore a brown trench coat and up close, I could tell that the sunglasses he wore were totally broken. His arms were splayed out to the
sides of the bench, his head pointed to the sky as his brown, stringy hair
hung in an absolute mess.

I tried my best to make my voice as soothing as possible. "Hey there,
buddy. How's it going?"

"No. Go away. Fuck off." His head didn't even budge.

I cleared my throat slowly. "Barnem. It's me."

This made him pause. "Grey?"

"Yup."

"Oh, hi."

"Hi. Can I—"

"No. Go away. Fuck off."

"I need you to hear me out. You have to come back. Things have
gotten ..."

He peeked at me. "Worse?"

"Weirder."

He crossed his arms. "Not interested."

"Look, last week—"

"Whatever you're about to say, whatever it is, totally and completely
does not pertain to me, Grey."

"Wrong! Totally wrong!" But that was all I could say on the matter. My lips felt instantly chapped, my throat stuffed with sand. This was the first time I had been in a public space since the attack, and it made me realize that I wasn't the same since it happened. I couldn't keep from shuffling my feet and looking around. I couldn't help feeling like something was watching close by. Even in the middle of Washington Square Park, in broad daylight, with over a hundred people going about their business around me, I felt like too many ears were tuned into my thoughts; like they could hear the worst parts of me. Was my voice too loud? Did I smell?

"Okay, all right, Barnem. But why don't you stop by the apartment with me for a few minutes?"

"What for?"

And then the dam broke.

"Because the freaking demon ate someone and my sister's here, ready to make my life a living hell, and on the way here, I gave a kid selling candy on the train a dollar for these little crackers but it was mostly air in the bag," I yelled without taking a breath. I could feel my face turning red. "So I asked for at least fifty cents back and you know what he told me?" I finally stopped to take a breath.

Barnem's head popped up. "You're an idiot."

I looked around. "Wow. Good guess."

But this wasn't what the Seraphim meant at all. The update I gave him must've lit a serious fire under his ass, because he stood up from the bench, stretched his back, and said, "Fine. But let me take a piss first."

He hopped over the partition for the dog park and started unbuttoning his pants. I tried to get as far away as possible, but instead ended up running into someone with a carved clock on his forehead. It was the creeper from the newscast, the cult leader. Up close, the carving in his skin was nothing like it looked like on the news—the way the skin was ripped into, the darkness of the scar. His buddy, Phil, mentioned that he had done the job with a paperclip, but it looked more like the work of a rusty nail.

I backed away. Every part of me was shaking. "Can you be a peach and not step on my air there, buddy? Thanks."

He kept staring. I remembered right away the last person to stare at me that way.

From behind me, a cheery voice started speaking. He was larger in size and had red hair. "Okay, Phil. Just waiting for you lawyer … to … call … me—"

Then he stopped and started staring, too.

My nerves got the best of me. I felt like I was being strangled again, being beaten on. The way their eyes bugged out of their faces, that slack jawed expression—the last guy to stare that hard ended up a demon-doggy treat. Then a cellphone went off.

"RUN, BITCH. OMMAGAHD. RUN, BITCH, OMMA-OMMAGAHD."

Phil slowly picked up his cellphone and said, "I'll call you back," then hung up.

"No need. It's your phone call. I was actually leaving," I said, and pushed through them. I was banking on them not attacking me out in the open, but who knows if a demon would care about that at all.

Luckily, I found a few cops nearby that were busy trying to arrest Barnem in the dog park as he kept shouting, "But you let the mongrels do it!"

A few minutes later, I picked up the public indecency ticket, my stern-faced Seraph, and hauled ass with him to the train. As we made clear of the park, behind me I could spot Phil and his friend talking to the other cultists who also began to stand and stare.

We rode the train to Queens in silence. He didn't seem to be in a talking mood at all, opting instead to rest his head on the edge of the window. I sat there, not being able to tell if I had forgotten how much of an uncaring bastard he could be or if he had mastered the practice in the weeks he had gone missing.

He was still wearing the same clothes, and still smelled of wet feathers, but now laced with other fine fragrances such as month old armpit funk and, for some reason, brie.

Halfway home, Barnem gave me the good news.

"You're going to hell."

58

I shook my head. "Yeah. Hi to you, too."

Barnem didn't blink.

"Whoa! C'mon now, Barnem. That's kind of harsh. Even coming from you." Taking in the serious expression on his face, I backed away. "Wait. You mean it? I'm going to hell? 'Hell' hell?"

"Saying it twice doesn't make it worse," Barnem groaned.

"Yes it does! Especially hell, Barnem. *The* hell. Lake of fire, valley of moaning souls hell! Why didn't you tell me this before?"

"What is it with humans and their places of endless torment and suffering?" Barnem mumbled to himself. "You all describe hell like it's a small town in Wyoming. I've been to Wyoming and I'm sure hell isn't half that bad." Spotting the blank expression on my face, Barnem sighed. "Yes, Grey. Hell."

An older woman boarded the train car. She wore a beige wool sweater and perfectly ironed gray skirt. "Hello and God bless," she started, in her thick Caribbean accent. She held stacks of neon-colored pamphlets in her hand, written in font that screamed homemade. "I come to talk to you about the *Bible*, about the words in the *Bible*, and the everlasting love God has given to you this afternoon."

Hearing her sermon was making things infinitely worse. Barnem went into his coat pocket and whipped out a small pack of sunflower seeds.

"You didn't want to know before. Didn't want anything to do with this whole mess you started. And now you're all ears, eh?" He grabbed a handful and dumped them into his mouth. "You entered a pact with a demon, Grey. What else was supposed to happen?"

I waved my hands about because I had nothing to say.

"The Beast is evil incarnate. The embodiment of unspeakable evil. The Shades, the pieces you scattered around after killing Gaffrey Palls, are poison to the soul. Whatever good is inside of you, whatever light you carry, gets snuffed out. I've seen it. People possessed by a Shade go mad, crazy, within days, some in only a few hours."

"But I'm not ..." I didn't want to say it. I have always sworn off the word.

"Yeah, you're not," Barnem replied. "But the other folks out there

5 9

aren't so lucky. I made the mistake thinking that the Shades you let loose would get the fuck out of Dodge. But if what you're saying is true, they haven't. They're here in New York. And they have their sights on you."

The preaching woman spoke over us, getting louder and louder. Sweat broke on her forehead and a croak grew in her voice, but she soldiered on about the worry we carry on ourselves, on the fires that await the fallen.

I had never felt so much pressure, in my chest, my shoulders, my head. I was used to beating down the worries of getting mauled to death by a tiger while hailing down a cab on 50th and Lex. Now I had to deal with being sent to hell when I die. This was on an entirely different plane.

I tried to keep the words from knotting in my throat. "So then why? Why bother coming back if I'm such a lost cause?"

"Ah … because, you fought off not one but two attacking Shades, Grey. Two. And call this a hunch, but you don't seem like the kind of person that's going to take a little thing like eternal damnation lying down." Barnem smiled. "And I'm here to help."

"He's eyeing you," the woman said emphatically as her MTA sermon was drawing to a close. She was staring at me. "He's looking upon you. Watching over you. Powerfully. The *Bible* says He's infallible, He's powerful, He's mighty. The source of all Salvation. And He has angels who bow down and serve him. The messengers of His light."

"I'll take one of those pamphlets," Barnem said, raising a hand. The lady seemed as shocked as me. I tried to read Barnem's face, his eyes, the crook of his mouth, but I couldn't tell anything from looking at him. He looked tired, run down. A typical non-caring New Yorker.

"God loves you," she said, handing him the pamphlet, voice trembling.

Before I could ask what the hell that was about, Barnem sloppily spit the mangled shells into the bright green paper, right on top of the words, "His Word Is Love".

He turned to me and said, "I'm your best shot at surviving all of this, Grey. Trust me."

As we boarded the elevator to my apartment building, I fetched my cell and fiddled with it. Barnem had left me alone the rest of the ride, maybe so that the weight of the entire shitstorm could hit me all at once. I didn't let it, though. I couldn't risk falling apart, and I managed to quickly bury the voices swirling in my head. And this is major. Like earth shattering. Because this was coming from me—someone who once saw another kid carving into a tree and I threw my boot at him because I felt he was carving into *me*.

I'll admit that it was Barnem who made it possible. He was crass, uncaring, and pretty high on the asshole scale—hovering around a 8.5-8.7—but he had a point. Sure, there have been some seriously shitty moments in my life, but I've only gotten this far by never throwing myself a pity party. My mom taught me that. There are better ways to spend your time. I learned while having to navigate every damn public place like a live minefield. It taught me that I wasn't going to survive worrying about my screwups for too long because there are billions of other things to worry about. I had started this and even if I was going to be eternally damned, I needed to make things right. For my parent's sake. This was my fault and I had to step up to make sure it doesn't happen to anyone else. It was going to take the two of us.

Barnem stopped the elevator door with his hand before it closed. "Say, Grey. That sister of yours. You tell her anything? About doomsday and the demon and so forth?"

"Don't worry. She's on a need to know basis, and that's how she'll stay." I flicked the phone's screen on and saw that it read ten missed calls from the she-witch herself. "Besides, she stays away from this place like the plague. It'll be easy to avoid someone when they are nowhere to be found."

"Right ..." Barnem slid out of the elevator and back out into the main hall. Scratching the back of his head, he grumbled, "I'll take the walk up if you don't mind."

"Wait! What happened to being the only person that could help me?" Flustered, I kicked the door as it closed. Leave it to Barnem to have me regret even a shred of goodwill toward the guy. I went back out in public for what, easily the most half-assed angel on the planet? I felt like an exposed nerve as the familiar chill seized the side of my head, my jawline. My panic can come in two forms. Either I exploded in large, blossoming, fiery fucks across the sky or, and this is when things get really unbearable, a thick paralysis sets in, molasses in my bones. I started pacing, breathing, trying to shake it free.

I was able to dump most of it off by the time I reached my poncho door. But as I pushed it aside, what was there to greet me plunged me right back into the cold cement.

Ten sets of luggage sat around my tiny apartment, surrounding a pudgy little woman who stood as I walked in. Even though I knew she was younger than me, the blue dress drenched in a heavy fur coat, the caked on makeup, the doily thing on her head that was so small that it could only be a hat for a small section of her hair made Petunia "Ingrid" Grey look more fifty-two than twenty-five.

Saint, the rat dressed as a dog, narrowed his little beady eyes at me as his owner asked, in natural fashion, "Amanda, dear. How are you? Why aren't you picking up your phone? And what happened to the door?"

A couple minutes later, I sat with my spine so straight that it was painful, palms melded to my knees, fingernails ripping into my flesh, and a terrified smile on my face.

"What do you mean, you're staying here now?"

Petty rolled her eyes. "Oh, don't be so melodramatic."

She was still dressed like she was born around WWII: conservative skirt, small blazer, a tiny hat, all in this ash gray color. As much as she reminded me of mom, she dressed older than her in every way.

6 2

"This isn't funny," I said, "Not as a joke. Not as anything. What happened to the—?"

"Oh, honey, please don't mention that God awful hotel. I will not speak of that awful place."

"Fine. But you can't—"

"It was like hell on earth, if hell was a half star room with a four star price tag. I specifically asked to check on the bed sheet thread count. And they lied! Just tossed out some number. As if I couldn't tell! No decency in this world, I tell you. Zero. None left."

"And another hotel?"

"All booked, I'm afraid. Plus they're charging price is outrageous."

"Price has never been an issue before. What about what's-his-face?"

"If you're referring to my husband Brad, dear, he's away on business. He moves where the money moves, I suppose, and I don't care to ask. He has our finances on a short leash during this trip and I would rather shop than argue with another secondhand servant at some glorified hovel."

As I set my nails into my palms and caught Petty looking at them, she added, "You still do that thing with your hands?"

Infuriated, I popped right up and shouted, "That's it! You can't stay here, Petty!"

"Oh, I know." She looked around. A breeze blew in from the hallway and lifted my poncho door up. "It's a risk, for sure."

"No," I growled. "I'm saying you *can't*. Cannot. No space at the inn."

Petty looked back at the closed door leading to the room she and I shared as kids. Mom and dad always slept in the living room in the fold out bed in the couch. Petty perked up a painted eyebrow. And as she looked back at me, something snapped.

That was it.

It's funny how thoughts of pure, unadulterated evil can make you laugh, make you cackle like a witch deserving of a house dropping on her. My odd, side of the mouth huffing, the glazed look in my eyes, must have made me seem like I had gone from zero to full psycho because Petty leaned away from me.

"Why didn't I think of it before," I asked out loud.

"Well, I don't know," my sister started to say, but I shhh'd her. I shhh'd her hard.

"Stay," I begged her. "Stay, stay. Stay-right-there." Saint gave me an odd look like I was talking to him.

I walked slowly to my roommate's door and placed my hand on the doorknob. I was still laughing when I gave it a turn. Throwing it completely open and knowing the ramifications of such, I walked back to the living room, feeling the demon trudging behind me, probably half asleep, but still towering over me.

I took a seat next to Petty.

And I waited.

I thought about how ridiculous I was about the whole thing. Barnem, Petty, Donaldson. All of these people shoving themselves into my life when I absolutely didn't want or need them to. And here I was, hiding the one thing that was a sure fire way of giving them the full flaming middle finger. Maybe I was delirious, but here was my "Get Out of Jail Free" card to trump all cards. Petty would run out screaming and I could carry on with the usual terribleness of my life without her. This was one thing that I had learned early to never do, and the one thing I had decided to throw to the wind in that moment: never show people your demons.

The tall, lanky shadow yawned and then sat cross legged on the floor, rubbing the lazy sheen out of its large yellow eyes.

A tremble ran through Petty as she looked at him.

He sat slouching off to the side, dozing off again.

Petty didn't scream. She only blinked at him.

Then, finding the words, she pointed at him and said, "You got a roommate?"

Realizing that I had been holding my breath the entire time, I exhaled before nearly passing out. Through the coughing fit, I said, "What the hell!"

"Hel-lo," she said right into its face. "Can-you-please-move-your-crap-from-that-room?"

I snagged Petty by the wrist before she could continue and pulled her through the poncho and out into the hallway.

"You don't see a major problem with that...thing in the living room?"

"Of course I do," she said earnestly. "I mean it's kind of you to offer— um, I want to say an Egyptian immigrant— to room with you. But if mom and dad find out that you've rented out your room, they'll flip, Amanda. Absolutely. Flip." I couldn't believe what I was hearing and Petty, sweet dumb Petty, put her hand on my shoulder. "Was it money concerns? Did you fall behind? May I offer—"

I slapped her hand away. "I don't need your money, Petty!" I was so shaken up, I was trembling. I wasn't crying. I was furious.

"Oh," she said and laughed. "I'm not giving you money, dear. I was offering to help you check Mom and Dad's backup savings."

I gagged. "Their *backup*? What backup?"

"You don't remember? Mom and Dad's backup savings. It's on a bank card, probably in the closet of the room your 'guest' is staying in. Mom stored it for a rainy day. I say you should find it and I'll check how much is on it first thing in the morning. If it's enough, I'll use it for a flight back home— no harm no fowl, I can tell where I'm not wanted— and the rest can go to you getting that guy of yours to move out. Soon as I get back abroad, I'll have hubby replenish the savings and Mom and Dad will never know." She patted my back. "How's that sound? You'll be okay here? Can you stand a dinner with your younger sister tonight?"

She called for Saint whose little paws skidded across my wood floors and through the poncho. She fetched him from the floor and tucked him under her arm. Just before she walked away, she spun around.

"Oh and I'll swing by Lou and see what he can do about this door. Fix it up for you, okay?"

I didn't know what to say. Dealing with Petty had always been a chore. I wasn't sure what was going on.

"Petty."

"Ingrid, dear. That name..." She lightly tapped her ears.

"Why'd you come? Why'd you come all the way here?"

She smiled, forcing her makeup to bunch up on her skin. "To check on my big sister of course. Now don't forget to bring the card tonight at dinner. A place nearby. I'll text you the address."

I pushed aside the poncho and stepped inside my apartment feeling emotionally spent. Had I been wrong about Petty this entire time? Had I been too hard on her? I shook this off as I stood over the body of my demon roommate, dead asleep, mouth wide open and its fat gray tongue plopped out onto the floor. Petty hadn't been able to see him for what he was, and this made me nervous.

Taking the opportunity to look for the card, I finally got to take a look inside the back room. The walls were painted black with purple curtains lining the only window. The bed— the one that used to be my bed— was covered in a soft, crimson bedsheet. A cheap lamp, sans a shade, sat in one corner of the room. But other than that, nothing totally out of the ordinary. Honestly, from the makeup of the room, I couldn't be sure if I had rented out my room to a hellspawn or Prince. No sacrificial altar. No phantom blood stains. And this always drove me crazy about the shadowy bastard. The few times I felt like I was going to step into something truly dark and awful, there was absolutely nothing to show for it. Nothing. Until of course something truly horrible landed on my lap in a way I couldn't see coming, like getting attacked in an alleyway.

As I looked through the baskets in my closet filled with my mom's manilla envelopes, the ones she had dumped all of her important papers into, I couldn't help but feel like Petty had somehow given me an out. This money could have set everything straight. She would be able to leave and I could go on living in the apartment without a demonic-sourced income. Sure, according to Barnem, I was going to hell and I couldn't avoid it. But at the very least, if I was going to help Un-end the world, my life needed some traction.

As I contemplated the proper ways to break up with a roommate from the seventh ring of hell, I found an envelope with my mom's writing on it entitled "Family Funds". Petty wasn't lying. In the envelope was a bank card rubber banned in a pizza menu with the pin code written on the flap.

I shoved the card in my wallet and walked by the demon as it lay drooling on the floor, the television off for once. I stood there in disbelief. How come Petty couldn't see it? How the hell was that possible?

I whipped out my phone and took five pictures of the thing snoring in the loveseat. Going into the gallery and swiping through the pics one by one made me feel nauseous with every flick.

Every single picture I took was of someone *else* lazying about: a slender man in a suit with a red beard, a round faced portly postman, an older Mexican lady with gray hair. I instantly remembered my internet fame and how quickly both the creature and my face was scrubbed. What kind of power did it really have?

Suddenly, the television turned on scaring me half to death. The demon stirred and groggily turned towards the screen. That familiar music from that kid's pirate show started to play.

"*Captain Cross,*
Whisk us away on advent-uuure.
Captain Cross,
The sea winds are a-blowing,
Fore the mast,
And change ye sails.
Oh, Captain. My Captain.
Land ho! Land ho!"

Captain Cross still seemed in a bad mood this episode. He kept getting upset every time some kid cut him off and was especially hard on Caitlyn with a Y and her choice to wear two different colors to band up her ponytails.

"There was a place called Sodom and Gomorrah…" Cross started to say.

The demon sat and watched this, and for some reason, so did I. It was a pretty awful show and should have been cancelled already, if it wasn't on the chopping block already. But I immediately felt drawn to it, like the scene of an epic car crash.

In my hand, I kept flicking through the pictures. A female lumberjack. An Amish guy with a du-rag. What the hell was going on?

Fortunately, I knew only one person who had the answers. Unfortunately, the guy was a complete dick.

So I went with my second option to try to help me out.

67

As soon as I got to Donaldson's door, I immediately sensed something was wrong. His door was partially open, and through the crack I could see what appeared to be grocery bags thrown on the ground, scattering most of the food all over the floor. This put me on high alert. What made me kick down the door and enter the apartment was the cell phone smashed on the ground, shattered glass scattered all around.

Okay, I'm also kind of a creep. I wanted to see into this guy's apartment. But everything had set me on edge and I would be damned if I was going to let someone back into my house without knowing where and how he lived. And yeah, a demon could have been hawking him up as a hairball while I stood in his hallway. I had every right to barge in.

Donaldson's apartment was the same layout as my parents' home, minus the furniture. In fact, it didn't have one piece of furniture to speak of. I couldn't see into the back room and the bathroom, those doors being firmly closed, but the living room had nothing other than room to live in. No loveseat, no couch. No TV or radio. There were three dirty plates in the sink, one used pot on the stove, and nothing else but large canvas bags pushed against the walls. Donaldson had a job working as a manager at Book & Ende, the largest bookstore chain in New York. However, that didn't explain why he had been living several floors above me for almost an entire month, but his apartment looked like he hadn't moved in at all.

Below the door in the back, a shadow glided one way and then the next.

A hand fell on my shoulder.

Swinging blindly, I threw a right hand which landed like a gong against the space between Donaldson's jaw and his ear. He stumbled backward, trying his best to stay on his feet. It was an awkward hit, but one that I could tell made him see stars.

"Ow!"

"Don't sneak up on me!"

Donaldson flexed his chin and checked that his earlobe was in one piece. "Says the person breaking and entering."

"Entering but not breaking. The only thing I almost ended up breaking was your pride." I gestured with my chin. "What's in the other room?"

He looked at me reluctantly at first. He stood there, and I quickly saw myself getting my ass unceremoniously kicked out of this man's apartment. But instead of getting angry, Donaldson turned the doorknob to the back room and pushed the door open so that I could see.

The room looked far more lived in than the rest of the apartment. There was one unmade bed there, a set of small speakers, a dresser by the back window, and a laundry basket overflowing with dirty clothes. The wispy drapes were wafting in the wind blowing in from the window.

"Do I pass your inspection? And want to give me a better reason as to why you're here again?"

"I saw your bags, um, on the floor. And your phone ..."

Donaldson cursed and picked it up. "Yeah. Had my hands full bringing this stuff in from work." He paused. "Was in a hurry when I got in." He paused a second time. "Had to pee."

"Oh. I need ..." I started shaking, my internal dial slipping from fight to flight. "I just needed ... you to come downstairs. For a second. No big deal. I ... have to go," I said and dashed for the door. I felt like an absolute jerk and wanted to get out of there as soon as possible. I hadn't had someone decent to talk to in so long that I forgot that there are right and wrong ways to have people hate you. Petty had put me on edge, too, and look how that blew up in my face. I considered myself one huge fuck up that needed a proper place to sulk in.

Donaldson cut me off at the door and pushed it closed with his hand. Then he walked toward me. Slowly.

Seeing this put me in defensive mode again. Why didn't he let me leave? What was that expression on his face? What was he going to do?

Instead he went and pulled a bag of frozen peas from his freezer and stuck them to the side of his head.

"Okay. Now I'm ready to go."

Frustrated, I had to ask, "Why are you so nice to me?"

Donaldson shrugged. "You didn't know? I'm part angel, Grey."

I nearly choked yelling, "*You are?*"

But by the crooked look he shot me, I knew that I had definitely screwed the pooch.

"We should go," I said, changing the subject.

"Yes please," Donaldson groaned. "Before my peas start defrosting."

Three minutes later and I found myself in an astonishingly ridiculous position of watching television with Donaldson on my right and the demon on my left.

"*Coming next month to the BCA, it's The Stud. Watch as our handsome, self-made millionaire, Darius, CEO and founder of Soap for the Homeless, and avid buck hunting enthusiast, looks for love among twenty technically desperate women. Watch as he narrows down his search to the final few. And with five ladies left, Darius is going to have to make some hard decisions.*

"Darius: '*I don't want to hurt any of the ladies' feelings. But also, I don't want to hurt my feelings.*'

And what happens next is so ... un-believe-able.

Random woman: "What is mononucleosis?"

The Stud. *Only on Channel 6 BCA.*

I turned away from the screen to watch Donaldson's face. From the moment he spotted the demon on the couch, he never averted his eyes. His eyes went from confusion to immediate shock.

"Holy shit!" He rubbed the back of his bald head.

"Yeah?"

"You got a roommate?"

I groaned. "Oh my god, Donaldson. You are a big, steaming pile of not helpful."

Looking at me, confused, he stood up, and leaned toward the black Shade on the edge of my couch.

The demon, noticing his proximity, sat up and narrowed its yellow eyes. Donaldson reached out his hand as if to touch him and suddenly the demon's skin grew darker, rigid, as if growing scales. It climbed onto all fours on the seat and, setting its ass into the air like a giant cat, a ripple formed around the demon's head and it hissed, quickly flashing all ten thousand of its teeth. Purple smoke poured out of its throat and its yellow eyes burned so hot that there seemed to be small embers in them.

As I was about to tackle him to the ground, Donaldson poked out his hand for a friendly handshake while yelling, "Hola! Me llamo Jeffrey!"

I grabbed him by the shirt and luckily, the demon dropped back down in its seat.

"Are you out of my mind?"

"What? Did I not conjugate the right word? Shit, is it 'Tu me llamo'? No, wait …"

"Focus, Donaldson! You're going to explain to me, in detail, what you see on that couch."

"On the couch?" Donaldson looked back and pointed, but never got to answer.

"Boowww!"

The sound scared both of us half to death. The demon had screamed, bellowed really, and it sounded like a fog horn. It was so loud that Donaldson and I quickly covered our ears as my windows shook and threatened to burst.

Growling in frustration, the demon slammed the controller so hard that it bounced across the living room, inadvertently setting the television on mute. Grumbling, it stomped its way back to its room but not before shooting Donaldson a look. I couldn't tell what was behind it, where it was coming from: anger, joy, fear. All I knew was that Donaldson himself didn't seize up or grow scared; he stared right back into those big, yellow eyes. When it slammed the door behind itself, he casually said, "That was weird."

I didn't respond. I couldn't. I was too busy seeing what had cut into the demon's show. It was a flashing a banner that said: "Breaking News: Bodies Found in the Hudson". My body glided around by itself. I couldn't feel myself floating to the loveseat and sitting down. I couldn't feel where Donaldson had gone. I only knew that the silent image on the screen would forever be burned into my eyes. That my life was officially crashing down around me and no amount of shutting-in would save me.

The newscast had blurred out the lady's face they had dragged from the Hudson, so I wasn't sure how old she was. But it was still easy to see that her blonde hair was sopping wet and that her skin was a dull, sickly color. And on that skin, carved into her forehead with what I could only imagine was something crude, were four letters that made me rush to the bathroom, climb into my bathtub, and close my eyes before the panic attack took away my ability to move.

Grey.

She had my name carved into her forehead.

DONALDSON KEPT KNOCKING on the door as I pushed farther back into the tub and drew the curtain. While I understood why he was upset—when the person you're standing next to goes white as a sheet and then locks herself in the bathroom, it should be cause for alarm—I didn't understand why he cared so much.

The tub was cool but I still felt like the air hanging around my shoulders was trying to strangle me. It was like Gaffrey Palls was haunting me, like he was continuing to squeeze the life out of me. With the blood in my veins still burning hot, I ran the cold water, clothes and all. The cold shock cut into my skin, but this calmed me, allowed me space to leave my body for a bit.

I'm not sure how long I was in there, floating in that emptiness between my ears, but by the time I came out, Donaldson had left and the demon was collapsed on my couch again.

I ran up the stairs, two by two, and banged on Barnem's door. It only took a few seconds for him to open up. I expected his usual drollness, some kind of pushback for me even being there. But he took one look at my face and said, "I saw. It's all over the news." He opened his door and let me in.

Knowing how much Barnem cares about things—as in how very little he cares about a damn thing—gave me an idea as to how the guy lived his life. So walking into his apartment, I mentally prepared myself for the worst. A television on a milk crate. A castle made out of beer cans ruling over a corner in the living room that was growing a thick mold that I hoped was kicking in for part of the rent. An empty plastic milk gallon sitting by a crate for when he had to piss and didn't want to go all the way to the bathroom.

None of these things were there.

Instead, the Seraph's place had more going for it than mine. Newish furniture, stainless steel fridge and stove, a mounted 50" flatscreen TV, a dishwasher humming in the background. He even had a coat rack with a nice hickory finish holding up the dingy overcoat he always wore.

"Where did you get all of this?"

Barnem must have gotten so lost in thought that he forgot I was there because he jumped nearly six feet in the air. "Christ almighty!"

"Is that an exclamation or a job reference?"

Gathering himself, the Seraph stared at me and got a beer for himself. "You know those spaces people rent to store things? The ones that you can go to an auction when folks can't pay up?"

I looked around. "You won all of this stuff at auctions?"

Barnem cracked the can open and took a large gulp. "Hell no. I stole all of this. I brought it up because a show like that is coming on soon and I want to watch it, so let's talk, Grey. Let's talk about this … carver."

I froze. "You don't want to talk about my roommate?"

Barnem burped. "Trust me. It's the same thing."

A lump grew in my throat.

On his marble countertop, he pushed over a thin laptop, which was already on the news site that broke the story.

"Hilary Clamp. Know her? Heard of her?"

"No," I said, skimming through the article. "Wait. She wasn't the only one they dragged out of the river?"

"One more. A Harry Somethingorother. It's all in there. Real grisly stuff. All of them burned pretty bad. Disfigured, the works."

I couldn't believe what I was seeing. *These people had died, had been murdered—*

"And each and every one of 'em got your name carved into their foreheads," Barnem said, cutting into my thoughts.

"You have to tell me, Barnem. I need to know what's going on. What the fuck did I do when I killed Gaffrey Palls and let these things out?"

Barnem swirled his beer, downed most of it, and threw himself into his plush leather couch. "Know the *Bible*, Grey? Ever read it?"

"Which one?"

"Doesn't matter. Same principle for most. What would *you* say the *Bible*'s about?"

I threw my hands up. "How about the Sparknotes here, Barnem? Life or death."

"All right. Here's my brief synop. I like to think that the book is only about a beginning and an end, with the stuff in the middle being dressing, filler linking both points of the timeline. If someone ever asked me for a five word summary of the *Bible*, it would be 'Something happened. Something will happen'. To beings like me, and even to your roommate downstairs, we consider the *Bible* a sort of How-To pamphlet, an official Employee Manual, if you will. It lays out our roles, explains the Do's and Dont's, and it's all to one end. It may seem like shit, but the moment you or me or *anyone* comes into existence, our main purpose is to bring this world one step closer to its destruction. I'm not here to spread love, or enforce peace, or ... play the harp. Like any major company, our sights are set on outcomes at the end of the fiscal year." He drew the can to his lips. "Except, of course, that the end of the fiscal year revolves around the severing of your timeline and the complete and total annihilation of life and death."

"So these demons," I began, "they're here, in New York, why? You're telling me because humanity was at the end of its run already?"

"Damn near knocking on it, Grey. Damn near opening the lid to the rapture and wrath. I told you. What Palls had in him, what he was carrying, was a defiler of men's souls. The Beast eats away at anything it touches, anything it takes over. The Shades corrupt humanity. They bring out the worst in your race and can raise some serious hell while doing so. But when they merge into one host, like they did in your friend Palls—"

"Not my friend."

"I get that, Grey. No need for the claws. Look, my job was to slay the Beast when it was fully formed, and after thousands of lifetimes, I almost did. Almost." Finding his can empty, Barnem grabbed another beer and still didn't offer. "I've seen a human host take four Shades before melting. Shit, Hitler had five living in his skin and look at what happened to him."

"Hitler? He committed suicide."

Barnem scoffed. "What? No! Adolf got out of Germany at the tail-end of the war. Moved to a small farm in the French countryside, changed his named, and even shaved that stupid little mustache of his. Grew mut-tonchops instead, but he didn't have the head shape for it. Managed to settle down. Died at the ripe old age of ninety-two. Shame, too. Three days before his youngest daughter's wedding, he stepped on a nail and contracted tetanus." Barnem shook his head and then peeked over at me. "He went to hell, Grey. Same place you're going."

"Oh, thanks," I muttered, throwing my head in my hands. "Clever celebrity endorsement you did there. Who's your marketing firm?"

I sighed and stared at the picture of the woman I didn't even know but who died because of me. "So I'm going to hell. This woman, Hilary Clamp. Is she going as well?"

Barnem shrugged. "But there will be more. She's not the first and not the last."

I grew nervous. In my mind, there was only one true sick, evil dick capable of this. I had to ask, "What if Palls didn't die? What if he's the carver?"

Barnem didn't even hesitate and said with conviction, "No, Palls is gone. But we have another problem. Another Shade has found a host."

"Oh great."

He flicked over to another open tab on the laptop and tapped on the screen. "Been seeing this guy on the television more and more."

I had to squint to dig the guy's face from out of my memory. I had seen his fake tan and whitened teeth before. But where?

"His name is Mason Scarborough. Runs a kids show or something? Dresses like an effeminate sailor?"

"Holy crap! Captain Cross is possessed by a Shade? I wondered why his show was getting weird. And don't look at me like that. I was only watching it because my roommate keeps watching it."

Barnem sat forward. "What else has it done? Anything weird?"

Remembering my sister and Donaldson's reactions, I showed Barnem the pictures on my phone. He swiped and handed it back unimpressed. "Shades aren't stupid, Grey. Even without a host, they can hide in plain sight. The only reason you can see its true form is because of the pact you made with it. And I can always see them. To everyone else, it doesn't register."

I felt so lost. How could I screw up so badly? I mean, I know *how* I could, I never expected that I would manage the size and scope of such a thing. Slumping in my chair, I mushed my hands into my face until my cheeks hurt. "This has all gone to hell, and no the phrasing isn't lost on me, thank you very much. I have a psycho after me. And you're telling me Captain Cross is possessed with more demons on the way. I'm never going to get my life back, am I?" I looked up at Barnem as he stared out of the window. "What should I do?"

The Seraph sighed. "You can jump on a plane headed in any direction. Stay in someone's house. Change your hair color, your name, the way you sign your checks. Don't answer the phone. Don't have human contact. Never go out at night. Pray often."

I took out my mom's bank card. Petty wanted to meet in about an hour for this thing that could do nothing to save my ass. I was out of options "You really think all of that would help, Barnem?"

"Not one bit," he replied, and tipped his can at me before taking his last sip.

14

PETTY DABBED THE edges of her mouth with a napkin and ordered dessert.
I entertained myself by pouring more salt into my water and using a fork
to swirl it up into a big cloud. The restaurant was a new eatery within
walking distance from my apartment; a swanky French/American fusion
spot, which meant that they cut up croquettes and called them "Frencher
Fries" for $11.95. The damn napkin I had folded on my lap was made of
better material than my bedsheets at home. I really wasn't in the mood
for her, or public scrutiny, or fucking bread baskets that came with oil and
vinegar instead of copious amounts of butter. But there I was, trying my
best to be civil when all my soul was needing at the time was one good
self-implosion. I was teetering on it the more Petty didn't reply to my
question. Even after I handed her my mom's card. Whatever money was
on it, I had no care for. I needed my sister to answer.

"You want to come back with me? Back to the UK?"

"I need ..." and this grated the shit out of me for saying so, but I still
managed, "I can't stay here. I need your help." When she blinked at me, I
added, "Ingrid."

Petty nearly soiled herself hearing the name come out of my mouth.
She was wearing this plum blouse and black skirt. It made her look regal
(like a regal bitch, but still ...). Most importantly, her hair was in a tight,
unforgiving bun; one that pulled on her scalp. The Petty I knew had wild
hair, hair that would swallow a comb, curls that made her brown hair explode outward like a fiery mane. Also, I hadn't realized how much weight
Petty had lost staying over there. She was nothing like the sister I grew
up with.

"Oh, Mandy." Reaching out, she patted my hand, but the way a stranger would do to a dog she had found with no intention to keep. "I don't think that's a good idea."

"What?"

She seemed honestly blown back by my reaction. "Come on now. You? Moving in with me? I live in Winchester, darling, not some gross motel."

I tried to hold it together. "If it's your husband, what's his face—"

"It's not. Look, I know it's been hard on you. I don't have to imagine, my dear. I already know how hard it is living with our parents, living in this city, without going completely crazy."

"I'm not crazy. I didn't say that."

"Now, Mandy. No one called you crazy," she said, raising the "patronizing" to one hundred. "I'm agreeing with you. *This is me*, agreeing with you. I'm on your side. I've supported my big sister throughout everything, don't you forget. I've seen how bad you can get. The ticks, the episodes."

My left hand started shaking. "Don't call them episodes, Petty. You don't know shit."

A waiter came by to ask if I could lower my voice. I glared at him until he slid the fuck away.

Petty only shook her head. "Honestly, Mandy, always making a scene. It's no wonder you hardly go to places like this and frequent that … burger place instead."

"Burly's? Last time I checked, Petty, we both ate there as kids!" I slammed the fork down, making the appropriate amount of mess on the table between us. Reaching into my back pocket, I pulled out the card and my mom's info and tossed it into Petty's salad.

"I don't want a dime of it," I shouted, standing up. "If it'll make you go away, far the fuck away, take the whole thing. And I think you should take some of that money to a good surgeon while you're here, Petty. See about getting that silver spoon pulled out as soon as possible."

Petty only tittered. "Clever. But I was not born with a silver spoon in my mouth, deary."

79

"Never said it was shoved in your mouth," I tittered back.

I was going to let this be my parting shot, finally leaving this whole thing behind me, but Petty snagged my forearm as I tried to walk by. She clasped it so hard that her nails nearly broke through my skin.

I could see it in her eyes. Something went off in Petunia "Ingrid" Grey. Suddenly, with her accent hanging on for dear life, the Queens girl came out of her. "You've always been funny. Funny, funny. Amanda is always cracking jokes. But you know what's not hilarious? You know what's kind of sad? Borderline pathetic? How about the amount of years I had to put up with Mom and Dad coddling your ass after your episodes, your breakdowns, your meltdowns? Or the fact that you can't keep a job to save your life? Oh, oh. I know. How about how Mom and Dad decided to homeschool you, which meant *I* had to be homeschooled? They never wanted to put their foot down and own up to the fact that their oldest was ill and needed help. They never asked me. Me! I was the *normal* one, and they trampled over me running to pick your ass up every time you fell flat on your face. It was always about 'Mental Mandy'."

The last barb cut so deep that it made me lightheaded. Prying her stupid fingers off of me, I stormed out of there. Part of me wished I had not given her Mom's card. Part of me wished that I had ordered the snow crab, or pelican soup, or at least the fucking braised swordfish to slap onto Petty's tab. I wanted to punch something, anything.

It took me forever to purge Petty's stupid face from my mind, the way her eyes were turned up at me from the table *I* had ruined. Part of me wanted to go back and flip out, but I didn't want to give her ammunition. *A normal life? Episodes? She's never even seen what I can do in an episode. She doesn't even want to know. Uh oh, here comes the crazy again! Punch, punch, punch, die, bleeding die.*

A few blocks down, after finally wrestling her out of my thoughts, I took a breath. Petty was taking her expensive bags, her fufi ratdog, and getting the hell out of my life. I considered myself the royal idiot for thinking that she had somehow changed. Petunia Grey—the godsend of kin; the patron saint of the perfect life. This was the woman who had an on-line profile with more pictures of her bags and shoes than her actual face.

Passing a small fruit stand, I spotted one of the community papers and stopped. Hilary Clamp was on the front page. The picture they posted of her was one of her smiling in a nice blue flower top. She was my age, I'm guessing. Seemed social, happy with her life. I don't know where I was pulling this from. Maybe most of it was pooling inside of me, making me sick. But what else could I do? Instead of letting the entropy set in right then and there, I pulled my hood over my head and hurried home.

And that's when I noticed footsteps picking up the pace behind me.

It was still pretty early. The sun had gone down but not totally. Tons of people were around, but every time I glanced back, there was nobody there, or there were too many somebodys to pick one nobody out. I dipped into a few stores to see if I could shake the feeling only to come out and feel it again. Those same steps closing in.

Finally I ran, full speed, like a maniac down Brook Avenue. My plan was simple: make the next hard right—which would leave me a straight shot right to my apartment—but then spin around and wait at that corner, catching the would-be tail by surprise.

The first part worked. I swerved around the corner, then hit a 180. But when I came around in my "gotcha moment" my pursuer turned out to be two people who half-assedly dove behind a nearby mound of trash. Not before I spotted their faces.

Realizing who these jerks were, I got ready for a fight. As I got closer to their hiding spot, I heard:

"RUN BITCH, OMMAGAHD! RUN BITCH, OMMAGAHD!"

"Are you kidding me?" one voice whispered to the other. "Are-you-kidding-me?"

The second voice replied, "I'm sorry. Thought it was on silent."

"Your damn mind is on silent. Go check and see if she's still there."

"I am!" I shouted.

"Goddammit, Phil."

"Get a fucking life, Gary."

"Come out, you two," I snapped, shoving my hand in my coat pocket. I carried my can of mace on me, but I wasn't sure that in this case, it was enough. "I have a gun on me and I'd rather not shoot you until you tell me why you're following me."

"Wait. Would she have a gun?"

"I don't know, Gary. Dammit." The bald guy from the Bryant Park cult stood up with his hands in the air.

"Where's Tweedle-Dee?"

The second guy was much taller but chunkier. He was the red-haired guy from the park as well. "I'm Gary."

"Phil," the other guy said.

"Phil. Gary. I'm the girl who's about reached her asshole quota for today so you'll have to speak up. Firing from my pocket tends to increase my chances of hitting testicles for some reason."

Phil and Gary glanced at each other, trying to figure out what to say. I had to admit, sure they were following me, and yes they had gone all creepy back at the park, but they both were pretty pathetic looking. And I know pathetic looking. They looked closer to being one of those guys who becomes famous for the ridiculous way he died. A tipped over port-o-potty or trampolining during a lightning storm. That kind of stuff. Part of me was about to relax when I spotted the carving on Phil's head.

Whipping out the can of mace and pointing it at them, I started blurting, "Fuckfuckfuck! It was you!"

Gary lowered his hands. "Oh, she only has mace, Phil. She can't really hurt us if—"

I lobbed the can and it struck him right in between the eyes. Gary doubled over. "For Christ's sake!"

Pissed at myself for tossing it, I threw up my fists. "Oh shit. Oh shit. Oh fuck."

"Wait, wait," Phil shouted. "Okay. What are you talking about?"

"You did it. One of you. Or both of you. You killed Hilary Clamp. And that other guy."

Greg stood up groggily, a red welt growing between the top of his glasses and right below his eye carving, and turned to his friend disapprovingly. "Aw, Phil. You didn't?"

"No, you idiot."

"Oh."

"I don't know Hilary Clamp or ... that other guy. We haven't killed anyone. Promise."

"Bullshit. You were staring at me in the park. And you carve into your own forehead. Sounds like a creep psycho murderer to me."

"But I'm not," he insisted. "I'm not any of those."

That's when I noticed that Gary had walked up beside me, whipped around, and started rubbing his chin. "Hmm. You know, and call it a hunch, but I think I believe him."

I threw a shot to the big idiot's kidneys and pushed him away. "Get back there, you moron!"

"Right, right. My bad." Gary took his place beside his friend who only looked at him mortified.

"Look. Yes, we saw you in the park, okay? We did. And yeah, we stared because," he looked at Gary, "because of reasons. But that doesn't make us murderers. No one killed anyone. And we aren't here to kill you. We promise. Not here to hurt you in any way."

I watched them for a few seconds, my heart still beating in my ears. "So? If you're not here to hurt me, what are you here for?"

Phil and Gary looked at each other and nodded.

That's when Gary smiled and said, "Your autograph."

SO THERE THE three of us were. I wanted them nowhere near my apartment, so I pulled them into an organic tea bistro thingy that used to be a shoe shop. Regardless of its past or present, it still smelled like feet to me.

Phil seemed as reluctant to talk as I was. He sat hunched over, rocking a bit. He face was drawn, eyes bloodshot. Couple that with his ripped white T-shirt, the fairly worn leather jacket, and the carving of the eye on his forehead and you have your typical New York nutjob checklist.

Gary was larger than anyone at the table. Round and flabby in places with a large nose and pock marks on his skin, he didn't seem to have an evil bone in his body. With his swooping ginger hair and girth, he looked like a big, red panda. Out of the three of us, he was the most carefree, doting over how good his spinach/asparagus (goop) tea was tasting. Even with the bruising on his forehead from the mace can, he seemed like this was the best day of his life.

"I didn't come to break bread," I told them. "I want to know how you followed me. And why. Start there."

"We already said," Phil replied. "We wanted to meet you. As for the how …" He peeked over to his partner whose eyes were locked on the TV hanging over the overworked coffee barista. Mason was making news again, this time with a commercial featuring the slogan "Make New York Nice Again" and an Eagle with a monocle. A quick scan of the room revealed other eyes on the television and, more disturbingly, a few people wearing shirts with the same words printed on the back.

"Well …" Phil started.

I glared. "Well?"

"Your aura," Gary said sheepishly and then smiled.

I shot them both my half eyed glare and stood to walk away.

"Wai-wait! He's telling the truth," Phil insisted, though he winced as if he wasn't too happy about letting me know more. "Um. What's your name?"

"Not relevant," I replied.

Phil clicked his teeth. "Have it your way. If you really need to know, we can see the darkness in people, in everyone. I mean, hypothetically, you know? It's what we've devoted our lives to. To prepare for the arrival of the Beast." He gestured to the eye carved into his forehead. "Our group has been around for years."

"Your cult?" I asked.

"We are a group of likeminded individuals commonly seeking the arrival of a higher, more perfect being in hopes of garnering its praise when it eventually enthralls the masses and enslaves humanity," Gary recited from memory, and then added, "Oh, and every third Thursday of the month, we also host a book club."

"A *satanic* book club," Phil insisted, as if that made it any better. "Any way, a couple of weeks ago, we saw the video everyone was talking about. The demon hoax video. Except we knew it wasn't a hoax at all. It was our lord showing us a sign that he was here. And then I saw a bird."

I sat up straight. "A bird?"

"Big. Black feathers …" Phil seemed to trail off and then he shook his head as if static had erupted in his ears. "I blacked out. When I came to, the bird was gone but it wasn't *like* I could see evil. I could really see it. On everyone. Sometimes it's like smoke, or like a gloom on people's shoulders. I could look into their sin. And then I saw you in the park …"

Phil stared up at me as if hypnotized. His eyes began to widen as his cheeks seemed to be drawn in, leaving his face as discolored as a skull. "I've never seen a darkness like the one you have bursting out of your skin. It's like looking directly into the sun, but one totally eclipsed. You're like a pulsating heart of darkness. "

"Cool story," I said, but secretly squirmed in my seat. "The bird. You said it was gone when you woke up?"

"The bird was gone," Gary interjected, and Phil jumped slightly hearing his voice. "Phil and I are roomies," he said, as if this made things better.

"So you can see the darkness inside of me," I stated, trying my best to wrap this convo up. One of the Shades was involved here, which I knew could mean that either Phil or Gary was possessed by it. Which meant that I could have been sitting across a potential murderer. I believed them about not being the carver for some reason. They seemed too stupid to get anything done on that scale, so I ruled them out. But I was sure that Phil could have been possessed, waiting for the perfect chance to pounce on me. "What happens now?"

"Whatever you want to happen."

Both men waited for me to respond.

"I'm not following."

"But we are," Phil insisted. "We're a cult who prays to the darkest souls. And it looks like ... well, you're it."

"What's your first command?" Gary asked.

Both men waited for me to respond again. And the only smart thing I could come up with was, "Party in my house?"

I'LL ADMIT THAT it must have been a lot to take in. I don't blame Barnem for freaking out. Not one bit. The scene was double-take worthy, triple if you wanted to wrap your mind around it, to let it all sink in at once. Let me explain.

There I was, standing in the kitchen mixing an avocado salad. Okay, I'll be honest, I couldn't afford salad, so it was just avocado. Okay, it wasn't avocado per se. More of an avocado-like dip. All right, it was creamed spinach I found as part of my nonperishables. And since I didn't have chips, I sprinkled it over a bed of crushed corn flakes.

Oh yeah, I was in full hostess mode for my guests.

On the couch, two figures sat hunched over a small table. There sat Donaldson, very still, very patient—his eyes darting from his card to the game board and back. To his left sat the demon, holding onto his lone card with both claws, his rabbit-like ears turned back impatiently. I've never seen such an intense game of *Guess Who* in my life.

Standing behind them, off toward the window, was Phil surrounded by the Beguilers cult. They stood whispering amongst themselves, watching me like I was the last best person to dance with at the senior prom.

This was the scene. This is what Barnem saw when he walked into my apartment. He first noticed the door which Lou had come and fixed while I was away, thanks to Petty no doubt. Barnem opened this on his own, without knocking FYI.

"Finally got a door, eh, Grey? So what did you—"

He froze. Mouthed a few things. The next thing I knew, the Seraphim grabbed me by the shoulders and rushed me into the hallway. Clasping his hands together and putting them in front of his mouth, Barnem started pacing.

"Can you quit with the walking back and forth, Barnem? Making me kind of sick."

Barnem stopped, and before I knew what the hell was even coming, he threw a single punch directly into the wall out of frustration, one that led to an explosion of wood and shrapnel billowing out around us. When the dust settled, I watched as he yanked his entire arm out of the wall and clasped his hands together again.

"I'm sorry for raising my voice," he said.

I leaned over, peering into the hole, only to see everyone in my apartment peering back at me.

"I just had my door fixed."

"I said I'm sorry."

I glared at him. "There is a hole in my kitchen! 'Sorry' doesn't quite cut it."

Barnem wiped his face. He took a slow breath to center himself. When he looked up, he had this intensity in his eyes. The Seraph had come to a decision about something that he wasn't sharing with me yet. "I thought we had an agreement, Grey. I thought you were going to be a little more proactive toward fixing this shit. Fixing, Grey. I can't imagine any of that circus in there fixing a goddamn thing. Besides, we have bigger problems." Exasperated, he forcefully pointed at my house party that was now visible through the hole and said, "What. Thee. Fuck. Grey!"

"Which 'what the fuck'? The demon 'what the fuck'? The Beguilers?"

"All of it, Grey. Every inch of that room. The Beguilers?"

"The cult from Washington Square Park. Remember them? They want to be my followers." I tried to sound like it should have been flattering.

"What are ... When did ... Why would anyone ..." He stopped and started like this for a solid few seconds.

"In my defense, this is me trying to fix things. I brought them here so that you can help me figure them out. Like, whose side are they on? No? Bad plan?"

"Who's the new guy?"

 88

"Donaldson," I answered. "He lives upstairs."

Barnem looked so imbalanced, so teetering on the edge of completely losing his mind that I thought about walking away. I had called him down to see what advice he could give me with the cultists. But now I honestly worried that I had finally broken the guy.

After a long second, Barnem looked up at the ceiling. Then he did something I thought I would never see him do.

He laughed. He laughed so hard that he had to hold the edges of his ribs after a while. It made me uneasy.

"So I'm guessing this is good?"

Barnem wiped his face. "No, no. This is terrible. The worst possible news imaginable. We are all probably going to die terrible screaming deaths."

"Oh goody."

Whipping out his cell phone, he shoved the screen in my face. It was a scene from the Captain Cross show, dated the day before.

Captain Cross turned to the camera and asked, "What was your favorite part of the day?" After a few seconds, the camera cut away and flipped to a long shot of Cross and the kids sitting around him. This made him angry.

"Was it time to go to the long shot? Did I give you the cue? Almost thirty years of doing this and I've never met a cameraman as rude as you." Cross stood up. "You know. That's it. I'm done. Children, would you please do me a favor and knock that camera man's teeth in?"

The children each stood up and began tearing things off of the set to brandish as weapons. An oar off the wall. Rulers which were broken for their jagged edges. Even Caitlyn (with a Y) overturned her chair and broke off one of its legs. The small army charged at the camera, knocking it off to the side. Caught on the audio were violent sound effects—wet sopping sounds and a man's muffled crying. Then Mason, who watched the whole event off camera said, "Thank you. Now what do we do when we make a mess?"

"Clean it up!" the kids shouted in unison.

"Very good. Jonah, get a mop. Cassidy, an oversized garbage bag

should do the trick."

All the kids celebrated with a hip, hearty: "Yaaaaaaaaay!!!

The Seraph pulled the phone away and scratched his chin with it. "Mason has gotten out of control and it's up to us to take him out. If this is the power he has, to manipulate others, to control people, then he needs to be stopped before it can get out of hand."

"I know. And I also know I agreed to help fix this mess. Okay? I remember. Fire and brimstone. But don't you think that I'm not exactly qualified to banish demons?"

"Oh, you? No, you're pretty terrible. I think you're the last person in this world that should be banishing anything. But that's the beauty of it," he said, smirking. "We are going to let your roommate eat Mason."

"Really? We're going to sic my roommate on him? Isn't that kind of like murder? And won't that ... won't that ..." I made my best impression of a mushroom cloud.

Barnem only grimaced. "Is that a toilet overflowing?"

"It's an explosion. Won't that end the world? The demons getting together would form this beast of yours." I stood up. "What happened to you telling me to run? Get out of dodge?"

Barnem walked away instead of answering me. He strode right into my apartment and started poking around my kitchen, just like the old days. Holding up the bowl I was whipping up, he asked, "What am I looking at here?"

I smiled. "Party dip."

"Sure it is." Tipping it into his mouth, he walked right out of my apartment again as everyone stared. I felt stupid for following him, but we boarded the elevator and walked out into the lobby.

"When was the last time you've been out at night, Grey?"

I wanted to say not since the attack, but mentioning it would have made me feel worse. We walked out into the New York City air. For June, it was awfully cool. I wrapped my hands around my elbows and stood there, waiting for the Seraph to make his point.

"So you haven't looked at the moon lately?"

"The moon? It's right ..." I pointed at where I thought it should be, but found nothing. "Right around ..." There were stars out, more than you typically see with the city lights swallowing them up every night. But no moon. I crossed the street, scanning the sky, seeing if a building was running interference.

"You were right the first time," Barnem said, pointing at the patch of sky for my first guess. I couldn't see it until I really stared into the black space, but the moon was there, only entirely eclipsed.

"The Oddities have begun, Grey. And the last thing you need right now is another strike on your list. You're going to hell. The whole world doesn't have to."

"Wait. Why haven't I heard about this? The moon is gone, Barnem. Why aren't people freaking out?"

"We have a job to do. The both of us, Grey," Barnem said, rubbing his hands together. "And you're going to have to do it. Know why? Because the Shade inside Mason's going to want to swallow the other demons. And the more he consumes, the stronger he becomes. This isn't some idiot with a knife in an alley, Grey. He's a Shade, a demon with a chip on his shoulder the size of fucking Babylon. And if he *is* your carver, if he's the one sending you fan mail corpses, then the message should be loud and clear. He's going to destroy this city looking for the other Shades, looking for you."

I glanced at Barnem and then to the black blot in the sky. "Well, then. There's only one thing I can do now."

Barnem nodded. "Right."

"Run."

The Seraph passed his hand over his face. "Are you serious, Grey? I said that this is cataclysmic. That you can't run. You can't. Cannot. Weren't you listening to me?"

I threw my hands over my ears. "No. You were rambling."

"I wasn't rambling!"

"*Fine!*" I yelled. "I'll help you save the world so that you can eventually end it and stuff. I'm going back to my party."

"I appreciate you," Barnem called after me, scooping up more of the party dip goop.

91

17

BARNEM SNAPPED HIS fingers in front of its face six, seven, eight times. The demon didn't respond. He still stayed drooped in my father's loveseat, snoring.

Meanwhile, I was busy in the kitchen trying to repair the hole in my wall. I managed to sufficiently go through seven rolls of clear packing tape to seal it up, but you could still see people's odd look as they passed in the hallway.

I turned back to Barnem who stood there with his arms crossed. "So tell me again how this guy's our secret weapon? I think he's more of a danger to himself."

"Why do you do that?"

"Do what now?"

"You're always referring to it as a 'he'."

Watching the snoozing loafer, I shrugged. There was nothing male or manly about it. With its overly round head and wide mouth, its turned back, flappy years. I don't know why I called it a 'he'. It was barely human.

Suddenly, as if someone had called its name, the creature woke up, startled, fumbled with the remote, flipped through the channels, and finally landed on what it felt it needed to see.

"Why does he do that?" I asked. "One minute, he's asleep. And the next, he pops up with this weird radar."

Barnem tried to take the remote away but the demon growled at him. "He probably senses something. The Shades are prone to spectacle and your roommate is an antennae to the weird."

He tried one last time to snatch the remote away, but the demon threw it into its mouth and swallowed. I nearly died.

"Aw great. That was my only one, genius!"

The show we were now stuck watching was called *Bullet Points,* and it featured four suits talking to each other for an hour. One of the suits was our beloved mayor. Behind my own private apocalypse, the city was in the throes of an election in a few days. Mayor Collard must have been stumping hard for a second term because he was drenched in sweat. He was a man shaped like a kid's volcano science project: round at the base and narrow around the head with white hair along the edges like snow peaks. The interviewer asked him another question, and Collard jumped all over her for it.

"You keep mentioning it, so let me say this clearly. I don't care what my approval rating is. Ninety, nineteen, or nine. This city has been *my* city for *my* term. I've set out to do good by the people of New York and look at us. Out of a recession. Unemployment down. Tourism up. We are popular again. We even have the Pope visiting in a few weeks. First time in thirty years. The Pope, here."

The interviewer had stopped listening halfway through. She put her hand to hear her earpiece better and then she smiled nervously into the camera.

"For the folks at home, and our guest, the honorable Mayor Collard, we seem to have a special guest who has called into the show. Hello, caller?"

"This question is for our beloved Mayor Collard."

I hadn't heard the voice of Captain Cross in years, but I recognized it instantly. His cadence. His word choice. Mason had called in to the show we just so happened to be tuned to. I glanced over at the demon who leaned forward as if listening intently.

I wasn't the only one who knew that voice. Collard squinted up at the air. "Mason?"

"Hey, brother."

"G-good to hear from you. My brother is Mason Scarborough. *The* Mason Scarborough." He laughed. "What's up, Mace. Why … why the call?"

"Don't patronize me, Donnie."

Collard looked around nervously. Now he was drenched in sweat.

As if smelling the ratings boost, the interviewer pushed forward. "That's right. Mason, the legend of kid's programming, is your brother. 'Captain Cross, batten down the hatches'." She laughed.

Mason breathed on the phone for a few seconds. Then he said, "Yes."

"Tell me, and tell the viewers at home. Do you support your brother's second term in office? "

"Second term? Pah!" Mason sounded like he had actually spit into the phone. "No, you idiotic television suit. I don't even back my brother's first term. If anyone needs any reason to see why this city has become the tactless, slut infested, armpit of this great country, look no further than our beautiful mayor." The camera wasn't sure what scared shitless face to fall on as Mason continued. "Why don't you ask him? Ask him how he can account for the rampant crime in this city? Or the growing homeless population? Or the subway dancers who spin on poles during what they have dubbed 'Show Time'?"

The mayor looked at the camera, confused. "Okay, Mace. Let's talk some other time." Collard made the "cut" sign with his throat to have the station drop the call. No one did.

"No, I'm sorry. Sorry that the severe lack of decency, ethics, and yes, proper manners has driven this city into becoming a den for uncouth children, who in turn become barbaric adults. Where is the decency anymore? Where is the civility? That is why I am announcing my candidacy for mayor."

Collard scoffed. "This is some kind of joke, Mason. Are you drunk?"

"The election is in a week," the interviewer chimed in.

"The people will choose what's right," Mason insisted. "They are tired of dirty politicians and phony promises. I promise to make New York City good again. Just like it used to be."

Everyone on the panel stared at each other.

"What the hell does that even mean?"

Instead of answering, Mason started playing the "Star Spangled Banner" over the phone from something he must have recorded.

The demon stood up, stretched, got a plastic sandwich bag from my cupboard, and went to use the bathroom.

Barnem had a seat. "He's making his move."

I scratched my head. "What's his move again? I mean, what's his deal? He's possessed by a demon. So he goes into politics?"

"The Shade perverts the human host," Barnem says slowly. "Sometimes it's quicker or it gets drawn out. But eventually, anyone and everything around gets warped. It's like an aura of madness."

"Aura. That was the word that Gary and Phil used. Phil even said that mine was as large as damn lighthouse. But I've been near this guy longer than anyone. Why am I not bat shit insane like the others?"

Barnem shrugged again, this time with expertly less effort, but I didn't let him off. "C'mon! You're the angel here, right? You can't think of one reason why I'm not plotting world domination?"

As soon as I said this, as soon as it left my lips, I regretted it because Barnem thought the same thing and snapped his fingers. "That's it!"

"Oh hell no. No. No."

"You said it yourself, Grey. You fight demons every day. Been fighting them all your life."

"Personal demons, buddy. No way in league with ..." I fluttered my hands around. "All of this."

"But you deal with stress. Maybe you've managed to find a way around it somehow."

My hand was shaking as I pointed my finger in his face. "I ... what I have is not a super power, you got that? It's not a picnic. It's not a friggin' bonus I get to scratch into my resume under 'Supernatural Prowess'."

"You have a 'Supernatural Prowess' section on your resume?"

"The point, Barnem, is that sometimes I feel fine and sometimes I feel broken, less than, possibly dead. Sometimes I hear so many damn voices in my head that I forget what mine sounds like. Sometimes I get so angry that I want to tear my flesh up to let out the pressure. Sometimes I fall so deep into my own head that I don't eat or shower for days. Does that sound like some super demon ass kicking juju you want to place your bets on?"

The angel pulled himself up, slowly, and stretched out his back. I heard a few bones creak underneath his clothes. "As a matter of fact there, Grey, that sounds like exactly the thing I want to bet on."

Having no idea what he meant by this, the Seraph told me to pull up the most recent show of Captain Cross. It was the same one the demon had seen: the little psycho kids, the captain giving his commands. I was amazed they even aired this on television.

"Mason has some kind of unnatural influence and I'm guessing it's from the Shade," Barnem said casually. "I'm sure it aired because he wanted them to air it." The Seraph rubbed his chin. "So let's see what we know. The people around him did everything they were told. But when he called in now, they laughed at him. So that means he needs to be around you to have influence. Has to be in person. It could be through touch or proximity to his voice? Hard to tell."

I sat down. "So Mason can tell people what to do? Does that mean he's the carver or not?"

The Seraph shrugged.

I realized that we were up against something totally out of my league. Even with an angel working out the plan of attack, I felt grossly insignificant. What the hell were we supposed to do against a lunatic jackass who can order me to take a long walk off a short short pier and I would have to oblige him?

"Hey, Grey!" a muffled voice called. The last face I needed to see at that moment appeared in the makeshift tape window I had made. Donaldson signaled for the front door and let himself in waving two sheets of paper. "Have something to share. A few days ago—"

Spotting Barnem, Donaldson stopped talking. Barnem's face, for some reason, got really sour as he approached. "Jeffrey," he said, extending his hand, and when the Seraph didn't shake it, he added, "I live upstairs."

"Apparently you do," Barnem replied, and turned away.

Donaldson, unfazed, turned to me and held up the papers. "I know that the last time I was in here, you kind of fell apart when we found out about, you know, the murders. Hilary Clamp."

Her name was the last thing I needed to hear. I tried my best not to totally look like it, but a burning knot had seized up in my stomach. It felt like I had swallowed a hot stone.

Donaldson dropped his hand. "I'm sorry. Didn't mean to push this, but it made me feel bad."

"It's okay," I said, and tried to escape to my kitchen. "I'm all right. You should go."

"Wait. It's because of your name being there. I know," he continued pressing. "It's spooky. I ran a search on how many Greys there are in New York and found only two listed. But that doesn't mean you're this crazy's target. In fact, I don't think you should be so down on yourself about anyone dying."

The room started flaring up in greens and reds and purples. I tried shoving my head in the freezer, but the anger inside of me took over. I came out spewing fire. "Tell me again when we became best friends?"

Donaldson chuckled. "C'mon, Grey."

"No. Remind me. I would love for you to help me piece this together because it seems you think I'm one of 'those people' who constantly needs help. When did you become anyone that could tell me how I should feel? Since when did we become so chummy that you could inform me how I should look at life and death? Because it seems like we skipped a few steps."

The knot in my stomach twisted further as I got angrier and angrier. Part of me recognized that Petty was now out of my life, now (thankfully) thousands of miles away, but she had left something behind—a wound that was poisoning me. Barnem had backed me into a corner with the demon business, so I couldn't rage against that, I couldn't tell him to leave me alone, and my dear sister wasn't there to take the brunt of my frustration. That left my nosey neighbor.

"Donaldson," I told him firmly, "I rescind my invitation into my home."

Donaldson stood there, looked at Barnem and then at me. "You 'rescind your invitation'? I'm your neighbor, Grey, not a vampire?" His smile disappeared. "You're serious?"

He took a few seconds to digest it all. I realized, in that moment, watching the expression on his face, that Donaldson was falling down the same stupid rabbit hole I've seen other people disappear into. I don't mean to push people away, honestly. And I will never admit this to anyone, but I do get lonely sometimes. However, aside from my parents, I felt undeserving of anyone's attention. I would cycle through these two—wanting and rejecting—or maybe I was both simultaneously. I'm not even sure. Whatever was inside of me always made sure that control was never in my hands, which would make sure that everyone around me was emotionally spent after I was through. I saw this all in Donaldson's face, in the way he slammed the door behind him, his head passing my kitchen portal without looking back.

"I don't want to give you advice in how to live your life, Grey," Barnem started. He got up and walked to the door.

"But you're going to anyway," I cut in. "Out with it already."

"It just seems like that guy is kind of an asshole."

"All-right?"

"But not as much of an asshole as other people are assholes." Conceding that that was the best he could do, Barnem looked up at me and shrugged.

As he walked out of my apartment, I called after him, "You should write fortune cookies. I'm sure you would make a killing at funerals!"

Right after Barnem left, the demon popped out of the bathroom, walked right up to me, and chucked a sandwich bag with my remote sealed inside of it into my hands. The bag was wet.

Before I threw up on myself, a patriotic commercial for the Brand New Pundit Mason Scarborough came on with the words "Make New York Nice Again" in big glittery words across the screen.

I could only scrunch my nose at it.

"There's no way he can win," I mumbled to myself.

Four days later, Mason Scarborough was leading in the polls. It wasn't even close. In a matter of days, his brother went from obvious frontrunner to scapegoat for everything wrong in the city. This meant that with only one week until the city voted in its next mayor, it would take a miracle to stop Mason.

On paper, a miracle should have been quite easy with an angel on your side. Unfortunately, this is Barnem I'm talking about. Instead of coming up with a foolproof plan, he spent the afternoons coming to my apartment to practice summoning his holy sword, the one he claimed could slay the beast. This entailed a lot of ground quaking, air gusting, and floating three feet off of the ground, but it only ever resulted in him summoning a small silver butter knife instead.

It was frustrating and also annoying because after the twentieth time, I ran out of space in my utensil drawer.

According to him, his power—the same that had been MIA the night Palls came knocking—was slowly coming back. But as much as we need-ed his holiness to come back, Barnem seemed locked into having my roommate do the heavy lifting for us.

"But if he eats the Shade, wouldn't we be making this one more pow-erful?" I questioned, nudging the sleeping demon with a broom. "It just seems we'd be blowtorching our own faces to spite our noses." When Barnem squinted at me, I added, "It's a turn of phrase."

"No it's not. And besides, I'd rather this guy over Mason. At least he stands still long enough for me to slay him."

The demon popped up, snatched the broom from my hand, tossed it out of the window, and then collapsed again on the couch.

I took it as a perfect time for a break.

"You're saying we should get to Mason before he gets voted in, but have yet to tell me how that's even possible at this point. Mason is a celebrity. He's a thoughtless prick, but one the entire city's watching carefully. They are saying that he hasn't even given out his address. No one knows where he disappears to."

Ignoring me, Barnem focused himself, set his hands together as if holding a massive weapon, and out plopped another knife that could barely cut a piece of lettuce without dulling.

"Wait," I said, jumping up. "We need a way to track Mason, right?"

Barnem wiped the sweat from his forehead and nodded.

This is what my lunch looked like later that day: I was sitting in a place of honor in a darkly lit room with candles along the edges and surrounded by cultists.

Okay. Maybe some hyperbole.

The darkly lit room was the Fuscher-Ballard Community and Rec Center basement in the heart of Bed Stuy. The candles, in order not to break fire code, were actually electric plug-ins. My place of honor was a wobbly foldable chair. The Beguilers were probably the only real thing in the room, sure, but I was waiting for the cultists to finish their usual Tuesday meeting.

"So I would like to thank Tim in the back for being kind enough to let us rent out the space here at Fuscher-Ballard. I would likewise like to remind everyone to please fold up your chairs afterward to prepare for a Bat Mitzvah later this evening."

Spotting Gary from a distance, three cases of donuts stacked high in his large hands, Phil saw the perfect spot to segue. "*So,* this concludes our meeting. Don't forget that dues are coming up. And we have our Cult Family Mixer at the end of the month! The theme is: adventures in the rain forest." A few people in the group let out a "woohoo". "And last and never least. We are blessed tonight with her black radiance. With

100

the lighter of the dark flame. She has come." Phil cupped his hand over the carving of the eye on his forehead as if making a telescope for it and recited, "Of ruin. Of blood. Of pain ..."

And the other cultists finished with, "Come fire and wither my flesh to the bone. For his song is the cry of the strangled cribbed child. May the bitter milk squeezed of the rotten corpse serve at his bounty. And let my slit throat croak his ultimate gaze. Ye, Beast of the Crown! Ye, Raper of the Swollen Womb! Come swallow the night."

Then they all looked at me.

I shrugged. "Oh. Um. Ditto."

The small reception afterward wasn't too bad. The Beguilers were an interesting mix of people, nothing like I was expecting. I had this thought that everyone who joined a cult was white, average looking, but all different types of crazy. Instead, they all appeared to be average in the "crazy" department with simply average looks, representing every race and age, both men and women. Everyone was either five seconds from a ritual sacrifice or ten seconds from opening up a cheese booth at a Farmer's Market. The only thing that these random people seemed to have in common was a certain "lady of shadow." And they all took their time to come shake my hand and talk.

The conversations spanned everything, every topic. But it was always about what *I* thought about the problem. The MTA fares, the Pope visiting, a husband's lower back pain that his wife was worried about. It was all seemingly ordinary stuff that they wanted my opinion for. I don't know what I expected of having my own cult, but it sure as hell wasn't that.

As the crowd thinned, Gary came up to the table I was sitting at, shoved a cruller in his mouth, and smiled. I made sure Phil was off talking to someone when I tapped the big lug.

"Hey, Gary. You can see auras, right?"

His red eyebrows raised. He nodded.

"What are you two talking about?" Phil came out of nowhere. I didn't like the look he was giving me. Sure, he was singing my praises in front of everyone, but I could tell that he wasn't buying too much of my unholiness. I thought that made obvious sense: who would want an outsider coming in and stealing your thunder—or hellfire I guess, in this respect. The Shade said that there was another one of them hiding inside The Beguilers. And for me, his story didn't quite add up. The bird disappeared after showing itself?

I knew I had to watch what I told him. "Just asking about the membership numbers. These folks are all pretty cool. You, er, set up a good vibe in here considering it's a Revelation cult that celebrates the future enslavement of mortal souls. Ooo, are those krispy treats in the shape of swoosh marks?"

"They are shaped like the Horn of Disfigurement, that which sounds when the dragon prepares to eat the stillborn child of the Western world. And, yeah, they're for members only."

Gary's gaze bounced back and forth between us, but he didn't say anything.

"So," I said, breaking the pregnant pause, "where does everyone come from? All around the state, huh? Must be a tight group, then. Everyone knows everybody else?"

"Mhm." Phil crossed his arms. "We're legit, regardless of what you think, Grey. Nothing like Smilie."

"Smilie?"

"A cult that opened up when we did," Gary explained jovially. "Phil calls them 'posers'." Shyly he leaned in and whispered, "They've been a bit ... aggressive with our members on the outside."

"Cult gang warfare?" I chuckled but this only pissed the little guy off more.

Phil grabbed Gary by his flabby arm and pulled him away. "Cult leader meeting. Sorry, you're not invited."

Though Phil definitely acted weird and was number one on my list, I felt that I should check the other members. And this turned out to be the most awkward thing I had to do. Floating from one little island of people to the next, holding onto my drink while people rambled on about weather, about their worries regarding what their dogs are dreaming, pineapples. I walked out of there emotionally spent and wondering how anyone in the world could manage being social at all.

I'm not too sure how or why this was possible, but I left that cultist meeting feeling really good about myself. I mean, I wasn't delusional or anything. I wasn't going to be drinking the Kool-Aid anytime soon—both figuratively and in real life—but even in that first meeting, I understood the draw to the whole thing. Sure it gave off a "I'm weird, you're weird, let's be weird together" vibe, but as I walked out onto the street and looked around, I could tell that there was something else to it. It was the same as the guys dressed up in their Mets gear on the way to the stadium. The same as the folks handing out flyers and buttons and other nonsense for the mayor to get re-elected. I wouldn't call it hope. It's the rest stop before it where you get to use the bathroom, stretch your legs, or buy greasy fast food. A familiar place that is safe and warm and inviting before the deep plunge. It was then that I realized that most things in this society are Religion Lite.

I carried these thoughts with me as I made my way down the block. And it was maybe because of this that I didn't see the guy invade my space bubble until he was right up in my face.

He wore a pristine white suit, but his dirty blond hair and skin were a mess, like he hadn't showered in days. His face was a likewise contradiction. Where his eyes were bloodshot and puffed purple around the bottom, the way his mouth was turned up into a smile took up 90% of his face. The edges seemed to reach back to his ears. His lips were thin, so it gave a particularly drawn-on look, as if with a pencil.

Before I could blast him about minding his space, he held up his hand. Carved into the palm, scarred brown, was a semi-colon and parenthesis.

The next thing I knew, I was jumped from behind. A van door rolled open and a black bag was thrown over my face. Someone on the street screamed, and I swung every knee and fist and foot I could to get free. But with so many hands grabbing me, so many people pulling me into that van and slamming me down so hard that every bone in my body shook, I could only lay there and hear the engine rev beyond the celebratory high fives my kidnappers were dishing out.

103

19

I ONLY HAD one thing in mind when they pulled my black hood off. So as soon as my eyes focused, I quickly searched the faces surrounding me. There were over twenty people standing around me, so it took me a while. I found who I was looking for standing toward the back.

"Excuse me. I need to … yeah. Just gotta get to the back here. Pardon me," I asked of a small woman. She moved aside and let me go through. "Let me squeeze back here. One sec, one sec. Yes, thank you. Just have to give my friend something." I approached the messy guy that had served as the distraction on the street. He didn't seem alarmed, probably because my hands were zip-tied behind my back. He held up his hand again.

"May all the smiles—"

My knee to his groin punctuated his sentence. Something hot and wet flew from his mouth, pure vomit. But instead of dropping off to the side in the fetal position, he smiled even harder. Grinned even deeper on either side of his face. I had basically knocked this guy's nuts into his throat and he was still smiling.

"Leave her to me," a loud voice shouted. The cultists around me all did as they were told, walking passed me sporting those unnatural grins.

The space we were in seemed like a stripped down store cellar, complete with dangling naked bulbs and columns featuring chipped paint.

When they were all gone up the nearest staircase, he finally stepped forward, wearing a highly elaborate white robe with flowing gold tassels featuring little dainty bells on each end. The hood he wore over his face was also made of white satin, but only featured an opening for his large mouth.

"Amanda Grey. Been so long."

"If you're that kid who was forced by my parents to invite me to your birthday party when I was nine, I still stand by my story. That cake was full of spit before I got there."

He laughed. But it wasn't his laughter that I heard. I heard maybe twenty different voices coming from all around. "You're in the spirit now, Grey. Funny, funny. But I wonder ..."

Leaning in, he ripped the hood from his face.

"... how funny you would sound if I ripped out your tongue."

His head was white folds. Stripped of hair, the albino skin looked more like it had the texture of a leather handbag. The mask had no eyes because this creature didn't have any. His mouth took up 90% of his head and sported sharp teeth and purple lips.

"So a Shade running his own cult," I said, seeming bored. "Kinda cliché at this point."

He laughed again, and again the chorus of voices mixed with his. "Yeah, yeah. It's a living. In this city, you get it where you can."

"I feel you."

"You know, I had you come here not to kill you," he stated, walking away and dragging his pudgy white fingers in through the sleeve of his robe. He slowly began to undress. "I actually want to propose something to you."

"I'm almost sure you're not my type."

"You'd be surprised," he replied, and let the robe fall to the ground. He was naked, round, and pretty disgusting. Most of his skin was that awful white color, and even his shriveled penis seemed to be rotting. What made things worse was that he was pretty light on his feet, even with all of that dead girth jiggling around.

But the cherry on top of the rancid cherry were the mouths. Every inch of his body sported a mouth full of sharp teeth. His knees, his thighs. The mouths lined his neck and stomach. The whispers, the odd humming I first thought were refrigerators. These mouths were chattering, mumbling, making rude slurping sounds.

"But no, Grey. What I'm actually proposing benefits the both of us."

"Mutual benefit," one mouth chimed in.

"Collaboration," another added.

"I'm hungry," the armpit mouth whined.

"What can you give me that I would want? I already have one Shade tenant."

"Yes." The Shade got really serious. "Yes, him. That runt."

"Traitor."

"Mortal-lover."

"No, seriously. I'm hungry!"

"I have information on your friend, Grey. On all of us. Special information on how to defeat us."

"I know more than you think." It felt stupid flying from my mouth. Barnem hadn't told me shit about the Shades and seemed set on keeping it that way.

The Shade smiled. "Your mouth moves, but that's all lies."

"Lair!"

"I'm starving over here!"

Frustrated, the Shade yelled, "Fine," and went to a light switch. He flicked it on, but I didn't see what it was connected to. It was then that I noticed that one of those smiling bastards had ziptied my wrist while it was bent at the wrong angle. The fingers on my right hand hung there lifelessly; probably shattered my hand when they tossed me into that van. This gave me space to work with. I needed to find the right way to bend the loose bone.

A second later, one of the cultist came down. He didn't seem phased at all that this creature was prancing around naked.

"You run around with your little turncoat, catching us, and yet you still have no idea what we Shades really are? You might as well be a child throwing punches in the dark. For instance." He sashayed his way over to the disciple, who had been waiting patiently for the next order, and placed his hands on his shoulders. "Did you know that we Shades are separated by our motivations? Yes, when we are one, we are one being. But we are creatures of habit. Take me for instance."

"No, don't!" I cried.

But it was too late. The Shade opened its mouth, all of them, and inhaled. A black cloud poured from out of the disciple's skin, one which the Shade ate. After one large suck, the man fell to the floor. But then he popped up and his smile grew even greater.

After reveling and smacking all of his lips together, the Shade said, "I am the mouth of the beast, Grey. I eat fear, hatred, and unpleasantness. But look at what I've come to use my powers for. Look at him! Just look! He is happy. So happy. And you know he came in like you; with heartache and pain dripping out of his pores. Dangling from his ribs like cobwebs. That sister of yours leaving. And your parents. You feel abandoned here."

It knocked the air out of me. "How did you—"

The Shade propped up his palm to silence me. The mouth on it told me to shhh. "Do not underestimate the nose of the gourmet of pain and suffering. That's right, Grey. He came to me like you. And I drew it all out of him. I saved him, Grey. From his own little private hell. Me! Ask yourself: is this the work of an enemy? Hmm? Am I really all that bad?"

To his credit, the sheepish looking man seemed better; almost lighter. He glanced at his own hands and touched his face in pure ecstasy. But it wasn't hard to see what was wrong with this picture. "Happy or not, he didn't choose."

The Shade got flustered. "I beg your pardon?"

"He didn't choose. There was no choice involved. So it's ... I dunno, empty." I shook my head. "Let me tell you something that *you* obviously don't know. Some humans want to be miserable and well, maybe I'm sort of biased but, I think that's totally fine. I think it's okay. Contrary to what you or anybody else believes, I don't want to be happy all of the time. To me *that* sounds like hell. Happiness is supposed to be ... ice cream and dogs you name Buttons. Things that eventually end. Happiness ends."

"You're not listening to me," the Shade growled. "Happiness *doesn't* have to end. Look at this marvelous specimen of a pure joy. And this was my third time draining him today."

The disciple held up both thumbs.

Then he jammed both thumbs into his eyes.

I screamed. He went thrashing to the floor as he dug deeper and deeper into his own skull, laughing the entire time.

The Shade sighed. "They always go for the eyeballs first," he said, then flicked the light switch a few times.

"I'm not making a deal with a Shade." I quickly corrected myself. "Another. I'm not making a deal with another Shade."

"What is your deal with the runt? Hmm? Did you agree to feed him all of us, do all of the heavy lifting, while he sleeps away on your couch? Are you not paying attention? He is using you." He threw his hands on his rolly hips. "At least partnering with me, you'd see a few benefits. All I'm asking is to be left alone while you get the others, starting with the Shade hiding inside the Beguilers." He watched my body language carefully. Luckily, with my arms tied behind my back, I didn't have much room to squirm. "So you *did* know that the Eye of the Beast had created The Beguilers? Color me impressed."

"Mhm. Knew the whole time. So to recap, you can go fuck yourself." I got the rest of my limp wrist to turn and slipped my hand through the restraint, slamming the piece of plastic on the ground.

"Disappointment."

"Utter failure."

"We should eat her. All those in favor?" To which fifty mouths all shouted "Yay!" One mouth shouted, "Nay," and the rest got on him about. One of them even whispered to the other, "That's why he's back there."

The Shade rubbed his chin. "I guess you're right. I could eat her." But as I prepared for the worst, he added, "But I won't."

"What"s that now?"

He laid down on the ground and crossed his legs. "Oh, c'mon. I'm a lover not a fighter. I played the bluff and you called me out on it. I am defeated."

"Bullshit."

"No shit. I concede. *No mas.* Your attack was super effective. Just sign me up. I'm on Team Grey. Who am I sharing a room with?"

"No one. You're not coming to live with me. Why is everyone acting like I need help? Team Grey is *not* a thing!" I yelled.

There was a commotion of laughter upstairs. It sounded like a canned studio audience laugh.

"Admit it. You need me, Grey. If you ask me—"

"I didn't!"

"But if you did, I say we hunt down the Eye. He's always been a bit of a stalker, that one. Or the Arm. He's been snatching women down on the Lower East Side."

I groaned. "I can't believe I'm doing this."

The plump, rotting biscuit of a man gave me a golf clap. "Atta girl. And I want to say that you won't regret it, but I don't want that sort of pressure."

"Fine. Just … you can't feed on anyone. And you have to release your sheep upstairs."

The mouth on his shoulder actually booed me. "Getting bored by the second. All right. All right, fine. But I want to keep one. Just to carry my bags." The light in the stairway suddenly appeared again, and the Shade rolled over lazily. "Finally. I summoned you hours ago to clean up this mess. Just slap some sunglasses on him and get the guy to a hospital, will you? And oh, pack my good bag. Just a few robes and my good lotion."

Someone came flying down the steps and hit the bottom floor with a splat. A rush of footsteps later and I found myself staring at Barnem. His gaze bounced between the Shade's face and mine. "You all right, Grey?"

"Yeah, yeah. I'm fine. You're late as usual. Was just talking to … wait. What should I call you?"

But I never got a response. Instead, I looked up and saw that Barnem had driven his entire arm right through the Shade's belly, rupturing it like a balloon filled with black tar. The sheer violence of it all froze me where I stood. The Shade screamed, but Barnem hit him two more times and the slop flew everywhere.

And then my roommate charged in and started scooping up the broken flaps and limp body parts and stuffed them in his mouth.

I sat on the ground, dazed, watching the scene unfold in front of me, wondering if I was actually making anything better or if by some freakish fuckery of luck, I was making things worse.

THE NEXT MORNING, with my wrist rocking all the colors featured in *Starry Sky*, I slunk out of bed and dragged ass to the bathroom. My body ached everywhere. If there was one thing I could thank all of this demon hunting for, it was my first taste of cardio in years.

Of course, all I wanted was one day to myself, to exhale, to try to dump all of the nightmarish brain matter before it spread to the remaining healthy tissue.

And of course what I got instead was two people staring at me as soon as I came out of the bathroom.

Barnem stood by the window, arms crossed. The demon had turned my father's chair to sit and face me.

"You know, I can't help but feel that in some way, you're pissed off at us for saving your life yesterday."

"Leave me alone, Barnem."

"Yup. There's that feeling again," the Seraph said with a point.

My roommate launched itself at me but I quickly pushed it away. After eating another Shade, it had transformed again: now into a seven foot tall, stretched out version of a long human shadow. Its face was still incredibly round and its mouth was still big enough to stuff six cats into. But now it had rounded shoulders and long arms; legs with knees, and five shadowy digits on its hands and feet.

"I told you that I don't need you to fix every bone I break. It's called a hospital." I then remembered that I wasn't sure where my insurance card was. I went to a drawer instead. "It's called masking tape."

"Do tell then ..." Barnem picked his nose. "Let's say we don't show up to save your ass. How were you going to vanquish that Shade?"

"It had given up."

"Take it from me, Grey. I've been hunting these creeps my entire life. These things don't 'give up'. Centuries of screwing with mankind, orchestrating wars and murders and one whole season of *Friends*, and one talk with you makes it all a-okay?"

"Don't say 'a-okay'. It's dumb. And yes, it was giving me information. It told me how to find the next two Shades."

"It was trying to save its ass!"

"Well, aren't we freaking all, Barnem? Isn't that what we're all doing? Because the last time I checked, you were a Seraphim who didn't do his job when 'The Beast' of a Revelations came knocking on my door. And you, my shadowy friend. Aren't you using me to eat all of your best buds? Aren't the both of you using me because you can't do any of this on your own? " I could feel the demon and the angel grow silent.

"I don't need you," I snapped, grabbing a jacket and my keys. "Didn't need either of you back before this whole mess started and need you even less now. I'll figure out the demon stuff. I'll figure out my own life. I'll figure it all out. And you could be gone. And you can go back to hell. Thank you and good day."

I emphatically slammed the door shut behind me and stood reveling in my small victory.

Of course, this didn't last long.

Keeping my eyes down, and with both Barnem and the Shade watching me as I rushed my way back in, I walked back into my apartment to put some pants on.

Then I left.

21

"WE WOULD ALL like to thank Karen for her gushing review of this book," Phil said to the group. "Very informative. But I think we all agreed to stick to chapter books."

"But we shouldn't discredit the magic of a good Dr. Seuss book," Karen replied heartily. "I'm serious. It's filled with magic. *Fox in Socks* is clearly a sixty page incantation to inflict pestilence upon our enemies."

The group looked uneasy in their seats.

Phil sighed. "For the fourth month in a row, Karen, we are not—"

"No. Look, look. 'Fox. Socks. Box. Knox. Knox in box. Fox in socks.' It's all here. I'm not making this up. It's all here."

For the next three days, I kept returning to The Beguilers. I went to their "Darkness Evocation and Resume Typing Seminar", an Unblessing of Children ceremony followed by a family movie night screening of *Free Wily*, and of course, their Book Club meeting. Sure I started going to flush out the Shade for myself, but oddly enough, it always felt good to head back. I guess it was our kinship of sullen souls. Or maybe it was that taking out the Smilie Cult had made me somewhat of a rock star. No one gushed over me, mind you, they weren't those kind of people. They listened to me intently when I spoke and respected my space. The family night was a potluck and everyone brought in the worst dishes I have ever seen in my life. I don't know what depression and zero culinary skills have in common, but all of these people seemed like kindred souls to me. I guess that's the allure of a cult in the first place: a bunch of people who are absolutely lost and scared, and decide to buy cups and rent a coffee machine and watch movies of leaping orcas. Even some of the Smilie followers flocked to The Beguilers and didn't seem to care that I had destroyed their dreams. They seemed kind if used to it.

Phil, on the other hand, was getting more and more pissed at me as I started showing my face at the various meetings. He had gone from freakish fanboy to furious fifth wheel in a matter of days, and I could understand why. As founder of the cult, I was making the guy look pretty damn irrelevant. Then again, there could have been a darker reason. The Smilie Shade was pretty satisfied with sitting back and corrupting people. Just because the first demon was (literally) hell bent on seeing my head on a spike, that didn't mean the others would be so proactive. Mason was running for mayor, the skin Shade built a cult, and my roommate once belched the entire jingle to a pickled mayonnaise commercial. I knew that I needed to check him in case he was the Shade, but the guy didn't want anything to do with me. So I took to getting to know everyone else myself.

With leads running dry and everyone turning out to be "normal", the Mason problem was getting worse. What everyone took as a joke his first week was suddenly making every news show and paper headline the next. It turned out that Mason was built for politics. This little punchline of man—of which the actual joke was "What is orange and orange, and orange all over?"—was seemingly rude enough, thick-headed and completely disconnected from human reasoning, to be perfect for the camera. It was never *if* he was going to say something that was borderline sociopathic. *If* never came into play when Mason Scarborough was in front of the media, and it made it impossible to choose one. My personal fav was his reply to a reporter that had asked him what he would do if the city faced another teacher walk-out. Mason proceeded to go on a forty-seven minute rant of why the guillotine was created. Then he ended his tirade with, "Thank you. Next question."

Figuring to kill two Shades with one stone, I came up with a plan that I knew Barnem would absolutely shit himself if he knew. But since I had pointed out the general direction I wanted him to piss off, I didn't need approval. The only problem was that the key to the whole thing was Gary, and getting the guy by himself was torture. Shutting down the

Smilie cult had made me something of a celebrity. Some of its former disciples had joined, and that meant everyone wanted to talk to me.

Between the handshakes and compliments, I also had to dodge Phil as much as possible. The man's glare was now turned up to eleven. His entire face scrunched all the way to the center of his bald head, with a thick vein throbbing by his temple that seemed to get bigger and bigger as the night went on. I needed Gary, not Phil, if I was going to get to Mason first.

After two hours, my opportunity fell right into my lap. A rep from the center had called Phil away to talk about how they could turn down the chanting after 8 p.m. ("But that's what everyone looks forward to," he said, frustrated.) and I was able to pull Gary to the side where no one else could hear.

"I need you to do me a favor. But we would need to leave right now."

Gary nodded again and hurried off to get his coat.

"Oh, and electrical tape," I called after him.

In the cab, Gary rode in the front seat to best give our driver directions. Next left. Next right. I was already lost but at least Gary knew where he was going. I was busy using the thick gray tape to bound around my wrist, keeping the loose bone from sliding too much.

"You sure you know where Mason is?" I asked Gary.

He laughed. "Just up ahead."

"RUN BITCH! OMMAGAHD! RUN BITCH! OMMAGAHD!"

The sound of that ringer had me wanting to claw my ears out.

"Gary."

"Sorry, sorry. That's me." Gary reached for his phone and picked it up. After a few odd non sequiturs, he handed me the cell. It was Phil's angry voice on the line.

"Where are you?" he screeched.

"Gary's helping me with something. We'll be back soon."

"No! You can't go out without me. That wasn't the agreement."

"What agreement? Calm the fuck down there, Phil."

He screamed in my ear, "I said tell me where you are or I swear I'll hunt you down myself, you little—"

I hung up the phone. Phil had always creeped me out, and this was proof positive that the guy was either a Shade or working with one. I made a mental note that after I confirmed where Mason was staying, the weird bald guy who had carved a damn eye into his forehead was next.

As the cab pulled away, Gary and I looked at the building in front of us.

"He's staying in a hotel?"

It wasn't exactly a hotel. It was billed as a hotel, but it was in worse shape than a hostel. To me, it was the worst excuse for a rented living space I had ever seen. The O and T in the lit up "HOTEL" sign were out; the windows were barred and some were broken; the air conditioners were leaking blue liquids onto the sidewalk. A prostitute and her street-side agent both stopped in front of the doors and were actually scared to enter.

Gary said that there was a large spot of darkness burning on the fourth floor, so we took the rickety elevator up.

"Let me do the talking," I told Gary who, as always, complied without complaint. In my mind, it was very simple. I was going to play the adoring fan role and ask Mason if I could get an autograph. Whether he gave me one or not, I would have found out where he lived and therefore be one step closer to beating him. I didn't think twice that Captain Cross was staying in a shabby looking hotel. Remembering the rundown set and general shoddiness of the kid's show was all I needed for a reference. Mason wasn't making a dime dressed as a TV pirate. To me, living in a shithole like the one I was walking into, with the scummy looking desk attendant eyeing me and the elevator having seizures on its way up, was the kind of thing that would make Mason Scarborough want to throw his life away to a Shade for. It definitely justified why he would be a vengeful prick willing to get possessed by a demon.

The carpets on the fourth floor hallway ran from sticky to soaked to nonexistent. I tried my best not to touch anything as the air smelled like someone poured burnt beans on a wet dog and then tried to flush it.

Gary stopped us at 4J and shot me a thumbs up. I knocked.

Hearing footsteps approaching the door, I fixed myself as much as I could, flashed my most fanatical smile, and started "heartthrob" screaming as the door opened. Unfortunately, a second scream, this one of pure terror, replied to mine when the door finally swung opened.

"Mandy?"

"Petty?"

My sister was dressed in wrinkled sweats and a large T-shirt with what appeared to be a huge spaghetti sauce stain on the bottom. Her hair was tossed up in a messy scrunchie. She tried slamming the door on me, but I was too quick. I put my shoulder into it and pushed in time to burst in.

The room was a mess, with every piece of luggage Petty had brought with her strewn around the room. Saint, his fur mangy and wild, picked his head up from the pile of clothes he had turned into a fortress, probably to protect him from the rats.

Petty didn't know where to go. "Shit."

"Shit is right, sister darling. I would love to know why the hell you're still here."

She looked panicked. If we weren't on the fourth floor, I am damn sure she would've tried the window. "How the hell did you find me? I-I-I …"

I quickly scanned the room and spotted three dresses hanging up. Only three dresses: the one she had come in, the one she wore to my apartment, and the plum one from the restaurant. I only needed one more piece of incriminating evidence and, luckily, she was wearing it.

"Petty. That stain on your 'I heart NY' sweater. Only one thing can make *that* stain on clothes. Only one thing, Petty!"

"Um. Why, whatever do you mean, deary?" Noticing the blotch, she stretched the bottom of her sweater and tried to scratch it out with a nail. "Oh. Vodka truffle sauce is such a pain to—"

"Only one chef makes sauce like that. And his name ends in Boyardee, bitch!"

Petty threw her hands up in frustration. "Okay! O-kay. What do you want me to say here? What? You have me by the balls?"

"Have you by the … Petty. Where is your accent?"

"Oh shit."

"RUN BITCH! OMMAGAHD! RUN BITCH! OMMAGAHD!"

"Gary!" I shouted. "This is a highly stressful situation I'm dealing with here."

Gary walked in from the hallway holding his phone again. "It's Phil. He's downstairs in the lobby." He jumped back on the phone. He jumped back off. "Never mind. He's on his way up."

"Craaap!" I was split by wanting to pummel my good for nothing sister and having to defend myself against a loon. "Gary. Go stop Phil at the staircase. No! Wait! On second thought, stay here." I picked up an umbrella and pointed it at Petty. "Don't you dare let her leave."

Gary crossed his heart. "Got it!"

I ran around the bend in the hallway as the loud clank of the elevator signaled the opening of the door. Phil rushed out, and with a head full of steam, charged at me.

"I'm going to kill you!"

"Love to see you try," I said, and swung the umbrella at his head. It was fairly easy to dodge, but instead it connected with the side of his head with a dull thud. His whole body corkscrewed in midair and then went crashing down. But he leapt up, immediately holding his swollen eye.

"Ow! What the hell, Grey?"

"Uh. Huh?"

Phil ran passed me, wobbling but headstrong, and I chased him in a slightly confused trot. After running into my sister's room, he froze in the doorway, and then fell back on his ass. His face was pale as he turned around and threw up.

I jumped over him and what I saw in the room made me lightheaded. I dropped the umbrella.

Petty was on the ground, her head turned to the side, eyes bloodshot and open. She wasn't moving. She wasn't breathing. There were thick bruises forming on her neck, which seemed violently gnarled to one side. She looked like a doll—lifelike, but completely wrong. Totally wrong.

Gary was straddling her.

117

He turned around, eyes glowing, mouth ripping open. "I didn't let her leave."

And then his voice started warping. "I didn't let her leave."

The rest was a full frontal nightmare. He lunged at me, skin spreading against the air like a blanket, growing impossibly wide like a wave of black tar. I turned back into the hallway to run, but the weight toppled me to the ground. I felt my feet slide into Gary's gaping mouth, my muscles growing tighter as I tried digging my nails into the ground. White blotches scattered around my sightline and all the sound around me became muffled.

The last thing I saw, running on all fours toward me in the hallway, was my roommate—its golden eyes beaming like headlights, fire leaping from its mouth.

22

"MANDY?"

This voice seemed to be calling me from far away.

"Mandy?"

Like echoes. Bouncing around in the dark.

"Mandy, can you hear me?"

Something startled me awake. It was dark when I opened my eyes and my body hurt like all hell. I couldn't tell where I was, or what had happened to me. But I recognized that voice.

"Petty?" The word was lost in my throat; it came out sounding like a croak. I was dying of thirst.

Out of the darkness to my right, something moved closer. It floated as if unattached to this world or the next. In the dark, the silhouette appeared black and white. It came into view: a torso, arms. There was wild dark hair around the shoulders. This person sat down next to me and the mattress sagged on that side with their weight.

"Petty?"

"Yeah, Mandy. It's me."

When I reached out, I felt her arm, then shoulder, then hair. She was real. I wasn't dreaming. However, I still couldn't see her face.

"Petty, it's dark."

She didn't reply. I tried to listen to her breathing, but couldn't.

"Petty?"

"Yeah?"

"The last thing I remember ... I remember seeing you dead."

"Yeah."

"Yeah."

In the silence, in the darkness, something made me feel uneasy. I tried sitting up, but even more bolts of pain leapt through my body. Nothing seemed broken, but then again, nothing seemed to be connected to me. I needed something to drink. My head was swimming in the shadows of the room.

"Why are you here?"

"W-where else should I be?" Petty stammered.

Strings of memory started coming to me, forming loose knots, broad pictures. "You were supposed to leave. You were supposed to be long gone. But I found you. I found you staying in a crappy hotel—"

"I can explain," she began, cutting me off.

"... probably the entire time. Probably sucking up Mom and Dad's savings." I dragged myself up. Pain ripped through my back and legs but it only goaded me on. "If I didn't see you die, if that was a dream or a nightmare or whatever it was, then how come you're here? How come you didn't go back home?"

"Okay, Mandy. L-let's calm down, now." She shook her head in the darkness. Maybe she was looking around.

"Where's your stupid accent now, Petty?"

She got up and I tried grabbing her, but I slumped out of bed and hit the floor like a wet mop. My eyes were getting adjusted and my surroundings were no longer fuzzy. We were in my room—our room. The room we shared as kids in my parents' apartment.

I slowly dragged myself over to the light switch.

"You died, Petty."

"Wait. Amanda. There's something you need to know first." Seeing that this wasn't stopping me sent Petty into a panic, screaming, "Barnem, get your ass in here!"

"How do you know—"

"You have to relax, sis. The Shade nearly killed you.

"How do you ... know ..." The words were sloshing around in my mouth but weren't coming out. I tasted a pang of wetness, and as I reached for the switch, I realized that the blood I was tasting was dripping down from my nose.

"*Barnem*!

I got to the light before she could call him again.

The bulb going on was like a nuclear explosion against my eyes. I braced myself against the wall as even my ears screeched. With my senses coming back down to earth, I could only see Petty standing in the middle of the room, her face buried in her hands.

Tackling my sister, I hugged her. I don't know what came over me. I was pissed, angry, relieved, concussed, delirious, and lonely. It was everything. Everything rolled into one. I didn't say anything. I held her small frame, my face drowning in her hair that was now loose and wild and free.

But something wasn't right. Not only was Petty not hugging me back, but she was freezing to the touch. Looking at it in the lamplight, I saw that her skin was beyond pale, almost white. Her fingernails were jet black.

I backed off.

"You're not …" I was trembling. The walls to the room churned. "You're not my sister."

Petty lowered her hands and dropped them to her side. Her face was white as well, as if her skin was a blank canvas. As she opened her mouth to speak, I saw that every tooth was blackened and her tongue was gray. But what stood out were her eyes—black ovals with brown pupils at their centers.

I couldn't tell if she was screaming at me or for Barnem as I hit the ground.

I woke up in the room again, tucked under some blankets, and with a bucket of vomit sitting nearby, possibly mine. The moment I stirred, the figure sitting in the darkness moved with an immediate focus. It handed me a cup of water which I grasped with two hands to guide to my mouth.

"Please don't try getting up again," Barnem said in a half whine. "You're what, a hundred and twenty pounds with keys in your pocket? You look light, but … Jesus."

It took me forever to form the words in my mouth, to push the breath out of my throat, to mold the sound with which he could finally hear me as I told him, "Fuck ... you."

"No, seriously. It's pretty incredible how much you weigh when you consider that you've lived off a diet of ramen noodles. You must have the most compact fat cells in modern science."

I let him revel in his stupid quip while I gathered myself and rolled onto my back. "Did I just have a nightmare?"

"That wasn't a nightmare," the Seraph said slowly.

I sighed. "The 'fuck you' was for something else, FYI."

"Oh?"

"At the start of this all, right when Palls showed up, so did you. After living upstairs for years, poof. Here you are. Then after disappearing for weeks, there you are again. Right on my television. You were sitting in that park."

"Okay." The Seraph was sitting in one of my foldable chair, tipped back against the door, hands behind his head. I couldn't see his face so I wasn't sure if he was going to be serious or smiling or even shocked by what I was about to say.

"I always wondered if it was all coincidence."

"Spit it out, Grey."

"You showed up because you knew where Palls was going to strike next. You were sitting on that park bench because you knew Gary was a Shade. Those damn secrets you keep locked in that head of yours puts everyone—not me, but *everyone*—in fucking danger. And now my sister ... And now Petty ..." When the words couldn't come out, I gave up.

"It was for the greater good."

"Spare me the sermon."

"That's just like you, you know? Can't believe in a high power, one that has this all set to a plan already."

"Right. A plan." I used my arms to slide my heavy legs into place. "Not sure if this is possible. You probably know, but to that I'm going to say 'Go to hell, Barnem'. And I'm going to mean it because one of these days, I'm going to have the energy and the space to punch you right on your fucking face."

The Seraph snickered. "When that day comes, Grey, I'll let you."

We both sat silently in the darkness. I couldn't trust him. Maybe I should have never trusted him. But he still had more answers that he wasn't keen on sharing. "What the hell happened to her, Barnem? What happened to Petty?"

The Seraph sat up. "Hell if I know the details, Grey. You might blame me for keeping secrets, but even I don't understand it all. What I do know is that your Shade came and saved the day. *Again.*"

I closed my eyes as I relived the sight of my roommate bounding toward me like a giant hellcat. But then I saw the images of Petty's broken body on the floor of that apartment. The welts on her neck. The life leaving her eyes.

She hadn't left the city. She lied and had been there the entire time. I was starting to feel the anger surge inside of me again, but mixed with grief, it only began to flood my lungs with pressure. I wanted to cry, but I also felt that it wouldn't change a damn thing.

Barnem cleared his throat. "You know, I might be the last person you want to get advice from right now, Grey. I get it. I also don't give a shit, so here it goes. There are things I do that are quote/unquote human. I eat and shit. I don't hiccup but I do sneeze and cough. I can get drunk and high. Man, can I get high. Woo! But there are other things I can't do. Like sex. What's the big deal? Or dreaming. What's up with that? Or ice cream."

I scoffed. "You're telling me Seraphs can't eat ice cream?"

Barnem grimaced. "Huh? No, no. Lactose intolerant."

"Ah."

"But kin ..." he began. "Brothers. Sisters. Sons, daughters, aunties, nephews. First or second cousins thrice removed. Everything about blood. About family. It's a mess. The whole thing. I mean, it kind of makes sense. If the *Bible* was a reality show that only featured its brothers and sisters, you would have at least ten seasons of material."

I sighed. The entire thing was a mess. I knew Petty showing up was going to really screw things up. But I would have never known how epically it would go down.

"She needs you now, Grey. She's outside waiting to talk to you. How that talk ends up happening, or even if it goes down at all, is up to you. But let me say one thing and I'll back off, let you breathe a bit. You've had more people try and kill you in this last month than most of the dictators I've met over the centuries. And yeah, you got some grit. I can't say I would have ever thought someone like you would still be breathing after all of this. But the stupid truth staring you right in the face is that you aren't going to do this alone. You're going to need me. Hell, you're going to need that shadowy thing outside if you want to keep that head attached to your shoulders. You have people who want to support you and have been there. You went all the way to the park to get me off of that bench, remember? So maybe for the first time in your life, you should start depending on other people. Let us help you."

He put his hands up and let them fall into his lap.

I slid the rest of the way out of bed and my knees shook under my weight. I clasped the wall, slid, slipped, and Barnem caught me.

"Let's go see your sister, Grey," he said, and guided me to the door.

23

CONSIDERING THAT IT involved a demon, an asshole Seraph, a negligent prick who let someone get murdered, the person who got murdered, and me—our little "family meeting" was like any ordinary one.

I tried keeping my calm. Tried to keep my composure. What didn't help was the way the demon, Phil, and Petty were acting: like three kids pulled into the principal's office for participating in a homicide. I tried to keeping it all together.

And I lasted a good minute.

"I'm going to fucking kill you."

Sitting side by side on the couch, the three of them wondered who I was talking to. Phil, questioningly, pointed to himself.

"I mean all three, but let's start with you and how you lied about the visit you had from a 'big, black bird'." Phil held his hands up. He looked so distraught that I started feeling sorry for him. Thankfully, that didn't last long. "Speak or I'll beat you with whatever energy I have left," I said holding up my fist. This, of course, was a half assed threat. It took everything out of me to swivel my elbow, prop up my arm, and bare those knuckles. The demon had tried to possess me and I was learning how much a thing like that takes its toll on you. But half assed or not, I could tell from Phil's face that it was extremely effective.

"Okay. Look. I'm ... I never knew, okay? Never knew it wanted to ... It said that you were important. That wasn't the agreement we had. No one. No one was supposed to die." He dropped his hands over his bald head and started rocking back and forth. "I don't ... I can't feel any more sorry than this. I mean it. I needed something, I dunno, something good to happen to me for a change." He was so shaken up that tears were rolling down his face.

Petty saw this and gave me a look with those blackened eyes to back off. But I didn't.

"What happened? Why did it attack my sister?"

It took Phil some time to calm down. When his rocking became more manageable, he replied, "I told you before. It's like an aura, and yours is big. Really fucking big. It can cling to things—people you know or stuff you wear. Your sister ..." Phil turned his head toward Petty. "I'm sorry. It told me that it only wanted to get to know her, to get to know Grey and team up in the future. We were supposed to take our time letting her know. That's what we agreed. I worried about it, I did, but none of that was supposed to happen. Never to hurt anyone. We were never supposed to hurt anyone."

"All right. It's okay. We understand," Petty interjected.

"You don't get to say anything. Nothing."

She rolled those dead eyes.

I turned to the demon. "And you? What do *you* have to say for yourself?"

The creature's yellow eyes darted around the room. The first time it had eaten another demon, it had changed from blobby to this guy. But if it ate the demon disguised as Gary, I wondered why there was no change this time. Why did it look exactly the same?

I turned back to Phil. "What did he do?"

"He saved her life," Phil insisted. "I watched him tear that other demon a new one, bite it to shreds. He even stuffed the whole thing in his mouth. The entire bird. But instead of swallowing ..." Phil started getting antsy again. "I don't know what he did, okay? Only he knows. But to me, it looked like he chewed up the other demon and ... gaveyoursistermouthtomouth."

"He ... what?" I screeched.

The demon shot Phil a nasty look for ratting him out, but quickly set its ears down when it spotted me giving him the evil eye.

"You're telling me that my younger sister is now possessed by a creature from hell? This is what you're telling me?"

126

Damn near ready to shake apart, Phil couldn't find the words to reply. And that's when Barnem finally put in his two cents. "Actually, it's not as bad as that."

I wanted to laugh but my mouth couldn't form the smile to make it not sound like a madwoman's cackle. So I scoffed and sat back. "Oh? Do tell."

"Actually, Petunia *is* dead. You can tell by all of the …" Barnem spun his hands around his face and body, silently trying to imply *all of that*. Then he finished off by saying, "Her body has expired, but her soul is being anchored to the corpse somehow. Maybe the demon inside of her is the only thing powering the body." When I gawked at him, the Seraph then realized. "Oh no, wait. That's waaay worse than what you originally thought, wasn't it? Yeah. My bad."

Petty's gaze bounced around at all of us. "All right. So I might be dead and all, but I'm still *in the room*. What does that mean? I'm a zombie now?"

"Ahhhh!"

"Not a zombie," Barnem explained casually. "Zombies are reanimated flesh. You're more like … I dunno, a refurbished corpse?"

"Gahh!"

"Refurbished? Like a phone?"

"UHhhh!"

"Sure. If the phone had a low data plan and was powered by a network of pure unspeakable evil."

"That's it!" I shouted. "That's it. That's it! Get Out! You get out!" Spinning toward Barnem, I added an emphatic, "You *definitely* get out."

One by one, they all got up to leave. But one shove to her chest made Petty realize that even though I was through hearing from the weirdos in the room, I was now ready for a sisterly heart to unbeating heart.

As it neared the door to its room, the demon turned around and gave Petty a nod and a chest bump as if to say "stay strong." But as soon as it caught me staring, it scampered off and closed the door behind him.

Being in a room with her, after everything she'd said, after everything that had happened, was excruciating. On one hand, she was more like the sister I knew. She acted less stuffy, her accent was present but not overbearing (the right level for her years abroad), and she didn't dress like a Mary Poppins stunt double.

And on the other hand, she was a possessed corpse.

"I messed up. Way before this. Way before coming back. I really, really fucked up," she said, cutting me off before I started my barrage of questions. She slumped into the chair as if trying to disappear into it. She kept staring at her hands; bending her fingers, clacking her black fingernails together.

I don't want to say that it made me break in any way—I was still livid—but how do you stay pissed at someone so down on themself? And dead.

With my arms still crossed, I sat across from her. "What happened?"

Her eyes widened as if remembering something painful. Those black orbs didn't blink, they stared off into space. I also realized, sitting so close, with the sun from the window falling on her dull skin, that Petty's hair was different, too. It lacked the bounce and curls she had when she was living, hanging instead like a thick curtain. There even was a change of its tone; darker, almost a mat black. The whole thing bothered me so much that I tried to focus on anything but her face.

"I was out walking one day, popping into the usual boutiques they have nearby the flat that we stayed in. Shopping for nonsense. Halfway through, I felt this pressure, right in the back of my eyes. So, thinking it was a migraine, I went to fetch a few pills from my purse. But the damn bottle slipped right out of my hand. Just like that. One second, I had it …" She laughed, but in no way because she found it funny. "The damn thing landed like an atom bomb. The can rolled one way, the pills scattered all over. All over. All clacking at once."

I knew, even before she finished, what she was describing. "A panic attack."

She winced as if I had struck her across the face. There was so much that she was wrestling with at once, and I realized that it was because that this was the first time she had spoken about it. To anyone. To herself. When it started, I couldn't look at her directly. Now, I couldn't tear my eyes away. It scared me. The way her face and body changed through everything she said. Everything. So familiar.

"I ..." She sat upright and fixed herself. "I didn't think much of it. Stress, I thought. I didn't tell anyone. Didn't feel the need." Her face softened. "When it happened again, it was at a dinner. In front of guests. Blake ... You can explain away dropping one dish, but I guess when I couldn't explain why it had happened fifteen times, he figured that he wasn't up to trying to explain it to other people." Then this flash of rage appeared as she said, "So he left me. Me, goddamit! Idiot, shithead, fuck-face. Threw me out with only my clothes and the luggage with my name etched into the handle for company."

And then she fell apart, but not in any way that I could recognize. Her face contorted. Her eyes bugged out. She flashed some gray tongue. She started making a "gal, gakk, gakkk!" sound.

"Petty. What are you doing?"

She went back to looking normal. "I was trying to cry, but I don't think my tear ducts work."

I went and had a seat next to her. She quickly leaned into me as I extended my arm.

"I'm a fucking screw up, I know."

"Yeah. Yeah you are."

"And I said some terrible shit to you before."

"Yeah you did. But you know what's more important?"

Sighing, Petty nodded. "That I'm your sister."

"No! Oh God, no! Please. That's gross. That you make sure you pay Mom and Dad back. That's what's important. You can be stupid with me all you like. But that money..."

"The money!" Petty jumped up and started walking in circles. "Okay. So you remember when I said I spoke to Mom and Dad? A few weeks ago? Right before I came? So, I did. They called frequently. Once a week."

I didn't like the sound of this. "What are you getting at here?"

"It's, uh ..." She started hopping on one leg, as if the words would fall out of her like a ketchup bottle. "So Mom's backup account? The one I asked for? It was actually backup account number two."

"I'm lost."

Petty took one big breath. "They left money in an account for you that was supposed to help you pay the rent and cover expenses while they were away, basically emergency funds that they told me about it and I was supposed to tell you about, but then the whole fallout with Blake happened and I really needed it, so when she gave me the info to share with you, I just emptied the account and lived out of a flat in the shittiest neighborhood that had crime and roaches and weird times when the street lights weren't working and why are you picking up that lamp?"

I pulled the plug out of the wall and checked the weight, tossing it from hand to hand. "Oh nothing. Please, continue." Petty only backed away and I said, "Oh, are you done? Because the gist of this amazing revelation, and you can correct me if I'm wrong, dear sis, is that you lied to me about Mom and Dad and then stole money. Money that would have helped me pay the rent and therefore *avoid this whole damn demon mess in the first place!*"

Petty stood up straight and tried to sound as sweet as possible. "You know, I feel like we are forgetting the touching moment we just had on the couch. The hugs. The feels. We should go back to that."

Before I could re-murder my own sister, we both heard a man scream in the hallway. Instantly, a face popped in the hole in my kitchen.

I couldn't hear what he was saying over his snarling. It might have been in Polish. Or maybe he was speaking in tongues. And his face was going from blueberry to plum pretty damn quick. But it was pretty obvious what all the screaming was about.

I hid the lamp behind my back as the Grey sisters waved to our super, Lou, who barged in baring his teeth.

"Grrrrrrey!" He froze as he spotted Petty. He stood there, trying to process this dead girl. You could see the tension in his flushed cheeks and brow. "Petunia?"

It was the only thing he got out before my sister acted shocked and slapped on that terrible accent again. "Lou, my dear. How are you? How is your wife? To what do we owe the pleasure?"

My sister the liar.

PETTY HAD NO choice but to stay with me. It was a serious strain on our relationship and I barely had any time to really unpack most of it ... okay, all of it. But I blamed this on Barnem who screwed this whole thing up. With the election four days away, and our master plan to take out Mason Scarborough reaching a complete standstill, I threw myself into the planning to take my mind off of things.

And by "planning" I mean sitting and watching Barnem pace around for hours.

"You're starting to wear out my floor."

"Funny," he replied sternly. "Just as funny as it would be if this entire city would turn into cannibals. Or if mad men ran the streets in packs. That would be hilarious!"

Petty sighed. "Is he always like this?"

"No, no," I said, skimming through my phone for news on Mason. "He's usually worse."

The two stopped to stare daggers at each other.

Petty sucked her blackened teeth. "Some angel you are. Hey, aren't you supposed to have a halo? Or a harp?"

"I have your harp right here, you rotting—"

"I found something!" I sat up, feeling my heart race in my chest.

Stopping what he was doing, the Seraph peered over my shoulder. "You found something? On Mason?"

It wasn't about Mason. Not at all.

I cursed my stupid mouth and stood up.

"I'll be right back. I have to see someone. But first, I have to pick something up."

Donaldson looked at me through the crack in his door. "I regret to remind thee that I am rebuked from thy home. We shan't talk."

"I made a mistake." I could tell by his face that he was about to say something, but I jumped in first. "Yes, yes. I'm just as shocked as you. Save the smarm. I made a mistake." I had two things in my hand. One was a brown paper bag and the other was my phone. I pushed the phone against the crack, showing him the pic of Hilary Clamp.

Donaldson sighed and let me in.

As I walked in, I noticed that there were tons of plastic bags everywhere, each one sporting the logo of the bookstore Donaldson worked for. Booke & Ende was pretty well known for its readings and signings, but the bag's contents didn't look very book-ish. They were filled with streamers and disposable plates and thick letters for banners. "Bookstore bat mitzvah?"

He groaned. "I wish. Stupid event at the job coming up in a few days." He stopped talking right away. I had broken a line between us, the way we could both just talk and let things fly. Now he was definitely more guarded. More than that, I could tell he didn't want me there.

"Hilary Clamp," I read from the news article, dated only two days prior. "Wanted in three different states with her partner. Robbed two stores. History of violence. Once held up a lady and her five year old at gunpoint. This was all before she was fished out of the Hudson. You were trying to tell me that when you came to my apartment."

Donaldson shrugged. "What's your point?"

I tossed him the brown bag and he caught it against his chest. I pulled up one of the stools as he carefully opened the bag. Peering inside, he suddenly looked like a kid on Christmas.

"Oh my god."

Five minutes later, Donaldson and I were both enjoying a burger from Burly's. But not just any burger. Oh, no. I had them put together the legendary "Burger Burger." Between the large bites of this burger stuffed burger, I asked him, "So? How does it taste?"

"Like grease. Like sweet, joyous grease and a future cholesterol reading that's going to make the doctor look at me and I'll be all like, 'I know the plight of my people, Doc. But it was oh so worth it.'"

"It's an edible abomination," I agreed.

I didn't have to go further. As soon as he had let me into his apartment, I knew Donaldson had forgiven me for acting like a jackass. Maybe even before. I wasn't sure how or why I knew this. Donaldson was smart and definitely cautious with other people, so I couldn't blame it on his ignorance. It was just that, for some reason, he had this odd healing factor when it came to me. Like I said, I didn't have to go further than enjoy this time, but I felt he deserved it.

"I'm not easy."

Donaldson nodded. "Newsflash."

"I'm serious. My sister is staying with me right now. And as much as it bugs me, it also reminds me that there was a time when it was just the two of us, plus my mom and dad. You know, small circle. Until recently, it's stayed that small."

"Now it seems like the world is ending, huh?"

I blinked at him. "Sure."

Donaldson wiped his mouth. "Look, I get it. I just didn't want you suddenly seeing yourself in Hilary Clamp. She was just some woman who made a bad decision and got mixed up in the wrong thing."

I blinked a second time. "Sure."

"I'm serious. All I'm saying is that you shouldn't work so hard to be or not be someone, Grey. I can tell it's hard enough being you."

I was ready to toss him a quip to lighten the mood. If there was anything I hated more was a goddamn compliment. But I didn't have to think of anything to change the subject to because there it was hanging out of the bag by my feet.

I held up the banner. "'Make New York Nice Again'? Oh shit!"

"Yeah. That's what I'm working on. Floor plan, ticket sales. He's a bit of an idiot, this Mason. But he bought out the bookstore for an event in three days. Can you believe it? The day before he inexplicably gets elected Mayor of NYC and he's throwing a party for himself to meet and shake the hands of the 'real people of this city'. The guy's a joke."

Wide eyed, I pointed my Burly's Burger Burger at him.

"Donaldson, I have a plan."

Barnem shook his head. "That's the worst fucking plan I have ever heard in my life. And I've lived for several thousand centuries."

"It's the best plan!" I insisted. "And it's the *only* plan. Donaldson gets us tickets. We get in. And then we wait until Mason goes to the bathroom or goes to the coffee table or whatever, and we jump the guy."

The demon snapped his fingers as if this was a brilliant idea.

"No. It's a terrible idea," Barnem sniped.

The demon turned to me, shaking its head as if I was the one being ridiculous.

"Who the hell's side are you on? Look, Barnem. It's a small venue. A bookstore. We just need to find a small, quiet space for our shadow guy here to do his thing. What can go—"

"A-hem!" Phil raised his hand to ask a question as if he was still in school. "It's coming with us?"

I had demanded he put his life on the line for this, and Phil was more than inclined to help make things up. Seeing how the Shades worked, he didn't want that to happen to anyone.

Barnem nodded. "You've proven that demons outside of contracts with people can blend in, so it's a safe bet that no one at the event will know. We can sneak our demon guy in and have him lay low. If I can't slay the Shade inside of Mason, then our friend here can eat it."

My roommate gave that last part two shadowy thumbs up.

"So this is it, I guess." I looked at the people I was planning this little adventure with and a thick migraine started to set in. Sure, for the first time in my life, I was onboard with people stepping in to help. But sitting in the room with me was a chicken-shit cultist, a useless demon, and the worst angel in the history of all angels ever. Regretting ever agreeing to this, I threw my head into my hands and hoped that my death would be a painless one.

25

The event was pure spectacle; so much, in fact, that it was both gaudy and awe inspiring. The bookstore of Booke & Ende was a great looking one—not that I frequent them too much. However, it sure wasn't the big, obnoxious ones that seem more like malls, or the tiny independents who sell six books in a space that smells like coffee and broken dreams. Booke & Ende was right in the middle: the second floor being a narrow balcony of tables and lamps; the main floor spanning outward with high ceilings and walls lined with books. Unfortunately, the entire space was filled with the most idiotic ignorance (redundancy intentional) I have ever seen in my life.

The main area was adorned with full frontal Americana: glimmering stars hung from the ceiling; little mugs were handed out with 3D fighter jets that, when you turned them sideways, screamed across a nameless desert, their jet streams spelling "Liberty" across the blue sky; mobiles of miniature eagles spun to the tune of the "Star Spangled Banner".

But this was nothing when you considered what they did with the actual space.

The floor was one giant American flag, with the stage being painted white with white seats— the audience rows were sectioned by colored stripes, both blue and red. The lectern from where Mason was going to speak was all flagged out. Just to the right, there was this strange box surrounded in a black curtain.

It was the single ugliest thing I'd ever seen in my life, and the people around me were eating it up.

We sat down—Donaldson, me, and my roommate, with a seat open for Barnem—in a red aisle.

"You sure this was okay? Getting us in and all?" I whispered to Donaldson.

"A perk for setting this whole thing up. A simple bookstore hookup," he said, staring down at his mug. "Wasn't easy, but I managed to squeeze out two more. Phil said he's bringing a guest."

Before I could grill him on who this guest was, she sat right beside me.

"Petty?"

"Hey, sis."

I was so pissed that the words couldn't come out, so I simply brandished a large fist in Phil's face.

"She insisted!" he exclaimed.

"You brought my dead sister here?" Donaldson gave me a glance, and I fumbled around. Through clenched teeth and a fake smile I said, "I mean, she typically wouldn't be caught dead here. Petty? Why the fuck are you here?"

"I'm bored, Mandy. And Phil here hooked me up. What do you think?"

I'm guessing she meant the makeup job. Her skin wasn't a dark gray anymore. Most of it was under a sweater and coat, and her hands and neck were plastered with pounds of cover-up. "He painted my nails, and look ..."

Petty smiled. Her teeth weren't black, but also not quite white either. "We used White Out," she said enthusiastically. "And we couldn't do anything about the eyes, so ..." She tipped the sunglasses she was wearing so that I could see those dark, hollow pits. "Amazing, right?"

Phil waited for a compliment. I just cracked my knuckles, making him flinch a bit.

A few minutes later, Barnem walked in and took a seat.

Taking a really good look at my row of miscreants, I groaned.

In a short span of time, my life had gone from fairly simple—sure aggravating, sure nerve wracking, but ultimately simple—to this hideous freak show. I had gone from a darling recluse to the most popular anti socialite on the planet. And now these people were sitting beside me

Barnem shook his head at his surroundings but seemed to be in a good mood. That is until he leaned forward to tell me something. Spotting Petty sitting next to me, he nearly lost it. He got up, sat down, slouched, got up again. The Town Hall had already started so I couldn't hear what he was saying over the blaring of "America the Beautiful". It involved a lot of cursing, I'm sure. She wasn't part of the plan and, to him, this whole thing had just gone to shit even before we made our move. A small security detail descended on him, forcibly asking the Seraph to sit down. A few seconds later, he was dragged out kicking and screaming.

The event started with ten people in suits walking on stage. They remained standing as an announcer came over the sound system. After some garbage, he finally got to the point of the entire night.

"And here he is. The 'tell-it-how-it-is' man of the people. The absolute voice of our nation. The man with the vision to make our city the greatest single populated state on the planet. The future mayor of this great state, Mason Scarborough!"

I didn't think anything could be stranger than the decorations around us, but Mason turned out to be the strangest. He walked up to the podium still decked out in his pirate getup from The Captain Show. Same black tights and shiny shoes. Same stupid hat with curling feather. He was dressed as a clown with a spray tan while taking the stage as a politician and no one seemed to care. The damn place went wild.

With him were the children from the TV show; stern looks in their eyes, weapons still in their hands. Caitlyn (with a Y) stood along the edge of the stage like she had been doing this since 'Nam.

The audience went wild. Women, men, children. There were two large television screens on either side of the stage which were focused on Mason's citrus-colored face.

"Why the hell is he so orange-y?" Phil whispered.

"It's like I'm looking at the sun if the sun gave itself cancer."

The five of us laughed. Caitlyn (with a Y) made the gesture that she was keeping her eyes on us.

To the right of his lectern, the box beside it came alive. The black curtains on it parted and exposed a small stage. And out popped Cracker Barrell the parrot puppet.

Mason cleared his throat. "Dearest constituents and voters, I stand before you on the edge of a great change in our great city. Tomorrow, because of your support, your votes and furious calls, I will assume the city appointed statehood of Mayor of New York City."

The crowd cheered.

Mason lost it.

"Don't cut me off! What is it with people cutting me off before I finish speaking?" he screamed.

The crowd was eerily quiet. Mason dropped his head. "Right. Please, all of you, punch yourselves in the face."

Everyone looked at each other.

Mason repeated himself. "For the sake of this country, you *must* punch yourself in the face." There was a long pause, and then he added, "Go on. I'll wait."

One by one, the crowd did as they were told. First only a few people. Then ten or twenty. Then the sounds of each knuckle meeting face passed along the audience like a wave of brutality, rolling like wild popcorn bursts. Some landed on the chin, some on the eye or cheek. Luckily, Mason had specified only one punch, but each one was hard, forceful. A baby nearby was barely managing to make a fist.

My small cohort was the only one not to follow suite, possibly because of our connection to my roommate. Well, actually I had forgotten about Donaldson. Unable to resist, the place where fist met his cheek bruised instantly.

Petty looked at me and whispered, "What's the plan here? How are we going to take him down?"

"*We* are doing nothing!" I hissed back. "*We* are not a *we*. *You* need to go home and let *we*, I mean us handle this, okay? I know what I'm doing."

"Fine!" Petty pouted and crossed her arms.

"Fine!" I turned to Phil. "What the hell should I do?"

His terror-filled face said it all.

I had to step up and address my team of misfits. "Okay. Okay. Let's not freak out here. So Mason can influence whoever the hell he wants and there are about a thousand people here. What do we have? A bunch of nobodies. All right. That's fine. That's cool. Plan hasn't changed. We're still just going to wait until his little speech is over and pounce on him after. Find a nice quiet spot. Should be possible, right?"

Satisfied with the crowd's silence, Mason continued. Using a clicker, the image of New York City came up on the large televisions as he spoke.

"Our city. For years it's been the home of countless indecencies. It houses the most liberal trolls of our nation. The big 'fat cats' of Wall Street control our very lives." He stared out into the audience for effect. "But that is only because we let it. We must bring the decency back. We-must-make ..."

The crowd responded with the rest of the asinine slogan, "Make New York Nice Again!"

"Where was I?" Mason asked. "Oh right. I plan to make New York City the model state for the entire world. Once we reach that amazing existence, I will make sure we stay that way. And there's only one way to do that." Mason pressed the clicker again and a large circle was raised around the image of the city. "We will build a wall. We will keep the rude, obnoxious people out. And we will make up for the foolishness of our previous leaders!"

The audience started clapping as a man was led on stage wearing a black hood over his head. His arms were lashed behind his back. They kicked him to the ground and he knelt to the gasp of everyone watching.

The hood came off and the Mayor, Mason's brother, stared back at us. He had tape over his mouth and a terrible bruise around his temple.

Petty and Phil glanced at me, but I was panicking, too.

"But first, some house cleaning," Mason said before coming out from behind the lectern, removing a pistol he had wedged into his belt, and firing it point-blank into his brother's head. There was an violent spray of blood as Collard rocked back and then collapsed.

"That execution-style murder was crackerlicious!" Cracker Barrell exclaimed to the laughter of the audience.

Mason belted the gun again and walked back to the microphone. "Tomorrow, I win the seat of mayor. But I have decided that waiting for such a time wouldn't be prudent." He paused and licked his lips. "Well, I hope no one made plans tonight because we must overthrow every power in the state by morning."

A huge clamor broke out. Several doors opened and four carts were wheeled into place at the front of the stage by security guards in SWAT gear. Each cart was overflowing with lead pipes, bats, butcher knives, barbed wire. A small bar opened up on the side, setting out homemade molotovs.

"Begin with local law enforcement and then work your way up. If you have a gun at home, on your wall, in a closet, bring it out and use it. If this government wants to take your arms away, then you send them the bullets first. Gut every last one of them. String them to light posts. That will show those religious freaks, those pagan zealots, faceless terrorists, those politico talking head wackos what happens when you make the citizens of this magnificent place angry. We will burn this entire city to the ground. Let's see those bastards try to blow us up then! A broken bone heals stronger and … he who laughs last. And so on." Mason shrugged and drank from a water bottle. "Please listen to Cracker Barrell for further instructions."

"Line up, mateys, one by one," the puppet squawked as everyone began standing. "No pushing. No shoving. There are enough weapons to go around. Please be considerate and leave the lighter weapons for the children. We ordered pizza!"

The crowd celebrated, but I wasn't sure if it was because of the free pizza or the free tools to physically maim other human beings.

Donaldson got up and started filing in with everyone.

"Okay, this sucks," I said, and noticed everyone looking at me for guidance. My roommate was even staring at me with his big, yellow eyes while fiddling with his shadowy fingers.

"All right. It's fine. We're still good. No need to panic, right? We still have the element of surprise. We just need to …" I watched the lines forming, on the left for the weapons, on the right for pizza. Both ran close to

141

the stage. "We just need to get in a line. I'll take the right with Beelzebub here. Petty and Phil, take the left."

Phil looked up at the security guards. "They're armed. Mason is armed. Shit, that little five year old with the missing front tooth is armed."

"Doesn't mean anything if they aren't expecting us. You two make a distraction when you're close enough. I don't care what it is. Then that leaves it open for us to rush the stage and tackle Mason. He's the one we need here. The moment our guy eats him, everyone will snap out of it. Mason is the key." It sounded like nonsense gobbledygook logic to me, but everyone quickly got up and moved into position. "Wait! No one has a better plan? No rebuttals? Oh, god. We're going to die."

I stood behind the demon on line and we moved with the crowd, slowly at first, only steps at a time. At the other end of the hall, Phil and Petty were moving a lot faster. They were faking a pretty hilarious conversation, with Phil jumping around like an idiot and Petty throwing her head back to laugh.

It was pretty convincing.

I tried getting their attention, but they just kept going on and on. By the time I realized why it seemed so natural, Phil was given an axe, Petty a stick wrapped in barbed wire, and then they walked away, completely forgetting what they were there for.

Not that it would have mattered much because the next thing Mason said was, "Can someone do me a favor and kill Amanda Grey? Yes, the woman standing right there. And her demon friend, too. I would appreciate it."

26

As the entire crowd turned on me, I barreled my way to the stage. Someone tried to swing a long chain at me but it smacked the person behind him instead. Shoving a few others down, the ones in line who were slower to react, toppled a large section over, giving me some room.

There was a commotion on the other side the stage. Petty and Phil must have gotten their lives together in time to actually participate in the fracas. Then a voice was shouting over all the others, this one coming from the entrance, as Barnem seemed to be raising his own hell. The combination of all three was an unplanned, unmitigated disaster. But it got me where I needed to be.

On stage with Captain Cross.

"You don't need to do this, Mason. People are screwed up without you treating them like puppets. You're talking about killing innocent people. Thousands."

Mason's tangerine face barely registered anything past his frown. "You're trying to appeal to my humanity?"

"No I'm not," I said plainly, and then asked, "Is it working?"

"Absolutely not."

"Oh."

"But it's an honorable attempt coming from you. I know all about Amanda Grey, and I expected far less from an uncouth, reckless young lady."

"You're welcome." I said kept an eye on the audience. The bodyguards were pushing through the mob. They were going to be on me in mere seconds.

Mason rolled up the sleeve on his right arm, pulled the Cracker Barrell puppet on it, and propped up his elbow to make the parrot stare at me as he spoke. "This *is* my humanity, Grey. Do you know how many years I gave to trying to change this world through its youth? When the real problem lies right up top. Politicians are just children playing dress up. It doesn't take a demon to see that. So what if a few thousand people lose their lives? What matters is—"

"Wow, Mason!" I yelled. "That's great. Tell me more."

The gamble paid off. Mason blew his top, screamed, started pacing. But before I could charge the guy, one of the SWAT guys leapt in from my blind side and grabbed my ankle while reaching for his gun. But then the demon's mouth closed around his head and clamped down. The wriggling body emptied an entire clip into the air. The shots must have woke a few people up because a panic broke out. Only a few people were still ready to fight. The others were rushing toward the exits, trampling each other just to get away.

I spun around and stormed toward Mason.

He lazily held up a hand. "Stop."

I slowed my running.

I took one extra step.

I stopped right in front of him.

And then I punched him in the throat.

His white wig spun like a top as he shuffled backward. This was the perfect opportunity for my roommate to eat him while he was off balance. But I turned around and it was still trying to pry the dead SWAT guy from his teeth. Noticing me watching, he held up one finger.

"One minute? We don't have one minute!"

In the back, Barnem was fighting his way up but making little progress. Phil and Petty were busy wrestling with two security guards. Well, Phil was in a chokehold and Petty was on the guy's back.

"Kick his ass, Mandy!"

"Still don't need your help, Petty!"

Mason caught me with a sucker kick to the lower back and I went down.

144

Barnem was shouting my name, and though I could hear the bodies he was managing to throw around, his voice was still far away. So as I turned around and felt the barrel of the gun Mason had set against my forehead, I was quietly able, within those fractions of a second, to quickly skim through my life and summarize it into two letters.

Eh.

Two shots rang out and I flinched. Only after the second did Mason's head snap back, followed by his body tipping into the lectern and then the puppet theater. The entire set piece—wood panels and curtains—collapsed on him in a heap.

My ears were ringing and the world spun slowly, blurring every time I turned my head. The chaos around me was displayed in moving vignettes: the remaining scuffles were between security guards and the NYPD; people had thrown down their weapons and were scattering; Barnem had gotten through the carnage and was leaping up on stage; the demon had finally freed himself of his last meal and was following suit; Donaldson pushed his way to the stage to where I was. But the most telling was seeing the smoke pouring out of the gun Petty had snatched from the security guard. Her black eyes were large, in shock, and some of the makeup on her cheek was rubbed off where she had been punched.

Barnem got me up and checked on me, his words still muffled behind my screeching ears. I wanted to make sure this whole thing was over, so I made sure to point out where Mason was so that the Shade couldn't get away. My roommate cracked his knuckles and started cackling as he approached Mason's dead body.

"Hey, Barnem."

"Yeah, Grey."

The demon began removing the debris to get to its meal.

"On a score of one to ten, ten being 'Awesome' and one being 'Fuck My Life', how would you rate our plan? He's going to eat and get stronger now. This is all on us if he gets out of control."

Barnem didn't reply.

Rubbing its shadowy palms together, the demon opened its mouth over Mason. But then it was punched, struck so squarely and forceful that its head caved in like someone had used a sledgehammer on a black foot-ball. The punch itself came with a dull shockwave that sent the demon's body hurtling through the air. It smashed into the overhead projector, bounced through the bottom of the second floor balcony and into the back wall.

Barnem grumbled and stood up. "Can I get back to you on that?"

"Sure thing," I said. "Take your time."

The only thing up out of the rubble was Mason's arm, the one he had struck the demon with. But on that hand was Cracker Barrell.

The puppet stared at us with vile sewn hatred.

Barnem spat and tried to come off calm. "Give it up, Mason. There's no way you can win here."

The puppet looked around. "Tonight was brought to you by the letter 'D'."

Barnem looked back at me. I shrugged.

"'D' is for 'disappointment'. For the 'destruction' of plans." Mason's back arched from the ground as he was pulled up to his feet without bracing himself with his hands. Now in full view, it was pretty obvious that he was very dead. Petty had struck him in the shoulder and the side of the head where the eyepatch sat. The bullet hole was large and glistening with black blood. From out of his eyes, his ears, his nose, it poured in thick spurts. Meanwhile, Cracker Barrell the puppet was still moving.

"But, Amanda Grey," it said, as black feathers stuck out of the stitch-ing, as it started to bulge and swell in size, "right now is all about 'disfig-urement'. 'Disembowelment'. 'Decapitation'."

"Demon," Barnem growled, pointing too dramatically for my tastes, "prepare to be slain." The Seraph set his hands together and a blue burst of energy leapt out like he was holding lightning. Before the smoke lifted, Barnem charged, plunging the summoned weapon into Mason's breastplate.

When the smoke dissipated, the weapon was roughly the size of a small dagger. A very dull dagger.

Cracker Barrell screamed bloody murder and Barnem let out a yell of triumph.

And then they both looked down.

The dagger had barely made a hole in the costume.

"Do over," Barnem declared, but was instantly swatted away by Cracker Barrell. The impact came with a loud sickening CRACK that sounded like the Seraph had been broken in half. His lifeless body flew across the room and landed with sick thud against a pile of folding chairs.

"Stupid. S-s-stupid. S-s-s-o stupid." Mason's body spasmed as it vomited up bucketfuls of the black blood. Then the puppet on his hand started to expand, growing ten feet, twenty feet, two stories high. Even though some its sewing popped, and the black feathers below the ripped material becoming exposed, the goliath still looked like a massive hand puppet, but now with a wingspan longer than my entire body.

I felt someone beside me. Petty raised her gun and fired until the entire clip was empty, but the giant parrot just sucked in Mason's body like a wet noodle.

"I know this might be a bad time," my sister said as the enormous puppet took a step toward us, sending tremors through the ground and howled, "Greyyy!"

"It's just that being dead gives you a new set of perspectives. I'm not making any sense here," she said as we dove to the side of the giant beak. The impact caused the wooden floor to explode. "And I know I've been kind of a jackass to you. To Mom and Dad."

Enraged, the parrot parted its mouth and dark flames shot out. It caught me so off guard that a stream climbed up my back and arm. As I screamed, Petty tackled me, smothering the flames. Only some of my neck and the back of my hair was singed.

"Our relationship is strained because of it. I know that. You know that. Everyone knows that."

"Petunia," I said in a way that was so my mom. This made Petty stop and take notice. "Can we, um, table the 'sister reconciliation'? I'll try to set up a brunch or a painting class or whatever. Raincheck."

"Right." She laughed as if it just dawned on her.

As I got to my feet, I wondered if death had made my sister both more aware of her surroundings *and* somehow even more self-centered

Donaldson leapt on stage with us. He had a pretty terrible cut above his eye, but he was alive. Which unfortunately meant he had questions.

"Grey—"

"Save it! Synopsis: the pirate mayoral candidate was being manipulated by this gigantic possessed fire breathing puppet."

"Actually, I was going to ask if this was your sister." He extended his hand and Petty shook it. "Jeffrey Donaldson. I live upstairs from Amanda."

"Nice to meet you." She leaned back and gave me the approving nod.

"I swear to god, Petty, that had better be the rigor mortis setting in." I shoved them both back, making sure they kept their distance. "As a matter of fact, why don't both of you just back off and give me some space to breathe? We got this." I pointed around the hall—to the demon in the smoking crater on the second floor and the unconscious angel by the chairs.

"Maybe we should—" Donaldson started, but I waved my hands until he stopped.

"How about we—" Petty tried, but I made coughing noises until she shut up.

When they were both silent, I said, "So now I'm going to go do my job, whatever that means, and neither of you is going to need to butt in. I got this."

I turned around and was immediately eaten by the twenty-foot parrot.

The whisper was coming out of empty space. I couldn't feel my body, my fingers, my feet. I wondered if this is what death felt like. But then there was that voice.

"*Psst. You know this is all your fault? All this death and destruction?*"

"*Who are you?*"

My voice seemed to echo though there was only pure white. Endless nothing.

"*Me? I'm no one.*"

"*Ah. No one. That's something only a douchebag would say.*"

The whisper chuckled.

"*He-he. Such a mouth. Even in the end.*" And then it said, "*You should give up, you know? This would all just go away.*"

148

"*So is this the end or do I have to give up? I'm confused. If you're here to taunt me, at least be consistent.*"

"*He-he.*" The same odd laughter. "*He-he. All right. Don't listen to me. But look at where you're at. Look at where you've landed.*"

I was ready to say that I couldn't—that I couldn't make out an inch of my surroundings—but then the white space fell apart and black ink began pouring in. In oceans. In leagues. And when it collided with the empty space where I had been standing, I felt my body. The world was rolling, throbbing, squirming, slipping. Everything had a black sheen. Everything was encased in the darkness. The world was dripping wet and encased in pulsating organs that spit the dark blood everywhere. I was in the belly of a killer parrot about to be digested.

As soon as I realized this, it was as if my confines took notice. The black blood latched itself to me, bound my arms and legs, dove into my throat and eyes and ears. I felt as if it were trying to pull me inside out.

And then the voice said, "*Told you. Yeah. Totally sucks to be you right now.*"

I tried to struggle. I tried prying my body free, but every extra movement hurt.

"*Psst. Grey.*"

The dark liquid started filling my lungs. I was drowning.

"*You're going to die now, Grey.*"

I started blacking out.

"*Or you could not. He-he. That's your choice. You could die pathetically here, now. Or die pathetically ... ehh some other time.*"

I was closing me eyes. They were closing. But I was also balling up a fist. Balling it and setting it back. And feeling how my organs burned and how my blood curdled, and my bones vibrated underneath my skin. I set my fist back and threw that punch like I knew where it should go, like I knew whose face it should land on. It was a punch I threw a million times in over twenty years. And as it came to a stop, the world I was in ruptured and I spilled out into the violent light.

Hitting the ground, I threw everything up instantly. I couldn't see a thing, but I heard sounds nearby, mostly wet dripping. Everything came out of me onto the floor as I took a much needed full breath of air. I was covered head to toe in the goop, and either I was crazy weak after almost being digested or the stuff actually weighed a ton.

The first person I spotted was Donaldson holding a dented folding chair. And then Phil trying to look badass with a gun. Beside him was Petty holding her arm, which seemed to have been ripped off. Even my roommate looked filthy and beaten along the edges of its body.

And each and every one of them seemed to be gawking at me.

"Hey," I said, still not having much of a breath for anything else.

That's when I noticed, none of them were looking at me.

I turned to see that I had punched my way out of the parrot's belly. Blackened, hissing guts hung out of the giant hole I had used to exit the stupid thing. Cracker Barrel had not moved or made a sound. And then, almost a half a second later, the entire creature keeled off to the side and crashed into the ground.

I slid backward myself but Donaldson caught me and set me down.

The first thing I asked, for some reason was, "Barnem?"

"He's alive. Beat badly. Just—"

"The voice ..."

Donaldson looked at me strangely. He said something but I didn't have my head on straight to make sense of it. Loud jets of steam cut him off as they burst out of the parrot's body. And it began to shrink.

I pushed off of Donaldson and limped over to where the puppet sat, ragged and torn. Mason's emaciated corpse was still attached to its lower end, and they both sat in a smoking pile of the dark tar.

"You ... have no idea ..." Cracker Barrell croaked as it spit out blood. "No idea ... why he stays around, do you? But if you did know, if you were to find out ... then how much—KRGH!"

My roommate had gone and stomped on the puppet's head, which was fine by me because I was done with ominous messages. And as it picked it up, it was pretty damn obvious by how mangled it was that, though it wasn't dead, it definitely wasn't talking anymore.

As the demon slid the parrot/crow and its master into his mouth, and just as the large lump of this heap settled in its belly, I thought about the voice.

The voice I had heard.

Even though my roommate's flesh began to bake and bubble. Even as sparks of hellfire blew from its mouth and fissures formed on its round head. Even as I stood watching the walking horror transform in front of me, I stayed removed from it all— just a passenger in my own body.

At first, I had thought that it was the demon inside Cracker Barrel talking to me. Wishing I would give up. Trying to make me settle. But it wasn't. This voice, the one I had heard in that empty space, wasn't trying to kill me. The feeling gnawed at me. The voice. The dread. The anger. The fear. I could hear it in the voice, even as it mocked me. Even as it laughed. In fact, I realized, that it all had actually sounded ... familiar.

And just like that, the would-be mayoral press conference of Mason Scarborough came to an end just as black beams of ultimate evil signaled the revival of an ultimate evil.

SHOCKINGLY, TWO DAYS later, I found myself in my apartment watching television by myself.

How did I know I was alone?

Oh, you can bet your ass I checked!

In the bathroom, the back room, even under the couch. No-body. No one. It was so damn amazing that it made me ridiculously nervous for some reason. Then again, it could have been what was on the screen at the time.

Mason had won. I'm talking an epic landslide victory. The biggest margin in the history of the city. Even with the murder of his brother in front of hundreds of people. Even with being *dead*. Cracker Barrell had been the creature of power, of influence. But Mason wasn't possessed by a Shade at all. This meant that the thousands of people who went out to vote for the guy *were actually voting for him*. No dark influence. No mysterious happenings. Just citizens exercising their democratic right to be incredibly idiotic.

Oddly enough, I understood their reasoning.

I had spent a week as a deity of my own cult, and I saw in the people mixed up with making that terrible decision one lone resemblance they were searching for something. I don't think they were looking for an answer, I just think they were hoping there was an answer to begin with. Their lives weren't where they wanted it. They were sad, depressed, angry. They needed hope, first and foremost, that there was something better out there.

Maybe Mason was the perfect guy for that job after all. He was used to programming kids, having them recite one form of gibberish after another and labeling it knowledge. Those kids became registered voters or disciples who were just looking for the same thing—a larger than life person who claimed to hear them when they were screaming into the darkness.

I turned the television off.

Zero. That was the number of newscasts and online journals that said anything about what really had happened in Booke & Ende. Mason had not allowed news cameras in the rally and nothing was ever brought up about the security cameras. The few folks that brought up the giant sewage spewing parrot were written off as part of "fanatic media". The videos and recordings of the event were scrubbed, of course. No one had seen or remembered the giant talking parrot or the woman who punched her way out of its stomach. The consensus was that Mason had snapped, ran out and kidnapped his brother and executed him in front of hundreds of people. The public response?

"At least this is a guy who gets things done. That's what we need in our officials."

Awe inspiring.

I only wished Barnem could have been there to see it all go down. He was still in the hospital, in a coma with more bones broken than anything they've ever seen. I had beat that Shade, by myself. To hell with his "greater good". I just needed him to wake up. To get out of his bed. To come back to the building, back to his apartment.

So that I could punch him in the face.

The peace and quiet was reaching out at me from all sides. I tried humming. I tried using a handball and bouncing it to myself from off of the taped hole in my wall. How long was this going to last? I had spent another wet and wild week head to head against demons. And now what? Where the hell was everyone? When were they going to come and spoil it?

Feeling like the walls were closing in on me, I headed right for the door and to a place where I could clear my head.

Our super, Lou, had three major rules for the building.

No smoking in the hallways because you can give all the babies and dogs in the other apartments cancer.

No handball in the front of the building. Go next door if you want to do that shit.

And absolutely no one was allowed to go up to the roof. Not for safety concerns, but because he would go up there himself. That was where he escaped from nagging tenants and an equally nagging wife. I had been going as a kid and never ran into him.

Out in the chilly Queens air, the stars were out again in full force. It didn't take me long to spot the moon, either. It was the first time in I don't know how long that I had seen it.

We had done it. Sure, my sister had died and was now a host to a sealed fiend. Sure, Barnem ended up in the hospital. Sure, the world had now just gotten a whole lot weirder with humanity one step closer to total annihilation.

But we had done it.

We had staved off the apocalypse for another day.

But there was still something nagging at me, still lingering about the whole Mason fallout, and I couldn't talk to anyone about it.

The voice I heard in the creature's stomach. There was no explanation for it. Something was talking to me, to me directly. It spoke to me as if it knew me. I had no idea what it meant. Where it was going to take me. I had spent all of my life with my parents telling me that I wasn't "Mental Mandy", that I wasn't crazy. But how could I explain any of the things I had seen? The things that I had done? The World Wide Weird was in my apartment, 24/7. Mine. But the voice … that was something closer.

A creak nearby made me spin around, and Donaldson popped his head out of the gated door.

"There you are. Petty told me you liked to come up here."

"Did she now? Shocked she remembered."

He stepped out into the night with me and looked up. "Can't remember when was the last time I saw the moon that big."

"Mhm."

Donaldson rocked back and forth on his heels. "You could have told me," he said, finally broaching the subject.

"Nope!"

154

"I was putting my life on the line that day. I mean, I didn't know that of course. But it would have been swell to know."

"Duly noted."

"What's your problem?"

I pounded my head with my fists. "What's yours? Social pariah? 'Nope, I'll just hang around'. Oh, your sister's dead and now she's not'? 'Cool, bruh'."

He slid his hands in his pockets. "I've never said the word bruh, bruh."

"See? I-don't-get-you."

He nudged me with his shoulder. "You don't?"

In the middle of our silence, Petty and Phil came up.

"No, no, no. Go downstairs."

"Do I eat?" Petty asked.

I rolled my eyes. "How would I know?"

"It's just that Phil …" She froze. "It's just that we want to go out to get something to eat and—"

"Oh helll no!" I stood in between them and nearly shook Petunia to death (again). "This guy is crazy. No offense."

"None taken," Phil assured me.

"He led to you being killed and consumed by a being of pure darkness."

Petty thought about it, ruminated, replied, "No relationship is perfect."

"GAH!" It was an epic gah. A final gasp at the heavens. I turned them both around and shoved them toward the door. "Go. Please go. Go. Shoo. Please. Please go shoo. Go before …"

No sooner had I forcefully gave them their exit and slammed the door behind them than I spotted the demon sitting on the edge of the building right where I had been standing. With lavender-colored skin, his face was slender and human-like: chin, nose, mouth, ears. He even had a ragged mop of short black hair on his head that was punctuated by the elongated horns curving toward the night sky. His spaded tail wagged back and forth. His upper body had the build of a young man, which he had covered in my old S.O.a.D shirt. His lower body was back to the hooves, but now surrounded in black wool.

"No, no. This was *my* time."

The demon turned his yellow eyes toward me. Now at their centers, there were tiny black dots which stood as its pupils. The dots rolled with stubborn attitude.

He rose and walked up to me.

Glaring, he put up one finger. Stuck to it was a sticky note.

I plucked it off and read it.

You suck.

He had signed the bottom.

D.

He gave Donaldson a fist bump and strutted back to the edge of the building.

"Worst roommate ever," it said in a voice that sounded like a revving chainsaw. It then sprouted two black bat wings and took to the air, gliding around the building until it was out of sight.

I yelled after him, "I don't suck. I totally don't suck. You know who does? The person who finishes the juice and puts the empty bottle back in the fridge. That's who sucks, my friend. In some countries, that's a war crime."

I turned to Donaldson to see if he was on my side, but instead he went back to staring at me.

We were alone on the rooftop again.

There was a long silence between us.

"So I asked you a question," he said.

"Did you?"

"RUN, BITCH! OMMAGAHD! RUN, BITCH! OMMAGAHD!"

Donaldson gave me a crooked look.

"It's catchy," I said, and quickly answered my phone. It was Petty. Again. "I already told you, sis. I'm really not up for this right now."

"Mandy." Her voice sounded echoey, hurried. "Okay. I treated you like shit. I get that, okay? I know."

"Where are you right now?"

"In the bathroom. Mandy, I need you to come downstairs, right away. Like now. Right fucking now. I'm in trouble."

I groaned. "Does it have anything to do with dark creatures pining for the fall of humanity?"

"No, but—"

"Byyye, Petttty!" And I hung up.

I hated myself instantly after and Donaldson could read it right on my face.

"You should go. We can talk later. I'm sure there'll be other romantic opportunities."

But I assured him, "No. No there won't. Because this isn't even romantic. It's ... it's ..."

Behind Donaldson's head, a streak flew across the sky. I had never seen one before, so I blinked as I tracked it flying across the horizon.

A shooting star.

Donaldson was looking somewhere else and missed it, but had the same shocked reaction. And then I spotted a second. And a third. Stars started falling from the sky, slow at first, but then picking up speed, leaving trails against the night like claws on canvas. There were dashes of light everywhere and it was impossible to see where the stars were landing because they made no sound on impact.

That was the night a third of the stars were stricken from the night sky.

Donaldson and I quietly stood there watching the sky fall.

When I got to my apartment, Petty was standing in the living room talking to someone relaxing my father's loveseat. It wasn't the demon or Phil. Even when he turned around to greet me, I almost didn't recognize who he was until I really focused on his face.

By then, the second familiar face came out of the bathroom.

"Mandy! We're home!" Dad yelled as Mom came and hugged me around the waist.

157

EPISODE THREE:
THE DEVIL YOU KNOW

HE WOKE UP screaming, clawing at the night air. Sitting up in bed, he saw that there was a perfect halo of sweat and urine soaked into his expensive sheets.

He sat there, listening to his own breathing in the quiet of his chamber. There were candles all around the room, tiny tongues of flame that broke up the darkness. He had been sleeping with them, against the council of his advisors and the house crew. The agreement to have one attendant peek in every hour to relight or just check in on the candles was hard fought but earned. Ever since the visions had gotten worse, over a month ago, and since they all came as dreams, he had started distrusting the darkness when he awoke.

"Grey, what have you done?"

He said this aloud both to hear his own voice and to break up the dense silence around him. Wiping the sweat from his brow, he reached out and fumbled for his glasses. By the time he found them and slipped them onto the bridge of his nose, the posted guard gave his door a light rap and asked him if everything was all right. He assured the young man that he was not in any immediate danger but needed an attendant.

The visions had gotten worse. Everything. Everything was spinning out of control. But it all was so clear. He couldn't forsake his calling. Not now.

Calling off the attendant, he washed himself with a wet rag and went to his writing desk, a large oak monstrosity that he liked to avoid because he always felt small sitting at it. From the lowest drawer, he produced a small box with an ivory handle and set it onto the bed. There were four latches and a combination lock he had to get through, but he did so with ease. This was something he had been practicing since the visions surfaced.

Inside, in small velvet pockets, were two pistols. Gold leaves had been fashioned on the barrel and the handles themselves had Latin script wrapped around in loops. Looking at these marvelously crafted weapons of salvation, he wondered what had gone wrong with humanity. How had the evocation of the End of Days come so soon, so promptly? It was almost as if some stupid idiot had flicked a switch, like he had started it all on his own. On purpose? Was this a grand scheme or just dumb luck? He would have to go. He would have to go there and decide the fate of this person immediately.

He tucked both weapons into the band on his waist, threw his robe over them, and rushed out of his chambers, startling the guard. The young man began running beside him.

"Pack my bags and order a flight," he told the guard. "I've put this off long enough."

"Your—" He stumbled over himself, tripping trying to keep up, but only avoided falling flat on his face because the man, twice his age, caught him.

The man smiled at him. "What is your name?"

The guard stood up straight. "My name? Oswalt Krug."

The older man smiled. This man who was supposed to serve as his guard was so young, so nervous. He reminded him much of his own childhood in service, flying on blind faith and a need to work for others. In the wake of the horrors he saw in his visions, his heart opened to this young man in a way he could not even explain. Krug, he knew, was a name tied to Germany. So he spoke to him in his most polished German.

"Oswalt."

The sound of his mother tongue, the one he had probably heard in his home as a child, settled the young man. He had such coldness in his eyes, but not in a way that it should be feared. He believed and he believed with all of his fiber. Straightening himself, he replied, "Y-yes, Your Holiness?"

"Do me a favor and pack your bag as well. I am appointing you as my attendee. I will need someone to trust."

Oswalt lightly bowed his head. His demeanor now changed, the young man was ready to stay by the older man's side. "I will. And where should I tell the plane we are going, Your Holiness?"

"To the belly of the beast, young Oswalt," the Pope told him as they matched cold stares. "Queens, New York."

I SET MY keys into the door and just stood there, giving him a big enough window, a freaking invite with his name splattered all over it, to draw closer to me. After a long night of partying, we both reeked of alcohol. I could smell it on him as he pushed up on me from behind, curling his arms around my waist. With my hair loose, he set his chin into it and inhaled. Before he could push in farther, I spun around and playfully tapped his lips with a soft finger. This made him laugh and lean in, but I turned the doorknob before our lips could meet and we both stumbled into my apartment.

I tossed my keys off to the side and watched as he took in the aesthetics of my apartment.

"Nice place you got here." The vodka shots he had downed were strong, but I guess not strong enough for him to follow up and say, "You got a hole in your kitchen wall."

He then broke out laughing, and so did I. Kicking off my heels, I brushed them to one side and slid onto my couch. I lifted up my dress enough to scoot my exposed legs underneath me. He came and joined me.

"I gotta say something. Can I say something?"

"Please do." I carefully plucked my gold earrings off and jingled them in my hands.

"It's just ... ah, I dunno. You don't seem like the kind of girl that'll scoop up some random guy in a bar and bring him all the way home."

"Well," I said, resting my head on the side of the couch, "first of all, I'm a woman not a girl. And second of all ..."

"Second of all?"

"That makes me capable of doing what I want, when I want to do it."

I was afraid that this might have been going a bit too hard, that it might rub him the wrong way, but he just flashed his smile and nodded. "It's just not safe, you know. How do you know I'm not some crazy psycho?"

I pouted. "Are you a crazy psycho?"

He sighed and closed his eyes, resting his head at the same angle as mine. "I am, actually. And I've come to murder you, Amanda Grey."

I chuckled. "Have you?"

"But not before I gut you. Rip you open."

"Mhm."

"Yank your guts out with my bare hands."

"Ooo."

"Dig out your eyeballs and skull fuck you."

"Not really hygienic, but not here to judge."

"Bleed you into your tub just to wash my balls in it. Smash all of your teeth in with a hammer. Tear your skin off and use it as wallpaper to decorate your shitty little apartment."

"Ah well. What was your name again?"

"Franklin."

"Right. So, Franklin, I get you want to kill me. Zero spoiler warning there. But don't talk shit about my apartment."

From behind, Petty drove the aluminum bat right across the space between his neck and his cranium, resulting in the *clop* sound of meat and bone. His entire head bent off to the side, which would have killed a normal son of a bitch outright.

Son of a bitch, he was. Normal, he wasn't.

With his neck broken and the bone poking out into the air, his right arm shot out and grabbed me by the throat. His left arm snatched the dented bat from Petty's hands. Instantly, a second set of arms, these with ash-colored skin and thick muscles, sprouted out of his chest. Arm #3 grabbed Petty in the same chokehold and #4 wagged its finger at me and then fixed Franklin's slicked black hair, even with his head slouched onto his shoulder.

"Tsk tsk, Grey," he muttered. As he stood to his feet, we were both picked up off the ground, hanging there like Christmas ornaments. "Good try. A for effort. But you should never use yourself as bait." He looked back at my sister. "Or at least bring better backup."

His second left arm hoisted the bat back and clobbered Petty across the face with it.

"Ow," she said, but didn't mean it. Her black skin was caved in and the blow had seemingly broken her skull, but Petty being a vessel for a demon and all? You could tell that it was only an inconvenience. Franklin held her by the throat, but Petty no longer breathed air, so it wasn't doing anything other than keeping her in place.

Furious that the first person he wanted to murder was un-murderable, he launched her across the room and she crashed against the wall by the back room. Petty hopped up, cracked skull and all, and dusted herself off.

"You're an idiot if you think I'm the backup," she laughed. And then pointed to the door to our back room.

But no one came out.

She looked at me with her dead eyes and then back at the door. "One sec." She opened the door and disappeared for a few seconds. She then came out and walked up to the spot where I was hanging and whispered, "Yeah. Um. He's missing. What was Plan B?"

I coughed. I wheezed. I turned purple. Purpler.

Franklin tried to curse at us, but Petty told him to shhh while she deciphered my message.

Petty stared at me intensely. Blinked. "Yeah, no. Don't understand you."

"Tha-wuth-plen-beee," I squeaked out.

"Oh." Petty pulled out her cell phone and began typing. Even with arm #4 giving her another hefty swat that sent her flying across the room again, Petty hit the wall like a bullet but managed to hang onto her cell phone.

"Petty!" I gasped.

She held up a broken finger for an extra second and continued typing.

164

A long minute later, my roommate walked in. With ripped jeans and a thrift shop bought military jacket over his skinny frame, he calmly strode in and paid us no mind. I could have strangled him if, you know, I wasn't being strangled.

Petty jumped up and finally became useful. Reaching into the black floppy hair that was covering all but one of his purple eyes, she tugged his earbuds out and shouted, "You're late!"

He groaned. "Late for?" Turning his head, he finally spotted me hanging from the demon's clasp like a fish on a hook. "Was this today?"

"It is! It was!" Petty exclaimed.

He yawned. "You said Thursday, no?"

"Et ... ehhhhh ... et."

He only squinted at me. "What is she trying to say?"

"I have no idea, it's probably that it *is* Thursday! Today is Thursday."

"No it isn't."

Franklin, caught up in the whole debate, chimed in. "No. She's right. It's Thursday."

My roommate strode up to him. He gave him a once over, scratched his chin, and then gingerly tore one of the arms from the socket. Franklin roared as a hot jet of black blood sprayed up to the ceiling.

"Please stay out of this," my roommate said, pointing the stump at him.

Franklin dropped me and started flopping on the ground as his wound gushed. I took a second to gather myself and got to my feet. "That's it! House meeting!"

"What?" Petty exclaimed.

"Right now?" was my roommate's bored response.

"Right. Now!"

Petty and my roommate looked at each other and groaned. My sister pulled up a chair and sat down. Meanwhile, my roommate plopped right down on Franklin's chest. It took me a few seconds to realize the sound I just heard were a few ribs breaking.

"We have rules in place—" I started to say, but my roommate cut me off.

He shot his hand into the air. "I move to have Grey voted out of leadership of the household. All those in favor …"

"We are not voting on that," I said, and Petty quickly lowered her own hand. Taking a few breaths to get back to a normal talking voice, I resumed. "There are rules in place. I thought this was obvious. And they are in place for all of us to be safe. Safety and just general courtesy. I ask you to close your door when you get dressed. I ask you to be on time when we are attempting to catch a demon. I ask that you knock before walking into the bathroom. And recently, the sulfur smell. The sulfur smell has just been getting worse."

"That's not me," my roommate stated when he saw that I was eyeballing him. He was still holding Franklin's arm and was playing with it, seeing the hand flop back and forth. Ever so often, he would dangle the severed arm in a way that it slapped the possessed man below him on the face.

"Oh. That's me," Petty admitted sheepishly. She still sported the caved in skull. Her eyeball was drooping out onto her chin. "Phil's dad is into taxidermy, so he picked up a few things. It's to curb the rotting. Some of my back keeps peeling off. And my teeth—"

"You know I have a name," my roommate said, talking over her.

"What?" I replied, but quickly got a dark look instead.

"—but he did a good stitch job on my right knee. Check it." Petty proudly flashed the sew-job her boyfriend gave her to keep the skin around her shoulder blade intact. It was stitched with neon-colored string with tiny hearts linked at both ends.

Even Franklin started talking in between the globs of blood streaming from his lips. He was cursing, or least seemed to be, in a language I don't know. My roommate reached back, and without a care in the world, tore another one of Franklin's black arms off. To me he looked like that cruel kid who plucks the legs off of bugs, you know, just as practice for his future niche as a sociopath.

"We are *not* focusing," I snapped at both of them. Dealing with demons should have been easier with more help. That's the only reason I decided to even allow these two to help fix the whole Apocalypse thing that I had started. That and they were both accomplices to the crime. But they were also both self-centered and immortal which, in my big ass book of horrible combinations on this earth, was right up there with the worst this world has to offer. Right up there with talkative cabbies.

"What time does Mom and Dad get back?"

"Three hours," Petty replied after checking her phone. "Maybe less, depending on what the 7 train is doing tonight."

I glared over at my roommate. "D."

"Yup."

"We have kind of a mess here."

"Yup."

He got up and closed his eyes. And when he reopened them, he opened his mouth. Black, shark-like teeth protruded outward like a steel trap. Seeing his doom, Franklin started screaming, pleading. The beak of a black crow peeked out of his broken neck, but D slammed into it with his spaded tail.

Ever since the nonsense from two weeks ago, when we were dealing with parrots and politics, he had been going by that name. He had also been consistently hostile toward me, which had never been the case before. As I watched him pick up and drag Franklin to his room to be devoured, I told myself that there was a time that I thought that D was protecting me. Ever since he got into this new form, I wasn't sure what team he was playing for.

What made me even more worried was this last Shade and what it would do to him. His body was already going through its odd metamorphosis. A small column of smoke wrapped itself around his head and neck. His horns were growing right before my eyes. His wings sported edges of pure flame. I had just assembled an all-powerful demon right in my living room.

"Anyone ever tell you not to stare," D called over, coldly. His eyes were changing. There were red rings encircling his black iris'. Above his head, a ghostly halo of black energy was forming under my apartment lights.

I wanted to say something at that time. Tell him thank you. This was it, the last demon we would have to worry about. I wanted to ask him what was going on. But before I could muster the strength for it all, he just flicked his tail and the blood leapt off of the walls and ceiling, forming a bubble that he plucked out of the air and began chewing like bubblegum. The glass from the windows snapped together in midair, and the furniture shook itself to the right shape. He left the place looking like we hadn't just intensely mauled a possessed man in the middle of my living room.

"D?"

"I'm not doing the dishes," he spat.

I cleared my throat to speak, but I couldn't find the words. D's change was getting worse and worse. He was eight-feet tall. He sported tusks. He had black claws that could pluck out my guts with ease.

"Uh, Grey," he said in a thunderous voice. "Want to tell me what this about? I gotta be someplace."

"I—"

Suddenly, this form of D collapsed into itself and swirled into a black vortex of balls of pulsating light. Petty gripped my arm as layer after layer of skin peeled away from my roommate as the energy he was firing in every direction shook the entire building.

And then it all snapped into place.

A man with black hair and ripped black jeans stood where the unholy black hole had appeared. He had slicked black hair and a sharp face. His skin was red, but not "devil red" … more like slightly over-tanned. He was my age, maybe older.

D slid his hands into his pocket and groaned. "I have to get going," he told us in a deeper voice than I had expected. He kept his head down as he passed me and closed the door of his room behind him.

The thought of this new, adult D scared the living crap out of me.

Petty was thinking something completely different.

"Holy crap! He's hot!"

I closed her mouth for her. "I'm *not* listening to this. Start cleaning before Mom and Dad get home."

Petty and I got to work on what was left over from the battle: a few broken plates and some ceiling plaster. As I swept, I glanced over and saw my sister kneeling down to fix our rug. Just below her collarbone, her skin was peeled open. Behind the flap, I could see the faint start of a ribcage but nothing else. No blood, no organs. Just darkness inside and bones. Like someone had stored a science project in a closet.

"Petty," I said, and made a gesture to her top.

My sister quickly tried to fold it back into place. Laughing nervously, she told me, "Just don't make 'em like they used to.

I tried to get back to work but Petty was still eyeing me.

"Problem?"

"No. No problem. Like absolutely nothing. Everything is fine."

"Okay."

"Okay."

I went back to sweeping. There were bloodcurdling screams coming from D's room, the sounds of more arms being torn out. We just talked over it.

"You've changed a lot, you know?"

"No I haven't."

"Yes you have. The Mandy I know would have never put herself out there like you did tonight. I mean, c'mon. The bar. The makeup, the dress. And here you are! You've done it! You caught all the Shades and life can get back to something … semi-quasi-normal-ish."

When I didn't respond, she just managed a very forced *hooray* with a side order of jazz hands. "You should be proud of that, Mandy."

"Mhm."

I wanted to agree with her. I wanted to be able to look back and say that things had changed, that I had changed in some shape or form, but most of it was hard to see at that moment. I had caught the last crow— Shade #5— with only marks from the guy's fingers still burning my neck and all of my appendages in order. I should have been happy. Fucking ecstatic, even. But had I really sealed away the evil? Could my life go back to the semi-ordinary? It was all kind of … simple.

Sure, my sister was still dead and possessed, a Shade was still living out of my back room while my parents were there, and they guy who needed to tell me what my next steps were was in a coma. But other than these things, it was now over. Wasn't it?

Seeing that I had gotten lost in my own thoughts, Petty chucked one of the pillows at my head.

"So we should hang out. Soon."

"Hang out?" I stayed focused on my sweeping, avoiding her gaze.

"Yeah, you know. Catch up. Talk a bit. Like what are you doing tomorrow?"

"Things."

"You're always doing things. When's a day when you're thing-less? Thing-lite?"

I tossed the broom aside. "If you haven't been paying attention, my plate's always full, Petty. Always. My life is a fuckery buffet and I'm perpetually in line for seconds."

It had been a while since I spent time with her, but Petty changing the subject so quickly told me that I had said something wrong.

"You and D are still at it?"

I tied my hair back and kept that answer to myself, choosing instead to fetch a dustpan. I didn't want to get distracted by any of it. D and I weren't on speaking terms anymore, but maybe it was for the best. With the final demon caught, and all of the biblical revelation stuff TBD, what was I really looking for now? A friend? I've had my fill of people. And it wasn't like D was going to stay around now that he was an all-powerful incarnate of evil. I should have been happy about it, too. I should have been freaking elated. But even without saying any of that, Petty could pick up the concern on my face.

I could tell that she was going to go there when we both caught a faint jingling of keys that fumbled with the front door lock and then fell to the floor. It was like we were kids again and were caught doing something that we shouldn't be. Petty and I started running around in circles, frantically trying to fix the furniture that had been tipped over.

"Honestly," I heard my mom's muffled voice say, "you and those keys."

"Yeah, yeah," my dad replied in a huff. "There's just so many of them

170

on the daggone ring. Mailbox, front door, outside door. This key's for a lock I don't even have anymore. This key … I don't even know what this key's for!"

Petty was shaking and pointing silently at her face. There was no way we could pass that off with our parents, so I quickly turned her around and started shoving her into the bathroom.

"Hurry up, I've been wanting to use the bathroom since we got on the train."

I caught Petty by the hair in mid-push, and spun her around. She reached for D's door but we didn't have time to knock on it. Dad was just turning the key as I flung Petty out of the window, her hair disappearing as the front door swung open.

"Mom. Dad. Hey. How are ya?"

Instead of looking happy to see me, my parents were aghast. My dad mouthed a silent *oh my god*. My mother screamed and covered her mouth.

Had I missed something? A broken wall? A body part? Don't tell me it was another bone protrusion.

"Mandy," my mother exclaimed, flushed in red. "You're wearing a dress!"

"I'm just saying, for years and years, people have been talking about it like it's some big thing. It wasn't. Nowhere close."

My mother just shook her head. "He's been complaining about this since he made us walk out of the show early," she told me.

"It had a bunch of people dressed as animals," my dad said to drive his point home.

"It's called *Cats*," my mom assured him. "It had cats in it. Who goes to see a show called *Cats* and complains about there being cats in it?"

My dad, frustrated, put his fork down. "I'm not complaining that there were cats in it. I'm complaining that there were only cats in it. No story. No plot. Just cats dancing. If I wanted to see three hours of prancing felines, I would feed PCP to the strays down the block. Cheaper tickets and far more enjoyable. How much did you pay for those tickets, Mandy?"

I could tell Petty was loving this. Sitting across from me at the dinner table, she kept shoving food into her mouth just to muffle her laughter. She and I were thinking the same thing: this was like old times.

"Don't mind grumple-stilskin over there, loves. Ever since we got back …" She put both of her hands up like she didn't want/need to say more.

My parents were retired teachers—my mom elementary and my dad college. My mom retired early and homeschooled me when our zone school was no longer an option. My father was that gruff professor that because of his dark skin and silvered beard, looked like the kind of guy who would start you off with an 'F' and leave it up to you to impress him. But he was a sweetheart. He just asked for things to make sense.

And obviously, he was a dog person.

My mom was that small Jewish lady with brown to almost red curls who let you skip her in the checkout line just to be nice. She would also count your items in the *10 Items or Less* line and shout you out if you're not following protocol.

Having them around this late in the game was nerve wracking, but also sort of a godsend. I needed this. Really. Besides the constant freakout I was going through having them around 24/7, I needed to remember what it was all about. What I had written my soul a one-way ticket to hell for. My family. Mom and Dad. Petty ... when she wasn't being annoying. Catching the Shades had been both psychologically scarring and emotionally draining. I had seen so many things, met so many people, and I didn't hate most of them. My tiny little world had seen its own little Revelations, but at least the world would go on. I felt like I'd lived more in that short span than in my entire life.

I looked around that table and thought that if I had to make that choice again, if everything had to hang on that big fat decision I made over a month ago, would I do it? Would I make it all over again?

Hell no. No fucking way. Not in a million years.

"Someone came looking for you, Mandy," my father said.

Gooseflesh.

"Someone came here? For me? Like ... who?"

Dad shrugged and Mom took over. "Tall young lady. Model-like. Super hot."

Petty dropped her fork and Dad grumbled, "Not this again."

I buried my face in my hands. "What am I missing here?"

"Your mother ..."

"Mom thinks ..."

"Hush, you two." My mom grabbed me by the wrist. "I might be a lesbian."

If I didn't know that it would send me directly to the pits of fire and torment, I wanted to die right there and then.

"Honey," my dad started to say.

"Part-time lesbian. Only part-time. I've been reading about it. Some call it 'late blooming'."

"Late blooming? You're fifty-three, Nora. Missing the Q10 bus by ten minutes, that's late. Deciding to use the crosswalk when that red hand is up, that's late. What you're describing is so late that it's early for something else." Flustered, my father turned to me and explained. "She spotted one of our guides, one, got a little crush on her, and now she's picking out what she's wearing to Queens Pride."

"She was adorable."

"And she's been hitting on anything in a skirt since we've been back."

My mom dabbed the side of her mouth with a napkin and whispered, "Hater."

Mortified, Petty excused herself as her cellphone rang. My parents and I sat in silence listening to the conversation.

When she got back, she let us know what we already knew.

"Gotta go. Date night."

"Is that why you're wearing so much makeup?" Mom asked as Petty hugged her. "Seriously, Petunia. Next time, you're going to stay for all of dinner. Sans the makeup and sunglasses."

She hugged Dad and of course he offered to give her somewhere to crash. "Mandy rented out the back room, but you got a place to stay here. I don't understand why you're in a hotel if your family's right here."

"Just until I go back," she told him. "Not going to intrude."

"Hmm. Fine. You need any money?"

Mandy paused. She was looking at me, planning her response. I took the knife I was eating with and made a slow pass against my neck. Zombie puppet or not, I wanted her to picture the amount of thread needed to fix a decapitation.

"No!" she shouted. And then dialed it back. "No, Dad. All good. I'll stop by tomorrow." And she left.

Checking the time for myself, I realized that I had missed a call from the hospital. I wolfed down the rest of my food. My parents' dishes were empty, so I cleaned up for them and slipped them into the sink.

"We're proud of you."

My father's words collided with my chest. The fresh bruises from my latest tangle with a demon tingled.

"You what now?"

My mom smiled at me from the table as my dad stood up. "We didn't put you in the best of situations when we left. We admit it. We kind of wanted you to fly on your own for a little bit. But it wasn't easy for us."

Behind his back, Mom pointed to my dad, mimed him crying, and then him crying so much that it filled up buckets that needed to be thrown out.

"It wasn't without some screw-ups," I replied, averting my gaze.

"You lent your sister some money, and it came back to bite you," he said. "You did what you had to. Got yourself a roommate when I know having to talk to people is your least favorite thing in this world. And this city just so happens to go completely nuts all of a sudden."

I kept a straight face.

"Thanks, Dad. And I promise it's only temporary. D is moving out at the end of the month. I'll move back into my room, and everything will be … back to normal."

My dad smiled and shushed me away from doing the dishes.

I had somewhere to be, too.

And for some odd reason, I was really looking forward to going.

FINN'S WAS ALWAYS filled with teachers in the late week. The bar hung a dusty chalkboard sign outside, dubbing its special happy hour "Thirsty Thursdays." For three hours, you could enjoy five dollar beers—all you had to do was prove you needed alcohol because you taught in one of New York's public schools. Of course, the bartender could tell that Donaldson and I weren't teachers. We could barely be in charge ourselves let alone burgeoning minds. But he still felt the need to question us about our areas of study.

"Poetry," was Donaldson's answer.

When I was asked, I said, "21st Century Occult. First round, please." While the guy flipped open both caps and passed over our beers, I figured out how to keep our previous conversation going. "Your turn, chum."

Donaldson looked up from his beer. "Okay. What fictional place would you want to have brunch in and why?"

I didn't even hesitate. "Mordor."

"Mordor?"

"It's the worst place on earth. Imagine ordering food there. Big flaming eye in the middle of the place and still lousy service."

Donaldson gazed dreamily into the distance. "I'll admit, the nachos there must be awesome."

"Mordor nachos."

He tilted his cup and clinked it against mine.

Donaldson and I were at a weird point in our … shit, I have to call it a relationship. I don't want to say that we were going out on dates, because I'll be damned if it was. I would just say we met for drinks and food on the regular, minus the flirting or anything else. We came to depend on each other in some weird way. He needed to blow off steam, finding zero success or even interest in his job. I needed ... well, I needed alcohol. Lots and lots of alcohol.

"You seem out of it," he said. He had developed an annoying habit of being right lately.

"To be 'out of it', good sir, would suggest that at some point in my life, I would be 'in it.' And the last time I checked, the only thing I've been in is shit, and shit is the only thing I'm always in. I'm always just standing in it."

"Metaphorically?"

"Metaphorically. Scategorically. Same difference." I tipped the beer bottle and got nothing but air for my troubles. I tapped for another round.

"More pressing question, Grey."

"Yup."

"How is it that a self-proclaimed social recluse is on her third beer and I haven't finished my first?"

"It's all Dad," I replied, cradling my next round. "He taught me how to enjoy a beer. Starting at seventeen, he would hand me one whenever Mom served steak. Said he didn't want me to be a lightweight when I went to parties. Guess he was preparing me for being the social butterfly that I am today."

Donaldson nodded. "So you're done, right? No more demons or crows? Is it safe to say the whole end of the world thing is TBD now, or can I stop paying back my school loans?"

I shook my head. "Nothing weird has happened. No 'Oddities.' I mean, D's still around and of course, Petty is still kinda not alive, but I won't be sure until Barnem wakes up." I sighed, remembering what I had to do later. I had been visiting the hospital every day since he got his ass kicked into a coma. He was a mess. Broken bones, internal injuries. The guy was pretty damn fragile for a Seraph.

Donaldson nodded. "And D? How's he doing? I was supposed to come over and play dominoes this weekend."

When I didn't answer, Donaldson went into his coat and pulled out his cellphone. A few swipes later, and he produced a small blog website for me to scroll through.

"'Roommate from Hell.com?'" I glanced over to Donaldson who took a long sip of his beer. Scrolling through, there were stories after stories of people sharing their worst, most damndest clashes with their live-ins. Vanishing toothbrushes and sexual horror stories ran for page after page.

"Two thousand posts in one night," Donaldson told me. "Nearly killed the damn Internet. But it all started with this post." He flicked it again and there it was: a poster by the name of LivedinEvil66 who had started the thread with five posts.

"'*A.G. has to be the single worst cook I have ever met, and I once spent a week living under a California underpass making quiche in a boot.*'?" I read aloud. "A.G? A.G? How long as he been writing this blog?"

"A month."

"A *month*? And wait one flaming minute! *I'm* the roommate from hell? Me?" Donaldson made a face like he regretted ever telling me, but I wasn't going to let him off the hook that easy. "What sense does that make? He is *literally* a roommate and he's *literally* from hell. I fail to see how this is even remotely fair!" Flustered and suddenly hot, I started flapping the neck of my T-shirt. "I don't get him. I-I don't. And it's not be-cause I don't try, you know? He's kind of a dick now. To me of all people. Like, what did I ever do to him?"

"I get that."

"I put a roof over his horns. I put quasi-edible food on the table. And *I'm* the 'roommate from hell'?" I huffed and looked up at the bar tele-vision screen. A big news crawl for the Pope's visit going down in a few days scrolled along the bottom. "I'm nice! I've been nice."

"Right." I could tell he wanted to say more so I glared at. "Look, okay, all right. All I'm going to say, and you should already know this … not coming out of left field, Grey, but you don't do well when people try to get close. Especially men." He slid me a side glance while drinking some more. "By the way … you clean up nice, Grey."

I spat a big fat raspberry at him. "No. Nope. Not going there."

Even as we spoke, two women sitting farther down the bar were staring in Donaldson's direction. They must have taken one good look at his dark skin, bald head, and tight shirt and were both whispering and glancing. I could smell them ovulating.

"I'm just saying," he began, "some people out here care for you. Like, honestly. I don't want to see anything happen to you. Your parents adore you. Your sister idolizes you but doesn't know how to show it so you two are just awkward. I think that *thing* Barnem does from time to time means he doesn't want you to die. And D's saved your ass more times than you can count. And since you've made it abundantly clear that all of this gives you the heebie-jeebies, some folks don't know how to show it."

"First of all, D doesn't care about me. He's a demon looking out for his own self interests. Second of all, this conversation has a regretful undertone that has very little to do with my little demon problem. Sounds like a personal problem."

Donaldson took a glance over at the bathroom line, giving me the opportunity to catch the eye of his two stalkers and mouth the words "herpes" while pointing to my lips. The women looked away and so did I just as Donaldson turned back into the conversation. "Look, I get it. That ship has sailed—"

"Has sailed, has a flaming arrow fired into it, and is now standing as affordable housing for deep sea crabs."

"—but it doesn't mean people will stop caring about you." He took the last sip of his beer. "And I'm not talking about myself. D cares about you, in his own way. You both have stuff in common. Like ... you both bring the social equivalents of warmth and light of a three day wildfire."

"Compliment!"

"You can't declare what is and isn't a compliment, Grey."

I stuffed my mouth full of bar peanuts, right in front of Donaldson's face just to hear myself chew over his blabbery. And yet still, his stupid logic had me thinking about everything, every single exchange I've had with my roommate. And I got sucked up into my thoughts because Donaldson and I didn't speak for almost five long minutes.

Suddenly he mumbled, "The problem with a menu listing an item

179

called 'Mordor Nachos' is that it's confusing. First, I would expect it to come shaped like a volcano. Secondly, what do I do with it? Do I eat it? Do I drop my jewelry into it? There's too many questions. There's just too many."

In the middle of my rebuttal, my phone's alarm sounded again.

"You off to see him?"

"Mhm." I got up thinking that the stool was moving and that I was drunk as hell. But then I saw the glasses rattling, the other patrons looking up at the lights as they flickered on and off. It was a mild earthquake. In NY! Most of it didn't last long, and the entire bar laughed and got on with their lives. I had to, too. Donaldson offered to come with, but I waved him off.

Natural disaster or not: I had somewhere to be.

32

Hospitals make me break out in hives. Everything seems sick, disease ridden. I don't touch doorknobs, handrails, elevator buttons ... nothing, nothing, nothing. I'll pee on myself and set fire to my body to dry it up before using a bathroom in a hospital. I'm not catching ass plague.

Barnem's room was on the fourth floor. He hadn't been carrying ID when he got his ass kicked, so I gave the hospital a name for their records. I tapped the chart that read the vitals of Dörk Sowerpüs and took a seat by the bed of the sleeping angel.

And I just sat there, flicking through television. In an odd way, this brought me some weird comfort. Barnem and I had a huge falling out just before this all went down, but that seemed inevitable with our personalities. If he was my guide to getting my life back, he was epically shitty at it.

Again, like clockwork, was another promo for the Pope's visit, this one from a press conference his holy one held right on the tarmac in LaGuardia.

He was a little man, dressed in the pristine white holy garb that looked like majestic curtains. He was completely bald and his eyes were bunched together at the nose which itself was as slim as a doorstop.

"I come to America, mainly I have come to New York, on a mission," he said through an interpreter. "What this mission entails will be explained soon. But for the time being know that my prayers are with all of you and with everyone in this great city."

"Got here kinda late, padre," I said to the television. "Grey's got this. Just one more demon to put back." I set my swimming head down on Barnem's bed. "Yup. Easy peasy. Like breaking a lamp. Just gotta ... crazy glue the pieces back. Good as new. Good, good, good."

I fell asleep mumbling this, right at the foot of the bed.

In the morning, I brushed my teeth with my finger, did some shit with my hair, and walked out. I was still wearing that stupid dress Petty let me borrow, and coming out of that hospital felt like I was taking the weirdest walk of shame ever. Things only got weirder when I spotted who was waiting for me outside.

I can't tell you how I recognized him, but I did. I hadn't seen him since we caught the last Shade, and his transformation that night was totally off-putting. I remember him as a short, goblin demon, and now he was this seven-foot … *man*. I thought the teenage Shade was worse because of his attitude. But this final form of my roommate was the scariest yet because he seemed human. I hadn't been prepared to face this in any way. Yes, I secretly preferred the monster demon form to a man my age living in my apartment.

D was standing by the doorway with the absolute gravest expression on his face as soon as I walked passed the sliding doors. When we got to the train, he said, "We need to talk, Grey."

Not wanting to show how this made my skin crawl, I replied, "Sure. Talk. Why were you at the hospital?"

He narrowed his eyes spitefully. "I've been going every night."

"You go? Every night?"

"Every night since he's been there."

"So," I mumbled, feeling like a jackass for pressing him so hard, "what did you want to talk about?"

"I don't need your permission to do things." With that, D gave me his back. Was he telling the truth? And why did he looked pissed off that I was there? Was it because of Barnem or me?

"I'm just kind of on edge now," I told him, trying to lighten the mood. "I feel like there's a big friggin' target on my back every time I walk outside." I glanced around the train car. I wasn't sure if it really was just my nerves, but the guy in the far seat was listening to my convo and the homeless man shuffling in from the next car with the bandaged face and trench coat was just standing there, either being the laziest panhandler in the history of this city or he was waiting for something. Why the hell was he so tall?

"You're paranoid," D stated as we got off on our stop.

We walked passed the silent bandaged guy and he didn't reach out and grab me, which I was grateful for. However, he did have a familiar smell. Damp feathers.

"We have to talk, you know? We haven't since Mason and ... you know. Squawk-squawk."

"Please don't ever do that in public." He glanced around, his gaze spinning around worriedly. "All right. You want to talk? So talk."

This was beyond difficult. I still wasn't used to dealing with someone so damned hard headed and anti-social. *Now I know what Barnem feels like*, I thought.

Walking into our little block in Queens, we found the kids were playing out in the street as an open fire hydrant flushed everyone's valuable water pressure everywhere. It was the kind of thing I saw as a kid in July. Weird to see it in April.

"We are close to putting the kibosh on this whole demon mess. Barnem didn't know anything about your ... about demons. A one track mind, that one."

"So?"

"I'm just asking for information. On demons? On how possession works? At least for Petty's sake, it's worth trying to understand."

This broke down his defenses. Petty and Donaldson; the three of them were like peas in a friggin' pod. It angered me to no end.

"What I did for Petty was a forced possession. Her soul is bound up in the Shade, kind of encased. It can't leave her body unless I release it. Or I die. Or something like that. Look, I suck at explaining things. And as to why I did it? I just think Petty is cool. That's it."

Cool. If I wasn't lost and confused about D's personality before, I sure as hell was after he called my sister cool. I wouldn't call her cool and we're related.

We crossed the street and he took the time to resettle himself. "Shades and demons are different. Vastly. Demons can be pushed out, exorcised. Shades are bound by contracts with the host. There is usually a point of entry into the body, and then a binding contract with a human. That's why the crows are usually inside, though I'm guessing Mason was too much of a prude. The relationship between a Shade and its contract ... it's more than picking up milk in a store. It's not an exchange of goods. More like ... it's more like a partnership."

"Worst partnership I've ever heard of."

This infuriated him. "I'm not talking anymore."

But that only set me off, too. "Fine. And fyi, I don't need you around to tell me when I'm being paranoid. Life hasn't exactly taught me that it's all palm trees and sunny days."

"The world isn't conspiring against you," D snapped angrily, and then muttered, "Not everyone wants to kill you, you know? You're not *that* popular."

"Hey, you! You Amanda Grey?"

We were right in front of my building now, and we both turned to see a woman leaning up against a parked car as she chewed slowly on a drinking straw. Skinny jeans and boots. A midriff blue and red plaid shirt exposing her slender stomach. She sported dead blonde hair that was cut short in the back and shoulder-length in the front, tucked nicely under a cowboy hat. At her feet sat a beat up instrument case, base by the size of it. The leather was tattered and busted open in some spots. Stamps from different countries were scattered all over it.

Seeing how slender and flawless her face was made me think of my mom (oh god), but more so because this woman was pretty. And pretty damn flawless. Like an airbrush come to life. I immediately prepared for a fight, but D sighed, "She's not a demon, Grey. Just go see what she wants," and slipped his hands in his pockets and walked off. The mystery woman turned her chin sideways to watch him walk away.

"Good to see you, cutie," she shouted over at me.

I stopped and squinted in her direction. "We've never met."

"Can't say we have."

184

"That wasn't a question. It's just that usually the people who've called me 'cutie' still sport the bruises around the trachea."

However, this didn't deter her from laughing and pushing off of the car to stand next to me. You hear about supermodels being tall and leggy. This woman's proportions were crazy. Leaning over the car had hidden that svelte nearly seven-foot frame.

Part of me realized that my mom had good taste.

The other part told that first part to shut the hell up.

Slipping the straw from her lips, she crossed her arms. "Gotta admit ... was expecting something else." She sighed, bit down on her straw again, and walked back to her instrument case. After popping both of its locks, she flung open the lid, kicking up a large dust cloud in the process.

"Are you looking to sign up with the Beguilers?" I asked. "We moved the book club to Fridays, but the meetings are still the same. You can sign up online for our newsletter and— *Holyfuck!*"

Holyfuck was the only way I could even come close to describing the size of the weapon this woman had pulled out of that case. It was a scythe twice my height and with a blade half the length of the car.

"Wowww. Look at that," she said mockingly. "You know, Barnem said that it would take something big to make you shut up." She lifted the large weapon slightly, with no effort at all, and let the handle drop back down to the sidewalk. Even though it looked made out of wood, the force split one of the concrete plates and left a small crater around the handle base. "Luckily, I'm a size queen."

"Wh-who are you?"

"Ah, well. I used to be employed as the Angel of Death. But while I'm waiting for unemployment to kick in, I guess I'm your new roommate."

PETTY'S WHITE SKIN and blackened eyes said it all: she was furious.

"I'm sorry. That doesn't explain why you brought her *here*."

So I agree, she had a right to be upset. When she wasn't cursing me out for bringing the Grim Reaper to her doorstep, she was looking out of the corner of her eyes at the leggy blonde sitting a few feet away.

"Look, Petty. Mom and Dad were cool about the part-time roommate. They understood that. They are not going to understand me having someone else bunk up out of the blue," I explained, wringing my hands.

"Right." After another quick look, Petty asked, "And why does she have to live with me again?"

"Because your sister put me in this mess in the first place," the woman on the couch interjected.

I could see the fear in Petty's white eyes. "I-I'm sorry. Are you thirsty? Hungry? I have a box of wheat crackers. They're kind of dry but I've been dipping them in maple syrup. It's not terrible."

My sister. A Grey after my own heart.

"I'm a corporeal being, love. We don't eat."

This immediately stood out to me. "You don't eat? Barnem is always shoving food—"

"Barnem is totally something else." She stood up, propped her hands on her hips, and strutted over to where we were sitting, letting her boots double clap against the floorboards. "I don't want to break up this meeting you two lovely ladies are having, but there's a certain urgency to this issue. Barnem didn't have time to explain, I'm guessing, but the Pope is here to kill you."

Petty shot me a look.

I slowly raised my hand.

When Death called on me, I said, "Yeah. Appreciate you taking my question, by the way. Um. What the fuck?"

Death knelt down to our level. Even on her knees, face to scared face with us, she was still incredibly tall. She took Petty's hand. My sister shrieked when she was touched but let her grab it. She set her palm flat and placed two fingers on it as if to demonstrate something.

"This world may be the playground of God and the Devil, but our roles in all of it are like threads, a tapestry if you will. You make a hole in that material, it all gets weak. Eventually all of it's going to unravel."

"I'm sorry," Petty said pointing to her palm, "what is this illustrating?"

"Oh, nothing," Death laughed. "I just wanted to hold your hand."

Petty snatched it away while the woman continued. "We are coming to the end of it all, Grey. The Pope ... well, the old guy's just doing his job."

"His job is to kill me?" I shouted. "The Pope? The guy in the gown and pointy hat?"

"How can she avoid this?" Petty asked earnestly. But Death looked at her as if she was a puppy in a windowsill.

"Even dead, you're adorable," she replied, bopping her on her white nose. "Nothing can change. There's never *change*. Who taught you two religion? C'mon now. That's the whole principle behind the darn thing. It's the reason people sign up in droves. Something happens for a reason. Nothing happens for a reason. Every prophecy gets fulfilled."

"So ... what? You're saying that I was supposed to invite Gaffrey Palls in? I was supposed to get a roommate? Petty was supposed to die?"

Frustrated, she stood up and sighed. "You're cute, but hard-headed. The prophecy is that your world will end, darling. Prophecies happen. That's what they do. The Pope is just doing what he's meant to do, what he's supposed to. Like the good little knight."

For some reason, I started to taste bile. It had rushed up my throat, flushed against the back of my teeth. My insides felt like someone had taken a fistful of my intestines and was twisting and crushing them.

"That's impossible," I muttered, swallowing the hot wretch. Petty looked at me weird. "We're one demon away from repairing ... from patching up that hole you're talking about."

The Angel of Death covered her mouth as she laughed. "Ah no, no. That's not how life works, Grey. Trust me."

"But Barnem said—"

Again. The pain. Now it was scratching. A rat gnawing its way out of my ribcage.

In her southern twang, Death told me, "Darlin', all you did was drive us up on a cliff and put us in park. The number you did to the design, the Grand Design, I'm talking big picture stuff, isn't fixed with a band-aid. Oh no. There was an order this was supposed to happen in. Removing one stage has basically thrown the whole playbook in a paper shredder. Now the universe is scripted after a cut up poem. Time and space are collapsing. The Oddities are appearing. Now everything's going to happen at once. Even if you do manage to call off the Apocalypse, the world will never be the same. *You* will never be the same. And I'm talking outside of the whole 'soul burning in eternal damnation' thing. Aside from that. Along with that."

I still wasn't feeling well but I could see that the revelation of my fate had hit Petty hard. I realized in that moment that there were a few things we needed to talk about.

Beyond the sweat, I asked, "And you? You're ... the Angel of Death."

"*An* Angel of Death," she said with a wink. "Well, actually, that was last week. What I am now is ... 'between opportunities'. When everybody's going to die, you don't exactly need a reaper of souls. Higher management called it 'redundancies'."

Petty shook her head. "God fired you?"

But Death seemed bored. "God? Honey, if only. I've been alive for an eternity and—" She pulled out her cellphone. "Hey look at that. Literally an eternity and a day. Say, does this place have wifi?"

My sister, quietly losing it, puckered her lips. "Look around. The wallpaper is dog-earing and that couch is only in one piece because of masking tape and pantyhose."

"Hmm." Death tapped her chin. "So that's a no?"

But that discussion was cut short by a sharp knock at the door. Petty scooted off to check on who it was while the Angel of Death plopped down in her empty seat across from me as I tried to steady my eyes.

"I'm not going to keep calling you Death. I kinda need a name."

"Oh yeah," she replied, thinking for a bit. Then she extended her hand and introduced herself as simply, "Cain."

I grumbled. "Out of all the names?"

She thought about it. "What? I love Cain. It's a strong name. Ahh. Reminds me of the good ol' days. The simpler days. When the faith and the soul were both one. When people saw God everywhere and never questioned His divinity. It was a better time." She stretched her arms. "That and I love Dean Cain. Man has aged beautifully. Fine wine."

Slapping me on the knee as if that should be a thing that should be celebrated, she then got up and went to her instrument case. Petty returned in time to steal her seat back.

"Who knocked?"

Petty seemed less concerned with this so she scurried through it. "Some homeless guy. Christ, this hotel is the worst. But what about her, Mandy?"

I sighed. "Yeah. I hate flirty people."

"Flirty people? Flirty people? Mandy, an unemployed Angel of Death is in my room. Wait. You don't think she's here to collect my soul since I didn't die, do you? Because there's no take-backsies."

"I'm here for something else," Cain said, holding out her reaping weapon again. The size of it barely fit in the room. I think I heard a noise like a mouse caught on a glue trap, but I'm not sure if it was an actual rodent or my sister sitting nearby.

"No need to crawl out of your skin, ladies. I'm here to help."

She tossed us a cheery smile and picked up the television as if it were an empty plastic bag. Dropping it on the floor, she then drove the weapon's handle through the top, breaking most of the frame but not the glass screen which quickly flickered to life with static. Ignoring Petty's grumbling ("It only had three channels but I'll still have to pay for that!") Cain then gradually tipped the blade. Ghostly blue lines appeared in the air, and every time the scythe glanced one, another set of voices and blurry images came through the screen. Most were unintelligible, and the rest I wish I never saw or heard. Murders, car accidents, someone drowning. It was the most morbid channel surfing session I've ever been a part of.

"As cool as it may look to you ladies," Cain explained, "the sacred tool of a reaper is not a weapon. It's a tuning device that ... ah. Here we go."

The scene on the low quality television was of a dark room. There were dozens of candles lodged into small ivory plates placed all around the room, but it was still difficult to see the center of the room where just the faint outline of a bed sat. To me, it looked empty until someone jumped out of the sheets screaming and scaring the bejesus out of me.

"What is—"

"Shh!" Cain demanded.

Out of breath, the man—whose face I barely recognized—seemed to be calming down from a nightmare. And then he said something into the darkness.

"Grey. What have you done?"

My stomach dropped.

I watched as the man fumbled through the darkness and patted around for a while before finding what he was looking for: his glasses. With shaking hands, he brought them to his face.

Of the numerous times he showed up on TV, he never wore glasses. But as soon as he put them on, someone called to him through the door.

"How is this possible?" Petty asked before I could ask.

"You may think you have all of this figured out, this whole 'mortality' thing. In fact, I think it's quite cute. I won't blame you. But the ethereal stuff? The way Heaven and hell work ..." Cain threw up a hand to silence me before I could ask anything. "Look, I hate being the one to tell you this, but you're both very very small. Tiny specks. Gorgeous specks, if you ask me, but specks nonetheless. If you knew what the afterlife was like, you would never have signed up for this."

Deflated by our sudden glumness, Cain sighed. "Okay, okay. Party pooper. I'm an Angel of Death. I've been told I don't have proper bedside manners blah blah blah. Let's start over." She cleared her throat. "This thing? Oh I just turned your TV into a see-er."

"A seer? Like a prophet?"

"What? No! A see-er. See-er. It's sees … well, stuff actually. See it picks up the strings of fate—strings of decisions which lead to a person's death, to be exact. The tool of an Angel of Death, which I checked out *without* permission when I resigned, thank you very much, is used to sever these strings. But if I tip it just right, I can see the intertwined fates of two people."

"That's the Pope," Petty said just recognizing him. "On the news … he landed in New York this afternoon."

Cain groaned. "This must have been from last night." She tried to move the scythe along the blue line but it only distorted the picture. "Well this sucks. It's not even a live feed."

"Can't you skip ahead?"

"You would think but no. I can rewind but not fast forward. Gonna have to let it play."

"What's your deal?" I asked Cain.

The large woman slapped a hand on her hip. "My deal?"

I watched as the Pope hid two pistols in his waist and walk out of his room. "Yeah. Why tell me this? What's your connection to Barnem and when did he tell you about me?"

"Like I said, sugar, I am no longer employed by the afterlife. Trying my hand at the private sector. You know … seeing what's out there. Barnem and I go way, way back. Long way. He asked me to help with your pirate problem. Back then, I was still employed, 9 to 5'ing it. A slave to the system and whatnot. But I left right after I got ol' Barnem's message. He called in a favor."

"And right after, Barnem fell in a coma."

"Still not paying attention, are you?" Cain bristled. "It doesn't work like that. Honestly. Barnem told me to not explain too much about how eternity works, but you're completely in the dark and I'm guessing you won't be trusting me any other way. So pay attention. There are spaces of being that you know: hell, Heaven, and Earth. You're obviously from the mortal realm—Earth. You eat, fuck, poo, etc. I'm a being of Heaven, which means I don't do any of those things and are therefore better. It also means I can communicate with the all powerful Celestial." She said this with an odd mocking gesture with both of her hands, and when we looked at her blankly, she added, "Celestial is the inter-office email system we have in place back at HQ. It's how Barnem contacted me. Anyway, hell is all the rest. If you're not mortal and you're not like any of the departments in HQ, then you're a demon."

"Like D."

"D?"

"Her roommate."

Cain had an odd expression on her face. "It has a name? Yeah, that can't be good."

"Just finish. What does this have to do with Barnem? And the Pope assassinating me? I'm done with all the demon stuff. I caught the last Shade."

"Barnem is a being of Earth with divine purpose, much like your Pope. Since you've been sitting on your hands down here, and with Barnem on the shelf, Fate called an audible to pick up the slack. The Pope is obviously here to finish the job. That means killing you, this D, and anyone else who gets in the way."

"And you tell me this *now*? Where were you a week ago when we were up against a nightmare parrot?"

Cain only flicked her hair. "Barnem sent a message, but I just didn't get it. I mean, it's just a bitch because you have to login every time. And when you change your password and forget you change your password. And then you press that button 'forgot password', but then it sends it to an email you don't know the password for. So you press the button and—"

"A-hem!"

On the screen, the Pope was talking to a young man who was posted by his door. The guy was roughly my age with slicked back hair. He introduced himself as Oswalt. The Pope said he had to come to New York.

"Why are the words and their lips different?" Petty asked.

Cain tapped her scythe. "Dubbed in English. And the point to all of this, dollface, is that Barnem asked me to help and that's what I'm here to do. The Pope is on a holy mission to end your life. The see-er is absolute. So if we're seeing this, he *will* succeed or die trying. You need to catch the last demon, quick and fast."

My immediate thoughts went right for Mom and Dad. I wasn't prepared to die, but they were far more important.

"Phil has a car?"

"Sure, but—"

"Call him to come pick us up. I'm going to pack Mom and Dad's bags and fly them somewhere, anywhere but here. Just in case."

Petty held her arms out before I could walk by. "Wai-wai-wait! Stop, cease, and desist. Tell me why she has to stay with me?"

"Because."

"Need I remind you that since you picked your roommate, there have only been two types of people you've met. Two! The good guys and then the guys that want to tear your throat out. How do we know which one *she* is?"

"Good point."

"Finally."

"Hey, Cain. Are you one of the good guys or the bad guys?"

The Angel of Death thought about this question long and hard, and just as she was about to answer, a large thump shook the nearby window. From the feathers and bloodstain, it was obvious that a bird had slammed into the glass and broken its neck. The woman then turned to us and shrugged.

"Good enough for me," I said.

"But, Mandy—"

I shoved a purposeful finger in her face. "Uh-huh. Petunia Grey, you owe me. Big time. Now I didn't want to use the whole 'You put me in this mess when you stole Mom and Dad's money' card. But yup. Gonna use it."

"Don't."

"Nope! Here it is!" I grabbed an invisible card out of the air, turned her palm over, and slammed it in there. Petty threw a fit.

Cain, watching our squabble, pouted her lips together and called out to us, "Goin' somewhere, Grey? I'm supposed to be escorting you around. Protecting you."

"How about no? No need."

"Suit yourself," she said, eyeing my sister. "At least I'll be in good company."

"How about no to that as well." Petty snagged me before I left. "Look, Mandy. Slow down for one friggin' sec. What's this about? Hell?"

"It's nothing you need to worry about. I gotta—"

But her grip stayed fastened to my arm. "We haven't talked, Mandy. Not since Mason. Not since I got to be … this."

I quickly turned away from her and started walking to the door. "We will talk, Petty. Promise. Just not now with the world still ending and stuff. Let's get Mom and Dad as far away from here as possible and then we'll talk. But I need that car so don't be late."

I wasn't blowing her off. I wasn't trying to, really. It's just that even after the clusterfuck of a month I was going through, I didn't have time to deal with … feels, my own or my sister's. There was a lot to unpack and very little time to sort through it all. Still, I did feel bad about dumping this on her lap. I ended up turning around, wrapping my arm around Petty's shoulders, and saying, "I'm going to ask now, okay? Can the former Angel of Death stay in your apartment?"

Petty bit her black lip. "Fine, fine."

"Great. Trust me that this is all part of the plan. I want her out of the way while I fix this, sure. But also … you're already dead. You can't be deader."

Petty opened her lips for a rebuttal but couldn't find one.

34

HAVING PROPERLY DROPPED off my new angel problem onto my favorite sister, I formulated a fool-proof, idiot-proof, Armageddon-proof plan to clean up my life. I would go and get my parents, pack them both "Get Out and Go" bags, and buy them a second honeymoon to any-place-not-New-York, just to get them as far out of the city as possible.

After a short trip on the train, I made it to the building in record time and set my keys into the door. The smell of cooking was filling the hallway, which I figured was Mom's way of getting the family together. I knew that the trip abroad had really affected my parents; that they missed us all being piled on top of each other in that little apartment. I also knew that it would take some serious acrobatics to get them both to pack up and leave again.

Of course, I also had to consider that Cain was just screwing with me in some way. I mean, sure those images from the see-er were pretty damning. And I already had my worries about my relationship with D. God, just the fact that I *had* a relationship with a demon was the end-all/be-all of all worries. All of this ran through my mind as I set my keys into the door because I wasn't a thousand percent sure where anyone's loyalties lay. Cain made it known what she believed: the extinction of the human race was inevitable and no amount of crappy crazy glue could put it together. The night I killed that lunatic Gaffrey Palls, I'd just changed the expiration date on something already attracting flies. As crappy as my life was, I couldn't agree. There were a few people here that didn't suck and I was ready to bite and claw and kick my way through to prove it. Besides, there weren't any crazy signs or Oddities going around. Cain said something was coming, but from where? Considering I had personally seen to it that they were locked away, and that there was only one more left to scratch off of that list, I thought I was doing pretty damn good for myself. Pope or not, if I got to the demon first and put him away, he wouldn't have business with me.

I just needed to prepare, and that meant getting my parents as far gone as possible, like Area 51 or Guam.

This was all running through my mind as two loud voices approached from down the hall. That's why when I glanced up at them and saw what they were. I froze, the last thought stuck in a constant buffering loop as I tried to process what the hell I was looking at. I stood there, watching the two approach, two eight-foot-tall roaches glistening in the hallway light. One laughed to itself as it fumbled with the keys to the apartment three doors down. The other threw itself up against the wall. I didn't realize until it was too late that it was glaring at me.

"Hey," it shouted, throwing one of its legs beside its mandible in order to call to me. "Hey, you. Something wrong with your eyes, honey?"

The roach at the door hissed at it. "What are you doing?"

"Don't ask me what I'm doing. Ask her what she's doing. I'm just asking missy-foo over there if she has something wrong with her eyes because she's staring hella hard."

The roach leaned back just to notice I was there. "Hi. Oh hi, neighbor. Don't mind him. Happy hour was a very happy hour." It said this by miming taking a drink with its skinny brown appendage.

"Don't 'hi neighbor' her," the drunk one said. "And yes, mind me. Mind me. You know, that Mason guy was right. People are just rude nowadays. Rude. I would have voted him for mayor. For freaking president!"

Luckily, the door finally opened and the hostile roach was pulled in by its wing, followed by the door slamming shut behind it. The large thud left me to my thoughts in that dark hallway. Thoughts that went something like, *Okay. Well. That just happened.*

With a little more motivation to get the fuck out of there, as soon as I swung the door open, I called my parents, "Mom and Dad. Super, super surprise for you. Get dressed so we can lea—"

196

"Lea—" was all I could get out and "Lea—" was as far as I was going to get.

A familiar young man, who was sitting on the couch, snapped his sunglasses-shielded eyes toward me.

Mom waltzed right of the kitchen and set the last plate on the table. She was wearing a pretty amazing flowery dress. "Oh, honey. We are *not* going out tonight. We have," she gestured around, "very special guests over for dinner."

I turned to the young man who stood slowly, but I quickly realized that it wasn't for me. Instead, he was paying close attention to the older man stepping out of the bathroom, wiping his hands on his shirt.

"If we are ready to eat, I believe it is only right that I say grace," the Pope said.

35

He was a short man, slightly hunched over the way men with age curve into the world. He was wearing cargo short that showed off his wrinkled—and yes, pale—knees, and a striped polo shirt. He looked very ordinary. I mean for a Pope. I don't know what I mean. The guy beside him was the same one from the vision Cain let me see. Oswalt, he said his name was. A long way from the black and white suit he was wearing in the vision, as he passed my mom's mashed potatoes, he wore salmon-colored shorts, a plain white V-neck T-shirt, and moccasins. Unfortunately, everything from the neck up was still all secret service-y. Hair slicked back, sunglasses, mean mug.

"You know, I have never been to New York," the Pope said.

"Oh my. That's hard to believe, your Highness," my mom replied. She clearly forgot what a Pope was to be called. I think this whole thing had her mind whirling.

But the man laughed. "James. You can call me James. I'm ... on liberty. You know I fought in World War II? Was part of the squads who helped set up triage centers after the U.S. hit the sand in Normandy. There was one guy, a young kid from Manhattan. Big mouth. You say it like that, right? He talked a lot. Never stopped talking. He used to talk up New York like it was a paradise." James nodded to himself, lost in that memory for a bit. Then he planted his fork into the meatloaf and said, "So tell me about yourself, Amanda."

I nearly bit my tongue. "Me? Bleh. Nothing. What?"

He glanced upward. I can't describe the amount of pressure I felt from just his eyes. It really was nothing, not even close to a glare. But there was something behind his half-opened eyes. I somehow got the feeling that my answers were really going to effect the way this dinner turned out. He obviously knew who I was, and Cain told me that he was looking to kill me. I just didn't know his game.

"I'm a nobody." I dropped my gaze down at my plate.

"Everybody is a nobody," he replied, wiping his mouth. But he didn't follow up or explain. He calmly went back to his food. The man was definitely the Pope. He even spoke like the Bible. He was Bible-babbling me.

I could tell that his private security was staring holes into me from behind his shades. His head was always angled toward me and he ate…really…slow.

"Mandy is our oldest," Mom said, and grabbed my arm. "She's come a long way, fighting demons."

The Pope, er James, and Oswalt both stopped chewing.

"Mom!"

"Oh, it's true. I mean we all have those things that stick to us, right? Those things we have to overcome? Mandy has been amazing at seeing through her personal troubles."

Our guests quietly went back to their plates.

Just before I could figure out where to steer the conversation, D walked out of the room, completely oblivious to the absolute paleness of my face upon seeing him. Both James and Oswalt stared as this young man sleepily dragged his feet from his room to the living room. There he checked on this large potted plant he had bought the other day. A demon with a green thumb—I can't even wrap my mind around it all.

After checking the soil and watering it, he then plopped right down on the floor with the TV remote. Old habits die young.

"And who is …" The Pope's voice trailed off in mid-inquiry.

Oswalt's chair screeched as he pushed it away from the table for a better look.

"Ah," my father said. "Just the young man who's renting out the back room. A friend of Amanda's."

"Not!" I found myself yelling, and then trying to cover it up. "Not … really. Guy, man, person. He is, um, crashing … staying, renting the room in the back. He is. Is he? Yup. He is."

James didn't turn to look at me. He just made a muffled "ah huh" sound in his throat. Ah huh, yes I understand? Or ah huh, there's the little demon fucker? There was no way for me to decipher which it was.

A commercial came on. It was hard to tell what it was at first. The black and white image of a cow tied to a post. A little girl walked up to it. She picked up a shotgun, pointed it at the creature's head, and the screen went to black to the sound of the blast. The golden arches slowly came on screen.

"Hey, D. Would you like to eat? We can scoot over."

My mom. Oh my god. My mom.

"I'm good." D rolled partially over to look at the table. From his upside down position, it seemed like he finally recognized that we had guests. "Who's the dinner party for?"

"I guess that would be me," James said, and stood to his feet.

I went from having a slight headache to feeling like I was trying to power through a concussion. I made a motion to stand, but Oswalt spun around to face me. I was suddenly aware of the position of his hands. There was the one grasping the fork. The other was below the table.

"You must be pretty important," D said very matter of factly.

"Nowadays, not so much," the Pope replied with some softness in his voice. He didn't approach. He kept his distance. "Do you recognize me?"

Blindly pointing, D replied, "No, but those are the good plates. Mrs. Grey only breaks those out for special occasions."

There was so much "wrong" in that sentence that I immediately had to drop it or else my head would explode.

"I see." James set his hands behind his back but still did not move. "TV. I heard the American stuff rots a person's soul."

"Depends."

"Depends on?"

"Primetime or cable. Now, reality shows? Those are the work of the devil."

James laughed as D fiddled with the remote, flipping it this way and that. He had no idea what the hell was going on and I wanted so bad to shout at him, or strike him with a car. Maybe something between those two.

"May I?" James said, pointing to my father's seat. Dad nodded and I nearly fainted. This was escalating past what I could take. Oswalt never took his eyes off of me. Now I all I could do was watch. Now I was just along for the ride. The eternal struggle of Light and Dark, watching reality TV together.

"What is this woman's problem?" James asked after watching for some time.

"She didn't kiss Chud, that's the platypus looking guy, after their first date," D explained. "He kissed the first four women in the first episode, so he expected more. It's all been downhill from there."

"Hmm. And now? Why is he handing her a phone?"

"Because he voted her out. So now she has to call her own cab home."

"Hmm-hmm. And the other woman, smiling back there. She is … the blonde?"

"Oh, that's Kindy. Spelled like Cindy but said like Kindy. She wants to learn to be a foot plastic surgeon to help kids in Third World countries. She's also kind of a bitch."

"Oh, I see."

I was mortified. My parents also sat there totally confused, but that's the thing with Mom and Dad. Something will confuse the ever living crap out of them, but they would just accept it as law. They constantly rewrite the rules of the world, which is where I guess I got most of my reasoning from.

They watched the entirety of the episode. The whole thing. Mom cleaned the Pope's plate while Oswalt ate very slow just to have a reason to sit at the table with me.

"Fascinating," James said, rapping his fingers against the arms of the chair as a form of applause. "I can see it. I can see the draw. Though it certainly lacks the enriching entertainment value. Me. I was born in Poland, in the capital, Warsaw. You can imagine the difference. Cameras were different. Society, extremely different."

"Humor," my father added.

"Of course. Humor was radically different." James paused and turned just his eyes toward D. "Ai auzit gluma despre preotul care a intrat într-un bar?"

The entire table fell quiet. Everyone lingered on how D would respond, but the demon took a sip of water, looking bored.

"Ou diriez-vous si je demande en français?" James re-tried. I caught pieces of this one. My father spoke French to us when we were kids.

This time, D turned to look at him.

James was only smiling.

The tension in the room was steadily climbing. By their tense bodies, I could tell that it was even affecting my parents, and they had no freaking idea the gravity of the issue.

"Quomodo autem nunc vado punchline iterum?" James tried.

"Waqal: 'Rbama la yjb 'an 'akun qad dakhalat fi hadha alqifs fi al-maqam al'uwala'," D replied dryly.

The shock on James' face was enough to make me stand. Oswalt jumped out of his seat to head me off. I was just lining up a proper fist when we were both stopped by laughter.

The Pope was laughing. Tears were flowing. Sweat lined his white hair. After a long minute, he was able to bring it down to a chortle. I didn't understand the exchange between them, but it totally sounded like the structure of a dick joke.

"That's it," James began, "that settles it. Family Grey, this evening you all will be my guests." Before my mom could lose it, he shook my father's hand. "And you will stay with me tonight. No need to decline because I will not hear it. They have rented out an entire hotel for me. Just endless halls and empty rooms. I'll give you one. You'll be home tomorrow afternoon. Oswalt, call a car to pick us up."

The young man did as he was told. Mom and Dad were beside themselves, and of course would never say no to a Pope. My mom sneaked in a hug and pinched my cheeks.

"You handle the apartment. You help your sister. You meet new people. You see what happens when you put yourself out there, honey? Things happen."

"They sure do," I mumbled.

I knew that I needed to stay with my parents at all costs, so I went to grab a sweater. But that's when I heard, "On second thought, Oswalt."

James set his hand on his escort's shoulder. "Call a car for the Greys to go on ahead. I would really like some time with young Grey herself."

James smiled.

I didn't.

It was odd watching my parents go without me. I knew that it was accomplishing what I was going there for, to get them out of harm's way. But watching them leave, scoot into the black unmarked truck that came to pick the Pope up, and seeing it drive away made me feel lonely. Absurdly. The most I've ever felt. I mean, here I was about to get murdered by the leader of the Christian following, and my parents had just driven off thinking that they would see me in a few hours.

Oddly, he didn't even want to talk to D. An incarnate of darkness, and the Pope really wanted some "time" with me?

I sat in my living room, waiting for James to come back after insisting on escorting my parents down. That left Oswalt standing by the door. I tried asking him a few questions about the Pope's business with me, but the guy barely acknowledged me. I then sat there wondering if the Vatican had blessed the stick before shoving it up his ass.

A knock at the door broke the silence and I immediately remembered that Petty was supposed to come; she was the last person that needed to be there. Luckily, my super Lou's voice followed.

"Came to say hi and start fixing hole in kitchen, Grey. Your mom asked me to stop by."

Even through those thick sunglasses, I could tell that Oswalt was agitated. I needed Lou to go away so I shouted through the door, "Not today, Lou. I'm in here having lots of sex so come back tomorrow. Now, thank you!"

I could hear Lou audibly gasp. "You are … I mean, are you sure?"

"Yes, yes. I'm sure, Lou. A lot of the sex is happening."

"I'm in here, too," Oswalt said to my disbelief. His accent was thick and oddly pornstar-ish.

Lou sulked around a little bit, uncomfortable and not sure what to do with himself. But then he apologized and promised to come back at another time, awkwardly saying, "Have fun. I mean, no. I mean, I'm leaving now." And then his footsteps died away.

As Oswalt checked through the peephole to confirm, I shot a text to Petty in a flash with the easiest message I could get out.

Bad dont come

Oswalt caught me but I feigned checking the time. When he stuck out his hand to take my phone, I put it back into my pocket. He was silently staring at me, wondering about taking the phone by force, when James returned. The old man closed the door behind him and Oswalt the good guard dog stood in front of it. D's door was closed so I wasn't sure what my options of rescue were.

James set his hands behind his back and walked calmly to my father's chair. Grabbing the back of it, he said, "The path of the righteous man is beset on all sides by the inequities of the selfish and the tyranny of evil men."

I chuckled. "How did I know this talk might start with scripture?"

James scrunched up his nose. "Scripture? No, no. *Pulp Fiction*. They were giving it on the plane ride over and I saw it twice. Love Tarantino. Ay! 'Zed is dead'."

Pushing the chairs only a foot apart, James took a seat and leaned back. Then, as if remembering something, he drew two guns from his waist—the same silver pistols Cain showed me in the vision—and placed them on the coffee table that Oswalt fetched for him on silent command.

"He doesn't sit," James says of him like a doting father. "I tell him to sit, he does so for five minutes, and then … pops back up again. Frustrating. By far, his worst trait."

Pointing to the revolvers, James crossed his legs and let me take them in. They were much larger in person, and by the sound they made against the wood when he set them down, they seemed to weigh a ton.

"I was going to use them. I still may use them."

"So this is a threat?"

"What this is, Amanda," he countered only with a tinge of anger, "is a discussion in which I recognize the short span of time we have been given. And I choose to spend that time escaping pleasantries. Would you rather pleasantries?"

"Never heard of the word. Please continue."

204

"I simply wanted you to see these as proofs of my faith, and nothing more." When I gave him a silent nod, he continued. "I have seen you. In visions. In dreams. This is what is connected to the title I hold. It's what all of my predecessors have wielded as well. It is what gives us the preparation to protect the Church. It's also robbed me of sleep every single day since taking on the role. Tell me, Amanda Grey. How do you sleep? Do you dream?"

"Like any other person."

"Visions?"

I didn't want to mention what Cain had showed me. Of D tearing his heart out. It might sour this. So I replied with another question. "How did you explain needing to meet me? My parents were weirder than usual."

"Ah." He smiled. James' smile was funky. The edges of his lips came up to such a degree that it smoothed his skin. It was like laughter made him twenty years younger. "We are reaching out to communities. Getting to know people as part of outreach. Pure chance I chose this building. Just fate."

"And what's the real reason? You flew all the way here for advice on sleep?" I kept myself from staring at the gun.

James didn't seem like the type of guy I could get a rise out of. He was oh so patient, even taking the time to listen and digest fully what I said before responding. I would call him a saint but … I won't go there.

"The vision is said to have been passed down from the age of Christ, from Christ, you can imagine. It is chronicled in his walk in the desert. When he saw his death. It is called, in our circles, Sancta Sedes."

A lump grew in my throat. "Death."

"And life," James added. "You can't have one. There will always be both."

"And why tell me?

"Yes, you. You Amanda Grey. I've seen what you've done, but only brief flashes. Only minutes. Only decisions." He turned his head to the side. "I want to know your story."

I sighed. "If you know all of the juicy details, what else is there?"

"I don't know. How about everything else?" Seeing that I wasn't going to respond to that, he asked, "Have you thought about seeking confession?"

"Confession? No, no way. I don't mean this as an insult, but me talking to a guy who is sitting there judging me, won't save my soul from eternal damnation."

He seemed amused by this. "Fine, fine. I won't presume to know what you are going through, but I will offer you a suggestion. You may not want to tell me your story, but you need to tell someone. The confines of a confessional may not heal your situation, but it may help other things."

And with that, James stood up.

I wasn't the only one stunned. Oswalt's face turned sour and drawn. He asked something of the older man in German. But James wasn't having it. He ordered the young man to retrieve the pistols and conceal them as he walked himself to the door.

I headed him off. "Whoa, whoa. You're leaving? That's it? A chat about dreams and some life advice and now you're gone?"

"I came to meet you. We met. I will tell your kind mother to phone you the address when we arrive. I would really like it if you were there." James shot me a thumbs up and tried to walk away. But I wasn't the only one floored by the whole thing. Oswalt started shouting in German and pointing at me. James, still calm, responded and set his hand on his shoulder. But this only enraged the young man more. He swatted aside James' hand, stormed over to the small table, and turned one of the pistols over so fast that his arm was a blur. The opening of the gun pressed so hard against my forehead that it was obviously leaving a mark.

"Sie müssen sterben. Teufel! Teufel!" When he saw that those words meant nothing to me, he gritted his teeth and jammed the gun in harder. "You are evil."

"Oswalt, right?"

The young man's hand shook.

"How did you—"

"Here's something you need to drill into your head about me, real fast. This has been the most difficult month of my life. Probably the shittiest month on the face of this planet. I've been strangled until my eyes wanted to burst from my head, sucker punched, and swallowed by a possessed hand puppet. To top it all off, the only place I'm going if you pull that trigger is hell. Signed and sealed. No connecting flights. So if you think for one goddamned minute that shoving a gun in my face is going to make my life crappier than it is, you're out of your mind, asshole."

I snatched the gun right out of Oswalt's hand and he backed away. It was one of those moments that I should have been a badass, but secretly I was hyperventilating. A hand slid the gun out of my grasp. I never saw James move toward me.

He smiled and put the weapon back in his waist. "I guess you're right. Who needs to talk about their problems nowadays? Though I could have done without the cursing of my God."

"In the moment," I grunted. "Like, sorry and stuff."

James asked his lap dog, who only stood there, pale and out of breath, to wait outside. Instead of arguing, Oswalt spun around and hurried out of the door.

James tapped his chin, a gesture that told me that even though he smiled through the entire thing, the confrontation had rattled him. "You two are alike. It's a shame he doesn't see that."

My jaw trembled as I tried to speak. "You know that much about me to make that statement?"

"I know that you blame yourself for all of this mess. I know you've been fighting to put your life back together." Taking a long breath, he came and stood beside me. His eyes: the pressure was gone. He looked tired and worn now, as if he had aged years in my apartment. "So you don't want to talk about your life. That's fine. But take it from someone on the outside. A kind observer. Your life and the decisions you make are your own. Up until now, you've been fighting tooth and nail to get it back to the way it used to be. You just want your life back. But time cannot change. You are now forever different."

"That's been a recurring theme today," I remarked, remembering the matching sentiment of one Angel of Death.

"So maybe you're going about this all wrong." James threw his hands up. And then he said, as if to himself, "'The mind is its own place, and in itself can make a heav'n of hell, a hell of heav'n.'"

"Don't tell me. *Reservoir Dogs?*"

James—the Pope who was standing in my living room—laughed. Then his brown eyes grew distant. He wanted to say something but I could tell that he was trying his best to shape the words. "I used to read this poem over and over again as a boy. It was my favorite poem. I felt for the person in the story because he was me. I felt important but was told by the world that I was one of billions. I wanted to be loved. And when I realized, when I really realized, that the man I had been reading about was Lucifer, when I took in the weight of his crimes and the reach of his ambition, I only loved the poem that much more." James opened my front door and, with his hand still on the knob, told me "That is the bitter part of evil, Amanda Grey. It's far easier to laugh with the Devil than cry with God."

As the door closed, I walked over to the window, shaking. There was something turning in my gut. A pain? An emotion? I needed air and slid onto the windowsill to have a breeze hit me.

He didn't kill me. He didn't even kill D. But why? Because he liked him?

Below I could see Oswalt holding open the door of the black SUV called to whisk the Pope away. Just as he appeared, a homeless man walked over to the passenger side. He was large and wore a thick sweater and sweatpants with stains all over it. I couldn't see his face. Oswalt tried pushing him away, but James calmed him down, pointed with his hand to pay the man, and jumped into his ride. Oswalt did as he was told and got in on the other side.

If I would have known then what I know now, I would of hung out in that window for longer. Instead, I picked up the phone and called Petty.

36

AN HOUR LATER, Petty showed up to the apartment with Cain in tow. I was so caught up in what happened that I had forgotten all about the former Angel of Death. Not expecting her, I slammed the door shut on her face before she could step in. A light rap later, I let her in and, uncaringly, she slinked her long body on to the couch. This time though, the news that the Pope had showed up had made her stern-faced. Petty was almost delirious.

"What did he say? Did he say anything? What happened to Mom and Dad?"

"Slow, slow, slow. One bit at a time."

"No," she said and kept saying over and over. "No, no, no."

"I kinda sorta told her you were going to hell," Cain explained in perfectly tailored deadpan.

My sister grabbed me by the shoulders and shook me. "We. Have. To. Talk!"

"Look," Cain said, standing up, "I'll just show her. Would be infinitely easier." She flipped open her bag, drew out her blade once more, and looked at my television set.

Remembering what she did to the last one, I waved her off. "No! You can't break that. No way."

"Ease up," the angel scoffed. From out of the handle, she drew out three cords and plugged them into the back of the TV. "HDMI makes everything so much simpler."

Like last time, she leaned the scythe back and forth until ghostly blue cords appeared in the air. She went one by one, cursing her luck after her tenth or eleventh try.

And just like the last time the three of us were together, another knock at the door interrupted us. Flustered, Petty stomped over to check.

"You need to know something, Grey. Something important. Something maybe Barnem failed to mention." Cain's face was stern.

I croaked out a laugh. "Barnem's honorary title is 'Seraph of the Forgot to Mention'."

I could hear the sound of Petty sliding open the peep hole cover. "Hello? Can I help you?"

"You've come this far just watching your back for demons and crazies." Smirking, she leaned forward. "And you've done one heck of a job with that. I'm impressed. Honestly."

"And?" I said, pushing her to get to the point.

"Hello?" Petty asked again. I glanced over at her and she shrugged when no one responded.

And then an image on the TV snapped into focus.

It was D, standing with his hands in his hoodie. The space he was standing in was wrecked, and it took me a really long time to piece together where he was. But judging from the tipped over florescent light tubings, the medical supplies on the ground, and the tiled walls, it was most definitely a hospital. Not just any, either: St. Francis, the hospital Barnem was staying in. His room, actually.

At first, I could only see D. But what lay at his feet stood out to me more and more. I thought at first it was just strewn about garbage and then a lumpy black garbage bag. But then certain details leapt out at me. Fingers. Hair. That was someone's body. And the blackened skin, the long hair, the exposed breast sitting outside of the torn blouse. The corpse was Petty.

D stepped over her body and I suddenly came into view, standing a few feet from the both of them, blood soaking through my shirt, my fist bared to protect myself. Then D exploded with energy, and his legs and arms seem to stretch out and grow. Black tendrils of dark power burst through his skin and quickly swallowed me up.

"D did this?"

I felt like I was spinning, falling into darkness. There was a slight turn in my gut, as if someone had taken a handful of my intestines and balled it up into a fist. Her words hissed into static and I felt like the room, the people around me, hell even the chair I was sitting in had just melted away. All of it. All of the colors ran. All of the jagged lines, the circles, the dimensions. All of it.

Until I was left in a white space.

The same space I was in only once before.

And this time, the whisper—the half-growling behind what sounded like sharp fangs—told me two words.

Better run.

"Don't mean to interrupt the doom and gloom stuff," Petty said nervously.

Her voice snapped me into reality again. I was back. Back in my seat. Back in my skin and bones. Cain had stopped speaking and was looking over at Petty.

"Problem there, beautiful?"

"Right ... so. The same homeless guy in a trench coat that knocked on my door back at the hotel. He's knocking on this door. So it's either a severe perv alert or a friend of yours? He wouldn't be—"

She didn't get to say the rest.

A muscular arm burst a hole in the door with a fist that hit my sister like a freight train. She flew passed us, corkscrewed, and after a seismic shattering of glass, for the second time in a week, Petty flew out of a window.

What stepped into the apartment was not familiar at first. I didn't recognize it as the man on the train D and I saw when we rode back from the hospital. Not until he was up in my face. It was massive and the arm hanging out of the torn trench coat reached up and tore the rest of its clothing off. Over its toned, taut gray skin, it wore an armored chest plate with gold writing on the front. The writing didn't stay still. It writhed and waved, looking more like tongues of flame than sentences. The jeans it wore were bursting around the knees and thighs with gray flesh. Everything was at least close to human—a highly steroid-infused human, but human nonetheless—except its face. Its veined neck was topped with an angular box with flat edges. If this were its head, it sported no eyes or other facial features. It was all skin and boxed skull.

"Mind if I step in?" Cain pushed me aside. She had somehow retrieved her scythe and turned the large weapon behind her back before slicing the floor. Wood broke and beams buckled, tipping that entire section of my parents' living room right into the apartment below, with me along for the ride. I crashed against a far wall as the current occupants scurried for the door, the woman screaming down the hall. Several pipes had ruptured and water shot out of the wall next to me.

Cut off from what was going on upstairs, I needed to check on Petty and get some distance to try and regroup. All I could think about was the destruction of my parents' home. I had fought long and hard to save it, but in the end, I still saw it destroyed. My childhood home was now ground zero. I'm just glad my mom and dad weren't around to see it destroyed like that.

I knew I had to lock this loss away quickly. The demon was coming for me, was challenging me to end this, but I worried that letting it go might come to bite me in the ass. I scrambled down the hallway, banging on the closed doors of the building I grew up in, shouting for everyone to evacuate. Fire. Earthquake. I basically yelled them all. It didn't take much convincing. The explosions and the rattling foundation if the building put everyone in a panic.

I only got as far as the end of that third floor hallway before the ceiling came down, sending dust and wood and plaster toppling onto my only exit. But it didn't come alone. The creature was there along with it. I heard Cain scream and a flash of metal, but it was quickly followed by a loud crunch of bone and something wet hitting the ground. I didn't turn around to find out what it was.

I backed up as it swung its tree trunk sized arm at me and struck the front of the elevator, instantly caving in the metal. Retreating back with a small family, we ducked into an apartment and locked the door. The creature took the scenic route through the wall, catching me by surprise. The force alone knocked me over, folding my small body around the legs of a desk in one of the rooms.

It was after me and that was easy to see. I wanted to get it as far from the innocent family and their kid as soon as possible. They ran with me to the back, but I shoved them into a closet and then cut to another room. By the looks of it, it was a nursery for a girl. Scared, I checked the crib but found it empty.

Sighing a deep breath of relief, I ran to the window. The whole thing was facing the back corner of the building. I could see the neighboring community garden which meant that Petty had landed somewhere down there. Three stories, no obstructions. Jumping from that height, I recognized that I would hit the pavement both fast and hard.

I looked around the room for anything to use for a weapon. But then I caught sight of something that made me forget that a hellish demon was close to finding me. It was my reflection.

The mirror was broken, maybe after one of the serious explosions that had gone off. But I could see my face, my entire face. There was something wrong with the right side. The cheekbone was raised. The skin was flaky, like a log whitened in a fire. And my eye was a perfectly black shell.

Just as I screamed, the door flew from its hinges and struck me. The force sent me flying and like a ragdoll; it blew me right out of the window as thousands of tiny shards of glass sank into my skin. I must have corkscrewed in midair because I saw the pavement then the sky, the building, the ground again. I couldn't feel my limbs moving; I could only watch them wave in the air in front of me as my free fall picked up speed.

I felt that I was falling for years. I wasn't sure if my body had hit the pavement or if it would hurt went I plowed into it.

All I did know was that though I wasn't ready to die, a part of me had let go; had slowly begun to give up. Reality was speeding toward my face and I was racing to meet it with one splattering finale.

"Hell is waiting," I think I whispered just as I hit the concrete.

37

WALKING AROUND THE hospital Barnem was situated in was nerve wracking. It always seemed like everyone had somewhere to go, someone to save, someone to see die right in front of them

I guess that's what freaks me out the most about hospitals in general. It's a space where most people just up and die. Sure you got the bullet wounds, the axes to the head, and what I want to guess is the usual vibrating toy issue here and there. But you also have cases of people who walk in with colds and never walk out. In my head, there were dead people all around me all of the time in hospitals.

One of these dead people, a nurse, stopped me in the hall. "You look lost."

"I am. I'm looking for …" I drew a blank. What was I here for? Barnem? Was this his hospital? And even if it was, how did I get here? *The last thing I remember doing was … The last thing I remember. It was a sound. The sound of … shattered glass.*

Seeing the discomfort in my face, the nurse patted me on the back. "Oh, honey. You're supposed to be downstairs," she said in her thick Caribbean accent. "Take the elevator down. Bottom floor."

"Bottom floor?"

"Bottom of the bottom." She gave me a dainty shove in the right direction and ran off.

The elevator ride itself was extremely long. I mean that it didn't last long, it just felt like I was in that stainless steel metal box staring at my reflection in its walls for forever.

Stepping out, I was greeted by a thin Asian woman standing as a hostess by two wooden doors.

I'm dreaming, I realized, and this calmed me.

"Table for you and your guest?" the hostess asked, but I had no idea who she was talking about. I was there alone.

"I'm looking for the morgue. The nurse sent me down?"

"Of course. Follow me."

She grabbed two menus (still expecting me to arrive with company even though I was clearly alone) and led me through the doors and down another long hallway, but this one was filled with the sound of people talking and laughter seeping out of the rooms we passed. The place was pretty old, with gaudy carpets on their squeaky floors, tacky oil paintings of white people hunting and sailing and other irrelevant shit, and chandeliers of fake crystal. At the end of this hallway we stopped at two large white doors made of polished metal.

Handing me the menus, which sported crimson leather jackets and the gold outline of a candle on their covers, and she quickly left me there. With no other option, I pushed open these white doors that were twelve feet tall. It was difficult. I heard the bones in my arms breaking.

Inside was a long table made of white stone with tea cups turned over on black mats. The floors and walls were painted all white, and blank picture frames hung for me to question. The chairs sitting around the table were thirteen; long black fixtures without armrests and tall back ends that rose into the air. Of the thirteen, six sat on each side. The final one was right at the front.

I'm early.

You're late, a whisper told me. So I counted the seats, lost count, and then just threw myself into any random one. Turning my cup over, I saw that it was large enough to be a sizable bowl. I poured myself some tea hoping to be able to speak before someone showed up. Using two hands, I gulped it all down.

I heard chairs slide aside and asses land in them, but I couldn't see who they were because the oversized cup was so big and I was still drinking.

Then came this tap tap tap; a nonstop surreal sound that seemed to vibrate in my bones (if in my dreams I did possess such). Lowering the cup from my lips, I looked for the source of it. Tap tap tap tap. I looked to my right and saw nothing that could be making the sound. When I looked to my left, there he was sitting beside me. I dropped the rest of the drink on my lap.

Mason Scarborough had his cheek firmly sitting on his fist, finger tapping against the smooth table, waiting for me to notice him.

"Grey."

"You're … you're dead!"

Mason stopped tapping. "I am. And thank you for that reminder, Grey. I do get so sentimental thinking about those days. Like a rising warmth in my chest. Almost like vomit."

"Oh." I patted my chest and laughed to myself. "This is a dream. I'm in a dream. Like a drunky dream thing. God. Almost … yeah. Almost got me."

Mason was dressed in a way I had never seen. He wore a purple suit with thin yellow pinstripes. His hair, which I always remembered as something I can only describe as "hippy shaggy" was now tied back into this perfect blond ponytail.

"You dressed for a funeral, Mason?"

"You can say that, Grey. You can say that." He still sat slumped over—one fist on his cheek and the other was placed on his knee, elbow sticking up in the air. A crow sat on the back of his seat; the number 4 etched into its eyes.

The doors swung open and several people walked into the room. Each one wore clothes right out of the zoot suit era and each crow stood propped up on a shoulder. I recognized most without even trying: the bag boy/man with the number 2 crow wore a blue suit with white wingtip shoes; touchy feely Franklin's fashionable tux matched the black feathers of his number 5 crow. Gary sat just to the left of Mason bearing his number 3 crow and a cheery wave in my direction. He wore an auburn blazer and tie. There was one heavyset Asian guy I couldn't place at all. When he caught me staring, he turned his thin lips upward in a familiar smile.

"Smile, Grey. You will live longer." And he started laughing. The crow on his chair—which squawked along with him—sounded just like it was cracking up.

216

"It's you."

"Really wish you would have taken me up on that offer. We could have really kicked these guys' asses. Team Grey for Life!"

The other folks in attendance just grumbled. Each crow held fast to their perches on the back of their owner's chair. Around the odd table, only three seats were empty.

"Okay. Let's not waste any more time here." As he said this, the large doors flew open once more. Quickly, Mason grabbed me from my chair and dragged me to the floor, pinning my head to his hip as if keeping me from seeing who had walked in. I tried to struggle, but in this dream, old fragile Mason seemed to be freakishly strong. I was able to make out, just beyond the space beneath the table, the lower-half of the room's new arrival.

"Yo," D called to everyone in the room, and all at once, the other crows screamed at him. From what I could see, D was wearing an all-black suit with a vest. He slowly approached the table and carefully tucked his hands into his pocket with his usual laidback flair. Even in my dreams, D was kind of a dick. With his face not obscured, I tried to get a better view from under the table, but Mason's grip on my head was too tight.

"Ah. And now arrives our gracious host," Mason muttered, though his face showed very little care that D had arrived. "It's been so long. I wonder if you would be so kind to fill us in on your progress."

"You don't order me around, anymore. I'm in charge," D snapped. "Besides, there's nothing to report. The see-er has been quiet and they don't give wrestling on Thursdays anymore which has thrown my whole schedule off."

"Yes, yes." The giant crow on the back of Mason's seat eyed my roommate intently. "You must be in limitless torture in the living world. What news do you have to end all of this?"

D's hands flew from his pockets and suddenly the table nearly exploded over me as he shouted, "Let me remind you your place. I'm working on it and it will all be over soon. That's all you need to know."

It was the most vicious and violent I had ever heard my roommate become. A crack had formed right down the center of the table and tiny splinters rained down into my hair.

Unimpressed, Mason replied, "I'm sure. And what of the 'white knight'?"

This immediately rattled around in my head. Where had I heard someone called a knight?

The people around the table began laughing.

"He isn't going to be a problem," D replied, going back to his casual tone. This only enraged the Shades again and the room was filled with their cries. "Calm down," he told them. "Like I said, I have him. And since it's my time to be in charge, you have no say in this. You do as I say."

This silenced the birds immediately.

Mason sat up straight. "You're leaving?"

He was, in fact, and he walked straight for the door. But as he set his hand on it, without turning to face us, he said, "I only called you here to tell you that this'll be the last time our cheery little group's going to meet. After tomorrow night, things will end, one way or another."

"Oh, let's be honest." Mason smiled and slid his eyes toward me. "Can we be sure you will do what needs to be done? Can you kill Amanda Grey?"

D froze.

As I waited for him to respond, my body seemed to work on its own. I found myself standing, pushing my chair back. I couldn't stay quiet anymore. Dream or not, I wasn't going to be ignored. But something was behind me. Something fluttered just behind my ear and pecked at my shoulder.

Turning to face it seemed like it took ages. I felt as if time had ruptured, leaving my body floating on its own. I was turning to see, turning to come face-to-face with the one thing I never wanted to know. The one thing that had been haunting me for weeks. More than weeks. Maybe my entire life. I was turning but not fast enough. I broke a sweat in the short span, ripping against my muscles, shattering my bones.

And that's when I came face-to-face with my biggest fear.

Its large beak.

Its black feathers.

Its red eyes with the number 7 printed boldly in it.

A crow stood upon my chair.

I screamed and D finally noticed me. His face contorted. Fire and ash poured from his eyes and mouth like a swelling furnace.

As he launched himself across the long table, the world exploded around us. Suddenly, I started bleeding from the forehead and my nose. Pain swelled throughout my body as the table, the walls, and the figures in their chairs, fractured into tiny floating fragments, as if the entire thing were a reality imprinted on glass.

And then, suddenly, Donaldson's face came into view. I realized that I wasn't in the chair or in the weird room anymore. I was sprawled out on flat cement.

"Grey." His voice sounded drowned out. "Grey."

"I'm here, I'm here. Keep your shirt on."

Donaldson looked up at the broken window that I had obviously fallen from and then took a look around. "Is D here? He must have caught you, right? How else could you survive—"

"He's not. Just … just pull me up please."

The sound of loud explosions and falling brick gave me a perfect "Previously On…" to remember what was at stake. I wasn't sure what the hell just happened or where I had gone, but all of it was blatantly real. Mason, D, the crows. Putting this to the side for the time being, I started focusing on the here and now. The Shade was attacking. The same Shade that was absent from the meeting had come to face me head on. It blindsided me. Cain set herself to fighting it right after Petty—

"Oh fuck." I quickly tested my legs. While I was beaten up and bleeding in a few places, I could still move. What the hell did happen to me?

Out in front of the building, there was utter chaos as folks and families streamed out of the front doors. I saw all of the families that had lived in that housing complex as if it were a generational practice. Lou was helping people clear out, and one explosion after another sent bricks and entire walls falling on whoever was nearby. He held his stomach tightly with one arm, a crimson stain blossoming through his T-shirt. Wherever I had gone, it seemed like no time whatsoever had passed.

Someone grabbed me from behind and I quickly swung my hands. Used to that reception, Donaldson easily sidestepped it.

"Grey! It's me. Remember? Just back there."

"Shit!" I grabbed him by the shirt and dragged him along. I searched for Petty toward the side of the next door community garden. When we eventually found her, I nearly threw up on myself. Petty had fallen on the white picket fence squarely and taken two spikes: one through the chest that had tented up the back of her shirt, and a second through her upper thigh. The wood had not gone through cleanly and had snapped off.

With two hands, Donaldson and I steadied her up. There was no blood, but her black skin had been shredded. I turned her over to reveal her sporting the same terrified expression she wore during our entire conversation upstairs.

"You're going to hell?"

Remembering where I had just come from, I told her, "Petty. Now's not a good time." I couldn't tell her too much. I didn't know how. I looked around. Still no sign of D.

"Another demon? I thought we caught them all!" Petty groaned, though I'm sure this was far from what she really wanted to ask.

"Must've followed me here. Can you stand on that?"

"I can run," she replied. But then she saw me staring up, looking up at the broken window.

"How'd you get down here so fast? Did you fly out of that window? I heard a window break and something land nearby."

Before I could come up with a proper response, the wall of my parents' apartment burst outward. And with all the debris, Cain toppled onto the concrete beside us. There was a metal pipe jammed into her collarbone, but like Petty, it was a bloodless affair. It instantly struck me again how different she was from Barnem. The guy had blood and guts, flesh and blood (I know. I've seen them). So what made the two so different?

The Angel of Death noticed us gawking at her, rolled, snagged both of our hands and started running. I tried my best to pull out of her grasp, but she had me locked in her grip around the wrist.

"No time for heroics, darlin'. Who the hell is this?" she asked, pointing back at Donaldson who was barely keeping up beside us.

"He's fine. And you can let me go."

"No can do, gorgeous. I promised Barnem I'd keep you alive until he got back on his feet."

Even though I felt greatly outmatched by the thing thrashing around my apartment, mainly because this was an attack just like the first two demons—out of nowhere—I found myself flying without that safety net. D was definitely not showing up and I still had to wrap my mind around what I had seen, what I had found out about myself, back in that other world. Still, I wasn't ready just to stand around seeing the complete destruction of the place I called home for twenty-something years.

"Let go of me," I insisted again. "I've fought enough of these assholes already. We can't let this Shade—"

"No, Grey," Cain said, and for the first time, her voice held an ominous tone. "Not this time. I already told you that this isn't that type of game anymore. What just attacked us, what tried to rip you apart in that room, wasn't a demon. That was an angel."

WE DIDN'T STOP running for blocks and blocks. Until there was fire in my joints; bile in the back of my throat. When we did finally find someplace to crash, the sun was setting in the distance. From where we were, the New York skyline was barely visible. But above the skyscrapers, the sun seemed to be rocketing back into the sky, which was redder than usual, instead of setting downward like science had originally scripted it to be.

Tucking our little party in a small kids' park, we all collapsed by the swings. Only Cain seemed completely unaware that a ten block run should have had her hunched over, throwing up her guts. She was too busy looking at the sky.

"Tonight's the night, Grey. You either …" She stopped as if just noticing the metal bar jutting out of her chest. She tore it out with one hand and let it clang against cement. "You either catch the final Shade or this is the last night of human existence."

Donaldson, out of breath, waved at her. "I'm sorry. And you are?"

"Oh. Cain. Ex-Angel of Death. Jeffrey Donaldson, right? Yeah, yeah. You were part of my district."

"District?"

"Mhm. You never knew your dad, but he's dying. Moved out to Chicago. Caught the cancer. Your mom is already dead. Brain aneurysm at forty-nine. Now that one I remember."

Donaldson looked like someone had slammed into his lungs with a baseball bat. "What did you— Want to tell me how know that?"

Cain fiddled with her hair. "Oh. Yeah, sure. I collected her soul when she croaked. That was me. I took your mom away from you."

It was like a switch being flicked on. Donaldson, fatigue and all, got right up in Cain's face.

"I'm going to ask you again and you're going to give me some proper answers."

Laughing, Cain threw her hands up. "Careful there, tiger. You're cute, but you ain't that cute." It took wedging my body between them just to douse the situation.

"Oh right. That's a bit of a faux paus, dead mothers and stuff." Cain shot out her hand so that Donaldson could shake it. "I'm not used to the human aversion to death. Was in the business too long. No hard feelings."

Donaldson slapped her hand away, causing Cain to scratch the back of her blonde head with it instead. Just like Barnem, she seemed completely disconnected from human emotions. Maybe even more so than the grumpy Seraph. "C'mon. I didn't kill them, just collected for the greater good. And at minimum wage. Now if you want to be pissed at something—"

"What's going on, Cain? Why did you say that was an angel, Cain?"

"Because it was, Grey. Your dinner guest must have sicced it on us after he left."

Part of me thought this was only remotely possible. Sure the old man had shown some restraint with us, with D, and he even called off his guard dog at the last possible moment. But he said that he came over just to meet us? To meet me? I get coming to see D for yourself, but what I couldn't wrap my mind around was why was I so important? I'm the screwup in this whole equation. And if he really wanted us dead, why send the angel afterwards?

And then I finally remembered. The feeling I was getting. The slow crawl of something in my skin. It felt like a panic attack, but so different. So concentrated. And then the white space. The whisper.

I had a Shade in me.

Maybe this entire time.

Maybe my whole life.

I tried not to show it in my face, but Donaldson must of caught the fear welling up in my expression because he came and stood by me.

"So what's the plan?" Petty sat up from the ground and dusted herself off. We all stared at her. "What? This is all fine and dandy. So and so wants us dead. Blah, blah, blah. At this point, get in line."

Cain didn't respond; she simply turned toward the setting sun to watch it bleed into the sky in crimson trails. It was a severed boil on the face of a dying planet. After a long pause, she said, "I remember this. Remember all of this. It's like ... like the old days. God's wrath was everywhere, let me tell you. You couldn't get through one week without a plague. You could be sitting down to a decent lunch, all by yourself, and by the time you roll out your cheese and wafers, boom-boom-boom, leprosy. Locusts. It made dating impossible." And then, hilariously she added, "And the traffic!"

"What are they—" The question stuck in my throat. I tried to keep myself steady. "What are the Shades fighting for?"

She sighed and I thought she was going to go the Barnem route and just blow me off. But then she replied, "It's called the Subjugation of Wills. Basically a demon pact that keeps the hierarchy. See, the Shades are strong on their own, but just a hiccup of what the Beast is. And since the Shades all have their own little quirks and agendas, that's where subjugation comes into play. Think of it as a bus with all the little Shades riding on it. The bus itself is big and powerful on its own, but only the strongest Shade can drive at any given time. It's like they fight for the seat, Grey, and none in my entire career have gone and done what yours has. Just beat the others with such conviction. And that's what makes him dangerous. That's why you gotta catch the last one before he does. Or else."

"Back up. This is D we're talking about. Back there, that thing that attacked us was an angel. More like your kind, isn't it?"

Cain snarled her lip at Donaldson and rolled her eyes. "They're warrior angels. Grunts sent from on high to hunt down and slay the Shades. I'm more of an angel with career goals. C'mon, dude. We're from two different sections of the *Bible*. Sheesh. Generalize much?"

"So why did it attack us?"

"Obviously ..."

"Obviously what?"

"It's out to finish the job, slay the Shade in your sister and your room-mate. And I bet I know what you're thinking next. You're thinking, 'Why not lay low and let that angel do its business?' Simple answer: because it just tore through an entire building just to get to you. And I have even shittier news. That cluster of stars you saw falling all those weeks ago wasn't a cluster at all. It was an army. It's a holy legion: a whole army of angels. And right now, they're probably tearing this city a new one, killing any and everyone they come across. And you can't stop them. You can't kill something ethereal. What do you think about that?"

They continued squabbling for the better part of the five minutes we stood in that park. But even without raising my voice, as soon as I spoke, they stopped and stared.

"This is all wrong."

"Hm? Say something over there, gorgeous?"

"This wasn't supposed to turn out this way. This. This." I pointed to the sky, to the cut over Donaldson's eye. "I had it. I really did. For the first time in my life, I freaking had it all kinda-sorta figured out. Seventy percent of it, at least! Yeah I messed up, but I was always able to keep it together. Even when I was the one who fell apart. Even when I was one big damn dumpster fire."

Petty wrapped her arms tightly around her chest. "You okay, Mandy?"

"I got it back. The apartment. Mom and Dad. Even you, Petty. Even you came back." I gave the nearby kiddie swing a shove with my foot. "It all just toppled over on me."

Donaldson came over to console me. "I know it's a lot on you emotionally, Grey …"

I stopped him short with a disgusted look. "Thanks, but I'm not asking for a tissue yet." I grabbed the swing with one hand. "Just saying. Now that I know what I've come so close to having, I'm not going to just wait around for Donaldson to hug me. No offense."

Crossing his arms, he mumbled, "Ain't nothing wrong with my hugs."

"I've come this far by just punching people in the face, so let's go with that strategy. Cain, what face needs punching before the shit goes down?"

She beamed. "You know I never noticed this before, Grey, but it's your penchant for violence that makes you all types of adorable."

"Just tell me what do we do?"

"The final Shade. We catch it before D does, before he becomes all powerful. Then we get Barnem and he cleans up this mess. We do this as fast as possible and—"

I felt a tug at my side. Petty's black eyes were very large. "Mandy."

"Petty. We'll get to that talk. Just not now, all right?"

"No. It's not that. Remember how you were able to find me in the hotel? Remember Gary and why he attacked me?"

At first, I didn't follow. "Gary? Gary and I found you because ..."

Cain was still blabbing when I cut her off. "How did the angel find me?"

Cain paused. "Like I said, your buddy must've led it straight to you."

I shook my head. "That only makes sense for when it showed up at Mom and Dad's. But it knocked on Petty's door first, remember? And before that, I saw it on the train when I was with D. It's like it can track me. Like it can sense my aura. And if that's true ..."

Petty had realized before I had but we both took off together.

"Where are we off to?" Donaldson asked, trailing behind.

"I need you to go to the hospital. Get to Barnem and pull him out. Do that however you want, but just get it done. We'll meet back up at the apartment. Take Cain with you."

"You got it. But ..." Donaldson paused and he and Petty exchanged nervous glances. "Are we going to talk about what happened back at the apartment? How you fell out of a window and are walking around now all fine and dandy?"

Yes. Tell them, the whisper told me.

"Not now. I just need you to trust me. I'm fine."

They both took a minute to digest this as we rounded the corner and headed to the train. Donaldson finally said, "I don't trust her, Grey. Something feels off and we've already been burnt on what people are or are not telling us." After thinking for a few seconds, he added, "Maybe we should just wait for Barnem to wake up before we start our next demon hunt."

"I'm with you. And that's why I need you there. Keep her in check for me. Focus on Barnem."

Of course, I had my own agenda. Remembering the fate Cain had shown us, I was going to keep Petty as far from that hospital as possible.

Speaking of Cain, she caught up to us in a flash, almost running backward with crazy ease.

"You're really doing this? You're running *toward* the guy trying to kill you? Toward the danger? And all of you are just going along with this?"

"If the angels are after me, then it means they can sense aura, which means that they will kill folks exposed to Shades. My parents are in trouble. Petty and I will get them."

The former Angel of Death held her head between her hands. "Am I the only one who thinks this plan ... that this plan is all levels of terrible? What happened to nabbing the last Shade first? What happened to that, huh?"

"To hell with him. My parents come first. C'mon, Petty. Donaldson—"

"I'll go on foot. Let me see that phone." Taking it from me, he set my mom's message to memory. "That place is only four or five blocks from the hospital which is only a straight shot up from here if I run down a block or two. I'll get Barnem out of there and we'll meet at the apartment."

As my sister and I ran down the steps to the train, Cain just stood there gawking at us all.

"Worst plan ever!" she yelled. "And you know, coming from me, that's saying a whole lot! I was around when people thought Noah was just compensating for something."

HALFWAY THROUGH OUR trip, Petty turned to me and said, "Don't think I don't know what you did back there."

There were only a few people on the train, which seemed weird to be running during an apocalypse (especially since said trains barely ran on the weekends). It also seemed odd to go from screaming people holding on to their families for dear life to people selling candy car by car. But that's how we're separated here. That's how delayed we are to everyone else's suffering.

"What did I do back there, Petty?"

"You made me come with you here. As in not the hospital I'm supposed to be brutally murdered in."

"You won't die."

"You're right," she said, and made me pause to look at her. My little sister's skin was so black, like dyed paper. Her white pupils still made me feel uneasy when I looked at them for too long. "You don't have to treat me as fragile, you know? I'm not."

"No. No, you're not. But that doesn't mean you should be in the middle of a mess all the time. You act like you're indestructible."

"I am."

"You're not."

The train doors slid open and we hurried from the train, rose up out of the stop, and dashed down the block. From where we were, it was a three block walk from there. "I don't want to have this argument," I told her sharply.

"Fine. But what happened back at Mom and Dad's? How'd you survive that fall?"

I stopped short. "I don't, Petty. I just don't. I don't need this right now. What I do need, right now, in this second, is for us to hurry our asses over and pull Mom and Dad out of there and then shove them on a plane away from this city. Everyone. Everyone just get on a plane and go as far away as possible."

"I feel bad."

It took a lot to keep my temper down. "Petty, we don't have time.

"So then when? When will we have time for me to tell you I'm sorry. When will I have time just to talk to my sister? Why is that so bad?"

"Because ever since you left, you stopped wanting to talk, Petty. Remember that? Why haven't you figured out the freakin' obvious by now? I don't want to talk to you because I can't. Because at first I see my kid sister who totally kicked her entire family to the curb for years. And on the other hand, I see a walking corpse of that sister. Okay? Happy now?"

I thought Petty was going to tackle me to the ground, but she hugged me instead. She held the hug, and suddenly I remembered how she was when we were little. She was always a hugger. And after every hug she would ask ...

"Do you feel how I feel?" she whispered to me.

I felt this odd weight in my chest. Before I knew that it was a pain-wrapped sob, it flew from my mouth. I quickly slammed my mouth over it and pulled away.

"It's all right," Petty told me.

Centering myself before it got out of hand, I cleared my throat. "It's not. Not yet. But I'm going to make it right. I promise. Okay, Petty? I promise right after this we are going to sit down and ... and we can talk."

But Petty was looking up.

Spinning around, I saw a black plume of smoke wrapping around the block.

"Oh Jesus."

We took off running and rounded the corner in time to see the top floor of the building my parents were supposedly in—a ten floor mini-high rise— completely implode. A giant fireball rolled out into the night air. Below the charred windows, large shadows stomped around its lower floors as gunfire lit up some of those spaces. The angelic legion had arrived.

Whipping out my cellphone, I checked for the room number. Mom hadn't given me one.

As soon as we entered the main hall, people were too busy running out to care that we were going in. There were bodies of the security guards everywhere, some so badly mangled that they seemed made of clay. We didn't have the exact location of James and my parents, but it was easy to follow the carnage. We took three flights of steps up and came out in a hallway with flickering lights. The gunfire was louder than usual up here. I was just about to peek around a corner to check it out, but Petty held me back and leaned out herself. Two bullets entered and exited her head in an instant.

She looked back at me. "How about one more flight up?"

"Noted."

On the next floor, the hallway was littered with bodies. It made it impossible to walk without tripping over all of them. But after a few feet, we ran smack dab into another party trying to go in our direction, and it just so happened to be the folks we were looking for.

My mom tripped over herself wrapping her arms around my neck. Dad had lost his glasses and his clothes were filthy, but he seemed okay. Oswalt and James the Pope were coming up the rear with a few hotel employees.

"We holed ourselves up for as long as we could," James said. "Now it's all about getting everyone out. We need to go."

But, of course, it wasn't going to be that simple.

Spotting us, one of the angels stomped toward our small party. Oswalt fired at it, but all of the bullets bounced right off of its hulking body. At full charge, it crushed one of the hotel workers under its foot, knocked me aside, threw my parents nearly into another room, and just halted at James who held his hand up.

Oswalt called to him, but James replied reassuringly. He then gave me a knowing nod and Petty and I fetched our parents. Just before we hit the down staircase, I turned to tell them to come with us. But what I saw instead was James' body being lifted like he was a small twig. The angel violently jerked his arms and the older man's body nearly folded on itself as blood flew everywhere. Oswalt screamed and fired his gun until it echoed a very deep click-click-click.

I pushed my parents to follow me and we all ran down the staircase. Luckily, the main hallway was clear and we ran out into the street. Cop cars were already on the scene and a few ambulances were parked nearby. Checking on my parents, I noticed that Dad seemed okay but Mom's skin was clammy and her lips were pale. Wrapping her in my arms, I felt her shaking uncontrollably.

"She's in shock. Over here!" Dad took her from me and the four of us walked over to the nearest ambulance and sat her on one of the gurneys. The EMT's loaded her into the back and then went to ask Petty if she was all right.

"Okay. I get it. I look like shit. Keep it movin'."

We were all on edge. Those things were still sulking around, and I had just witnessed the Pope get mutilated by one of them. I looked down at my arm, which couldn't stay still, and I hoped—knowing what was inside of me—that I was just in shock, too. I knew I needed to keep my shit together. But what Petty came to tell me didn't make things any better.

"Just tried calling Donaldson," she said, taking the receiver from her ear. "He ... I can't get in contact with him."

I gritted my teeth. "That doesn't mean anything. He's probably too busy taking Barnem out. Or maybe he's already back at the apartment."

"Move! You need to move this crew out now!" a cop shouted, and out of the sky two of the angels landed on the sidewalk. Seeing that his point was a valid one, we all jumped into the ambulance. The EMT slammed the door shut behind us and the driver peeled away just as the gunfire began to roar. Over the blaring siren, we soon didn't hear anything.

"What is going on?" Dad asked. He was hanging over Mom who was nearly catatonic, but his eyes were clearly on me and Petty.

I thought about lying. I really did. But I was ready to tell them right then and there. That is, until the driver of the ambulance yelled, "We got someone following us."

Even with the ambulance flying down the street, there was a peal of tires as a second car pulled up beside us.

"Oh fuck. He's got a gun!" And suddenly, someone fired on us. I got down as much as possible. Dad tucked both me and Petty underneath him as the ambulance swerved. Just as it seemed to be close to rolling over completely, the driver slammed on the brakes. And that's when we heard the two sounds. The first was the gunfire, but it wasn't aimed at us at all. It was aimed at whatever was making the second noise on the top of the vehicle.

There was sharp seize of metal and suddenly an arm shot in from the ceiling. It grabbed the first EMT right from where he was sitting and pulled him out of the vehicle. After tossing him away, its second lunge flew right toward my face, but Petty leapt in front of me. Those hands, capable of ripping through the outside of the ambulance, palmed my sister's head and crushed it. My mom, awake during this whole thing, went limp. My dad yelled and kicked at the large arm as it dragged her lifeless body to the outside.

The EMT driver fell out of his seat getting the fuck out of there, leaving us at this creature's mercy. But the person firing, after a short lull to reload, was giving us cover. "Let's take Mom out." My dad didn't second guess me. He untied Mom's seatbelt and carried her out onto the street.

Outside, Oswalt was in one of the unmarked cars. His arm lay limp at his side, so he stood there firing with one with hand and loaded the magazines with his clenched teeth. With Mom walking but not entirely there mentally, Dad loaded her into the back. He had to scoot in with her to make sure she was comfortable, and that's when I slammed the door shut behind him. I saw that the angel was too distracted to come after us. Oswalt was shooting at it but he might as well have been tossing those bullets underhanded. It was focused on prying Petty open with its bare hands to get the Shade inside of her.

"Drive!" I slammed my fists on the top of the car to get Oswalt's attention. "Get them out of here!"

"He gave me orders," he replied. "Grey, he saw his death tonight. He wanted to give you a chance. We have a plane ready to leave the city."

"So go! I know what I'm doing."

With a hearty slam of the gas pedal, I saw my dad's worried face speed off. He suddenly became livid, and I could imagine his large hands nearly ripping the car seat out just to try to kill the man driving away from his daughters.

"I know what I'm doing," I kinda said again, but didn't know who was listening. Diving into the ambulance's driver seat, I stared at the steering wheel. I had never driven before in my life. "Okay. I don't know what I'm doing." I turned the key and hit the gas with both of my feet only to plow the ambulance into a parking meter and mailbox. Not knowing, or needing, the brake, I sent the vehicle down the sidewalk, glanced a parked car, managed a big fat unlicensed turn that hit the curb and set us back on our wheels, but then blew out one of the tires. By then, I had reached almost seventy miles per hour and dove out of the open door. The sidewalk ripped into my skin and my clothes, burning both badly, but nothing broke. The ambulance, with Petty and the angel still on it, slammed into a building. It tossed both of them some twenty feet, but the creature landed on its feet.

It already had most of her chest cavity open and there were wing flaps coming from inside. Petty hung motionless, arms and legs dragging on the floor.

I felt defenseless against that thing.

And that's when the whisper started up again.

"*Shame. So shameful.*"

"*Sister being eviscerated right in front of you like an old doll and the only thing you can do is watch.*"

"*Unless you want to kill.*"

"*Let's kill it.*"

"*Let's murder it.*"

Seeing the angel slowly mutilating my kid sister, I had to agree. "Let's murder it."

Inside of me, I felt this sudden rush of adrenaline. I ran right at the angel, set back a fist, and threw it with all of my force. The way my arm cut through the air boomed like an airplane flying overhead. All of the nearby windows shattered instantly as the angel with the mangled head caught the fist within its giant palm. But the force behind it was too much and the whole thing tore right out of its shoulder socket. Somewhere on the twentieth floor of the nearby building, that discarded limb landed.

The second punch I threw landed right on its waist. The blow was so clean that even though its torso was blasted off into a nearby parked car, its legs were still standing there.

Exhausted, I collapsed to the ground. I didn't know if it was going to come back, or if there were more in the vicinity. I just knew that this one was as dead as possible for the time being.

Righting myself, I tapped Petty who was lying face down on the concrete.

"The hospital, Petty. We have to get to the hospital and check on Barnem and Donaldson. C'mon."

She didn't reply.

"Petty. Stop playing. You're not dying here, remember? You can't die. Just … come on. Get up. Mom and Dad are flying out tonight. They're safe. You were right, okay? I couldn't do this by myself. I couldn't."

I tried picking up her arm, but it was dead weight.

I can't tell you how long I stood there. I didn't really feel like I was in my body at all. It felt like I was looking down at something happening to someone else. Complete disconnect. Even when I rolled her over and saw what the angel had done to my sister. She was completely torn in half, the tear running from her stomach to the tip of her chin. Her white eyes were still open.

"Petty? The hospital, Petty? Mom and Dad. Mom and Dad, Petty?"

I remember that I kept talking, I kept saying things. But all of it was disjointed. They were just sounds I was making.

Even when the crow poked its head out of her chest, my hands grabbed it by the neck and wing without me asking them to do so. Only instinct was carrying me through this; was showing me what needed to be done.

I pinned the bird down on the ground with my knees, never looking away from the sister I would never get to see again. The sister I had now lost three times in one lifetime.

 234

In that moment, I felt every pain all at once. And it was so wide, so deep, that it left me unable to see or sense what I was doing. So looking down, at the crow flapping violently in my grasp, I didn't think twice about what I had to do.

I grabbed it by the neck and sank my teeth into its black feathers.

I'M NOT SURE how long it took me to get there. I walked for a long time, semi-directionless at first, at half step most of the time. My leap from the ambulance had torn open blisters on my chest and my neck was scarred up. I put Petty's body on one of the rolling stretchers and kept it with me because there was no way in hell I was going to leave her there.

So I walked all the way to the hospital, shambled all the way there, I should say. I walked right in the middle of the street as only a few people were driving. With all the shit going down, the city had become a ghost town. You would expect that thousands of New Yorkers would be fighting and clawing to get out of the city, but I barely caught a few people even running fast. I guess it made sense, you know? Where are you going to run when the world is ending?

The automatic doors to the hospital didn't work. A man's corpse was caught between that and the wall, causing the constant thump of the actual door nudging up against his chest. I took the side door.

There were no angels around, but the entire place had been torn apart. There was no one alive. Doctors, nurses, patients, janitors—all of them were strewn about like garbage.

With Barnem's room on the fourth floor, I pressed the button for the elevator. The door slid open right away, even though there wasn't a car in it yet. And then like a comet, the whole fiery thing flew passed and exploded on the floor below. In a daze, I blinked at it and decided to take the stairs.

Heaving Petty's body up and climbing those stairs all on piggyback was nothing I'll ever recommend doing in your life, and I can't even explain how I was able to do it. I collapsed on floor three and stayed down for maybe five or ten minutes before continuing my journey.

Opening the door, I saw a man's body sitting up against the wall with his head down, chin buried into his chest, and a round halo of blood outlining the area he had been impaled to. Seeing Donaldson's lifeless body like this made me grow even more numb. Part of me had expected to find this, to come against my worst fears, but not so soon. I walked passed him and made my way to Barnem's room.

The entire place was in ruins, more so than any other place in the hospital. The whole right side of the room was missing and I found myself staring out at a city that was no burning in the night air. Scores of angels flying in rigid formations floated around the skyscrapers. Whoever had come to purge this hospital obviously had this room as its main target. And something told me that this wasn't the work of any angel.

I had to step all the way to the back of the room to see this because it was obstructed by a bed turned on its side. But it was there: my worst fears were confirmed.

Barnem, the only being capable of slaying the Beast, was lying on his stomach in pool of his own blood. The blood was easy to trace—the body was missing its head entirely. I choked back the bile and stumbled backward. But more than this, it seemed that he had one last thing to tell me, because at the end of his two bloodstained fingers, the Seraph had managed to write one single letter out on the floor.

D.

"Yo."

His voice blew the muteness right out of my body as a cold jet flushed through my skin. Standing in the doorway, my roommate watched me turn around slowly.

Even though I was scared half to death, I tried to swallow my panic as D strode into the space. His face and eyes, the way he stepped both within view but with a perfect space between us, told me that he was suspicious. He was on high alert and wasn't going to be taken by surprise. Not by me and not by anyone else in the world now that he had taken care of Barnem. I knew that I needed to tell him something before he

237

ended my life. I needed to stall, for some reason. Any reason. This was all proof that D had been just biding his time to tear the last Shade out of me, and now he had come to collect.

I lay Petty down and stood over her.

"What happened to her?" he asked.

I felt sick. "One of the angels."

He didn't respond. I could barely make out his face in the shadow. His hands were conveniently tucked in his crimson hoodie. Then he asked, "The Shade I put in her?"

"I have it."

"You *have* it?" D took a step closer. "I saw your parents."

My arm shook. "You what?"

"Getting on a plane. Getting out of here."

"What did you do?"

"Nothing."

"What did you do?"

"I told you. Nothing." He slowly pulled out one of his hands. "I can take you to them, though."

This enraged me. Giving no fucks, I slapped his hand away and stepped so forcefully forward so that we bumped chests. Hearing that he had been anywhere near my parents flipped my "Flight" to an almost permanent "Fight".

"C'mon. I'll take you to them."

Everything in my body was telling me to run as hard and far away as possible, but I stood my ground staring into D's black eyes. I never noticed, but there seemed to be violet clouds churning in the center. Looking into them was like staring into an alien planet.

"Barnem is dead—"

"Good riddance."

"So I guess the only ones left are just you and me. What are you going to do now?"

A black aura, as thick as smoke, billowed out of the Shade and started to fill the space around me. I backed away as the wind bursting out of him pushed me back and pressed me against the farthest wall.

D's body began to change. His horns spiked five feet into the air. His

238

legs curved back and grew black thorns. Veined wings shot out of his back. With eyes glowing a deep purple, he pointed a black claw at me and growled, "You know what has to happen now, Grey? The end of the line. And I'm not going to make it painless."

Something dark awoke inside of me as well. I went blind in my right eye. It was like a pen had burst and ink was streaming down the eyeball until my vision was completely gone on that side.

And the whisper came.

"It's either you or him now, Grey."

"Rip his face off!"

"Bite off his arm. His leg."

"Punch his head clean off."

"Now's your chance."

"End it."

"End it."

"Grey!" D's roar sounded like an explosion. My fist felt heavy and I glanced over and saw black tendrils wrapped around my knuckles. The shadow was thick like armor, yet I could still bend and flex the joint. Looking at the form D had taken—an eleven-foot goliath—I knew that I was going to die. But this hadn't stopped me when Gaffrey Palls beat me bloody. Or when Mason's parrot swallowed me. Or any of the other deaths I was booked for the last couple of months had been cancelled.

It took everything to will my legs to move. It was the hardest thing I've ever done. But I did. And the next step came easier. And the next.

Soon as I was jogging.

Soon I was running at full speed.

Quickly, I dashed across the broken room and found myself right on that hulking beast as D breathed fire. His wingspan was jutting out into the other rooms and the hallway. My fist came crashing down around its flaming skull with such a force that the most of the floor buckled under our feet. My entire shoulder slipped out of the socket right on contact.

D's head snapped back from the force but it didn't seem enough. He wasn't dead. He wasn't beaten. But at least he knew that I had the last word.

This is what I was thinking as suddenly, D's massive body dissipated into black wisps of smoke, and the male body that I knew hit the floor like a sack of wet garbage. The punch sent him sliding for about ten feet, tearing up the floor tiles, before coming to a hearty crash in the hallway.

Sliding my shoulder back in place, I got to my feet, leapt over the broken wood, straddled D's splayed body, and raised my fist to cave in his face.

But I stopped.

Out of my left eye, through my hazy vision and the only good eye I could see through, I saw two things that stopped me cold. One was that D was actually afraid of me. And the second, and probably most shocking, was that he was crying.

"*Finish it,*" commanded the whisper.

"*Finnnish iiit!*"

Hesitating for just a moment gave the demon the opening to grab my wrist. Back on the offensive, I tried to wrench him loose and land the killing blow. But instead of resisting, D tried to drive my fist down on purpose.

"Do it!" he screamed. "Do it already. Kill me. Just know that I went down fighting. Fighting for what I believe."

"Um ..."

Sensing the loss of my resolve, he said, "What? This is what you wanted, isn't it? This is what all of this is for, right?"

"Uh ..."

"What the hell is wrong with you, Grey?"

"What's wrong with *me*? That's my line," I shouted back. "You can't take my line."

"It's not your line. You're the one trying to kill me."

"What?" I fell back onto my ass. "This isn't making sense. You're the one trying to kill me."

"Why would I do that? You've already been through some shit already. Like ... like Petty."

I could tell just by the way he looked at my sister's body from where we were lying that he was highly emotional about the whole thing.

"Wait! So if you weren't trying to kill me, then what was with that uber demon transformation you just whipped out?"

D wiped the tears from his face. "I was trying to protect myself from the power hungry monster you've become."

"Oh! Oh! That's rich coming from the demon bent on global domination."

"I am n— No, wait. I am on paper. Okay. I am. But ... just not now. None of this, Grey None of this shit was me."

And for some reason, maybe it was the last of my sanity ebbing away, but I believed him. "You didn't do this. So ... so who killed Barnem? And Donaldson?"

"Jeff?" This took the Shade completely by surprise. He clenched his chest and slumped over on his side. "Jeff! Someone ... Jeff is dead?"

So much of this was hard for me to process. D was actually mourning Donaldson? Like actual feelings? Like more than me.

After a few seconds, he sat up. "You! You thought I killed him?"

"I—"

"Why would I kill Jeff? The guy was cool. Way cooler than you, Ms. 'Seek and Destroy Every Demon Hunter'. Don't think I didn't know what you and that Seraph were planning. Going to fatten me up and leave me last."

I looked back at the room. "So is that why you killed Barnem?"

"I did not kill Barnem!"

"But you said—"

"I said 'Good riddance' because the man was a pain in my ass. God! Stop saying I killed people that I didn't kill."

The building was suddenly struck by something that sounded like a mortar blast. D and I looked at each other as four and then five more explosions rocked the hospital.

"Angels. We gotta go, Grey."

"But wait," I said as he took my wrist and pulled me down the hall. "You said you saw my parents. Is that true?"

"I did. Thought you were there. Saw the kid helping your parents board a plane and he told me that's where you were headed. Hold on." Leaving behind the bodies of my sister, my upstairs neighbor, and the only guy I could call a friend, D dragged me by my neck through the nearest window and took flight with me across the Queens rooftops.

FLYING FROM WHAT was left of the hospital room allowed me to see how much of New York had been destroyed. There were large fires burning everywhere, sending thick plumes of black smoke into the air. I saw insects larger than horses respecting traffic lights as they scuttled about the streets. I saw purple storm clouds filled with locusts dump millions of the little critters on DUMBO. I saw angels in full armor patrolling the streets. It felt like I was living a nightmare.

I've never flown before, so D whisking me across the city clasping nothing but my wrists as my legs just dangled above streets and rooftops made for a rough trip. It didn't help that my pilot seemed to lose control ever so often.

"You can put me down now!"

My roommate's breathing became labored and once or twice, when he looked down to see if I was all right, his eyes rolled to the back of his head as if he were slipping out of consciousness.

"D!"

"I'm up," he groaned, shaking his head and adjusting his flight pattern. "You just kinda clocked me a bit … hard …"

We suddenly dropped into a sharp nosedive. In the chaos, I couldn't tell which way was up, but even as he was partially unconscious, D wrapped me up in his arms as we managed a sloppy barrel roll and burst through the side wall of a building. The force dumped me into the rubble of a living room and sling-shotted D head-first into a kitchen partition, bounced him off the ceiling, and halfway through the back wall. He let out one muffled "Ow" as the fridge tipped over on him.

"Made it," I heard him say as he slumped over.

My ears ringing and left cheek cut open, I dragged myself to my feet. It took me a few seconds to realize where D had "landed" us. The floor on the entire left side of the apartment was slanted due to it falling into the lower floor. Water was cascading down from the apartment above and I could still smell smoke from something burning nearby. My front door was nothing but a pile of splinters. The wall facing the street was completely missing and open to the crimson night sky.

My home. This was my home.

I wiped the blood with my sleeve and sat in the rubble. Holding my aching arm, I picked up an old picture frame that used to house a picture. The frame was broken and the picture itself was missing. Everything in this place was just dust and shrapnel now. Just lost.

"This is what I was fighting for," I mumbled to myself. "I did this all to save the home I grew up in and … it's all gone now."

The neighborhood was in worse shape, if you can believe that. Most of the streetlights were out, but that didn't matter—there was only wreckage to look at. The night sky was now completely red, giving the world an unnatural, sinister glow. The building was abandoned, no one was on the street, and most of the city was as silent as a corpse, minus a few police sirens wailing in the distance. Burly's across the street was on fire.

I tried remembering everything about my life in that space. I was a real person with real memories. Not all of them were great, sure, but I made sure to tell myself that they were at least mine. Regardless of what was inside of me at the time, I had lived my life with it gnawing away at my insides and managed not to self-destruct. Not to give into feeling like every day I was drowning a little bit. This was all in hindsight, I knew, but I needed it. I needed to know that part of me was still in control. Even after everything. Even after it all.

My cell phone was gone and my laptop was probably swallowed up by the debris. I wanted at least a little insight into what the world was thinking about the apocalypse I had started. The TV was on its side with a cracked screen, but it turned on when I pressed it.

The first thing to come on was the finale of *The Stud*. In it, Chud had

243

lined up the last three remaining women. Each one stood by an aisle with a cloth draped over it. The sound was out and it was hard to see through the cracked glass, but one by one, the ladies revealed large, blown-up ultrasounds of their uteruses as Chad first took notes and then held up a card with a one to ten rating on it. The woman who scored the eight acted as if she had just won a Nobel prize.

Every channel was like this; everyone on its regularly scheduled programming. The world was ending and people didn't seem to care. The newscasters were generally reporting things as if Armageddon was just another Tuesday. Hell, even the Powerball numbers were read.

I thought about my parents. I was hoping they were safe and out of the city by now, but I couldn't be sure. Oswalt didn't owe me anything, but if the short amount of time we spent in each other's space was any indication to his character, he was loyal to James. Knowing that I may never see them again hurt so much that I felt like my chest was about to explode. And then I used this. I used this pain to rip everything out of me.

Petty.

Donaldson.

It all came spilling out of me. And I sat there on all fours, rocking slowly, as the grief poured out of me. Like something had ruptured inside of me and there was no way of putting it back. I sat there until I had no more. Until I felt empty.

When all of it had poured out of me, D was sitting nearby, his back up against a wall. There was a heavy crack in his skin around his forehead and a thread of black blood poured down his neck.

"Why me?" I asked softly. D responded with a slow shake of his head, but I wasn't having it. "Why me!" I yelled again.

"I don't have that answer."

This both infuriated me and made me want to keel over and start crying again. "How long?"

D's face told me that answer already. "I don't know, Grey. You're asking the wrong person. The night Palls came in here, the night this whole mess got set into motion, was the first night we met."

This answer wasn't good enough. I stood to my feet even though I felt as if my legs were lashed to stilts. "I had this thing inside of me the entire time, so why didn't I turn out like the rest?"

D looked over the broken wall overlooking my neighborhood. "I'm not the one to ask."

Sitting there, right in front of us on a jutting metal beam, was a crow. It was a slim, curved bird with a ruffled feathers. Its black beak had silver at the very tips and was roughly the size of a greyhound. The number 7 was imprinted into its eyes.

I dragged myself to stand in front of it. When I was just a few feet away, I asked, "Are you proud of yourself?"

The Shade blinked, but remained silent.

Looking passed it—at a New York being swallowed by fire and destruction—I laughed. "You know, I thought my life sucked before this. I thought, nothing can be worse. I mean, just a few months ago, before all of this mess started, I just would've rather stayed indoors. I didn't need friends. I didn't need anybody really, and I kind of chalked it up to the luck of the draw. Just what I was stuck with, randomly, out of the blue. 'Little Mental Mandy' would be something I lived with to the end of my life. And I sort of came to peace with that, in my own way.

"But then that wasn't all true, was it? I did have a choice. This entire time, I had a choice. Except, you never let me see it. You blocked it out of my brain, somehow, I don't know. I don't know if that is even possible. But it was you. You, the entire time. Buried in my bones and skin. You never got to me like all the other people because they had never known what it was like to be trapped inside your own body. But I did. And I'm not saying that you recognized that, and that we had some connection, but I like to think that you tortured me throughout the years and then found yourself a prisoner." I laughed. I actually laughed even though tears were rolling down my face. "You were in your own little hell inside of me, weren't you? That would be really fucking fitting."

The Shade never took its eyes off of me. D didn't say a word.

I wiped my face again. "I don't know what I was expecting talking to you right now. I just figured that for once, I should. That like everything I've been up against in my life, I should acknowledge that you even exist before I promise myself never to be swayed by your whispering, by your influence, again. I've beaten you already. I do it every single day I wake up. And I'll keep beating you until there's nothing left of me which, co-incidentally, might be a few minutes from now. I don't know. That's all I want to say, I guess."

Just as I turned away, the Shade spoke. It didn't whisper to me this time. Instead, it had a feminine voice. "You want a medal? On the backs of everyone who has died? On the billions who will die? On the idea that when you take your last breath and you will bite the big one, Amanda Grey, you will serve out the rest of your afterlife in hell until kingdom come? You're satisfied with that?"

"As long as I choose it."

The Shade flapped its wings twice and landed on the broken curvature of the farthest wall. "I can read your mind. I've been in there and let me tell you, it hasn't been pretty."

"If you're really in my head," I shouted, "then you know what I'm willing to do to find out the truth. So are you out here for a pep-talk or are you going to tell me what I need to know?"

D stood up holding his head, and my Shade nearly began beating it wings aggressively at him. "Don't trust it."

"Uh. Pot meet kettle," I groaned. "Just, one of you, tell me what the hell is going on."

D crossed his arms. "We Shades are shreds of something larger, some-thing darker. We've been forming over the recent millennia. But amongst us, there is more at stake. We are also at war with each other. Every time we form, our wills are at odds. This means that when one Shade absorbs another, they are forced to serve the dominant drive. This is as they are written in the prophesies called 'The Subjugation of Wills'."

Rubbing my temples from the numbness forming behind them, I re-plied, "I've never heard of that prophecy."

"They are written of Shades, so they are prophecies scribed in hell," D responded.

"Paged in Lucifer's bible, a book bound in flesh," the Shade added.

"Scrawled in the blood of sinners."

"Penned with the bones of angels."

"These scrolls sit in the chamber of the Dark Lord himself in the lowest, coldest part of hell."

And then D added, "I heard they were looking into e-book reprints."

"Ooo," the crow replied. "It's a good market for it."

"Okay!" I yelled. "Can either of you please tell me what this struggle, this 'Subjugation of Wills' thing, has to do with me?"

My Shade sighed. "She's even more annoying on the outside. It means that our un-holy war would bring pain and darkness to your world. There will be famine and disease and lines twice as long at the DMV. But something isn't right. This is too soon. There is a secret hand dealing these cards."

"Someone or something is forcing all of this to happen, and they're letting it all come down on your head," D explained. "Only question is why?"

My Shade spread her wings out. "You two don't need me here. I'm leaving."

This was in no way what I was expecting. My Shade had some serious confidence issues.

"Hey."

"What?"

I walked over and stood staring at it. It turned its head slightly at me. "I'm kind of stuck right now," I told her. "Because on one hand, I want to pet you. And on the other, I want to punch you so hard that your beak flies off."

The crow stood glaring at me. "I know what's behind that threat, Grey. I also know that there's a part of you that wants to curl up into a little ball and wait this whole thing out. There's a part of you that wants to track down your parents and just run and run and run. Makes more sense, doesn't it. These people, this city, has never done a thing for you. And in the long run, what does it matter? You're going to hell anyway."

When I laughed as a response, it asked, "What is it, Grey?"

"Nothing. It's just funny hearing that voice on the outside for once."

The Shade rolled its two 7's and a tear formed in its chest. The entire

247

bird flipped itself inside out and fell into a black puddle. Twitching, the dark pool crept along the ground and climbed into my shadow on the ground where it slowly dissolved.

"D. I saw you meeting with the other Shades. Where was that?"

Remembering this seemed to get D seriously flustered. "Yeah. You want to tell me how you managed to find yourself in the outer cusp of hell? That place is kind of waiting area for the damned. Used to be called the 'Hotel California' but now it's just a high-end Asian fusion coffee house/bed and breakfast. Things are changing all over the place. What were you doing there?"

"Oh nothing. I just fell from a building." D face palmed, but then quickly screamed as he touched his skull. "You all right?"

D winced again. "Oh nothing. Just a fractured skull."

We sat there for a few minutes without saying a word. I didn't want to admit it, but part of it was just enjoying his company. I wondered if in his own way, he was doing the same.

"I'm sorry about Petty."

I gave him a silent nod. "She's going to hell, isn't she?"

"We can't keep dwelling on this. What did you do with the Shade I imprisoned in her body?" Reading my body language, his eyes went wide. "Grey?"

"I wasn't going to leave it there. So I *sorta kinda* ... ate it?"

"You— No wonder you nearly split my head open!" D exclaimed. "Okay, well. At least it's contained. That means we have all seven Shades under control."

I walked right up to him and shoved him backward. "No! No! You don't get to talk like that. What are you planning? If you're some ancient evil, why are you helping? If you weren't going to eat me, then why have you been looking out for me this entire time?"

D threw his hands up. "Hey. I never said that I didn't initially intend to eat you. I totally did, okay? It's just that I ..."

A chill ran through my body. "You what?"

"I ... my entire existence, I've always been stepped on. I've never been the Shade of the greatest will. I've always been the bottom. But then, you gave me a chance. And I saw that you had been going through the same thing, in your own sloppy human kind of way. I'm going to beat these Shades and become king someday, and you'd better believe that when that day does come, my kingdom will bring a plague of horror and torment to any and all of your kind. But like, for now, I think I need an *Advil*."

I sighed and limped over to what was left of my kitchen cupboards. My mom kept a safety bag for emergencies. After a minute of rummaging through it, I found the right container and tossed the entire bottle over. D flicked it open with one finger and downed six.

"What's the plan?"

He wiped his mouth. "We need to flush out the person responsible. Something tells me that whoever this person is, they are watching our every move. Maybe not right now, but they've been watching from the very beginning."

Outside, thin flakes began to fall from the sky, but it wasn't snow. I held my hand out and a gray flake landed in my palm. It was raining ash. "I think we can use that to our advantage. I have two Shades and you have five. We might as well use them, too."

D sighed. "I don't like the sound of this. Please don't say 'I have a plan and it's just crazy enough to work'."

I smiled. "Oh god, no. We'll both probably die pretty painful deaths. But then again, what do we have to lose? The world can only end once."

"AND THAT'S IT," I said, leaning back in the wooden seat.

The priest on the other side of the screen didn't move or respond. He simply sat there, just a static silhouette buffering.

My throat was raw and dry after talking for so long. I'm not even sure how long it had taken me to get from beginning to end. But I did. Every piece, every facet. Donaldson, Petty, my parents, Lou, the Burley burger burger, scythe HDMI ports, the Smilie Cult, Mason, Gary, Cain, the Pope, my roach neighbors, the Beholders, warrior angels, Franklin the plant, Gaffrey fucking Palls, pet sacrifice, Bag Boy/Man, the Lie bra, me in a dress, "Make New York Nice Again", Oswalt, Hotel California (under new management), ramen noodle delicacies, the stars falling, Mordor nachos, angels who play harps, an actual "puppet politician", and Craigslist.

"I'm …" The priest trailed off. The darkness in the confessional booth smelled like cheap carpet and old books. "This was quite the story."

"Right. So," I rubbed my palms together, "how does this absolving thing work? Is it still twenty Hail Marys or is there a prayer that consolidates it all?"

"I'm …" The priest kept pulling on his collar and clearing his throat. "Can you wait? Right here. Can you wait right here?"

And then he bolted out of the confessional.

Sighing, I let my head drop back, allowing it to thud up against the wood of the backrest. Working my way through everything and trying to explain in detail was at first my way of getting some therapy out of this, and while I was hoarse, I did feel better. Lighter. James had a point—this confession thing was a greatly needed baggage drop-off site for the terminally stressed.

However, somewhere in between, and I can't point to one place in particular, retelling my entire story from the beginning, had made me question a few things. Maybe I had been too close to the blood and overall mayhem to fully process these things, perhaps I was too busy trying to stay alive while Fate was having a gay old time bashing me over the head for two months. But things had started standing out to me. Odd things. Peculiars. And though I saw many faces peering back at me in the darkness, one seemed to come up every single time.

At first, I laughed. After everything, I figured that's where I should start—just straight up laughing at the whole thing. I guess that the identity of the person who ruined my entire life (minus the reasoning behind it all) had been a bit too obvious, and that was probably why I didn't notice it sooner. If anything, I told myself that if there was any big lesson, any massive take away from the whole mess I had found myself in was that you can worry about a thousand horrible events happening in your life—a loose AC falling on your head, a faulty traffic light when you're already in the middle of a walkway—but it's the thing that'd closest to you that's really in line to slit your throat.

I sat in that booth for over ten minutes, half waiting, half dozing. When the priest didn't come back, I dragged my ass out of the confessional.

As I approached the front of the Saint Patrick's Cathedral, passing row after row of empty pews, my footsteps echoing throughout the empty church, I reminded myself that I saw this coming. Oh yeah. I knew he would show up. From the moment I figured out that everything, every bit of suffering I'd been subjected to, was plotted out, executed, and orchestrated by someone's twisted wet dream to frame me for the apocalypse. I was banking on him showing up, actually. After all I went through, every life I was blamed for uprooting— the destruction of homes, the city-wide catastrophes—I knew, I just knew that the scumbag who had set me up from the very beginning couldn't help but show his smiling face, right there, at the very end.

And there he was, waiting for me in the front row as I got out of the confessional. I didn't have to ask about the whereabouts of the priest who was supposed to be listening to me the entire time. Each row I passed as I walked up to the front of Saint Patrick's Cathedral was decorated with one or two of his limbs, organs, and/or other assorted body parts. I was so numb to it all that I walked passed each one without feeling in my skin, let alone any connection to the human carnage. The last pew on the right held his head: eyes wide open, mouth now frozen in mid-scream. I stopped to stare at it, realizing that I had spent hours in that confessional and had never seen this man's face before.

I slid into the pew next to the cause of my misery but said nothing to him. Instead, I looked up at the church altar. Behind it, the bold image of a crucified Christ gazed down on me. I paid special attention to his eyes.

"He looks sadder than usual," I said aloud.

Barnem clicked his tongue. "Melodramatic. He only seems that way to you, Grey. Because you don't understand."

Angrily, I turned to face him. "Then make me."

But this only made Barnem laugh. He looked nothing like I had last seen him. Sure he was dead the last time, impaled to a wall like an angelic shish-kabob. Now he wore a bulky iron chest plate, one that resembled the garb of the angels laying siege to New York City, but his was slightly more decorated as it sported a gold crest which moved and shifted around the gray metal, sometimes creeping over his shoulder as a lion, other times blossoming on his chest like a ball of flame. Barnem finished the ensemble with iron gauntlets over his hands, but also acid washed jeans and his thin arms completely bare. With his hair shaved off at the sides, and the rest of it propped up into an obnoxious mohawk, he looked like a lunatic cosplaying as an intensely deranged psychopath.

As ridiculous as Barnem looked, each finger on his gauntlet was stained with blood. That's when I realized that he had used his hands to create the priest's pieces.

The Seraph huffed at me. "Make you understand what, Grey? You barely understand what existence is. You barely know anything outside of yourself."

I knew I had to keep him talking. At least for a little while longer.

"Humor me," I said.

"All right. How's this for an existence? How about having to eat to keep up this mortal body? Hmm? It's frustrating. *And* gross, by the way. Mashing, crunching, gnashing. Balling gobs of meat and bread with saliva. All the time. That's all your damn kind ever does."

"Yeah, well—"

I acted like I was stretching, but I managed to draw the knife off of my waist and thrust it at Barnem's throat. But the Seraphim caught the tip just inches from his larynx with only two fingers and continued talking.

"Consume and repeat. And when they aren't eating, they are talking about eating. Or taking photos of what other people should be eating. It is *the* worst, I really need you to understand. The absolute worst. Framing my life with food."

There was a shattering of stained glass around us and suddenly we weren't alone. Twenty angels surrounded us, each fashioned in ash-colored armor. Up close, I could see that their skin resembled oddly shaped wax; misshapen heads without faces beneath their metal coifs. Their wings were tucked behind their backs and their weapons—swords, shields, and maces—stood at the ready.

"Funny you're so talkative, Barnem. I vaguely remember you saying that you hated rants. Was that a lie, too?" I asked, not giving a damn about my circumstance. I tried pushing the blade closer to his neck but found it impossible.

He sighed. "Is that what you think I did? You think I lied to you? No, no, no, Grey. No, no. To claim that I 'lied' to you in any way would make you important. No I *denied* you the truth. Huge difference. Immense. I denied you the truth because you weren't worthy of it. That's all. Would you bother wasting your time explaining string theory to a flake of dandruff?"

I set both hands on the knife and tried my best to shove it into his damn neck, even got up for leverage. Even leaned into it. Nothing.

"Done?" Barnem asked.

"Totally," I replied, pulling the knife away and giving it to him.

Taking the weapon, Barnem flicked it over his head and it clattered somewhere in the back of the church. He tapped the seat for me to sit.

I did and he stretched his arms out on the backrest like we were on a date.

"Aw, c'mon," he said coyly. "You and me, Grey. We've been through a helluva lot."

"Because of you," I muttered, trying to rub feeling back into my skin. "All of it."

"Remember when we first spoke about this, Grey? The first time you asked me? I told you, didn't I, what my role was? What I was put on your stupid little earth to do? I am *the* herald. *The* angel whose sole job is to end your world. Don't hate me for doing my job, okay? Take that shit up with management."

I laughed. "Is that it? Really, Barnem? All of the pain and suffering, the innocent lives, framing me for ending the world, and you justify it with a really shitty version of 'Don't hate the player, hate the game'?"

Barnem searched his memory for the right word, flicked up air quotes, and replied, "Holla."

I furrowed my brows as if in thought. "I wonder."

"Please don't do that."

"No, I wonder, Barnem. How much of your 'job' was Gaffrey Palls?"

The angel's face puckered. "Dunno what you're getting at."

"You don't? This whole thing started with a friggin' demon-filled piñata visiting me in my home while an angel, who just so happens to be its vanquisher, also just so happens to be living upstairs."

"So?" Barnem said indignantly and then threw his armored hands up. Then he added, "All right. Okay! So I might have jumped the gun with the whole 'Day of Reckoning' thing. Maybe a tad on the early side. But you … you of all people know how much of a joke your race is. Whoa. *Was.* Past tense at this point, I guess."

"You 'jumped the gun'?"

"And why does any of it matter? Today. Ten years from now. Ten billion." He clapped his hands together. "Your whole existence was headed in the shitter anyway. So what if I nudged the gas pedal a bit?"

I swung a nasty right which connected flush against the Seraph's face. He didn't catch or dodge it. He wanted me to hit him. The angels took a step toward me, but Barnem waved them off with two fingers. The blow bruised instantly, a small trickle of blood even crept out of his mouth. But otherwise, all my (well-deserved) sucker punch accomplished was propping the Seraph's head back to give him a view of the ceiling. On the other end, I'd broken my hand.

Barnem blinked. "You're testament to your kind, Amanda Grey. No matter how old you seem to live, you still wield power like children. Given the ability to build marvels, and instead you engineer double-sided dildos that sing 'Auld Lang Syne'. You're capable of crafting sonnets, or laws that defeat social injustices, but instead dedicate your language skills, time, and energy into typing your completely worthless opinions in the little space beneath cat videos. You should be thanking me. Yeah, you should be on your knees singing my fucking praise. Do you know what it's called when a higher life form dispenses the kind of justice I'm responsible for?"

I gritted my teeth. "Murder."

Barnem's head remained pointing up at the ceiling, only his brown eyes slid down to stare into me. "Mercy."

The seraph stood up from his seat and walked up on stage while the angels parted to give him space. Taking a deep breath, he looked around. "I'm going to be honest, and this may seem crazy to hear, but … churches give me the creeps." He planted both of his hands flat on the white clothed altar. "Just so big and hollow. An empty house. It's supposed to make you feel small and well … mission accomplished!" he yelled and two wings burst from his back. His voice echoed throughout the entire place, trailed, then grew silent as his wings disappeared again. "You have no idea how long I've waited for this."

"You have no idea how much I don't care," I shot back. "You're an angel, Barnem. You're supposed to be one of the good guys."

"Oh, but I am. I am the good guy. A goddamn hero. You know I watched you for a long time. A really long time, in fact. And I guessed, considering how shitty your life was, day in and day out, that you would actually see that. That you would actually side with me in all of this. Isn't that crazy? I mean, here I thought that you were as fed up and over this …

this uselessness of an existence. But not you. Not that Amanda Grey. She's a fighter, to the bitter fucking end, too. You fight, endlessly. You throw your fists at anything in your way."

"You bet," I replied. "It makes me that much adorable."

Barnem looked at me half eyed as the image of the gold flames on his chest crept back and forth. "Even now, it freaking escapes me. You, of all people, Grey. I thought you would really, truly understand how being forced to be around *these* people was a goddamn chore. And unfair! It's unfair to us, Grey. It's unfair that we have to watch their shows and listen to their music and eat their food and smile, when all we want to do is spit that shit out and say 'No. I'm not and will never be a part of you'. They push us aside. They call us difficult, pariahs, when in reality *we* are the normal ones. Us! We speak our minds. We think without being clouded and swayed by others. We fucking rock compared to their crappy little timeline viewing existences and somehow we are the weirdos? We are? Have you seen what they do for entertainment? Have you met the people they elect into office?"

"So the world is fucked up?" I said, standing to my feet. "We should be building one big couch that can be seen from space for every person who can use the therapy, not trying to light them on fire. You're attempting to justify genocide!"

"I'm trying to serve my purpose!" Barnem boomed. Running his hand through his mohawk, he then walked over to his sword and wrenched it from the ground. The blue metal seemed to sing. "I spent so long chasing the Shades, Grey. So long. But then I realized that I didn't need to work so hard. That's when I met Gaffrey Palls. And then it all clicked. My purpose. Palls did the heavy lifting and all I had to do was to … aim him, point the freak in the right direction." He started clapping. "And Palls was onto his last demon, the final piece, when you two met. And then you killed him."

Remembering that man's face brought a lump to my throat. I was seething. "So Palls was working for you?"

"Everybody was working for me. Even you in the end, Grey. Tell me, did that runt of a demon die a horrible death? How does it feel to be so black and powerful?"

"I thought you were dead."

He chuckled. "Oh, yeah. Well it's easy to kill someone and pop their head off like fresh fruit." He showed off his fingers. "But, even if I were to die, Grey, I'm an angel. My place is right here. Can't go back to Heaven. And I'm totally too holy for hell."

This made me have a shred of hope. Against my fears, I managed to stand up. "You staged it. Made me think you died just to pit us against each other."

"And you did. It took some time, you know. I had to kill a few people in the process. That Hill woman, for instance. I figured killing her and scraping your name in her forehead would be … I dunno, motivation. And it kind of worked. Almost got yourself killed in the process, but you got the job done. Bra-vo." Barnem dragged the white cloth off of the altar and began wiping his bloody hands on it. When he was done, he balled it up and threw it aside. "You have one more role to play, Grey. I hope your roommate died a horrible, screaming death. I can sense his darkness inside of you. It's gushing out. These guys, well, they're here to kill you. They're looking to kill anything touched by the Beast, whatever is inside of you now. I'm going to sick them on you so that I can see, for myself, if you really have the darkness. You will lose control. And then, I will slay you myself."

I stood up. The angels all took a step toward me but I didn't flinch, instead saying angrily, "Sorry to break it to you, Barnem, but I'm not going to lose control. D's will was strong enough to control it. I can control it now, too. What is it called again? The 'Subjugation of Wills'."

"Subjugation of Wills, eh?" Barnem drew into his poker face. "I blame you, up there," he yelled to someone behind me. "That's always been your problem, you know? You had one job: get her to fight the other Shade. But instead you took your time. If you weren't on my side already, I would have called you out on trying to undermine me."

I turned back to see that Cain was sitting on top of the confessional I had climbed out of, her scythe sitting blissfully on her lap.

"Come off it, Barnem. I'm only here for one reason and one reason alone. My job opportunities soar as long as the age of man ends tonight."

Then, when she spotted me, she twiddled her fingers and said, "Hey there, beautiful!"

"You? You helped this guy end the world for a chance to network a new job? Have you not heard of the Internet?"

Cain laughed. "I have a very specific skillset, Grey, one that only increases in value once the big party gets underway. Like do you know that the first part involves a culling? I mean absolute. A freaking fire sale on murders." As if realizing something for the first time, she sighed dramatically. "Oh man. If the Plague was like the Coachella of mass genocide, this is going to be an event. Massive!"

I was too busy paying attention to Cain that I missed one of the warrior angels making their move. It dove at me and drove its large sword right down on my head. I thought I dodged in time, but the full weight connected, and just like trying to head-butt a two story house, the sword drove my entire head into the ground.

It should have beheaded me, but instead I balanced the edge of the blade on my shoulders as I stood back on my feet. The angels all took a step back in shock. Only Barnem clapped his hands in amusement.

"That didn't hurt," I said aloud. "But what do I do now?"

"Just let loose," my Shade hissed. *"Show them what happens when you screw with prophecy."*

Feeling the complete power of the Shades inside of me was pretty much what I thought it would feel like to French kiss a wall socket, or dry humping an electric chair just as someone flips the switch. Tossing the sword aside, I landed one solid punch to the angel's abdomen. What's the insides of a warrior angel look like, you might be asking? Feathers and purple goo—pounds of it flew everywhere. The other angels were on me immediately, but this time, I was ready. One swung its ax for my face. Instead of ducking, I leaned forward, caught the massive blade with my teeth, and shattered it. There was nothing pretty about the way I attacked each one, but every punch and kick was accompanied by a black cloak of ash and shadow that extended out of my skin almost twenty feet. I tore one's wings off. Punted one through the high ceiling. This was the most power I had ever felt in my life and I was reveling in it.

Suddenly, Barnem kneed me in the face and pinned me to the ground, pointing his holy sword's tip right in between my eyes. My strength was immediately gone, the fire within me snuffed out when he touched me. As the only angel capable of slaying the Beast, I knew that the Seraph was loving every moment of this.

"Look at you, Grey! Look. At. You!" he shouted. "Glorious. This darkness. It's even greater than Palls when I first met him. Even darker than his black soul."

Unable to move, I had to play my trump card and pray for the best.

"You know, Barnem," I told him as I attempted to slide from under his weight. "You know that I told you back when Petty died that you owed me something. Whaddaya say you pay up? I already got one punch in."

"Ha!" This was catnip for the egotistical Seraph and I knew that he couldn't resist. In his mind, I was already beat. "You really are something, Grey. Like really. It's a shame you and the Beast got so close, now you have to go to hell because your soul is tainted. Would like to say that I'm going to miss you, but … that's bullshit. But that's really good, Grey. So good. I'm … You know what?" Smiling, he slid his arms behind his back. "Make this good. Pretend like this is the last thing you'll ever do in your life because—"

Somewhere outside, a large explosion filled the air. It sounded like a building toppling over.

Barnem smiled. "Well, yeah. I guess it will be the last thing. C'mon, Grey. Time to finally do something with that pathetic life of yours. Last licks."

The Seraph was too busy jawing to see me lift my leg up like a pitcher. The fist I then hit him with landed flatly across his face with the same amount of fanfare that the meteor that killed the dinosaurs had. The floor cracked around us as the Seraph's entire upper half made a small radial crater around my feet upon hitting the ground.

A large squeal of delight and clapping came from Cain's perch when it landed.

Barnem was ready to laugh it off, but I pounced on him and slammed my right hand over his open mouth. I raised my left hand in a fist behind my head, showing Barnem exactly what I needed him to see, and he reacted. Unfortunately, while I knew that I was risking a lot by attacking an angel head on, I didn't expect what happened next.

With one sharp cleave, Barnem severed my right arm off at the elbow. The pain that exploded through my body was at first like a hot flash. I felt like I was instantly drenched in sweat. What was left of my arm bled so freely that my legs instantly went numb. There was blood, so much. It was getting into my eyes, my mouth.

I heard Barnem gag and then open his mouth to let out this semi-orgasmic exhale. After coughing uncontrollably, he croaked out, "Now there ... there's a bit of violence that's been a long, long time coming."

From somewhere nearby, I heard Cain let out a gagging sound and then her feet hit the ground. "Whelp. Don't need to stay here for this part."

Barnem clicked his tongue. "Still can't stand the sight of blood? You know that's not supposed to be a thing. You're an Angel of Death."

But Cain kept walking. "I reap the souls. Never liked how they got there. Besides, I heard that the locusts are about to drop on Times Square. That's the sort of thing that if you're not early, you might as well not go." And the last I heard of her was the sound of the front doors creaking shut behind her.

There wasn't much I could see anymore. I was bleeding out but still trying my best to crawl somewhere. Barnem used his foot to turn my face over and face him. "You should be grateful for this, Grey. You should be grateful to me. Think about it. Your sad little existence now has value and meaning. Where would you be now without me, huh? Locked up in your apartment, rotting away behind your locked door? You were pathetic. And I made you necessary."

I heard the point of Barnem's holy blade land right by my face. "This is it, Grey. And just look at it like this: you'll get to be with them again. Sure it's hell and all, but you'll have your sister there. And Donaldson, too. The man probably shaded his entire soul just trying to get near you."

I stared up at the Seraph's mangled face as he drew back the sword.

Mixing in with the fear, the nauseousness, and the overwhelming pain, came another feeling that was strong enough override them all. It was as if something had taken my skin and was pulling it in all directions at once. As if all of the hairs on my body stood as sharp as needles. Barnem staggered as if feeling something, too. We were both suddenly aware that, even given in the large expanse of Saint Patrick's, the air around us had changed. It felt as if a blanket had swallowed the dying city outside and now a thousand eyes were on us. We were aware that we weren't alone.

THERE WERE WHISPERS coming from one of the back pews of the church; a male and a female voice. Barnem heard this and looked to the back. From my spot on the floor, I couldn't see who it was but the Seraph smiled menacingly.

"How'd I know someone like you two would be showing up?"

"Barnem," a cheery male voice called out. A few footsteps later and two figures were standing beside my bleeding body. I couldn't see their faces but the young man wore cargo shorts and sported these pristine white sneakers. The woman wore a white top and had sandals under her long black skirt.

"Ever since Cain told me who took over—" Barnem was cut off by the fist bump the male was offering him. The Seraph rolled his eyes at it instead. "I knew you two wouldn't be able to let this go without showing your faces."

"Barnem," the female said finally. She had actually been caught up staring at me. Both of them were barely human. I'm saying this and can barely comprehend it myself, but she was "off". It wasn't that her features weren't normal—skinny arms with light tone in the bicep; long, ridiculously curly brown hair flowing to her shoulder. Nose, mouth, ears—all present. But also, all crudely done. Every single one of her traits were stretched to their limit, pulled cartoonishly to a degree. Her arms and ears and neck were tube-shaped, as if filled with florescent light bulbs instead of bone. Her head was done as if traced with a plate in mind, and her eyes were perfectly round. Rounder than round: two long ovals sitting alongside a nose that seemed fashioned with a protractor. Her creepy eyes, with at the equally ill-conceived green retina, blinked down at me.

"It's great to see you. We were wondering if we could have a word?"

"I'm busy," Barnem barked.

"It will only take a little of your time," the male insisted, and instead of acknowledging Barnem telling him to fuck off, they both stepped over my pool of blood and found seats. The war angels around us had become still, almost like statues.

Barnem didn't sit. He only crossed his arms and waited.

"Would you like to start or ..." male weirdo began.

"I can," the female said. "You can chime in if I miss anything?"

"Of course. Of course. Oh! Wait! I'm sorry. I'm sorry. That one. That one bleeding on the floor. She should ..." He pointed at me as if I was a bag of garbage someone had forgotten to throw out.

The female leaned, in trying to whisper. "Should we meet with her separately before he murders her? It's all confidentially and stuff, but as a way of, you know, getting to know our consumer?"

They gave each other a high five.

"Love it. You're right. We would have to call HR."

"*Again*," Barnem shouted. He then brought his voice down as the hole in his face danced. "I'm in the middle of a ritualistic slaughtering. Whatever the hell you two have to do can't happen after?"

The male made a pained face. "Ooo, yeah. I'm sorry. No."

"Okay. Sent," the female said. She had been fiddling with a small device, a cell phone I'm guessing, and then dropped it on her lap as if deciding to not care anymore. The way she blinked those crazy eyes was severely freaking me out. "Let's just do it and when we hear back, I'll figure out the paperwork stuff on our end. That Angel of Death left already, too. Right? Could have consolidated all of our meetings, but guess we're not that lucky."

"Hey, mortal," I heard the male say in a cheery voice. "Care to join us?"

Before I could reply, one of the soldier angels picked me up and sat me upright in chair it had fetched. Barnem glared at me but remained standing.

Now in full view of them, I could really soak in the freakish way these two overly cheery people looked. With such arms and legs, they looked on stilts. Standing, they must have been ten or eleven feet tall. The male had a side man-bun and was clean faced, but everything about him was dumb to look at. I felt like I was staring at a New York City's street artist rendition of a human being if they were drunk, high, and had never met one in real life. The extra-long ovals at the center of his eyes were blue and were staring down at his phone as he tap-tap-tapped away with his exaggerated fingers. Then, crossing his legs, he set the phone aside. To his partner he said, "So I just contacted Katty ... you remember Katty? Christmas party last year? Had a little too much to drink?"

"California wildfires Katty?"

"That's her. That's her. She's funny."

"She's a bitch."

"She's a bit of a bitch, yeah. But she owed me a favor. And guess what?"

"What?"

"She gave us some extra time down here."

"Awwwesome." Another high five. The female looked at me. "It's so that you don't die in the middle of this Exit Interview."

"This is—" I sat properly, realizing that my lopped off arm was no longer a problem. The bleeding had tapered off. The intense pain had also stopped, as if muted, and I sat staring at the severed lump just below my elbow as if something horrifically traumatic had happened to someone else.

"So I'm Bill. This is Ada."

"Hi!"

"We are here to help you navigate the staffing process."

"And we're here to make things as painless as possible. Whoops, sorry, ay," the being known as Ada said, leaning forward and tapping me on the knee jokingly. "We appreciate your time and know that you have places to be."

"So. On a scale of one to ten, ten being pleasant and one being awful, how would you rate your experience on this plane of existence?"

Barnem spit. "I never thought I would live to see the day that the Enthroned would come down to Earth to handle shit like this."

The being known as Ada prickled, but her partner—the being known as Bill—cleared his throat and went into his pocket. "You know I forget that it's been a while since you've been back to HQ. Just to let you know, there has been a restructuring of the goals and focus and just overall policies of the company in an attempt to better synergize with the ever evolving needs of our core market."

"Is that fucking English?" Barnem took the card. "Glory? You re-branded Heaven ... 'Glory'?"

Ada beamed. "Check out the slogan on the back."

"'Glory is Bliss'? What does that even mean?"

"On a scale from one to ten," Bill continued, "ten being extremely satisfied and one being not satisfied at all. How do you rate the support the company has given you during your employment?"

"How do I rate the company? This company? The company that de-moted me to this hell hole in the first place? The company who locked me, a Seraph, in flesh and blood and shit and piss? You two have the *balls* to ask me that? After fucking aeons of fucking putting up with their stupid wars and disease and the Macarena?"

Barnem held up the card in his hand and then crushed it. Without saying a word, he let the wad fall onto the floor.

Ada tapped her chin. "So is that a zero?"

"Zero. Yes, zero. Now fuck off. I've got a job to do," Barnem said, pointing back at me.

"I guess we *can* wait until he's done," Ada not-so conspicuously whis-pered to her partner. Bill sighed but threw up his hands like *what can you do.*

Barnem dislodged the sword from the ground.

"This isn't right."

"Shuttit, Grey. I already told you that I'm not here to hear you beg."

"I wasn't talking to you. I was talking to them."

The creature known as Bill sat forward, genuinely interested. "Yes?"

"I'm not the Beast!"

As my voice echoed along the walls and high ceiling, behind me, I could hear that Barnem had stop short.

Out of fear that he was starting to figure things out, I walked toward the ones Barnem called the Enthroned, gripping the stump of my arm. Getting this close was proof positive that these two were nowhere near the spectrum of normalcy and it made it easy to chart them across their levels of weirdness: Barnem, ordinary; Cain, taller and longer than ordinary; and now Ada and Bill—freakish caricatures of the ordinary. They didn't even blink their eyes properly. Sometimes downward. Sometimes rolling upward with the lower lids. To me, the way they darted and tilted their heads to inspect me reminded me of giant birds.

"I am not the Beast. It's not inside of me. It's not whole."

The being known as Ada cocked her round head, once to the left and then to the right. "Your aura is completely black, child. Signs of the Beast are around you." Her cellphone rang and she held a long finger for me to wait.

Picking up where she left off, the being known as Bill tried to continue chastising me, but it wasn't long until his cellphone rang as well. Apologizing, he picked up the call. There was only one side of the convo that I could hear from both of them

"Yes. Yes, of course."

"I'm actually here with the both of them."

"No. She's still alive." (Ada winked at me.)

"Yes. He's here," Bill said, gesturing over to Barnem.

"I'm sorry. What now?"

"And you're sure about this?"

They both gave each other nervous glances and then hung up their phones.

Barnem took the opportunity that my back was turned to seize me by the back of my neck and slam me face first into the floor. But just before the sword came down over my neck to end it all, Bill croaked, "Stop!"

This only delayed the Seraph for a few seconds. He put a tighter grip on the hilt and drove the blade down.

"I said stop!"

Barnem went flying, struck by something I couldn't see. Whatever it was rocketed him through the front end of the church. Enraged, he stood up and yelled, "You have no right."

"*You* have no right," Ada explained. "You were about to kill this woman without fulfilling the rites. There is an order, Barnem. An absolute order. And it must be carried out."

"Just think of the paperwork—"

"Shuttup!" Voice shrill and now maddened, Barnem lost it. "I am charged in killing the Beast and she *is* the Beast. They are inside of her. I know it. She killed the demon and ... and ... and why are you all staring at me?"

Bill leaned forward. "What is that? That on your face?"

"It's ..." Barnem lifted a hand to give some excuse for the hole in his cheek, but suddenly froze when he noticed that something was off.

From out of this hole, a black beak nipped at his finger.

"This ... can't be." He turned to me and yelled, "When did you—"

Barnem frantically fell to his knees and crawled over to the pool of blood and severed arm that was his handiwork. Picking up my mutilated limb, he inspected the palm only to find the large, gaping hole I had used to shoot D right into his mouth during our scuffle.

He turned to me as the large black leeches formed all across his skin. "Grey! You b—"

He couldn't finish his sentence as D—having reverted to his original pudgy demon self—burst out of the side of his head with a large crack that exposed all of his teeth and scalp on that side. The Shade rolled in the air and landed on my shoulder.

Barnem, somehow still standing, was going to give the angels around him the order to attack, but he instead vomited several liters of black blood.

"What. Have. You. Done?"

Seeing the black tendrils coming out of the Seraph sent the the Enthroned scrambling at the sight of it. Ada scurried back, nearly falling out of her seat. Bill covered his mouth.

"Corrupted? A Seraphim?"

Barnem couldn't talk. His words were muffled behind the blood and by how bad his face had been butchered. The skin dangled like loose meat.

But he was pointing. Pointing at me and D.

The blood continued gushing down his neck, cascading down the silver chest plate, and soaking into his hair. The black leeches' wriggling intensified.

Barnem drew his sword as black boils burst all over his arms and face. With his only good eye locked onto the me—the woman who he had planned to kill since her birth, the woman whose life he regarded below everyone else's—he charged.

Ten silver spears pierced his chest from above, each one striking the floor of the cathedral so hard that it split the plates. The soldier angels were moving toward him. Barnem screamed at them to halt, to stop, but the black blood was now streaming out of his back in tendrils with piranha-like mouths, each one biting and snapping at the air around him. A battle axe sank halfway into his torso and seemingly stopped as it got lodged in his spine.

With these holy weapons protruding out of his body, his flesh collapsing slowly, the Seraph simply stared at me. I knew then that he hated me, maybe more than ever, at that one given point. And just in case he didn't, I figured I'd remind him.

"Hey. Hey, Barnem. Psst. So I was sitting here wondering what cool shit I was going to tell you before … you know, you die. I'm sort of inclined just to say that I'll see you in hell. But yeah! That's totally going to happen now. You and me. Roomies forever."

Barnem's million mouths let out a garbled wail, only to have one of the warrior angels stomp on his skull from behind. The Seraph's head split open under the weight of it and maggots spilled out of the broken skullcap.

"Well!" The sound of the being known as Bill scared the living hell out of me. I totally forgot he was sitting there. "I want to say that this was pleasant, but I also don't want to lie."

"Say, Bill," Ada peered over at me, "if Barnem was corrupted, how is the rite going to be carried out? She still needs to be killed. And all of the Shades seem to be present. You think we can call in someone to sub for the time being?"

"Possibly."

"No." I pushed myself off of the ground, slowly because I only had half the force, and stumbled over to the two beings. "Barnem cheated. He forced this, this entire thing to happen. This wasn't divinity or fate. Just one asshole's attempt at moving up in life."

Bill placed his fist under his chin. "We know. We were told so by the 'Powers that Be'."

"The Powers that Be is our marketing and research strategy team. Really cool bunch once you get to know them. They were the ones who called."

"That still doesn't change the fact that this needs to be done."

Thinking fast on my feet, I yelled, "It's an inconvenience."

Ada tittered. "Excuse me?"

"You heard me. The End of Days has greatly affected my way of life. Not in a good way," I exclaimed, pointing to my stump. "If you knew Barnem pushed the clock, then when was it actually going to end?"

"Hmm." Bill leaned his large face into me and checked his cellphone. "According to this spreadsheet … um. The world was scheduled to end … a week from next Thursday."

Ada sighed and swiped downward on Bill's screen.

"Oh right. I mean ten thousand years from next Thursday. Ooo that's a *very* different number." Before I could follow up, the being known as Bill interrupted. "Fine, fine. We'll keep the original date. But only because it's a pain to change the Event List once it's out. I think that everyone set their vacations around it and I'm not going to be *that guy*."

"I guess you'll need compensation for any damages one of our ex-employees carried out," the being known as Ada sighed and took out her own cell phone. "You won't die here, I'll call it in, no probs."

I didn't have to think; my mouth just opened and it spilled out.

"I don't want to be saved."

The being known as Bill raised one of its weird eyebrows.

"This isn't about me. I want … it's my sister."

"As you wish. Name?"

"I'm Amanda Grey."

"No. Your sister's name?"

"Petty ... Petunia Grey. Oh, and Donaldson. Jeffrey."

The beings known as Ada and Bill looked at each other.

"Well."

"Yes. Can you believe it? Self-sacrifice for loved ones. That's—"

"A means of redemption, I would say." Ada nodded feverishly. "Yes. This is grounds for total absolution of sins."

"Pious credit recovery."

"Yes. Quite."

"So?" I asked, totally confused. "Does this mean I don't have to go to hell?"

"Yes," Bill stated. "You have been absolved."

"Wow. W-well, thank you!"

"As long as you signed the User Agreement at the start of your life, we can rebuild your—" Bill tapped Ada and showed her his phone. "Ooo. That feature won't be rolled out in your reality until 2047. Sorry."

The being known as Ada tapped away at her phone, then slipped it away. "Okay. Petunia and Jeffrey. All Done. We have to go."

Suddenly, my body began contorting and bending themselves into knots. The power that D had granted me to fool Barnem—that of six of the seven Shades—was now going wild in my body. Short, dumpling D raised his spaded tail in the air and I felt the birds boring up from my insides, burrowing up my throat. Five Shades flew from my mouth, but D quickly sucked them up in one hearty puff. His body swelled through the phases of his transformation until finally his adult form was hunched over me. Just as he reached out, the warrior angels bore their weapons at him before he could zap me with it.

The being known as Bill pointed a long finger at him. "Don't mistake our dedication to quality customer support for weakness, creature. The mortal made her choice. If you in any way attempt to save her, we won't wait for a prophecy to smear your foul existence across the timelines."

Even with such an existential threat flung his way, D stood his ground. "You'd better watch who you're threatening, birdies. I don't take orders, especially from lowly, lower-middle management angels."

270

The being known as Ada tapped her fingernails on the wood. "Actually, the 'Big Guy' isn't in charge anymore. Sold his stock on this existence a *long* time ago. You're now looking at the new co-COO's of Glory Inc."

Bill tapped his coworker's lap and they both stood. "Well, we really must go. It was really nice to meet ... It was great to ..." His voice trailed off, and unable to lie, the beings known as Bill and Ada just got up and walked away. And from a distance, I could still hear them talking.

"Fine work. Some hang-ups aside, we really rolled with the punches back there."

"I know, right? But how freaky looking are humans? I kept trying not to stare."

44

As SOON AS the two Enthroned vanished, so did the other angels. And suddenly I was sitting in an empty church wondering how everything was going to resolve itself.

It all happened slowly.

Slowly sunlight began to shine in through the stained glass windows.

Gradually a small congregation began streaming into the church. They filed into the pews and bowed and prayed, thanking God for a new day. A few people even came up to me and asked if I was okay. I lied and said I wasn't.

"I got her. Move. Move!" D came and lifted me up. By then, the wound had started to bleed again. The pain began a steady crawl back into my system like a poison. He threw my good arm around his neck and tried to lift me up, but everything was rushing to me at once.

Realizing that I was dying and couldn't move, D slipped my head onto his lap. He flicked his tail at the people around us.

"No one will bother us."

And it did seem so. Either he wiped their memories of us or made us invisible because we were left alone.

"I want to call you reckless, a boiling hot mess, but I don't want to insult other boiling hot messes that have nothing to do with this."

The pain was reaching something unbearable. It was a sound. It was a violet heat burning my eyes.

I wanted to talk to him about what had happened—Barnem, Cain, the Enthroned. I wanted to let him know that I didn't blame him at all. And that I *was* being reckless and I was being stubborn. But I knew that he either figured this out or didn't care. Possibly a mixture of the two. Everything was ending now.

I mustered enough breath to ask, "What will happen to everything?"

"To the city? The world? Who knows. The angels all left. At least for now. Things outside are quiet." He looked up at the shattered glass and the light made his purple eyes burn. "You said that Cain warned you that things will be different. Well that's an understatement."

The sun was doing something amazing. It had broken through the thick sky like a knife and the actual rays were golden … even glancing off of the broken skyscraper that had been toppled over onto another; even reflecting off of the translucent wings of the dragons making their way toward South Street and shining down on the charred rubble lying on the street. It made it all beautiful for some reason.

"Did I do the right thing, D?"

"Who knows?" he replied, honestly.

I attempted to laugh, but couldn't find the energy to focus. "My parents. I tried telling them. I tried—"

"They'll be fine." D pulled the hair from my face. "I'll make sure."

There were tears in my eyes but I couldn't wipe them; could barely keep them open.

"D?"

"Yeah, Grey?"

I wanted to ask about him. Wanted to tell him what the Shade inside of me had said. If he was going to seal it or devour it when I died. About Barnem. About Petty. About Donaldson.

"Yeah, Grey?"

"You still going to take over the world?"

D laughed. "Enslave humanity and make the world worship me as bringer of unholy fire and destruction? I dunno. I missed the season finale of *The Stud*, so I'm kind of just focused on that. I really wonder if Kindy won."

My next blink felt like it lasted hours. When I forced my eyelids open, D was leaning in. Hanging just over my ear, he whispered to me, "I'll see you in hell, Amanda Grey."

It was odd trying to move my left hand, but I used the last of my energy to lift it from the ground. D sat silently, watching it ball into a mediocre fist. As the punch landed on his jaw with the mighty force of a thin ball of tissue paper, I quietly closed my eyes on the image of a demon smiling down on me.

Like someone puffing out the light from a candle, there was no gap between this and the release of pain in my body. As soon as this lifted, I opened my eyes and reached upward to grab D by his curved face.

But he was gone.

The church and the church steps were gone.

New York was gone.

I had awoken in a bed with thick sheets. The room surrounding this bed was decorated with wooden panels posted up against the walls which each held empty picture frames. Clocks with no hands ticked away. The wallpaper was red with gold loops all over. It was fucking hideous.

I hadn't noticed him at first until he sucked his teeth and let out a sigh so big that seemed to change the temperature of the room— a large man sitting hunched over at the foot of my bed. Dressed in a gray pinstripe suit with white wingtip shoes, he sat with his back to me.

He turned slowly to face me and I let out a scream the moment our eyes met.

"Nice to see you, too, Grey," Gaffrey Palls snarled. "Nice to see you, too."

ABOUT THE AUTHOR

Alcy Leyva is a Bronx-born writer, teacher, and pizza enthusiast. He graduated from Hunter College with a B.A. in English
(Creative Writing) and received an MFA in Fiction from The
New School. Alcy enjoys writing personal essays, poetry, short
fiction, book reviews, and film analysis, but is also content with
practicing standing so still that he will someday slip through time
and space. He lives in New York with his wife and a small army
of male heirs.